Praise for
Leslye Penelope

"A master class in fantasy world-building."
— *Time* magazine on *Song of Blood & Stone*

"Penelope delivers an engrossing story with delightful characters in this fantastic opening to a promising series."
— *Publishers Weekly* on *Song of Blood & Stone* (starred review)

"*Song of Blood & Stone* is a thrilling and complex journey through a beautifully rendered world that is imaginative, magical, and eerily similar to our own. A terrific read!"
— Daniel José Older, *New York Times* bestselling author

"High stakes and dire twists will keep readers turning pages, and it's clear that this is only the beginning of what's sure to be a thoughtful, emotional, magnificent series."
— *Booklist* on *Whispers of Shadow & Flame* (starred review)

"Set against a backdrop of myth and magic, *Song of Blood & Stone* is a sweeping tale of love, duty, and destiny that feels as urgent as it does timeless."
— Rebecca Roanhorse, *New York Times* bestselling author

By Leslye Penelope

The Monsters We Defy

By L. Penelope

Earthsinger Chronicles

Song of Blood & Stone

Whispers of Shadow & Flame

Cry of Metal & Bone

Requiem of Silence

Breath of Dust & Dawn (novella)

Hush of Storm & Sorrow (novella)

Echoes of Ash & Tears (novella)

THE MONSTERS WE DEFY

LESLYE PENELOPE

REDHOOK

Copyright © 2022 by Leslye Penelope
Excerpt from *The Ballad of Perilous Graves* copyright © 2022 by Alex Jennings

Cover design by Lisa Marie Pompilio
Cover illustrations by Arcangel and Shutterstock
Cover copyright © 2022 by Hachette Book Group, Inc.
Author photograph by Valerie Bey

Redhook Books/Orbit
Hachette Book Group
1290 Avenue of the Americas
New York, NY 10104
hachettebookgroup.com

First Edition: August 2022
Simultaneously published in Great Britain by Orbit

Redhook is an imprint of Orbit, a division of Hachette Book Group.
The Redhook name and logo are trademarks of Hachette Book Group, Inc.

The publisher is not responsible for websites (or their content) that are not owned by the publisher.

The Hachette Speakers Bureau provides a wide range of authors for speaking events. To find out more, go to www.hachettespeakersbureau.com or call (866) 376-6591.

Library of Congress Cataloging-in-Publication Data
Names: Penelope, L., 1978– author.
Title: The monsters we defy / Leslye Penelope.
Description: First edition. | New York, NY : Redhook, 2022.
Identifiers: LCCN 2021058428 | ISBN 9780316377911 (trade paperback) | ISBN 9780316378024 (ebook) | ISBN 9780316388467
Subjects: LCGFT: Novels.
Classification: LCC PS3616.E5387 M66 2022 | DDC 813/.6—dc23/eng/20211203
LC record available at https://lccn.loc.gov/2021058428

ISBNs: 9780316377911 (trade paperback), 9780316378024 (ebook)

Printed in the United States of America

LSC-C

Printing 1, 2022

*For Carrie and Della and all the women who,
when pressed to the wall, fight back*

If we must die, O let us nobly die,
So that our precious blood may not be shed
In vain; then even the monsters we defy
Shall be constrained to honor us though dead!

—*Claude McKay*

We are going to emancipate ourselves from mental slavery
because whilst others might free the body, none but ourselves can
free the mind.

—*Marcus Garvey*

1

THE CROSSROADS

Some folks say it wasn't just being born with a caul that made Clara Johnson ornery as a red hornet, it was being born at the crossroads. Her spirit, unlike most, had a choice to make right there at the beginning. Cold or hot, salty or sweet, lion or lamb. She came into this world through one of the forks in the road, and Clara being Clara, she chose the rockier way.

See, her mama and daddy was migrating up North from Gastonia, North Carolina, riding in the back of a wagon with her grandmother and two other distant kinfolk from down that way, when her mama's water broke. They was about to cross the Virginia state line, just outside a place called Whitetown, which didn't give nobody in that vehicle a good feeling, when they had to pull over to the side of the road—one of those roads that no Colored person wanted to be on at night—just so that gal could push that baby out.

Her mama was hollering up a storm and her daddy was holding a shotgun in one hand and his woman's hand in the other when he first caught sight of his baby girl—a slippery little thing covered head to toe with the birthing sac. Mama Octavia pushed her son aside and did what needed to be done, freeing the child so she could breathe and making sure to wrap that caul up in a sheet of newspaper and put it in her satchel.

Everybody was breathing a sigh of relief that mother and child were healthy—for a first baby she came out smooth and quick without too much bleeding or tearing or anything like that. And then that baby got to screaming. It was like to wake the dead. In fact, it did shake loose a few spirits who'd been hovering over yonder, waiting on someone like Clara to come round. And they're more than likely to do their hovering closer to a crossroads than not.

Mama Octavia sat back as her son's common-law wife tried to hush the child, and the menfolk watched the darkened road for signs of trouble. She scanned what little she could see by the moonlight and the lantern-light and caught sight of a pile of ashes and wax someone had left in the center of the crossroads. A shiver went down her spine like someone walking over her grave.

She realized her mistake, that precautions should have been taken when a child was born this close to a fork, but it was too late to do anything about it, and she didn't have the working of things the way her own grandmother had back there at Old Man Johnson's plantation, so she said a prayer for the soul of her grandbaby, hoping the child's little spirit had chosen well.

It wasn't long before she, and everyone else, found out exactly what Clara Johnson was made of. Or just what else her birth had awakened.

Clara Johnson paced the sidewalk in tight, agitated circles, trying in vain to release some of the pent-up anger welling within. "That pompous, arrogant sonofabitch," she muttered under her breath.

Her fingers coiled, pressing almost painfully against her palms, taut as the head of a drum with a tempting rhythm of rage beating against it. Like the *thump, thump* of fists meeting flesh.

Her grandmother's voice chided in her head, *You know you ain't about to fight no grown man.* Which might have been true, but that didn't mean she couldn't fantasize about kicking him in his family jewels and bruising up the face that the other girls in the office seemed to think was so handsome.

Footsteps sounded behind her, but wisely kept their distance. "Miss Clara?" a cautious voice called. She took a breath and turned slowly, grabbing hold of the trickle of calm that accompanied this distraction.

Young Samuel Foster stood watching her, more worry than wariness in his gaze. "Thought you'd left without me," he said, breaking into a grin. Tall since his recent growth spurt, with an ebony complexion, the boy would be a heartbreaker in a few years.

Clara smiled back and shook out her clenched fists. "And deprive you of the pleasure of my company?" She let out an unladylike snort. "Let's get going. Happy to leave this place behind for the weekend."

Samuel chuckled and fell into step beside her, heading toward Rhode Island Avenue. "Dr. Harley nearly made you blow your top back there. I thought for sure you was gonna let loose on him."

"Nearly did." Thoughts of the man in question and his smug, punchable face almost made her turn back. "Still might." Though higher on the food chain in the office than she, Harley wasn't really her boss, but he took great pleasure in ordering her around with his nasally whine and treating her like warmed-over trash. And while he had a good foot of height on her and probably one hundred pounds, he didn't know how to fight dirty like she did. "I'm sure I could take him. He'd probably be afraid to scuff up his shiny brogans."

Samuel shook his head, watching her carefully until the light changed, as if anxious she might really go back and start a fight. "Can't let folks like that get to you none, the ones always trying to tear you down. Nothing gets built up that way."

Clara turned sharply to look at him. From the mouths of babes.

That boy has more sense at fourteen than you do, her grandmother's voice lamented.

Blinking under the force of her scrutiny, Samuel changed the subject. "Big plans for the weekend, Miss Clara?"

She exhaled slowly, her fit of pique now almost completely dissolved, replaced with a welling sadness she refused to show. "A stack of library books is waiting on me. What about you?"

"Shifts at Mr. Davis's drugstore and making deliveries over at the print shop." His chest puffed up with pride.

"Didn't you hear, weekends are for resting?" She bumped him on the shoulder.

"Dead men can rest, until then I got to work. Got me some big dreams, Miss Clara." And a handful of younger brothers and sisters all relying on the paychecks from his various jobs, but he didn't mention that so neither did she.

"I ain't forgot," she said instead. "You gonna own one of these businesses on U Street. You figure out which one yet?"

He scratched his chin, considering. "Not quite yet. But I will."

"You keep going the way you are and you'll be working at each and every one of them."

That infectious grin returned. "I'll have one heck of a résumé, then."

Clara admired the boy's drive and determination—she wished she could borrow a little of it for herself. She was happy enough to have the one job. The big dreams she'd leave to him.

They chatted as they walked through the edge of the Washington, DC, neighborhood once known as Hell's Bottom. The intense poverty and crime had faded to the edges. Now the streets were well maintained and safe, filled with a wide range of Negroes battling the August heat.

Here were folks coming home from a long day of work whether in an office or labor yard, going to change, eat, and rest a bit before heading over to U Street for the evening. Maybe they'd take in a picture at the Lincoln or a band at Café De Luxe or maybe go dancing at the Palace. None of which Clara had ever done.

As usual, Samuel insisted on walking her to her door, though it took him several blocks out of his way. But he was resolute since it was the gentlemanly thing to do. After they said their goodbyes, he turned and ambled off, while Clara dug her key out from her purse.

The billiard parlor she lived above was still shuttered until later that evening. Miles, the owner, took Fridays off to "sleep in"—probably a good idea seeing as the place wouldn't close again until Monday morning.

Miles was a friend of her daddy's, and before he'd gone back down to North Carolina a few years ago, he'd asked the man to keep an eye on her. Miles owned the whole building and charged her a fair price for two rooms with heat and hot water, and though living here was often noisy, Clara had long ago been forced to learn to sleep through just about anything. The workweek was over and she wanted nothing more than a bath and her lumpy mattress. The heat and her receding anger had left her bone-tired. She turned the key in the door, ready to shut out the world for the weekend.

"Miss Johnson? Miss Clara Johnson?" Her shoulders tensed at the lilting voice calling her name. All she had to do was twist the doorknob and slip inside, pretend she hadn't heard.

It could just be one of her neighbors—the voice was unfamiliar, but she had more of a "nod as you pass by" relationship with them than a speaking one. Ruth Anne, the woman who ran the beauty parlor next door, often looked like she wanted to start a conversation. And it wouldn't be too unusual for folks to know her name—every Negro in the city knew her name at one time.

But the questioning, halting tone to the voice made her almost certain this was no neighbor. The urge to slide inside the narrow vestibule and slam the door in the face of her would-be questioner was strong. However, the husky voice whispering in her mind minced no words. *Gal, you better turn your narrow tail around and see what that young woman wants!*

Clara sighed deeply, and pressed her forehead against the wood of the door.

I know you hear me talking to you, Clara Mae. Best not ignore me.

"Yes, ma'am," she uttered under her breath and turned around.

The girl standing on the curb behind her looked like she'd been cut from the pages of a magazine. Her chestnut hair was smartly pressed and curled—immune, it seemed, to Washington's formidable humidity—with a fashionable cloche hat perfectly positioned on her head.

Her face was somewhat plain, but you'd never know it from the way she carried herself. She looked several years younger than Clara, maybe eighteen or so, wearing a green silk dress and shiny patent leather oxfords.

"Miss Johnson," she said, holding her hand out. "I'm Louise Wyatt, and I need your help."

A stinging sensation nettled Clara, uncomfortable and insistent, locking her into action. It wasn't due to the heat or the traffic; this was pure magic. She could not deny someone who came to her for help, that was the deal she'd made when she was about Louise's age—and one she could never ignore. Guilt for something that hadn't even happened yet attached itself to her like a suit of armor.

"Come inside, then," she grumbled and pushed the door open.

2

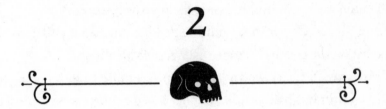

MISS LOUISE WYATT

Miss Louise Wyatt chattered all the way up the steps to the second-floor apartment. She apologized for calling at the end of a work-day, but this was an absolutely urgent situation and it just couldn't wait for the weekend. Clara unlocked the door, a headache already bloom-ing. She ushered the girl inside and set her purse down on the table. Next to it, a wooden folding cot rested against the wall, draped with a dirty apron that would need a good bleaching to be white again.

The owner of the apron stood at the stove, measuring coffee grounds into the percolator. Louise entered and took a slow look around the small space, then froze at the sight of Zelda. "Oh my!" she said, blink-ing rapidly.

Used to reactions far more severe, Zelda struck a pose at the stove with her hand on her hip. She was dressed in a pair of sports knickers buttoned below the knee, with striped socks and a man's button-up shirt. Her shock of fluffy, pale golden hair had been wrangled into a braid circling her head.

"Miss Wyatt, this is Zelda Coleman. I agreed to let her stay on my couch until she found a place of her own. That was six months ago," Clara said wryly.

"Y-you have a white roommate?" Louise actually took a step back.

Zelda, taking perverse glee in this assumption, bared her teeth in a frightening smile. "Why, I'm just as Colored as you are."

Clara slipped off her shoes and wiggled her pinched toes before taking a seat on the couch. "She ain't white, she's an albino."

Zelda crossed the space and sidled up to Louise to give her a good look. Her skin was pale as milk, but her broad features were unmistakably Negro. Brown eyes ringed with blonde lashes glittered with amusement. Zelda held out her hand and Louise stared at it for a moment before blinking rapidly and offering her own to shake.

"Oh, how...interesting." Louise's complexion, a cool buttercream with plenty of warm undertones, was much closer to Zelda's than to Clara's. Her bearing and manner shouted a so-called better class of people than either Clara or Zelda could lay claim to. She probably ran in the same lofty circles as that jackass at work.

"What was it you needed help with, Miss Wyatt?"

It took a moment for Louise to extract herself from Zelda's firm grip. She smiled nervously before perching on the seat of the wobbly armchair. "Please, call me Louise. You see, I—" She looked back toward the kitchenette, but Zelda had slipped out silently to give them privacy.

Louise took a deep breath. "There's a young man. Robert." A dreamy smile overtook her face. "And he was courting me."

The air next to her shimmered and a diaphanous figure began to take shape. Clara ignored the spirit, focusing on Louise's words. "He told me how much he loved me, and, well, I believed him."

"That gal gave up the goodies is what she did," a slightly hoarse voice announced. A sturdy body began to take shape, with arms crossed in disapproval.

"And?" Clara motioned for Louise to continue.

"Well, you see, after we, ah..." The girl blushed. "I was certain we were going to get married, so why bother waiting when it was practically all set up?"

"See? I told you." The older woman's face was now visible, though still somewhat translucent.

Louise wrung her hands. "But afterward, he stopped calling on me. There was always some excuse."

The spirit snorted. "Already got the milk, what he need the cow for?"

"Mama Octavia," Clara said through clenched teeth. "I can't listen to you both."

"Um, Miss Johnson? Are you talking to me?"

Clara shook her head. "No, my grandmother has made an appearance."

The girl's eyes widened; her gaze skittered around the room.

"You *are* here because you know I can talk to spirits? Did you not think there would be some spirits hanging around?"

Louise's lips moved but no words came out. Clara stood and crossed to the kitchenette to pour a cup of the coffee bubbling on the stove. "So is that what you came for? To get back your beau? Don't seem like the type of man who's reliable. Maybe you're better off without him."

When she turned around, coffee cup in hand, Louise was flustered, shaking her head back and forth. Clara really should offer the girl a cup, it was good manners and she wouldn't hear the end of it from Mama Octavia, but they didn't have much left. And Clara was the one who'd worked close to sixty hours that week, spending each and every one of them struggling not to put her foot where the sun don't shine on that overeducated, highfalutin gum beater, only to be interrupted by this foolishness when she really wanted to go to sleep.

"Oh, but he's perfect," Louise gushed. "Handsome and from the right family. He's at Howard studying to be an engineer. And besides..." She looked down at her clenched hands. "I'm in a family way."

Mama Octavia clucked her tongue and floated over to the window to peer through the sheer curtain, shaking her head the entire time. "These fast-tailed girls," she muttered.

It seemed to Clara that the boys in these situations were just as fast, but she'd never heard her grandmother slander them. "How old are you?"

She dropped her head. "Seventeen."

The coffee she'd just drank grew heavy in her belly. She placed the cup back on the counter. "Listen, Louise, I don't do love spells or potions, you should see Uncle Nazareth about that."

"I don't want to deal with that old witch doctor. I heard from Mamie Jackson, whose godsister's auntie said you helped her. And what you do really works. I need Robert back, Miss Clara, I just do."

A weight settled around Clara's heart as the girl went on.

"You've done so much for the community, helped so many people. And you bring hope. I mean, I was just a girl back during the rioting, but I remember—"

Clara held up a hand. "All right. I'll do what I can, but you have to know there's a cost. And it's probably more than you want to pay. Not money—I don't charge anything, but the spirits do. They require a hefty price."

Louise nodded, her perfect curls bouncing. "I'd do anything to get him back, you just don't know. If my daddy finds out, he'd be so disappointed in me. And he just might kill Robert. This baby needs a father, and I love him so much. And once we get married, then everything will be right as rain."

Clara doubted that, but as usual, what warning she could give had fallen on deaf ears. "All right, follow me."

Bone-tired and uncomfortably sweaty with no breeze coming in through the open window, she led Louise to what should have been the coat closet. Instead, the tiny space held a stool and table—an altar, covered in candles of different colors and widths. Thick wax was congealed on the surface of the wood. Colored fabric lined the walls, including the ceiling.

Clara sat on the stool and motioned for Louise to stand behind her. With regret gripping her chest, she struck a match and began lighting candles. For the return of a lost love, the spirit she needed to call would have to be a romantic. Summoning an entity with the wrong temperament would lead to an even greater disaster.

"So how does this work?" Louise whispered.

"I use the candles to invite an Enigma to come through to our world and hear your plea."

"An Enigma?"

"Some folk know them by other names. Genies, fairies, duppies, jumbies—they been called all kinds of things in different places. They're powerful spirits who like to play in the human world, make mischief, grant wishes. We ask one of them, and if they choose to, they'll give you a gift—a Charm that will help you solve your problem. But they'll also give you a Trick, and that's something you won't like so much. That's the cost of their aid. The Trick is like a debt you owe them until they feel like they've been paid back. Are you sure you want to do this?"

A look of concern crossed Louise's face, but then her hand drifted to her stomach, still flat as a board. "I'm sure."

"Now, once I start, it's important that you stay quiet. No matter what happens, don't make a sound unless I tell you to."

Wide-eyed, the girl nodded.

Clara turned back around and sighed. No getting around it, then. She stared at the flame on a fat red-and-white-striped candle. It burned steadily in a solid orange. Quieting her mind, she closed her eyes, but the vision of the flame blazed on in her mind. It danced, moving sinuously, slithering through the air like a snake. Like the serpent in the Garden of Eden, tempting Eve with knowledge that would come with a dear price.

The veil between the world of humans and the world of the spirits, *Over There*, was always perilously thin for Clara, but during these meditations it shrank down to nearly nothing. The sense of the unseen was stronger. The presence of invisible bodies surrounded her, their world existing on top of her own.

She stretched her senses forward, seeking a spirit that felt like love. This was how she'd always done it, how Mama Octavia had taught her to. Find the Enigma who wanted what the petitioner wanted; that was the best way to mitigate the consequences of dealing with the beings at all.

An insistent presence made itself known, but this one was all wrong. Nettling and aggressive, it pushed itself at Clara, but she avoided its energy. Romance and tenderness was what the girl needed, not this tenacious beast. Again she focused on the qualities of the spirit she wanted to call until she felt a more appropriate entity grow nearer. The telltale tug of a connection made her jerk on her stool. Her eyes flew open and the fat candle in front of her sparked with a white flame, which grew higher and higher.

Clara held up a hand when she felt Louise move behind her. "Welcome. Who do I have the pleasure of speaking with?"

"I am called Lalin, though some know me as The Moon."

Louise stiffened and brushed against Clara's back. The surprise of hearing a voice coming out of a white flame would hopefully help keep the girl's lips sealed.

"Our sister Louise Wyatt seeks the return of her lost love. She entreats you for your aid, Lalin." Clara spoke slowly and clearly, choosing her words carefully. "Will you bring him back to her so that they may be married and raise their family together?"

A figure began to emerge inside the flame—a woman's face. It was indistinct, just the suggestion of eyes, nose, and mouth, but it gazed to the side at Louise, who was now shaking.

"This is what you seek, child?" Lalin asked.

Clara turned her head. "Answer her," she whispered.

"Y-yes, ma'am."

The face of the Enigma retreated, falling back into the flame. The candle wax began pouring down faster than what was natural. The red-and-white rivulets bled like a jugular vein sliced open.

"And what will you give me in return?" The spirit's voice turned teasing, almost flirtatious.

"You will get your Trick," Clara said quickly before Louise could utter a word. "Your Trick and nothing more."

"Very well, then," Lalin pronounced with a sigh, the faint mouth pursed in a pout. "I will grant your desire. Your love will return in three days, chastened and desirous of renewing his affection with you."

While Louise's excitement was palpable, Clara tensed, waiting for the other shoe to drop.

"He will find you irresistible. In fact, all men will be entranced by your beauty. You will shine brighter than all other women."

Clara's heart sank even as Louise giggled with delight. "I've always wanted to be beautiful."

"And the rest?" Clara asked, weary to her bones. "The Trick?"

Lalin chuckled ominously. "All will look upon you with desire, but none will ever truly have your heart."

"That's all right, all I want is Robert. I don't have eyes for anyone else."

"Is that your will, Lalin?" Clara's voice was thick. Her dress was plastered to her back and she just wanted this over with.

"It is."

"Then be it so." Clara blew out the candles, ending the connection to the Enigma and sealing Louise's fate. Smoke danced in trails up to the ceiling and scented the air.

"Please let me pay you," Louise said, reaching into her purse. "I can't thank you enough."

"No, no money. I can't take money." Clara had a hard time looking the girl in the eye. Back in the main room, Mama Octavia still stood at the window, her back to them.

Louise hustled to the door, her eyes shining with tears. "Thank you again," she said before leaving.

"Please don't," Clara whispered, staring at the closed door.

Zelda reappeared with a fresh cup of coffee and handed it to her. "How bad was it?"

Clara settled on the edge of the armchair, one leg swinging restlessly. "Her man will come back and marry her. And she'll be irresistible to all other men—but none will truly have her heart."

Zelda tilted her head in question.

"*None,*" Clara repeated. "That will include her future husband, I'm certain. He will love her, but she'll never be satisfied with him. That's her Trick. A life without love. Men competing for her attention, becoming jealous, promising her the world. Giving it to her, even. But she'll feel nothing."

"Oh." Zelda's lips turned down.

"That girl is in for a heaping of sorrow."

Mama Octavia clucked her tongue and turned around. "You're just giving her the same deal you got. It's their choice to make it or not. Everyone has a choice."

"Not always a good one," Clara grumbled.

Zelda raised her brows, but she'd long grown used to Clara's habit of speaking to thin air.

"No," Mama Octavia said sadly. "Colored folks don't often get good choices, do we?"

Clara's shoulders slumped. She went off to her bedroom knowing her grandmother spoke true. She couldn't remember the last time she had a good choice.

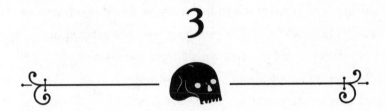

THE DISTRICT RUMBLERS

Rivulets of rain chased each other down the window in streams, not quite the downpour it had been earlier in the afternoon, but steady and persistent. From her perch on the couch, Clara tracked the umbrella-clutching people, undaunted by the weather, heading out to enjoy their Saturday all the same. Music from the player piano down at Miles's place wafted up through the floorboards, the notes melding together in a swinging tune.

The book on her lap struggled to hold her interest. She tapped her toes against the cushions, keeping time with the melody as her mind wandered far from the pages. It was due back to the library in a few days and she wasn't sure she would finish it—a rarity. Louise Wyatt's face, filled with gratitude, kept replacing the printed words.

Clara dropped her head in her hands. The guilt didn't let up, but that was nothing new. There had been more than a handful of Louise Wyatts over the years. People she'd had to help—curse was more like it. She tried to reason out how yesterday had been different. Maybe it was the fact that the girl had been seventeen. At that age, Clara's life had changed forever.

The little cuckoo clock her daddy had carved for her mama struck eight from its place on the wall above the table. It wasn't late, but Clara decided to take her sorry self to bed anyway. She'd just uncurled from the couch when Zelda burst in, sopping wet. She pushed her dripping hair from her eyes and grinned widely from the doorway.

"What you so happy about?" Clara grumbled.

Zelda entered the room, removing her jacket.

"Put all that in the bathroom, will you? Don't want to warp the floors."

When the young woman returned, clad in a fluffy robe that looked very familiar, she sprang onto the armchair, bouncing in her seat.

"I see you helped yourself to my robe. Might as well spill. What you been up to out there in this weather that's got you grinning like a fool?"

Zelda stuck her hand in the pocket of Clara's favorite robe and pulled out a wad of cash. Clara's brows rose. "Sure is a lot of money."

"You know that march those ofays was having downtown today?"

"You mean the Klan march?" For weeks, Colored Washington had been on edge with the impending descent of Ku Klux Klan members from all over the country. "Yeah, of course I know about it. Everybody knows not to go below M Street today. What about it?"

"Well, I got word from some acquaintances about a group of mug men from up in New York coming down to fleece them old pecker-woods, so I went down there."

Clara blinked. "Wait—you went down there? And you…"

Zelda nodded, still waving the chunk of cash. "Hoodwinked those hoods. I can pick a pocket better than just about anybody. Some of them New York boys got arrested, but I melted myself back into that crowd of white folks who came out to watch. Didn't nobody look twice at me with all that commotion going on in the street."

Zelda's grin was almost manic, and, not for the first time, Clara thought the woman she'd first met two years ago was more than a little touched in the head. Growing up in the circus would do that to a person, she figured.

"Girl, you is crazier than a loon bird. I don't know how you've survived this long."

Zelda laughed, throwing back her head. "So we got us some of their money, we should spend it."

"Your lunatic self got their money. What *you* gonna do?"

"Naw, honey. You been up in here moping about Lord knows what. I don't think you've had a night out in all the time I been here. Well, you're going somewhere tonight. We can see a show—there's a new Lorenzo Tucker film up at the Lincoln. Don't you want to go and stare at his pretty face for an hour or two? The Colored Valentino." Her voice turned dreamy.

Clara rolled her eyes. It had been much longer than half a year since she'd been out on the town, and she had no intention of changing that. "I don't wanna stare at nothing but the backs of my eyelids. I'm going to sleep. Say hi to Lorenzo for me."

"Oh no you don't." Zelda stood when Clara did and blocked her path. "You act more like you're sixty-three rather than twenty-three. I ain't never met a young woman who acted more old. I know you didn't like helping that girl yesterday, saddling her with that Enigma debt, but you can't hold it all inside like that. It'll explode if it ain't got nowhere to go."

Clara set her jaw. "I let you stay here 'cause I felt sorry for you. The YWCA was full and you ain't had no other options, but that don't mean you can tell me what to do. I ain't had a mama since I was six years old and I don't need one now."

Zelda remained unfazed by Clara's rising tone and didn't back away. "Well, call your granny, then, she'll tell you I'm right. Mama Octavia, you here?"

"She ain't here and she don't need to be."

"Well, it don't matter anyway, you're coming with me to the theater."

"I'm not going nowhere but to bed, Zelda!" Clara slid between her and the armchair, stomped into her room, and slammed the door.

An hour later, she was tucked under an umbrella, avoiding a puddle on the sidewalk as she walked down U Street. A line had formed in front of the Lincoln Theatre and they took their place at the end.

"You know Ruth Anne next door has a room to let up on the third floor."

Zelda regarded her innocently. "You want me to leave, I'll be gone tomorrow, but if you turn around one more time, you ain't never getting another wink of sleep tonight."

Clara crossed her arms mutinously. She'd lost track of the number of times Zelda claimed she'd be gone tomorrow. The pale-skinned harridan was the stubbornest person she'd ever met. Zelda had stood outside the bedroom door, singing at the top of her lungs some lewd blues song she must have picked up in the gutter somewhere. Clara had tuned her out for as long as she could, but when Miles beat on the door screaming at them to stop all the hollering, that his customers were complaining, she'd finally given in.

The ticket line was slow, but thankfully the rain had let up. Clara lowered her umbrella and looked up at the building they stood in front of, the Casbah. It was a popular nightclub two doors down from the theater, and the folk streaming in the front were dressed a sight better than Clara or Zelda. A pang of longing shot through her, but she ruthlessly squelched it.

"You wanna go there instead?" Zelda asked, noticing where Clara's gaze was stuck. "The band playing tonight is all anyone's been talking about lately. Best in the District. They say—"

"No." Clara chuckled dryly, silently cursing the woman's perceptiveness. "That's not for me. Besides, you think they'd let us in in these rags?" She motioned down at her threadbare raincoat and Zelda's battered shoes and cloche hat. "Those nose-in-the-air Negroes would eat us for dinner." She craned her neck, looking toward the front of the line. "They got a blind ticket-taker up there or something? This line ain't moved an inch."

Maybe that was a good thing. Maybe they'd be so late the ushers wouldn't seat them and she could go back home where she belonged. But her impatience warred with her misgivings; she stepped to the side to see around the long queue of people. Her movement took her squarely in the path of a laughing young woman coming up from behind her. Perfume clouded the air and Clara turned to apologize, then froze with recognition.

"Why, if it isn't Clara Johnson." The woman stepped back, sounding both amused and aghast at the discovery. Light brown eyes regarded her coolly from a face Mama Octavia would describe as "high yaller." There was nothing battered about the red rubberized poplin raincoat the woman wore with a matching hat. Nor the diamond earrings dangling from her ears.

"Addie Savoy." Clara's voice was toneless. She also recognized the two young women standing behind Addie, both similarly dressed. Thankfully, Addie was here with her girlfriends and not her jackass of a fiancé.

"Why, I haven't seen you in years, Clara. I'd thought you might have gone back down South. That was the rumor I'd heard, at any rate. But I see you're still here. It goes to show, you can't trust gossip." She fluttered her lashes prettily and smiled with bloodred lips.

"There's a lot of things you can't trust, Addie."

Zelda looked back and forth between them, her brow descending as she no doubt sensed the chilliness in the air. She stepped closer to Clara and squared her shoulders.

"Are you headed into the Casbah?" The woman's voice was polite, but the derisive glance she gave Clara's drab gray dress spoke volumes.

Clara glanced over at the doorway. "Isn't the band tonight supposed to be something special?"

Addie and her friends giggled. "If by *something special* you mean the biggest thing to hit Washington in years, then I suppose so. Israel Lee and the District Rumblers are indeed special. I just hope you'll be able to get in to see them. They do have a dress code, you know. They don't just let anybody in."

Rage and shame blinded Clara until Addie's shining jewels were nothing but a blur. Her spine turned to iron and she held on to her temper with as tight a rein as she could muster. "Well, if they'll admit a forked-tongue, scheming heifer like you, then I think I'll be just fine."

Addie's mask of politeness cracked before shattering altogether. The woman stepped up to Clara, no longer disguising her disgust. "Well, I'm lucky my daddy's a judge and not a jailbird like yours. Then again, the apple doesn't fall too far from the tree. And who you calling a heifer, you ol' coal-tar, dusty-butt jigaboo."

Someone was audibly growling now, Clara supposed it was her, but the rushing in her ears made it hard to tell. Her umbrella clattered to the ground as she grabbed Addie Savoy by her lapels with one hand and reared the other one back to strike. But before she could get any momentum going, she was wrenched backward by a strong grip around her waist.

"I think this alley has enough cats in it," a deep voice purred in her ear.

Clara twisted and writhed, not liking being manhandled by anyone, though the man's grasp was as gentle as it could be, given the circumstances. "Let me go!"

"You calm down and I'll let you go."

"What's it matter to you if I'm calm or not?"

"It doesn't. But does it matter to you that you were about to coldcock Judge Savoy's favorite daughter?"

"I don't care who that yellow bitch's daddy is."

"Think you'll feel different from inside the cage he'll throw you in?"

That forced the air out of her. The rage that had been fueling her escaped in a gush and she became dead weight in his arms. Zelda's shouts made her crane her head. Her roommate was cussing up a storm and being barely restrained by two large men several feet away. The man holding Clara had pulled her a few steps away, into the mouth of the alley next to the theater.

"Let me go," Clara said, calmly as she could. After another moment that felt like a short eternity, her captor complied.

"I'm all right, Zelda!" she called, and her roommate quieted.

Clara turned slowly and caught her first sight of the meddlesome man. Her lips parted and her eyes forgot how to blink. Lorenzo Tucker might have been a handsome movie star, but the man before her had him beat by a mile. He was tall, with skin the color of caramel, his square jaw freshly shaven. He smelled faintly of cigarettes and liquor, but beneath lingered a scent that made her suck in another breath just to figure out what it was. She realized she was staring and pulled away, stepping back.

Zelda reached her side and scowled at him. Unfortunately, Addie Savoy and her crew also approached, along with a small crowd that had gathered and seemed annoyed they'd been denied any bloodshed. Clara gazed at them all with darts in her eyes.

"Israel Lee, how can I ever thank you? You're such a gentleman." Addie Savoy gave Clara a wide berth as she ran up to the man—Israel—and oozed her coquetry all over him. "Good breeding goes such a long way. Some folks act like they're still in the jungle. Utterly predictable." She had the nerve to cut her eyes at Clara, while also having the good sense to keep Israel between them.

Clara's nose flared, and Israel's humored gaze shot to her. "Well, I'd suggest that some folks better not rile up the apex predators," he said to Addie conspiratorially, but his eyes were on Clara.

"Are you hurt, Israel? Will you be able to perform tonight?"

"I'm fine. She's light as a feather." He ushered Addie away, then tossed a look over his shoulder. "You okay there, lioness?"

Clara straightened her coat and skirt. "I'm fine. And you should mind your damned business."

He chuckled and winked at her before tipping his hat. Someone shoved a guitar case into his hands and the waiting audience swallowed him up. In a few moments, the alley was empty and everyone had moved on to more entertaining pursuits.

The rain began to fall again.

Clara took a deep breath. The adrenaline of the almost fight, the anger boiling within, the irritation of old, barely healed scars had left her drained.

"I don't think I'm in the mood for a picture tonight."

"Well, that was enough entertainment to last the whole weekend. But I wonder what Addie and old nosey Israel Lee will say when they can't find these?" She held up two wallets, laughing.

Clara shook her head and they turned around to head home.

GHOST GIRL

S ome folks is just born unlucky. You can blame it on the stars, or on a curse, or a mojo hand, but that's just the facts. Luck is real and some ain't got it.

Pearline Coleman was less unlucky than some, but that wasn't saying a whole lot. She was slew-footed, bucktoothed, with long limbs and a short torso. And she wasn't what you would call the sharpest tool in the shed. Her mama didn't think she'd ever get married, but Pearline found a man. (And some said if she could, anyone could.)

They met at a church revival in the refreshment tent. He was a sharecropper down in Fayette County, Alabama, working thirty-seven acres—the same land where his parents had been slaves. She worked alongside him and bore the man ten children, none of which had the good sense to die.

The first nine were healthy, more or less, but that tenth baby—only the second girl—came out the color of a full moon at midnight. The girl's daddy started thinking Pearline had stepped out on him, or gotten caught out somewhere by some white man. Folk didn't talk too much about the high yaller babies and who their real daddies were.

But the child wasn't yaller, she wasn't even white, she was whiter than a white man's white sheet. Doc Abram called the girl an albino, but didn't nobody know what that meant. All they knew was that she burnt to a crisp in the sun and her eyes rattled around inside her head like a jar of beans in a thunderstorm.

The year she was born, boll weevils invaded Fayette County, cotton prices fell into the cellar, and it didn't rain for ninety-nine days straight. Folks called her the Ghost Girl, said she was an omen or a body full of bad luck, but Zelda didn't pay them no mind. She raced her older brothers and sassed her older sister and learned to ignore the stares and whispers.

But twelve mouths are hard to feed, and while Pearline may have had enough love in her heart for all her children, she didn't have near enough money in her pocket to feed them all. So when the white man in the seersucker suit came by the two-room cabin they called home and offered her two hundred dollars—more money than they'd made the last two years combined—she packed off six-year-old Zelda with her one good dress and her hand-me-down shoes and sent her off to the circus.

The banners at the freak show advertised a *Monkey Girl from Mars* or *Snow Princess from Antarctica*. The words changed depending on the city and the whims of the showmen. She was dressed in animal skins or satin and lace and stood under the stares of a gaggle of peanut munchers.

The bearded lady adopted her and taught her her letters. The tattooed man showed her how to juggle, and the family of acrobats schooled her on how to pick pockets. There was bread most days, and a bath once a week, which made it a sight better than her home had been, and Zelda tried to make the best of it.

Before long, she became the one who stood up for her fellow freaks, asking for better trailers, more food, a rest day when they were too sick to perform. All in all, she was a real boil on the behind of the man in that seersucker suit, so he sold her to a carnival when she was sixteen. Her friends at the circus wished her well and worried over her—the two-bit carnival was a step down from their circus, and it seemed like her luck had changed for the worse.

But Zelda Claudine Coleman didn't believe in luck, good, bad, or otherwise. She was stubborner than a blind, thirsty mule and when she set her mind to something, nothing nobody said would change her mind. She made such a fuss about so many things that by the time she reached Washington, DC, in the spring of 1923, the managers of the carnival were almost ready to be rid of her. There were other Colored albinos they could buy who wouldn't give them so much lip—not ones that could juggle while walking a tightrope, but was that really worth all the hassle? Only thing working in her favor was the money she brought in. Money she never saw. So it was once again, with one good dress and a pair of hand-me-down shoes, that Zelda made her escape.

She worked on the streets, picking the pockets of the folks who looked fancy enough not to bother about the missing cash, and picking the locks to the houses of the widows or widowers in the obituaries for a place to lay her head. But one day when she ran afoul of a low-level gangster who looked fancy but was in fact bothered about his missing wallet, Zelda stared down the barrel of a derringer for the first time, wondering if she should start believing in luck after all.

It was then that Clara Johnson turned into the alley behind her apartment and called out the young man by name. "Wallace Granger, does your mama know you have that gun?"

"Clara, this ain't your business. This girl here stole from me."

"Is that true?"

Zelda nodded. "But I gave it back." She pointed at the cash sticking out of his jacket pocket.

Clara crossed her arms, tilting her head at Wallace Granger, who she'd known since primary school and was just about the worst teenage wannabe gangster in town. "Well, what you still holding the gun for?"

Wallace frowned and looked at Clara.

"Put that thing away before you hurt yourself, and go on home." The young man's hand wavered until he lowered the weapon. "Leave now and I won't tell nobody you got robbed by a girl." Wallace glared at both of them and then left.

Clara looked Zelda up and down. "I ain't never seen nobody like you before."

Zelda stuck up her chin. "And?"

"And nothing. Watch who you steal from, though."

As Clara walked back down the alley and into the night, Zelda set her mind to something new. That girl was going to be her friend, whether she liked it or not.

4

THE MONROE BOY

W hat is this?"
      Clara shifted to the side as stale breath wafted over her. A thin-fingered hand slapped a sheaf of papers on her desk, next to the typewriter she was currently using. She blinked up at the man leaning over her, trying not to breathe all that foul air he was spouting in her face. "Well, Dr. Harley, this appears to be your article on the St. Charles Hotel's basement slave pens. Perhaps you need to see an eye doctor if your vision is declining."

Her voice was sweet as punch, but from the desk next to hers Mrs. Shuttlesworth cleared her throat in warning. The office manager had lectured Clara about her attitude many times, but didn't being phony count as having a good attitude? It certainly seemed to for everyone else.

"My vision is impeccable, Clara. I'm referring to these lines in my article concerning details of the slave woman whose death incited a revolt there. I certainly didn't include this bit about her father and brother's presence in the jail or her fondness for singing. *The Journal of Negro History* is a scholarly publication. We publish well-researched articles, not fantasies. Your job is to type the words I give you, and occasionally fact-check, *not* add emotional flourishes devoid of evidence."

Clara's jaw clenched. She took a slow, deep breath to rein in her temper. Dr. Alphonzo Harley a.k.a. the Jackass was one of the first Negroes to achieve a PhD in history from a major university, a feat achieved at the age of twenty-five. A fact he never let anyone forget, least of all her. The other typists and stenographers in the office chattered over how he was the handsomest of all the researchers with his butter-yellow complexion and sea-green eyes, but Clara found him repulsive. He had all the charm of a rattlesnake as far as she was concerned.

"In my fact-checking, I found it necessary to make an edit and correct an inaccuracy in the article, Dr. Harley, that's all."

"An inaccuracy?" His brows rose.

She spoke slowly, enunciating clearly. "Because the *Journal* is so well respected and important to the race, it is incumbent upon us to humanize our enslaved ancestors. The young woman had family present who witnessed her death. That is an important detail not to be missed."

"There is no historical record of that. Where is the documentation to support this thesis?"

Clara's lips clamped shut. Her documentation was in the form of a man named Zeke who had been chained next to his son and daughter and listened to her singing voice grow weaker and weaker as death took her. The girl's name had been Annie. Her brother was Mason but they called him Sweet Pea. After seeing Annie's body dragged away and after the escape attempt mounted in the wake of her death had failed, they'd been sold off to a plantation in Virginia.

Clara had long ago learned to tune out the spirits who shared the world with the living. As a child, the noise had nearly driven her crazy—all those voices, all those shimmering entities floating through walls and appearing out of thin air. Now she knew how to block them out and ignore them all or focus on the ones who had something to say to her. In general, the ghosts didn't bother her. There were a few who wanted messages sent or had unfinished business to conclude, and other, darker spirits with mysterious agendas, but Mama Octavia offered a strong barrier against those who would pester her.

Zeke, however, had made a compelling case. He'd been looking in on one of his descendants, a girl who worked for the *Journal* but did more chattering than typing. He'd overheard Dr. Harley talking about his research for an article about the infamous St. Charles Hotel, known for its exclusivity and luxury, high-class amenities—including the underground dungeons where visiting slave owners could keep their property.

Zeke's heart had broken with the cold way his daughter was described and begged Clara to let her memory shine through just a little bit more. She knew she couldn't include Annie's name, but she'd slipped in a few details that made the girl less of a statistic and more of a person. Dr. Harley didn't often review his articles after having them typed. But noticeable errors in the copyediting of the last issue had left the researchers and writers paying closer attention than usual.

She knew whose fault that was and cut her eyes at the new fellow, Langston, who lounged at his desk in the corner. If she wasn't mistaken, he was reading a pulp magazine when he was supposed to be editing a document.

"The information I included was part of the personal recollections that the abolitionist group recorded. Those files were placed back in the basement, but I can retrieve it for you if you like." She'd spoken as civilly as was possible and held her breath now as Harley considered.

"I don't recall reading anything like that. Yes, I want to see it."

"Today? It's nearly six o'clock."

Harley looked at his watch. "Tomorrow, then. First thing."

Clara sat back in her seat. She'd have to forge the document tonight. It shouldn't take long, but she still had a stack of typing to get through.

When he didn't move on, she tilted her head. "Was there something else?"

He clasped his hands behind his back and rocked on his heels. "I spoke with Addie this morning. She related the...incident from the other night."

Clara's nostrils flared. She bit her tongue to keep from responding.

"Your presence here is an ongoing mystery," he went on. "You are not qualified, often unprofessional, and increasingly inept."

She grabbed a pencil and clutched it, imagining it was his neck. Her grip tightened as he continued.

"But if there is any repeat of the violence you showed my fiancée Saturday night within these offices, I assure you, Dr. Woodson will ignore the pleas of his friends and the charitable nature which led him to take you on in the first place and expunge you from the premises with extreme prejudice. Am I making myself clear?"

The pencil in her hand snapped in half. He jerked, glancing at it, and narrowed his eyes before turning and stalking off. Clara sucked in a serrated breath. Then crushed the two halves of the pencil into even tinier pieces and tossed them in the waste bin.

"You getting into trouble in your off hours, Clara?" Mrs. Shuttlesworth asked from her spot a few feet away.

"No, ma'am. I think he was misinformed." She wasn't even lying, really—she'd been physically prevented from getting into trouble by one nosey musician.

"You really shouldn't antagonize Dr. Harley. It isn't your place to correct the researchers' papers. If they miss something, it's on them."

Brushing the pencil debris from her hands, Clara took a steadying breath. "I know, Mrs. S., but his work is often sloppy. It's not just this, he takes all kinds of shortcuts just to publish more than anyone else. He treats the journal like a race."

"He's a highly educated man from one of the best families in the

District. You're a year shy of earning a high school diploma from Armstrong Manual's secretarial program. You're in no position to criticize." The older woman sighed deeply. "I'll ask Samuel to get those papers up from the basement."

"I haven't seen him at all today, are you sure he's here? He was supposed to run these over to the post office." She pointed to a stack of stamped letters on the corner of her desk.

Mrs. Shuttlesworth frowned. "I don't know. That's not like him to not show up and not say anything."

"You're right. I wonder what's held him up. Hopefully, he'll get to it tomorrow. I'll get those folders from the basement. They were all mixed together, so I'll need to find the right one anyway." And then add a fake account from Zeke. Not fake, she reasoned. It *was* a historical record from someone who lived through the event.

She rose heavily from her chair, knowing that she would be at work for quite a while longer.

As she walked home alone that night, the streets were mostly empty. Music rang out from a speakeasy across the way where the hard cases were making merry, but the majority of the neighborhood's residents were tucked into their beds. While she missed Samuel's jovial presence, Clara wasn't afraid of being alone at night. She knew how to protect herself and had done so plenty of times.

Ghosts from her memory, instead of from the spirit world, called to her. *Well, if it ain't the Little Sniper. Do you shoot every man who comes in your bedroom?* Whispered voices echoed along with the fear she'd felt in those long-ago days. Protecting herself could have consequences, as she well knew—especially when you were Negro.

She shook away the voices and picked up her pace, eager to get home.

Up ahead, a woman approached, tugging on the arm of a gangly teen. The boy seemed addlepated, walking under his own power, but with a listing, shuffling gait, barely picking up his feet. When Clara passed under a streetlight, the woman quickened, rushing toward her with alarming speed, the boy she towed scuffing his shoes behind her.

"Clara Johnson?"

"Yes, ma'am. Do I know you?"

"My name is Dorothy Monroe. I been looking for you. I need your help."

Her steps slowed, dismay making her body feel heavy like she'd been weighted down with rocks. Two people within a week of each other needing her help? She exhaled slowly and bid them to follow her into her apartment.

Dorothy Monroe was a sturdy, no-nonsense woman with rich brown skin and sharp dark eyes. Her son Titus was small and fine boned—the opposite of his mother—with a face suffering from the divots and pocks of adolescence. His knuckles were scabbed over from what was probably a recent fight.

Zelda took one look at the pair and gave up her cot without a word. She was probably headed downstairs to the pool hall to hustle some unsuspecting dopes. Dorothy chose to stand and declined any refreshment. Clara was feeling polite tonight, but also grateful nobody actually wanted anything from her limited cupboard.

The woman pointed to her son. "You see him. He been like this the past few days. He'll eat and drink. He can go to the bathroom on his own, but other than that, it's like he ain't there. Whatever makes the body and mind work together has just wound down like an old watch."

The boy's hands rested on his thighs as he hunched on the couch staring out at nothing in particular. Mrs. Monroe started to pace the wooden floorboards. The music from downstairs was low, an old ragtime tune from the player piano tonight. "It's like he been touched in the head, but he was always a smart boy. Industrious. Temper on a hair trigger like his father's, but a good boy overall." Her voice held deep anguish, but her eyes were dry.

Clara watched the boy carefully. The blinking of his eyes was curious, spaced out far apart, and even his breathing had a rhythmic quality to it. "Will he speak?"

"A word or two, here or there yesterday and the day before, but nothing at all today. His friends even came over this morning and he barely looked at them."

"Had he been anywhere out of the ordinary before this affliction began? Could something traumatic have happened to him?"

"On Friday, he went to baseball practice and to his job at the grocery store. That night he said he wasn't feeling too well and went to bed. In the morning, I couldn't get him out of it." She stopped her pacing and clenched her hands together tightly. "He won't answer when I call. He'll only eat if I put the fork in his hand, and Lord knows how long that will last. Got a dog he loves to pieces, but he won't touch her. I even tried to rile him by shouting in his face and carrying on. He knows better than to talk back, but, like I said, he got a temper, and his eyes tell it all." She crossed her arms. "He didn't even react. Not a flash or a grumble. I knew I had to keep an eye on him, so he hasn't left my side."

Something in her tone made Clara take notice. "Has he tried?"

"This morning. I turned my back for a moment and he stood up out of nowhere and walked right out the door. I let him, just to see where he would go. Followed him to the park on Vermont Avenue, but he just stood at the corner like he was waiting for something."

Clara's scalp prickled, an uneasiness coming over her. "What is it that you want me to do for him?"

"Can't...can't your spirits make him back the way he was?"

Enigmas could heal disorders both physical and mental, but there were limits. They couldn't make an idiot into a genius. Couldn't bring back the mind of a man who'd had his head bashed in and lost his faculties. Or maybe they had the ability to, but those kinds of things hadn't ever interested them enough to try. And even the promise of the Trick the person would receive wasn't enough to entice them.

Dorothy's voice wavered. "I'm willing to do whatever it takes. I've heard that sometimes... Well, if you let a spirit possess you, you can get more powerful work out of them."

Clara shuddered and shook her head rapidly. "You're talking about being Embraced by an Enigma. That ain't no parlor trick and nothing you ever want to agree to. It's not like the Pentecostals catching the spirit and speaking in tongues and then right as the river when the music ends. Enigmas are powerful and willful. They treat you like a puppet and take complete control." Her breathing sped up just thinking about it.

Dorothy sagged onto the couch next to Titus. "This is my baby. My only living son. Gave birth to seven—three died as infants. One was killed in jail. Two were lynched down in Mississippi before we come up here. He my last one. I'll do anything."

Clara's heart swelled and her throat thickened. Compassion for Dorothy's plight made her think about her own mother, something she tried never to do. If something similar had happened to Clara, what would Aurora Johnson have done to make it right? Well, something *had* happened to her, a lot of somethings, but the only thing her mama had done was leave a trail of dust in her wake.

Clara stood, pushing the thoughts away, and approached her closet. "Will he be all right there on the couch?"

"No, if I'm not watching, he'll get up and try to leave again."

"Well, bring him over here, then." She opened the door and sat before the altar. Dorothy stood behind her, Titus at her side.

Clara lit the candles and blew out the match. The flames flickered and swayed, reaching out for her like clawed fingers. She swallowed the sense of foreboding and closed her eyes, working to call a nurturing spirit. An Enigma who would care about Dorothy's quest to save her only living son—maybe Queen Esther or Monsieur Fos. She'd dealt with both of them before in cases of wayward children of one kind or another.

But minutes ticked by and nothing happened. Clara opened her eyes and checked the candles. They were still doing their odd dance, rocking toward her in a way that made the hair on her arms prickle.

Her shoulders slumped. Maybe if she hadn't felt so much for Dorothy—compassion, and sadness, and even a little jealousy—she wouldn't have done what she did next. She hadn't done it for anyone else who'd come to her for help, but then again, she'd never had a case when no one answered her call before. She avoided using her natural second sight for good reasons, reasons she ignored now, sinking deeply into the power she was born with to look Over There.

Folks around the world believe that being born with a caul gives a body powers. Clara's were mostly of the talking-to-spirits variety, but she could also sense things that no one else could see: energy, power, magic. But just because she had these abilities didn't mean she wanted to use them. She kept them locked up tight. People weren't meant to gaze out Over There, and doing so could get you an eyeful of something you weren't ready for. Or bring something back with you. The candles let her see without seeing, so to speak. The same divination techniques that charlatans and hucksters used to separate the desperate or gullible from their coins could also be wielded by someone with a true gift, whether it was scrying into water bowls, throwing chicken bones, or turning cards. Clara just liked fire; the candles focused and protected her, functioning like a one-way mirror, but she didn't strictly need them.

However, with the Enigmas silent, she peered through the veil between worlds and tuned in to the Monroe boy's aura. When she glimpsed the echo of his spirit Over There, she reared back in shock. Whatever was afflicting him wasn't natural. A normal disease, either physical or mental, would have clouded his energy with the murky tones of the sickly. However, this was a net of malevolent energy swirling around him like smoke. Its origins could only be in the spirit world. And the spirits themselves were avoiding both of them. Even the least powerful denizens of Over There were giving Clara a wide berth.

Knowing the risks, she tried again, without any intermediaries, eschewing the flame and wax and smoke, calling out with her own inner voice, one she knew could pierce into that other place. She shouted silently into the unknown—a dangerous activity since you never knew just who might hear. A true summoning was out of the question—that would put her into debt personally and she couldn't bear the weight—but she knew the Enigmas could hear her. They were just ignoring her.

The energy clouding Titus's aura was powerful and heavy. And coming from it was a thin thread of rainbow-colored light which extended into the beyond. That was what started this affliction, she guessed.

She had no further time to investigate, for the press of a familiar, terrifying presence made itself known to her. She shuttered her sight and sat back, breathing heavily.

"They won't come," she whispered.

"What do you mean they won't come?" Dorothy asked slowly.

"I'm not quite sure. They just…It's never happened to me before. Not in my entire life. I call and something comes. To have nothing… Whatever happened to your son is not something that any of the Enigmas want to help and fix." *Which means one of them is likely responsible.* That rainbow-colored thread led somewhere.

"So what do I do now?"

Clara blew out the candles and spun around on her stool to face the woman. "I…I'm not sure."

Even a bargain with an Enigma and the resulting Trick were at least *something*. To be able to offer nothing at all and to relegate the woman to uncertainty—it stung. "We could try again another day, but...I don't think it would make a difference. You could go see Uncle Nazareth. I don't know that he'd be able to help, but you could try."

Dorothy set her jaw and nodded in a manner of a woman who had known great loss and sorrow. She heaved a deep breath and turned to leave, with a firm grip on her son's wrist. "Thank you, Miss Johnson. I really appreciate you trying to help."

"I'm very sorry I couldn't do anything for your boy."

Dorothy waved absently with her free hand but didn't say anything else as she trundled out, her vacant-eyed son in tow.

Clara stood in the center of the room, unhappily staring at the closed front door. Failure nettled, leaving barbs under her skin. A snapping sound had her turning back to her altar. The candles she'd blown out had lit themselves again. The flames rode high, at least a foot in the air. They kissed each other, reaching out for her, gyrating and swirling together unnaturally.

A shiver danced down her spine.

She didn't dare chance another look Over There. Instead she rushed across the room and blew out the candles. Then she slammed the door shut.

5

THE EMPRESS REQUESTS

On Tuesday afternoon Clara easily found a seat on the nearly empty streetcar and settled in for the ride downtown. Outside the window, the overcast skies vowed rain. Her own mood was just as gray. Samuel hadn't come to work for the second day in a row, and she was beginning to really worry. He had no telephone—she was fairly certain the boy's family had no electricity or running water either—and no way to alert them if he was ill.

Mrs. Shuttlesworth had tasked Clara with one of his duties, traveling down to the Library of Congress to pick up a sheaf of documents the assistant librarian had set aside for the journal.

"Dr. Woodson is in particular need of those papers, so don't dawdle," the woman had admonished.

The founder of the *Journal of Negro History*, Dr. Carter G. Woodson, did not exactly rule his employees with an iron fist. But everyone from the educated researchers to the typists and stenographers lived in fear of *the look*—the one that meant that not only had you disappointed him directly, but by extension you had let down your entire race. Working for a man who had done so much for Negroes was a responsibility they all took seriously. Well, almost all of them. By rights, Langston should have been given this task in the first place since he was Dr. Woodson's assistant, but that man was more idle than a broken-down jalopy. He hailed from one of Washington's more important families and was just as spoiled and entitled as the rest of them—though without all the snobbery. So Clara went instead.

She enjoyed her work at the *Journal*; it was important and fulfilling and far preferable to scrubbing floors, even considering the presence of the Jackass and his sycophants. But she didn't feel that she fit there and wasn't certain how long she would stay. Of course, where else would she go?

As the streetcar creaked and rolled down 7th Street, the weight of a stare grazed her skin. A white man sitting across the aisle, his back to the windows, pierced her with ice-blue eyes. The trolleys were integrated and she could sit where she liked, but that wasn't why he was staring. And, of course, no one else could see him because he was dead. Had been for six years now.

He didn't come around too often, just every now and then, staring a hole in her head with murder in his face. She held his gaze, jutting her chin out and narrowing her eyes, to show that she wasn't scared of him, but she wouldn't win this contest and eventually looked away. He never had nothing to say to her and eventually would be on his way again. But his presence was just one more domino stacked in a set that felt like it was teetering.

All day she'd felt unseen eyes watching her. Tracking her as she left home and walked to work, as she sat at her desk and ate lunch in the tiny kitchen. Maybe it was this familiar ghost with all his animosity, but it felt like something more.

"Mama Octavia?" she whispered. There was no one living seated nearby to hear her talking to herself.

"Yes, baby?" Her grandmother wasn't always in earshot, but when she was, she would come. Her physical form materialized on the bench, tilting her head.

"I had to use my sight last night, directly. Now I feel...like something or someone is following me."

The older woman took in the silent sentinel standing watch. "I see that boy's back. You think he's got something to do with it?"

Clara twisted her lips. "Not really. Feels like something bigger."

"He need to give up and move along."

"You can try talking to him again, but he don't bother me none."

Her grandmother frowned, knowing better, but didn't contradict her. "What happened last night, then?"

"This boy—well, his mama—asked for help, something was wrong with him and the Enigmas wouldn't come. I needed to see what it was."

"And what was it?"

"Something bad. He'd been targeted."

Her grandmother peered at her intently. "I'll keep an eye out, baby. But if nothing came through last night when you breached the veil, then you're probably safe from them."

Clara nodded. But she didn't feel safe.

"I'll go talk to some folks Over There and tell you what I find out." With that, she was gone.

The streetcar bell jangled. At the next stop, the car filled up some. A pair of Colored women smiled as they passed, then settled onto the bench just behind her.

"So you think she ran off with that boy?" one woman said, her voice hushed.

"I don't know what to think." Anguish filled the second voice. "She's home for the summer from Lincoln. With just a year left in school, she could have graduated and married him. Why run off now? My sister is just beside herself. It's just not like my niece to act this way."

The first woman tutted in response. "Something must be going around 'cause I been hearing stories. Folk acting strange. We're having a prayer circle tonight for two children who just up and lost their senses. Ain't right in the head no more. Their mamas don't know what to do. I sense the devil at work."

"Could be someone working one of them juju hexes."

The other woman hummed in agreement. Clara listened as their conversation continued, and the ominous sensation that had been clinging to her skin since the night before only grew heavier. Was the strange illness that had afflicted Titus Monroe affecting other young people? If so, what did it mean?

Out the window, Clara gazed at a trash can sitting in the mouth of the alley. Someone was burning garbage and the smoke thickened before her eyes. It puffed up like a mushroom before dying down again, unnaturally. Then it began to pulse in a steady rhythm, like a heart beating. She turned away, her stomach hollow. Her gaze met the eyes of the ghost, whose vengeful expression bent into a smirk. He tipped his hat, a policeman's cap, and disappeared.

Clara's unease grew over the rest of the afternoon and into the evening. She couldn't concentrate on her typing and made so many mistakes she'd had to start the whole article over. At the grocer's after work, she strolled down the milk aisle and the bottles began to rattle on the shelves. She stepped away quickly, peering around to make sure no one else had seen, when the thick glass of one bottle cracked before her eyes. White liquid streamed out, frothing and bubbling like it was being boiled. She spun on her heel and left, leaving her basket on the floor.

On the walk home, streetlights flickered on and off as she passed. They were all electric—no fire to smoke and dance—but they were giving her a warning all the same. When the bulb of one light burst with a pop, scattering sparks inside the glass case, she jumped, then raced all the way back to her apartment.

Ruth Anne was outside the beauty shop next door, chatting with a client. Clara hurried up her steps and nodded distractedly at the women.

"Clara Johnson, when you gonna let me tame those naps?"

The beautician's hair was smoothed into a fashionable short bob, the curled ends reaching her earlobes. Her lithe figure was well displayed in a short-sleeved, asymmetrical day dress with the hemline barely covering her knees.

Clara looked around nervously, not wanting whatever was happening to spill over and harm these women in any way. "I'd just sweat it out," she said with a shrug. Her hair was pressed and pulled back into a simple bun as usual.

"You barely have enough girls in there for the clients you got, Ruth Anne," her client said, turning away. "What you trying to drum up more business for?"

Clara paused, her key in the door. "You lost some of your hairdressers?"

Ruth Anne heaved a sigh. "Hazel and Virginia didn't show up today. I just about worked my fingers to the bone trying to fit their customers in on top of mine. Not sure what the world is coming to, folks not showing up without so much as a by-your-leave." She threw up her hands in disgust and turned back to her shop.

Clara pushed open her front door and ran up the steps to her apartment. Zelda wasn't there, thank goodness. She didn't want to answer any questions. She changed out of her work clothes, careful of every button and zip. Anything could be turned against her at this point and a powerful spirit wanting to grab her attention could get very creative.

Since her grocery run had been thwarted, she cautiously scraped together a baloney sandwich and drank a glass of water all while staring at the closed closet door.

Mama Octavia hadn't returned with any answers, but if Clara didn't want the entire neighborhood to come crumbling down at her feet, she needed to address this situation. Someone obviously wanted a word with her, and she had a good idea who it was.

Girding herself, she entered the tiny closet, sat on her stool, and lit a single candle—a long red-and-black taper. Almost immediately the flame turned a spectral white and an indistinct face peered through.

"Clara. You try my patience."

She swallowed the retort she wanted to give, pressing her lips together and breathing slowly. "I take it you wanted to contact me."

The flame rose higher and the face grew more defined. A regal forehead and deep-set eyes. Cheekbones sharp enough to wound. This Enigma called herself The Empress, and she and Clara had history.

"You could have come last night." Clara kept her tone light as she was more than familiar with this spirit's temper.

"I could not speak freely in front of those people."

"Do you know what's wrong with that boy? What caused it?"

"I do. And you can help him . . . by helping me."

She was welded to the stool, an icy sickness spreading through her. A bargain was something she needed to avoid. The Empress continued, "Someone near you has acquired an item she has no business with. I need you to get it back for me."

"What is it?"

"A ring."

Clara frowned. How could a spirit use a ring? It wasn't possible. Under certain circumstances an Enigma could interact with the human world in a physical way, but Clara wasn't interested in creating any of those circumstances. "I don't understand."

"Are you familiar with a woman calling herself Madame Josephine Lawrence?"

"The opera singer. Of course. She owns half of U Street." Madame Josephine was a local celebrity from one of the hundred families that

43

made up the best of Colored Washington. After the Great War ended, she'd performed around the world and, when she returned to the District, had surprised everyone by marrying a notorious gangster, Bow-legged Mo. The two of them began buying up property and businesses. She was a woman completely out of Clara's orbit.

"Madame Josephine has this ring you want?"

"Indeed. And you must take it from her. She wears it at all times, so this is no easy task. But your reward will be great. I will make a new deal with you, even better than our last one." The smoky visage smiled, causing spiderwebs of dread to lace themselves across Clara's skin.

"Even if I wanted to do this, how would I get it to you? And how would you use it?"

The Empress grew testy. "Do you think yours are the only hands I have at my disposal in the human world?"

The spirit's evasion of the question caused waves of unease to fill Clara's belly. "And what does this have to do with Titus Monroe?"

The Empress's ghostly lips pursed. "The ring caused his condition."

Clara blinked. That malignant energy she'd seen surrounding the boy was magically made, and if this ring caused it, that was even more reason to stay away. "Are you saying that Madame Josephine attacked that boy?"

"No."

"Then what?"

"The *ring* caused his condition," The Empress snapped. "And the ring can reverse it. Do what I ask. We will strike a new deal."

Clara chuckled humorlessly. "What you're asking is madness. Madame Josephine is untouchable and powerful, with an even more powerful and dangerous husband. Even if I were a professional thief with money and resources and knew how to do what you asked, I wouldn't."

"Not for the sake of that child? The boy whom the ring has saddled with a spiritual affliction?"

Clara clenched her jaw. "It's not just him, is it? How are the spirits involved?"

The Enigma narrowed her eyes. "Just as there are wars between humans, we have wars here too. However, instead of a few mere years, ours can last eternities. There are battles for control, alliances and betrayals. We function much as you do in that regard. None of us are pure good or pure evil."

"You have free will," Clara murmured. "Just like us."

The Empress smiled. "Yes. And I am trying to right a wrong and save my people from tyranny...and free yours as well. Our conflicts can spill over into your world. Humans will suffer greatly if the ring stays in its present hands. I *need* it." The face in the flame swelled, the candle's fire expanding and lighting the wicks of all the other candles around it on the altar. Clara shrank back from the heat and the power, but could not give in.

"You'll have to get someone else to do it. I don't want a new deal with you, and I can't risk sacrificing myself." She stood quickly, toppling over the stool in her haste as the unified flame grew.

"I have much to offer you, Clara. Do not turn away from this."

Clara shook her head and backed away. "I'm sorry, I just can't."

She picked up a mason jar filled with sand from the corner and dumped it over the candles, snuffing out the flames. Her hands shook as the smoke filled the room.

The Empress's face took a long time to fade.

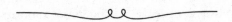

Clara's head swam as she backed into the main room. She turned and jumped to see Zelda sitting on the couch.

"When did you get in?" Her breath heaved and she placed a hand on her chest to slow her racing heart.

"Few minutes ago." Zelda stood and went to the stove. "Tea?"

Clara nodded and made her way to the armchair. It had been her father's and the leather was cracked and torn in multiple places. She imagined him sitting on it like he used to, filling his pipe with tobacco after a long day's work. She missed him something awful and wished he had a telephone so she could hear his voice telling her that everything would be all right.

She and Zelda didn't speak while the teakettle rattled away. Soon enough, there were two chipped teacups on the coffee table sitting next to the sugar bowl. The scent of chamomile and lemon wafted into the air, and Clara mumbled a thanks as she sweetened her tea.

"I think you should reconsider your situation." Zelda's voice had a little rasp to it, like she'd been somewhere shouting.

"What situation?"

"The one you're in right now."

Clara closed her eyes to keep from rolling them. Zelda had been rooming with Clara long enough to know about her powers and the debt she held to The Empress. They didn't often discuss it, though— and she had no desire to do it now.

"You know, I heard Nellie Caldwell was looking for a roommate since her sister is getting married. Maybe you should go see about that."

"Nellie Caldwell stuck her hand in my face to see if I was covered in chalk." She sipped her tea calmly. "I bit her finger. I don't think she'd make a good roommate."

Clara blew out a breath.

"You really want me to leave, I'll be gone tomorrow. But first you need to think about your leverage."

Clara rolled her eyes at the common refrain. Then her words sunk in. "What do you mean?"

"That Enigma of yours sounded desperate. Like she might be willing to do something drastic to get what she wants."

"That's what I'm afraid of."

"No, you're thinking like a rube. You need to think like a grifter. Desperate people make mistakes. They're easy to control because they're only focused on what they want or need. You can use that. She wants to renegotiate, well, what does she have that *you* want?"

Clara set her mug down and leaned forward, Zelda's meaning becoming clear. "She could end my debt to her. Remove my Trick."

A slow smile spread across Zelda's face. "Now you're cooking with gas."

Clara's mind raced with the possibility. Would The Empress really agree to it? Enigmas released debts on their own schedule, if ever. She'd heard of it happening a time or two, and if you ingratiated yourself with them and made a good impression, you could get rewarded. Truly rewarded, not the double-edged Charms that came with a Trick.

"She sounded that desperate to you?"

Zelda nodded. "It's worth a try, at any rate. What have you got to lose?"

Clara sat back in her chair. She could lose far more than she imagined. Enigmas were known for twisting words and meanings for their own amusement, but what if The Empress was desperate enough? Could this really work in Clara's favor? Doubts and suspicion— especially of the Enigma's motives—clung to her like storm clouds, but amid the tempest was a small beacon of hope.

Could she take such a great risk for an equally great reward?

6

SEARCHING FOR SAMUEL

Clara glanced up from her typewriter at Mrs. Shuttlesworth, who had begun tapping distractedly on her own desk with the edge of a ruler. Their gazes met across the short distance and worry was evident in the creases of the older woman's face. She wasn't just the office manager, she was more like the office mother, and even though they didn't always see eye to eye, Clara had always appreciated her maternal care.

"This is the third day that boy hasn't shown up," Mrs. S. said, looking over at the clock on the wall. "He's never been late or missed so much as a day before. I think something must have happened to him."

A similar concern had sunk into Clara's bones. Walking home by herself the last two days, she'd tried to brush off her disquiet, but for ambitious and driven Samuel, with his ailing mother and gaggle of younger siblings relying on him, to just not show up for three days in a row? Something was very wrong.

The Empress's visit was never far from her thoughts either. She didn't believe in coincidences. If Titus Monroe's condition had an otherworldly cause, and others were being afflicted as well, it stood to reason that the rise in missing people around the neighborhood was connected in some way. Hell, Titus would be missing too if his mother hadn't kept an eagle eye on him, practically chaining the boy to her side.

Clara's intuition was shooting off fireworks. She knew better than to ignore it, but she just didn't know what it all meant.

The phone on Mrs. Shuttlesworth's desk rang. "Associated Publishers, how can I help you?"

Clara pulled out the last page of the article Dr. Woodson needed done this morning, then stood. "I'm going to go by and check on him, make sure he's not laying up sick or something." Though that would actually be the best-case scenario. "Should have done it yesterday," she mumbled. But with The Empress trying to grab her attention, she'd been a risk to anyone she came across.

Mrs. S. smiled gratefully and mouthed a thank-you before turning her attention back to the call. Clara gathered her purse and turned to leave just as Dr. Harley entered the front office along with Glenda, Theresa, and Irene, the stenographers who often followed him around like a Greek chorus.

"A bit early for lunch, isn't it?" Both of his eyebrows were raised.

"I'm running an errand." Her tone was brusque. She did not have the energy to get into it with the Jackass right now.

"Isn't that that boy's job?" Glenda asked, her shrill tone raising goose bumps on Clara's arms. "Where is he anyway?"

"We don't know. I'm going to check on him and make sure nothing's happened." When Glenda opened her mouth again, Clara added, "His people don't have a telephone. They live back in the Dennison alley."

Four identical looks of disgust met her. It was like she'd said his family ate cats for breakfast. Harley shook his head. "I told Dr. Woodson hiring that boy was a mistake. There's a genetic inferiority that manifests among the lower classes. It's not their fault, but there's a reason they don't manage to get far in life."

The three bobbleheaded women nodded their agreement to his asinine statement. Clara was certain her brain was on fire. Was it possible for steam to pour from a person's ears? "Perhaps you should share your theory with Dr. Woodson, I'm sure he would find it enlightening."

"You know your job isn't to check up on recalcitrant guttersnipes," Harley added.

"What is your job, anyway?" Theresa piped up breezily. She picked up the top page of the stack Clara had just finished with her finger and thumb, as if the pristine paper might have been dragged through the mud at some point. "With the number of errors you make, it's a wonder Dr. Woodson keeps you on at all."

"He does have a soft spot for the less fortunate." Irene directed a cloying smile her way while at the same time eyeing her with disdain.

Mrs. Shuttlesworth put a hand over the telephone's mouthpiece. "I have Dr. Turner on the line. He needs to dictate an article and since you girls don't seem to have anything to do at the moment..." She left the statement hanging.

Clara turned on her heel and headed toward the door, a wicked smile spreading across her face. Dr. Turner was a brilliant researcher, but his thick Jamaican accent made taking dictation from him a nightmare. One of Harley's sycophants was in for quite the morning.

"I'm going to make sure your pay is docked for the time out of the office, Clara," Dr. Harley called after her.

She waved at him, extending her middle finger just a bit straighter than the rest, and walked out the door. A wall of August heat hit her, ratcheting up her already high internal temperature. She marched down the street like a soldier going to war, only the battle she wanted to fight was with a certain bigmouthed know-it-all. She was heedless of her surroundings until the bleating of a car's horn brought her back to the present. The pedestrian crossing light was still red, but she was several steps into the intersection.

"You all right there?" an old man called out from a nearby doorway.

Clara nodded and stepped back onto the sidewalk. When the 7th Street streetcar bell jangled, she realized she'd been so distracted she was walking in the wrong direction. She groaned and started to turn around, but a familiar figure across the street made her pause.

Zelda raced out of a building with the sign "Uncle Al's Billiards" above the door. She was dressed, unusually for her, in a prim white tea dress and patent leather flats. She ran halfway down the block before disappearing into an alley. A moment later, two men ran from the pool hall, giving chase. Clara sighed, cursing her misfortune to be saddled with such an addlebrained girl.

She raced across the street, slipping through the cars waiting at the stoplight, then ran down the block in the opposite direction to another entrance for the alley, planning to cut them all off. The narrow passage was lined with dilapidated sheds, wooden and brick garages, and clusters of overflowing trash cans. Up ahead, at the T intersection where the alleys met, Zelda came barreling across the cobblestones. She didn't notice Clara and executed an impressively acrobatic move—using a crate lying next to a one-story garage as a springboard, she practically bounced off the wooden boards of the structure's wall and landed on its roof.

She stood up there, triumphant, before her eyes widened to find Clara approaching. The men who'd given chase speeded around the corner and skidded to a halt once they caught sight of the two of them.

"For Chrissakes, how did she get up there?" the taller one said.

"We want our money back, you thieving wench." The second one pointed a meaty finger at Zelda. They were both in their early twenties, with crisp haircuts and clipped accents. Out-of-towners. Probably from up North.

"What I tell you about scamming the tourists?" Clara asked.

"I didn't steal anything. I won their money fair and square." Far from being scared, Zelda appeared invigorated by the conflict, with a disturbing grin spreading across her face.

"That true?" Clara asked.

The tall one folded his arms. "She hustled us. Acted like she couldn't play. Lost the first few rounds, then cleaned our clocks."

"Are you two stupid? What do you think a girl all dolled up to look innocent is doing at a pool hall at ten o'clock in the morning? If you all got scammed, it's your own damned fault. Use your heads next time." At Clara's words, the stocky one hunched his shoulders. "And what were you going to do? Beat the money out of her?"

"I'd like to see them try," Zelda said, barely loud enough to hear.

"You, hush."

The men shared a glance. Both looked ashamed, as they should be.

"Tell you what," Zelda said. "I'll give you the chance to win it all back. Double or nothing?" Her eyes were alight.

The shorter one looked ready to accept, but his friend shook his head. "You stay away from us, you witch. We don't want nothing more to do with you." They backed away and then left the way they'd come.

"You're going to get yourself killed one day. You ever thought of getting a job like a normal person?"

Zelda shrugged. "I have a job. And I'll never be a normal person, so why pretend?" She bent her knees and flipped over the edge of the roof until she was hanging from it, her legs dangling down. Then she jumped to the ground, landing neatly in a crouch. Clara winced, but Zelda rose, brushing off her hands, no worse for the wear.

"What are you doing here? Shouldn't you be at work?"

More warnings and admonishments would do no good. Plus, Zelda was two years older, she should know better. Clara just needed to get used to the fact that one day she'd find the girl splattered on the pavement somewhere with a bullet in her head. "I got an errand to run."

"What kind of errand?"

Clara ran down the situation with the missing Samuel. Zelda's expression darkened.

"Uncle Al at the pool hall said the girl who does his laundry hasn't been seen in a couple days. Thought she must have run off with some man, but I met that girl and she is one hundred percent bull dagger."

"Maybe she ran off with some woman," Clara mused.

"And leave behind paying customers?" Zelda scoffed. "Seems like folks are starting to go missing."

"Two of Ruth Anne's hairdressers didn't show up, and I've heard other folk talking about lost family and friends too. I think you might be right. People are going missing." A deep chill overtook the sticky heat surrounding her. "And I think the Enigmas might have something to do with this too."

Zelda lowered her brows and looked around the alley suspiciously, as if an Enigma would pop out from behind a trash can.

"I'm on my way over to where the Fosters stay to see what Samuel's people have to say. Maybe I'm wrong and he'll be there in bed with a bad cold."

"Could be." Zelda fell into step with Clara.

"Where you headed?"

"I'm going with you."

Clara stopped. "Why?"

"For backup."

When Clara went to protest, Zelda raised a blonde eyebrow. Clara blew out a breath and narrowed her eyes. Stubborn heifer. "Fine."

They walked west, crossing lively 7th Street again, though at this time of the morning most of the businesses were quiet.

"Think someone is taking them?" Zelda asked.

"Couldn't be for ransom. What's the point of taking a teenage errand boy, or a hairdresser or laundress?"

Neither woman had an answer. The two remained quiet as they crossed the neighborhood. Partly because Clara was lost in her thoughts and partly because this stretch of S Street was pristine and some instinct kept her from sullying it with her voice. Perfectly kept three-story brick row homes, their tiny fenced-in yards manicured within an inch of their lives, stood at attention like soldiers on the tree-lined street. Up ahead, a dark-skinned woman in a maid uniform swept the iron steps. The Colored people who lived in these homes were the kind who hired servants and met up at social clubs like the Pollyannas, had cotillions at the Colonnade, went to galas at the Whitelaw Hotel, and looked down their noses at anyone considered beneath them. Dr. Harley's words came to mind. *There's a genetic inferiority that manifests among the lower classes.* One of these houses belonged to him.

The neighborhood shifted slightly, three-story homes becoming two stories. Well-kept, but without the unblemished obsessiveness as before. These people worked and did well for themselves, but not so well that they had other folks to do their cleaning for them.

The classes of Negroes in Washington were well defined, and at the bottom of them lay the world Clara entered when she turned down an alley between two modest white brick homes. Invisible from the main streets, rows of shabby houses faced one another. Pocket communities like this one were hidden behind row houses all across the city. A dreariness clung to the air back here, and though it was morning, the sun didn't penetrate the tight spaces, leaving it looking more like dusk. These structures had no electricity or plumbing, a communal water pump stood in the middle of the cobblestones, and two foul-smelling outhouses announced themselves as the women drew deeper into the courtyard.

An old man sat on a low stoop in front of one house. A corncob pipe hung from his lips as his head lolled back against the bricks. Zelda glared at him suspiciously, but he barely opened his eyes as they approached.

"Excuse me. Do you know where the Foster family stays?" Clara asked.

The man didn't say anything, just pointed a dark, gnarled finger across the way toward a two-story structure with a boarded-up window next to the front door. It backed directly against the home facing the main street, but whether or not the residents there knew or cared about the people they shared a wall with was anyone's guess. Clara approached with leaden steps and knocked on the rattling door.

After a minute, it cracked open and a brown eye blinked up at them.

"Hello. We're looking for Samuel."

The door slid open a fraction more to reveal a tiny, brown-skinned girl whose hair was badly in need of a brush and some grease. The girl blinked at them owlishly. Clara realized she was staring up at Zelda.

An albino Negro was always a strange sight, but Zelda crouched down to the child's level and smiled. "You wanna see some magic?"

The little girl nodded. Zelda pulled a penny from the pocket of her dress and held it in her palm, then closed her fist around it and rotated her wrist a few times before opening her hand. The penny was gone.

Clara was afraid the child's eyes would pop right out of her head. She grinned a gap-toothed smile, apparently delighted. Zelda then pulled the penny from behind the girl's ear and the child dissolved into giggles.

"Ain't seen Samuel since Monday morning," another voice said from inside the gloomy residence. The little girl opened the door wider to reveal the room. It was small and cluttered with furniture. The dim light of an oil lamp revealed a bed in the far corner where Samuel's mother lay. A coughing fit wracked her before she could continue.

"He been acting strange. Sitting in the corner staring at nothing. Not lifting a finger or saying a word to nobody. Not like himself at all. Then he just up and left."

"He hasn't been to work," Clara said, sharing a glance with Zelda. "We were getting worried."

The woman's eyes closed. "I don't know what could have gotten into him. Maybe he's just sick in the head like his daddy. If you see him, tell him the children is hungry." As if to punctuate the statement, the little girl's stomach growled loudly. "He always does the shopping."

Samuel's mother appeared far less distressed than Dorothy Monroe had been about what sounded like a similar condition affecting their sons, but Clara reasoned that everyone dealt with things in their own way. Living here probably made people highly adaptable.

Clara thanked the woman and stepped back outside. Zelda handed the penny to the child, who clutched it like it was made of gold. The door closed behind them and they turned back to the bleakness of the alley.

A heaviness was forming around Clara's heart. It certainly sounded like Samuel and Titus Monroe were suffering from the same affliction. But why? And if this ring that Madame Josephine wore had caused this, what was the purpose?

A cat mewled somewhere nearby and a door opened across the narrow courtyard. Clara considered the next steps. There were some places the local teens congregated, she could try there, see if anyone had seen Samuel—maybe she could connect him and Titus Monroe. If this was an illness of some kind, or even a curse or a hex, knowing where they'd been struck would be helpful.

"Don't look." Zelda spun around to face the house. She tugged on Clara's arm, but it was too late. There was nowhere to hide, they were out in the open.

The man who had emerged from the home catty-corner to them was saying his goodbyes to someone inside. He turned away and the smile on his face promptly fell when he caught sight of Clara.

She took a deep breath and squared her shoulders. "Uncle Nazareth."

Dressed in a maroon suit with a white turban covering his bald head, the older man scowled. He marched his spindly frame over to them, making the string of cowry shells around his neck rattle.

"Clara Johnson. What'd I tell you about stealing my customers?" He raised a knobby finger to wag it in her face. Only the Lord himself kept her from grabbing that finger and twisting it clear off. She'd been raised to respect her elders, but respect had to be earned.

Just at that moment Mama Octavia shimmered into view. She took one look at Uncle Nazareth carrying on like he had no sense and started cussing up a storm, using words that even Clara would never repeat. And though he couldn't hear her, it was a wonder the man's ears didn't burn to a crisp.

"I haven't stolen any of your customers," Clara said through gritted teeth.

"I been in this city twenty-seven years, and I'm not going anywhere. No one asked me to, neither! And I never had no trouble until you come round. You don't even charge folks! Why come to old Uncle Nazareth when Miss Clara Johnson will help you for free?" He sniffed.

Clara shook her head wearily. "You know I can't charge nobody money. But trust me, they all pay plenty. And I do try to send them to you when I think the Trick will be too bad. Not that I think your hoodoo will actually help." She muttered the last under her breath.

He crossed his arms with a *hmph*. "You're the type of disagreeable gal folk put roots on every day. I got a mojo bag with your name on it."

Zelda shifted. She wasn't particularly big or tall or strong-looking, but when she settled her glare on him, he took a step back. "You threatening my friend?" she asked through a clenched jaw.

Mama Octavia cracked her knuckles and Uncle Nazareth glanced at the space where she stood. He couldn't see her, of that Clara was certain, but it definitely looked like he was sensing something. She'd always thought him a quack and didn't put much stock into his kind of rootwork, all style with very little substance, but maybe the man had a twinge of psychic ability. Or maybe all the menace directed at him right now was simply too intense *not* to feel.

Even with her Trick, there were some requests that Clara could refuse—killing or physically hurting people were included. She didn't know what Uncle Nazareth's boundaries were, and she didn't particularly want to find out.

"You just listen here," Nazareth said, fortunately keeping his finger to himself this time. "I'm trying to make a living. I don't need you pilfering my clientele."

"What makes you think I'm here drumming up business?"

He narrowed his eyes at her, but instead of answering, turned on his heel and stalked away.

"If that countrified Negro tries to put roots on you, I'll haunt him 'til his nappy hair grows back," Mama Octavia muttered. Clara smirked. "The damned fool couldn't spell his way out of a dictionary. Been peddling chicken-bone cures and reading tea leaves and calling it magic, putting real root doctors to shame. Some nerve he's got."

"I don't have time to worry about him," Clara said.

"What time is it anyway?" Zelda asked, holding up a battered men's watch. The glass was scratched but the leather band dangling from her fingers looked new.

"You took that from him?"

Zelda shrugged. "Could be it fell off his wrist."

Mama Octavia chuckled approvingly. Sometimes her grandmother was cold-blooded.

"Well, it needs to fall back on. We don't need no more trouble from that old scarecrow. Slip it in his window or something, make him think he lost it."

The pickpocket grumbled under her breath, but Clara ignored it. Mama Octavia turned and crossed her arms. "What you doing back here? You'll get your throat cut in one of these alleys, sure as I'm standing here."

"You're not really standing here, Gran. And I'm looking for someone.

People around the neighborhood are going missing, including a friend of mine. Were you able to find anything out Over There?"

"Not enough. Just a bunch of haints who can't find their kin. You're right about the missing. It's all anyone can talk about."

Many people's ancestors stayed close to their loved ones after passing. Most not as directly as Mama Octavia, though. "They're going someplace we can't see or find them either," the older woman said.

"When did this all start?" Clara asked.

"This past weekend sometime. That's when those I talked to first started getting worried."

"I saw Samuel on Friday and he was normal as can be. What could have happened this weekend?" Dorothy Monroe had said her boy started acting strange over the weekend as well.

Zelda frowned. "This weekend? Could it have something to do with that ofay march?"

"The Klan? Lord, I hope not." If the Ku Klux Klan had something to do with kidnapping Negroes, then they were in for a world of trouble. The cloud she'd seen corrupting Titus Monroe's aura and The Empress's confirmation of an otherworldly cause led her to believe the answers lay elsewhere. She didn't think a bunch of racist whites had access to Over There. Then again, what did she know about white people and how they operated? Just because Madame Josephine wore the ring didn't mean that a curse or hex done by someone else couldn't be using its power.

Zelda looked back toward Samuel's house, expression worried. "In the meantime, I'm going to stop by Miss Ruby's grocery and get some food for the little ones. Put those city boys' money to good use."

As Zelda slipped down the alley, Mama Octavia's expression darkened. "You be careful, Clara Mae. The spirits are troubled. Whatever's going on feels big. Powerful."

Clara nodded. "I feel it too. Growing."

Her grandmother faded, once again leaving Clara alone. She paced out of the alley and back into the sun. The last time she'd felt this weighted, pregnant dread, she was seventeen years old and her world was about to explode. Once again, it was as if the air held the scent of a storm coming even though the sky was still blue.

The thing that was coming would play itself out, the way these things always did. Knowing something was going to happen and being able to stop it were two different things. A shiver raced through her, overcoming the oppressive heat and raising goose bumps on her skin. She wasn't looking forward to it, whatever it was.

7

THE REANIMATED

The small patch of grass was a triangle bordered by three streets—
10th and U were perpendicular to each other, while Vermont Avenue sliced a diagonal line through the city, a spoke in the wheel of one of the city's many traffic circles. Park benches lined an area peppered with bushes and spindly trees. As far as parks went, it wasn't much, but the neighborhood kids liked to gather there, the girls gossiping on benches, the boys throwing dice and pretending to be grown.

It was a block from Clara's apartment and the place where Dorothy Monroe had stated her son Titus had gone when she'd let him wander. He'd stood at the corner on the bottom tip of the triangle, rocking back and forth and waiting. But waiting for what?

After going back to work to deliver the news of what she'd learned about Samuel to Mrs. Shuttlesworth, Clara had found it difficult to concentrate. So instead of heading home at the end of the day, she'd tried to retrace Samuel's steps. She'd visited his other jobs at Davis's Drugstore and the Murray Brothers Printing Company.

He'd been at the drugstore Saturday morning, doing inventory in the back, but had disappeared after lunch. And the deliveries he was supposed to have made that afternoon for the printer had to be taken by someone else. The pharmacist, Dr. Davis, had been deeply concerned about Samuel.

"You let me know when you find him," he'd said. "I've been hearing murmurings about people going missing, and Samuel is such a good boy. So much potential." He'd clucked his tongue as Clara retreated from the shop.

The manager at the print shop had already hired a replacement. "Too many folks wanting work to wait. One monkey don't stop no show, you know?" the man had said over the sounds of the machinery spitting out sheaves of paper.

And so Clara had headed to the park. It was the only other location that could hold any potential answers, if Samuel's disappearance was at all related to Titus Monroe's condition.

The place was mostly empty except for a handful of preadolescents who sat clustered around one boy holding a pulp magazine. On the cover, an illustration of a barely clad woman in the clutches of some kind of alien or monster or something was rendered in garish colors. Clara approached, tearing their attention away from whatever was on the pages. They all politely issued greetings to her.

"Y'all know Samuel Foster?" she asked. The boys shared questioning looks and then shook their heads. Samuel was a bit older than them anyway. "You heard of folks going missing around here?"

A redboned youngster with freckles peppering his cheeks spoke up. "My cousin Wendell. Auntie's been worried sick about him. Hasn't seen him since church on Sunday."

Clara blew out a breath and looked around. "I heard that sometimes folks will come here and stand around, not doing anything."

An uneasy silence reigned for long moments. Finally, a stout, dark-skinned boy said, "They don't bother anybody, but they come shuffling through, almost every day. Give me the creeps."

The redbone snickered, but a smaller boy shot him a look. "You were the one who said you thought they acted like one of the reinvigorated." The others murmured their agreement.

"The reinvigorated?" Clara asked.

The one with the magazine held it up. "It's from a story. A mad scientist loses his lady love to typhus and is obsessed with bringing her back to life. He steals her corpse from the graveyard and invents a machine that reinvigorates her. Only when she comes back, she's not the same."

"Touching the beyond has done something to her," the dark-skinned boy added, his voice full of reverence. "She's alive, but not alive. She doesn't speak or sing the way she used to and the scientist is upset."

"See, he brought back her body but not her soul," the first one continued. "So she's just an empty husk."

Half a dozen pairs of wide eyes stared up at her. Clara blinked. "So what happens at the end of the story?"

The magazine owner shrugged. "It's a serial. The end doesn't come out until next month."

She chuckled to herself, surprised that she'd gotten so caught up in their silly story. There were no mad scientists reinvigorating Colored people. She'd heard tales of Enigmas bringing folks back from the dead, old stories from slavery times said to have been told by some of the last Africans brought over in chains, but Clara didn't believe them. The spirits were powerful, but were they that powerful? And none of the missing had actually died. As far as she knew.

"Here come some of them now."

Several boys pointed to the opposite sidewalk where a young man and woman stepped out into traffic in the middle of the block. Appearing to be in their late teens or early twenties, they walked with stilted steps, eyes vacant; they completely ignored the cars honking at them as they shambled across the street. Drivers threw epithets and swerved to avoid them, but the two paid them no mind.

They approached the spot where the Monroe boy had stood, according to his mother, at the edge of the park, right at the intersection. Clara started walking toward them, but before she got close, a Model T roadster with a flatbed-pickup body pulled up to the curb. A bulky man with his hat pulled low jumped out of the passenger side, opened the hatch, and pushed the two afflicted people into the back of the vehicle, which was meant for cargo and such. Two teens were already seated there, all with the same blank expressions matching that of Titus Monroe. Then the truck took off.

Clara was locked in place, her jaw hanging open. It took long moments for her legs to start working. When they did, she raced after the vehicle, which turned left at the corner onto U Street.

At this time of the evening, the street was busy with folks returning home on their evening commute, or stopping in at the shops and eateries. With traffic relatively heavy, that truck wouldn't be able to move too quickly. Maybe she could follow it. At least for a little ways. Or she could find a taxi to trail it. But she didn't have much cash on her, and cabs weren't cheap.

She hurried across the street, keeping the vehicle in her sights. It was stopped at a red light, but then the signal changed and the cars surged forward. There was no way she could do this on foot, even with the heavy evening traffic. She began looking for a cab but didn't spot one among all the cars.

Disappointment weighed heavily. And the realization dawned that not only was someone afflicting people, but they looked to be kidnapping them as well. The Empress had stated that Madame Josephine was not responsible, but if she had the ring, and the ring was to blame, then certainly she must know who was behind this. Unless the ring was being used without her knowledge.

The sidewalk was full of people. Clara, standing still among them, was jostled and pushed. She moved off to stand under the awning of a law office, still looking down the street to where the truck had disappeared. But a familiar face caught her attention, causing her to stiffen.

Miss Louise Wyatt walked on the arm of a tall and dapper young man. They looked like a matched set, both expensively dressed and coifed, not the most attractive folks in the world, but they carried themselves with class and grace. Louise's man held several shopping bags and looked at her so adoringly, he was barely paying attention to where he walked. More than one person had to hustle out of his way or else be plowed down.

Clara backed into the doorway, trying to sink into the shadows. The two would shortly pass right in front of her and she had no wish to be recognized. Louise's expression was inscrutable. The girl was poised, but did not appear happy.

A passing gentleman tipped his hat at her, smiling admiringly regardless of the fellow already on her arm. Louise's man shot a challenging glare at him and quickened his pace. Jealousy hovered around him like a cloud.

Clara turned just before she could be spotted, feigning deep interest in the nameplate of the law offices. Street noise roared in her ears as she drowned in shame. Though she had neither struck the deal nor accepted it, and had given the warning she was able to—part of her Trick included no vociferous objections to the deals she facilitated—the part she'd played, the responsibility for the young woman's plight, burrowed into her chest.

Years of debts, people cursed, lives altered—the memories were a noose around her neck and with each new deal, it drew tighter. She was barely able to breathe at all.

She pressed a hand into the cool glass embedded in the door before resting her fevered forehead on it. The Empress could get her clear of this ocean of guilt. She could void their deal, toss out a life preserver to save Clara from the stormy seas, and leave her safely on a shore where there were no new Charms and Tricks to be the conduit for.

Much as she didn't trust the Enigma, and didn't want anything more to do with her, the possibility of freedom was too tempting to ignore. Accepting her Charm and Trick had led Clara from a prison of concrete and iron to another made of regret. Now, all she had to do to breathe fresh air again was something slightly impossible.

Clara stumbled into the stream of people on the sidewalk, barely seeing them, the roar of their voices drowned out by the volume of thoughts racing through her mind. She had no recollection of walking the short distance home and found herself inside an empty apartment.

She blinked a few times to clear the fog from her mind, then squared her shoulders. She didn't even take her shoes off before crossing the room, entering the closet, and sitting on the stool. Shaking fingers lit the single candle and the Enigma's ghostly visage came through the flame almost immediately.

"This ring," Clara said with no preamble. "Taking it from Madame Josephine will somehow stop what's happening to the people in the neighborhood? The strange affliction suffered by Titus Monroe and others?"

The Empress's smoky grin made chills run up Clara's spine. "The ring is the cause. Once you get it for me I will be able to reverse the effects."

"And how will I get it to you? I need to know before I agree."

"A simple ritual that may be completed with mundane materials. It does not require the blood of virgins, if that is what you are concerned about."

Clara snorted. She still had concerns about The Empress and her plans, but if she could help Samuel and Titus and the others and at the same time free herself—it was a risk worth taking.

"All right. I'll try to steal this ring, and in exchange, my debt is cleared, my Trick is gone. No more brokering deals for your kind."

"You would give up your Charm as well, you know?"

"Fine." The Charm was tainted, as they all were. She'd never wanted it in the first place, but she'd thought she needed it four years ago when she first made the deal. After using it once she'd vowed to never use it again, and that wasn't changing.

"Very well," The Empress cooed. "Get the ring and give it to me and your original deal will be vacated."

"And no new Tricks or Charms? I'll be completely free."

"You will be free, indeed, Clara Johnson."

Enigmas couldn't lie. They could twist and bend but not outright deceive. Clara recognized her own desperation but could sense nothing in The Empress's words to object to.

"Then I agree."

A cold wind whistled through the tiny closet, blowing Clara's hair back. It snuffed out the candle as well, taking The Empress's victorious laugh with it.

Clara wanted answers to whatever was happening to the people in her neighborhood. Plus, she needed to be done with this endless guilt. Hope and dismay warred within her. For now, she had to find a way to steal a magical ring off the finger of the most powerful and well-connected Colored woman in Washington.

8

MADAME JOSEPHINE

A full day later, Clara's ears were still smarting from the tongue-lashing Mama Octavia had given her. Her granny had read her up one side and down the other for agreeing to become a thief, as she'd put it.

"I raised you better than that, gal," the ghost had said, her final words on the topic, a disappointed scowl cutting grooves into her cheeks. She was right. Under normal circumstances, Clara would never have dreamed of doing anything like this, but the situation was far from normal.

Mama Octavia would eventually come around, but yesterday she'd faded away, ensconced in a cloud of disapproval, and wasn't speaking to Clara. Whose stomach was still upset from a combination of guilt and nerves. Seated now on a stool at the Howard Dairy Lunch, she stirred another spoonful of sugar into her coffee. The bitter brew did nothing to settle her roiling belly.

From her perch at the counter in the front window, she had a clear view of the street. Next to her, Zelda wolfed down a plate of bacon and eggs, regardless of the fact that it was going on eight o'clock in the evening. The restaurant had been staying open late on the days when there were big shows next door at the Howard Theatre. But Clara hadn't been able to eat.

Out the window, traffic had stalled on the narrow one-way street, and the spotlight illuminating the front of the theater glinted off metal and chrome. A red carpet had been rolled out onto the sidewalk in front of the theater's main doors, and the doormen in their crisp uniforms walked back and forth, escorting VIP patrons from their cars into the building.

Tonight was the opening of a new vaudeville show, and according to Zelda, the neighborhood gossip agreed that Madame Josephine would be putting in an appearance. Mama Octavia would be happy to know that Clara still couldn't believe she was actually doing this, and most of her was very doubtful she'd succeed. But she was determined to try to gain her freedom. In order to get close enough to the singer to steal from her, she needed as much information as possible. Detectives in the dime novels she'd read as a child were always following their subjects around, finding patterns in their behavior, and learning their known associates. So, while she was seeking to commit a crime instead of solve one, she was doing the same. Zelda, of course, had invited herself along. But it turned out she had a network of contacts that was very useful.

An impeccable ruby-red Hudson limousine pulled up and Clara stiffened. This was not the first limo that had arrived, but it was by far the nicest. Even the tires appeared to glisten with polish. A brown-skinned man in a black cap was visible in the driver's seat, but the interior was shaded from view by filmy curtains. Soon enough the occupant emerged—a burly man with hands the size of dinner plates and broad features. Clara's shock faded as the door remained open and the man bent, offering a meaty paw to the delicate arm that emerged.

Rings covered every finger of the hand, and the long, tapered fingernails were painted blood red. A diamond bracelet surrounded the wrist, and the rest of the body that slowly emerged was just as bejeweled and resplendent. The woman's dress matched her nail color and was the very latest in fashion, with a drop waist and a skirt shimmering with beads. Short-cropped hair, curled into a meticulous bob, was topped with a tiara that winked in the artificial light.

Madame Josephine stood to her full height, an impressively tall woman even if she only came to her companion's chin. She surveyed the scene around her, smiling serenely at the small crowd that rushed to greet her. She must be in her mid-forties at least, given the longevity of her career as an opera singer, but she appeared much younger. Her skin was a light cocoa, probably half a shade darker than a paper bag—the test which elites used to determine who was too dark for fashionable society. But that hadn't stopped her fame or popularity.

She received the folks who had emerged, practically from thin air, to greet her with a special knowing smile that hinted at secrets. Clara strained to focus on her hands, which flew as she talked, but though she could spot a number of rings, the woman was too far away for a good look at any of them.

Josephine's voice too remained a mystery through the glass of the picture window. Clara had heard the singer's arias on the radio, of course. She'd seen her drive by before, in a different automobile, and had once been pushed out of the way when her entourage had strolled down U Street, clearing a wide path for the celebrity. But she'd never truly been interested before.

"Is that Bowlegged Mo with her?" she whispered to Zelda. They were the only ones seated at the counter, but the eatery was still half full of people.

"No, he's not as big as a brick house. That must be a bodyguard." She sighed wistfully. "He could guard my body anytime." Clara raised a brow as Zelda gazed at the enormous man appreciatively.

Madame Josephine and the small crowd that had gathered around her disappeared into the theater, and Clara and Zelda wordlessly drained their coffee cups and left some change on the table to tip.

"Side door?" Clara asked. Zelda nodded.

The restaurant and the theater were separated by a wide alley, with the stage door to the theater located halfway down the long building. The door was "guarded" by a lanky youth smoking a cigarette.

"Evening, Billy," Zelda said, tossing him a dime. He blew smoke out of the corner of his mouth and grinned.

"Miss Zelda," he replied, sketching a bow. Then he pulled the door open for them.

The hallway beyond was teeming with people in various states of costumery. Musicians in suits lugged instruments, dancing girls scantily clad in beaded costumes stretched their long and limber limbs, two men dressed as bedraggled hobos painted each other's faces by the light streaming from a bare bulb overhead. A stout woman in an evening gown was doing vocal scales while a clown paced back and forth behind her.

No one stopped Clara and Zelda as they breached the hallway and entered a wall of organized chaos. The green rooms obviously could not hold the number of people performing tonight, but it gave the two interlopers even more cover. Clara peeked inside a room that was empty save for a man in an oversized yellow suit. He was blackening his already dark skin with burnt cork while muttering his lines and chewing on a cigarette.

"Is that...?" Clara whispered, eyes widening.

Zelda glanced in and nodded. "Yup. In the flesh."

Clara had not thought it possible for her to be overwhelmed by fame, but she blinked several times at the most famous vaudevillian comedian in the world before backing away.

Most of the doors to the green rooms were open, and Zelda peered in each one they passed. Finally she stopped at an entrance that was cracked open, with bustling activity audible within. She rapped three times on the doorframe before sticking her head through. Over her shoulder, Clara saw a space packed by women in various states of undress. Giant feathers strewn around blocked much of her view, though.

A dancer somewhat near the door looked over and smiled. She held up a finger and then made her way through the crowd of women to meet them in the hall.

"Estelle, this is Clara." Zelda made the introductions. Clara nodded; Estelle grinned. She, like the rest of the dancers in the room, was what Mama Octavia would call "high brown," too dark to be light-skinned, but not so brown as to offend. She was fine boned, with an upturned nose that made her look puckish, but her limbs were sinewy with the strength it took to be a professional dancer—and what's more, from the looks of it, one of the elite Howardettes.

"What do you hear, Estelle?" Zelda asked.

The woman looked up and down the hallway and led them closer to the stage, where the activity was a little less boisterous. "I can't talk long—we're the opening act—but the madame isn't easy to get near. She has her own box and her own waitstaff. Last time she was here, the manager tried to assign someone else to serve her because the normal girl was sick, but she wasn't having it. Sent her guard to get her drinks instead."

"Sounds paranoid," Clara mused.

"Ever since Bowlegged Mo got arrested."

"Wait, what?"

"You didn't hear?" Estelle's eyebrows climbed. "Her husband got himself caught rum-running in Virginia. Word is he's blaming a rival bootlegging outfit and increased his wife's security."

"When did he get arrested?" Clara asked.

"Couple weeks ago. But listen, if you want to talk to her about

72

sponsoring your show, doing it here ain't going to work," Estelle advised. In the distance, a man began shouting. "I gotta go. We even, Z?"

Zelda nodded and Estelle smiled her thanks before scampering away.

"Sponsoring your show?" Clara questioned.

Zelda shrugged. "Had to give a reason why I wanted the info. Something's going down with the bootleggers. If they're going to war, then Madame Josephine's going to be near impossible to get close to."

Clara grimaced as the band began to play the intro music. The odds against her success, already high, were climbing. What did she know about bootleggers and criminals? How was she going to get this done?

The dressing room door opened and the Howardettes, the premier Negro dancing group, raced by to take their places onstage before the curtain opened. Clara and Zelda flattened themselves against the wall to keep from being run over.

Applause filled the air as the audience caught the first sight of the dancing girls, who began their high-stepping routine. When Zelda went to move away, Clara grasped her arm and inclined her head. They edged closer to the stage, to a position where they weren't visible but still had a good view of the audience and the boxes stage right.

Sure enough, Madame Josephine sat alone, except for her hulking bodyguard, in a box that could seat half a dozen. From down here they could even see the doorway behind the box, which the guard stood beside. Then the guard stepped aside, letting in someone. The newcomer was tall, wearing a tuxedo and a charming grin. A grin which Clara recognized.

"Israel Lee."

He held a drink in each hand and settled next to Madame Josephine, handing her one. The two appeared quite comfortable with each other and Josephine laughed prettily at something Israel said. Though she was at least twenty years older than him, it looked like she was flirting.

"I guess with her husband in jail all bets are off."

Zelda shook her head. "Nah. She's a well-known flirt, and Bow-legged Mo and her seem to have some sort of agreement. She has toy-boys all over the city."

"Is he one of them?" Clara nodded at Israel.

"Hadn't heard. But maybe. He's the newest thing, and she likes collecting anything fashionable and pretty."

Clara wasn't sure that Israel Lee could be called pretty. Plenty of men could, but he skated the line. His jaw was a little too strong, his forehead too broad, and while his lips were sensual, they weren't soft. Nothing about him was soft. His good looks were clean-cut, but still strongly masculine. Clara realized she was staring and shook herself.

Two men in suits approached the box, stopping in front of the body-guard. They appeared to exchange words and the guard tensed. The large man seemed to expand slightly, shifting his weight and position to appear even more formidable.

While Madame Josephine took no notice, Israel Lee turned his head. Clara thought he was talking to the three men, who all looked poised for a fight. But apparently Israel was able to defuse the situation, for the two newcomers left and the bodyguard deflated his posture again. The entire incident left Clara wary.

Her nerves were rattled once more when a gruff voice spoke up from behind them. "Hey, what are you two doing back here?"

"Time to go," Zelda whispered, turning. A large man bearing a clip-board stared at them, bemused.

"We're on our way to our changing room," Zelda said cheerily. The man's eyes widened at the sight of her. "We're with the magicians. First time at the Howard, just wanted a peek before we get onstage."

She linked arms with Clara and pulled her away before the stage manager could get his tongue back. They scurried through the still-jammed hallway and to the stage door.

"What now?" Zelda said once they were safely out on the street. Billy was still at his post, puffing smoke circles into the sky.

"What we need is somebody who can get close to her," Clara thought out loud. "At least as close as Israel Lee can."

"You know anybody like that?"

"Yeah, I do. But I think it means I'll need to have another chat with The Empress."

9

THE FAIRY BALL

The True Reformer Hall stood on the corner of 12th and U Streets, just a block from Clara's apartment. Mama Octavia had told her of watching it being constructed as she walked baby Clara around the neighborhood in her buggy. Designed and built by Negroes, it towered over its neighbors like a proud sentinel. Inside were various businesses: a drugstore, a tailoring shop, meeting rooms used by various organizations, as well as a ballroom and concert hall.

Folks rented out the ballroom for parties and galas and society events where those from Strivers' Section or LeDroit Park came down to U Street to rub their long noses together. You could sometimes find Duke Ellington and his band playing on one of their visits back to their hometown from New York—though Clara had been a few years behind him in school and didn't see what the fuss was all about. Just another pretty-boy charmer who thought he was the bee's knees and was halfway decent on the piano.

Clara shuffled uncomfortably down the street wearing the beaded black flapper dress her neighbor Ruth Anne had lent her. The woman had also curled her hair—Clara still wasn't sure how it had all come to be. One minute she was standing in front of her closet wishing she had a fairy godmother to help her change her rags into a dress that would gain her entry to the ball—her ghostly grandmother having been of absolutely no assistance—the next minute, Zelda had dragged her downstairs and over to Ruth Anne's shop, and a curling iron was blasting her earlobes with heat.

The hairdresser's feet were a size smaller than Clara's, so her own simple, low-heeled oxfords would have to do, though they were not at all appropriate. Walking beside her, Zelda wore a wide-lapeled gray suit she'd borrowed from Miles. It didn't fit particularly well and Clara was glad they only had a very short distance to go since the stares Zelda usually received had already doubled in the past two minutes.

They joined the small crowd which had gathered on the sidewalk outside the hall. Tall figures in exquisite evening wear dwarfed them. Just as Clara spotted another woman in a man's suit, someone bumped into her from behind, pushing her forward.

"Excuse me, honey," a deep voice rumbled. A large hand clasped her shoulder to steady her.

She turned to find a clean-shaven middle-aged man in an exquisite jade gown smiling apologetically at her. The sight was undoubtedly unusual, but not unexpected considering where she was headed. "It's no problem," she replied.

The logjam at the door was slowly clearing, but the attitude of those awaiting entry grew tense. Clara looked over her shoulder to find a police car moving down the street. A collective breath was held until it had passed.

Once she'd breached the doorway, the reason for the jam was clear—there were two events here tonight. A woman stood on a chair in the entry shouting instructions. "Pollyanna social straight ahead. Fairy Ball upstairs."

The bulk of the impeccably dressed folks headed for the stairwell and Clara allowed herself to be swept up by the crowd. They paid their entry fee to the ticket taker—$1.25—and then entered the ballroom, quickly moving aside to get out of the flow of traffic.

Strings of twinkling lights adorned walls which were layered in pastel-colored gauzy material. Around the edges of the room, cocktail tables had been set up, but most of the crowd was out on the dance floor. Onstage, the band was rolling, playing a fast-paced tune that had everyone's feet moving.

The majority of the people gathered—whether male or female—wore women's clothing. Beads, silk, and satin reigned supreme and the array of hairstyles rivaled that of any fashion magazine. Just like with the gowns, those wearing suits or tuxedos ranged in size and shape. Clara suspected that some merely enjoyed breaking tradition, while others were overjoyed with the freedom of getting to explore a part of themselves they couldn't anywhere else. However, a fair number of the guests were masked to protect their identities. The Fairy Balls were an open secret, but that didn't mean the police couldn't decide to raid one at any moment.

Both white and dark faces peppered the ball attendees. The white folks must have come in through a different entrance, for she hadn't seen any out on the street. Overhead fans attempted to move the thick air, but weren't having much luck. But even with the heat and the crowd and the danger, folks were having a good time.

A wisp of longing brushed against Clara as she watched the people on the dance floor. She'd long ago shut the door on the normal things girls her age did. She didn't know the latest dances or which picture down at the Lincoln folks were excited about. Her penance. But maybe if she was able to pull this off, she would one day find herself on a dance floor like this one, cutting a rug and laughing and smiling like the people around her.

For now, she was here on a mission. She and Zelda stood at the edge of the room, scanning the place, when a commotion erupted behind them in the entryway. She glanced at the men arguing, then did a double take.

"Stay here," she told Zelda, then moved over to where voices were raised.

Two men wearing snappy suits, but obviously not attired for the evening's event, were confronting two others in tuxedos. Clara recognized the shorter man—though he was still barely old enough to be called a man—in the tan wool summer suit.

Wallace Granger had been a two-bit teenage gangster who'd grown up in the neighborhood. His run-in with Zelda a couple of years back had been the instigating factor in Clara's meeting the woman, and since then he'd gotten caught up in a lot more trouble. Maybe more than he could handle.

"That wasn't the deal," Wallace was saying, gesticulating wildly. "What I'm supposed to do with these cases?" Stacked behind him were two unmarked wooden crates.

One of the elegant tuxedoed men shook his head. "We canceled our agreement two weeks ago. Take them back where they came from."

"You don't cancel on Crooked Knee Willy," Wallace said, lowering his voice as if that would make him sound dangerous. At the mention of the gangster, Clara surmised that the crates were full of bootleg liquor.

"You do if he doesn't hold up his end. Mo's people offered protection for our business and events and actually delivered. I'm still paying off the lawyer from the last police raid we had after *your* boss promised we'd be all clear." The dark-skinned man must be one of the event organizers. He was straight-backed and regal-looking, his conked hair slicked back ruthlessly.

He didn't seem to be afraid at all of the gangsters he faced, even when the larger man beside Wallace shifted his suit jacket to the side to reveal a holstered pistol.

The organizer opened his own jacket—Clara couldn't see what he showed them because she was behind him, but from the shocked expression on Wallace's face, he must have his own gun.

Clara chuckled to herself and backed away. Her intervention wasn't necessary. It looked like the organizers had it under control. Though if this was further evidence of the growing beef between the city's main bootleggers and numbers runners—Crooked Knee Willy and the currently jailed Bowlegged Mo—then things were probably going to get worse, and that wasn't good for anyone.

She took another step back and treaded directly on someone's foot. "Oh, I'm sor—" Her apology died on her lips when she saw it was Zelda.

"I told you to stay over there," Clara hissed, grabbing her elbow and marching her away.

Zelda grinned. "You ain't my daddy. What, you trying to keep me away from him?" She motioned with her chin back toward Wallace Granger. "I ain't scared of him. Last time I seen him, told him I was gonna haunt him with my ghost powers."

She waggled her fingers and chuckled maniacally, eliciting alarmed expressions from passersby.

Clara rolled her eyes. "Why are you here again?"

"We don't go through this life alone."

Clara paused. The band ended their song at that instant, punctuating Zelda's words with an eerie quiet. A shiver ran down Clara's spine, heedless of the cloying heat of the ballroom.

Then the musicians started in on the next tune and the moment was over.

Zelda's gaze darted all around, taking in the mass of people. She hadn't noticed Clara's unease. The entry hallway had cleared; the organizers must have come to some resolution about their problem with the gangsters.

80

"How will we find him?" Zelda whispered.

Clara took a deep breath, focusing back on the task at hand. "He's got an Enigma debt. I can find him."

"And you trust him?"

"I don't trust anyone. But people tend to be predictable—that's something you can rely on."

If Zelda replied, Clara missed it as she sank into her second sense. She was still wary of piercing the veil, but it was necessary in order to locate the man she'd come here to find. She hoped that if she did it quickly enough, she wouldn't attract the notice of anything she'd rather avoid.

She braced herself as Over There came into limited focus. Auras popped into existence all around her and the people took on a subtle glow. Beside her, Zelda's pale skin assumed a bluish tinge. A riot of colors illuminated the dance floor, from passionate reds to imaginative purples and everything in between. She filtered them out to find the one person here with a burden hampering his energy. The weight of his Trick would turn the gentle light of his aura into an intense but muted cage.

"He's in the far hallway," she said, motioning directly across the ball-room floor. Crossing directly through the dancers would not be wise, so they skirted the edges, walking the long way around, and slipped through the open door.

The music was slightly muffled due to the thick carpeting in the corridor. Doors lined one side, but a bar had been set up out here, complete with stools. Those wishing to converse had a better chance of being heard outside of the main ballroom.

Her gaze skated across those gathered and landed on a Colored man with a cluster of white men in suits around him. His energy showed the telltale symptoms of someone burdened with a Charm and a Trick, but he wasn't what she expected.

Two years ago, a man had come to her seeking to remove his debt. He'd been of average height, with medium-brown skin and a craggy face "full of personality," as Mama Octavia would say. She'd recognized his name immediately—Aristotle Bishop was a former vaudeville star. She even remembered her father having taken her to one of his shows when she was young, though she hadn't recalled his act. Of course, she hadn't been able to help him, but had tried just in case.

An Enigma had come that day. Not the one to whom he owed a debt, but another, willing to exchange the debt for a new one. Aristotle had declined, thanked Clara, and gone on his way. But she'd never forgotten him.

This man had the same energy about him, but something about his appearance was different. Instead of middle-aged with a medium build, the man holding court before a half dozen entranced spectators was thirty at most, with blue-black skin—another one of her grandmother's sayings—a shade of brown so dark it reminded her of the sky at midnight.

He was elaborately dressed in an embroidered purple caftan that reached his ankles. Multicolored beads graced his neck, and he wore a round cap in a traditional African print of purple and red with a plume of feathers rising from it. Incongruously, a sash was displayed across his chest bearing what looked like military medals.

Clara blinked several times and extended her senses again. The aura was indeed the same, but the man himself quite different. Then she noticed a sort of shimmering around his features. She tilted her head, not quite understanding what she was seeing.

She focused on his face and clothing, and in an instant, both became diaphanous and insubstantial—she was able to see *beneath* them. Fortunately, there was another set of clothing there, and another face as well. This one she recognized.

"He's glamoured." She chuckled humorlessly.

"What does that mean?" Zelda asked.

"See that man there in purple?"

"The one who looks like Nyimbo, king of the Zulus?" Clara raised her brows, and Zelda waved her off. "He was a sideshow act cooked up by the circus manager. Found some old Negro with not too much in his head and dressed him up like an African king—or at least what they thought one might look like—and had him speak gibberish. The rubes ate it up."

Clara rubbed her forehead. "Well, that's our man." She motioned toward Aristotle. "His costume is his Charm." Zelda still seemed confused as Clara approached the group, staying at its outer edge.

The man in purple spoke with a lilting African accent which caressed the vowels. "It is indeed a shame, kind sir. And that is why I have come to the great nation of America. There are many here who could benefit from the resources in my homeland, and I do not come merely seeking aid, but the return on your investment would be great. It is not even an investment so much, you see, as a guaranteed source of income. All we seek is to keep our mines out of the hands of the colonizers."

He held a stack of official-looking documents in his hand and waved them around. The white men surrounding him were nodding, very engaged by his spiel. One pulled a checkbook out of his pocket. Aristotle held up a hand.

"I am sorry sir, I am only able to deal in cash. You understand, I hope, that the banking institutions are working in concert with those trying to deny us our resources. My home is a place of great wealth, but we do not trust banks."

Zelda shook her head. "I don't believe this. They're really falling for it." She leaned against the bar several feet away, eyes lit up with admiration.

Over the next few minutes, the rapt marks emptied their wallets to invest in a gold mine somewhere in Africa. When the party broke up, the "African" turned around to face the bar and ordered a drink. Clara took that moment to approach him. He tipped back his glass, swallowing the scotch, and then turned to face her.

"Did you seek an audience with Prince Abdul Menelik bin-Solomon, child?" Up close, the disguise was impeccable. Something far beyond what makeup could achieve. It was only with her second sight that she could spot the cracks and, with great effort, view the man beneath it.

"Actually, I'm looking for Mr. Aristotle Bishop."

He startled, then peered closely at her. "Clara Johnson." The false face smiled, and Aristotle threw back the rest of his drink. "What are you doing here?"

"I might just have a way to help you."

THE ACTOR

Aristotle Philemon Bishop took his first breaths the day the Civil War ended. He wasn't never sure if that meant he was born a slave or born free. But not three days after Big Mama slapped his bottom and his squawks echoed across the cotton fields, his own mama strapped him to her chest and started walking north.

Weeks later they reached Philadelphia, where she got a job as a washerwoman for a Colored family that had been free for two generations and looked down their nose at her skin and her rough hands but still recognized her as a sister. They also needed a wet nurse for their baby boy and that was work she knew well. Of the five babies she gave birth to, Aristotle was the onliest one she kept. The others had been sold to parts unknown.

The missus of the house once asked why she'd chosen such a big name for her son. "A Colored man ought to have a name he can live up to," she told her. And didn't that boy take it to heart.

He got the same schooling as the children of the highfalutin Negroes. Sat side by side in classes with white boys and girls too. His mama hoped he'd go on to college, become a doctor or engineer or something. After all, the missus's son was on his way to Oberlin College and was making his family proud. So Aristotle enrolled at the University of Pennsylvania and suffered through two years of classes, trying to turn himself into a scholar for his mama's sake when what he really wanted was to be a star.

When he showed up back home one day, hat in hand, face pulled down, she knew something was wrong. "I been kicked out of school," he said before she could ask. "They won't let me back."

Well, she geared up to fight, sure it was the fault of those white folks—though which white folks specifically, she didn't rightly know. He couldn't bear to tell her the truth—he'd been found in bed with a white boy and nearly arrested. Her love and hope for him were so strong and so connected that when he moved to New York and joined a vaudeville act, she keeled over in her washing tub and died.

Aristotle didn't never quite forgive himself for that. He gathered his grief and molded it like clay into the faces he used onstage. But it seeped through his pores, into the burnt cork that turned his brown skin a sooty charcoal. When he cakewalked or tap-danced or told jokes for an audience of hollering white folks, the guilt wafted around him like smoke. When he walked off the stage and back into the real world, to hotels he couldn't sleep in and train cars he couldn't ride in, that guilt flared with heat and light. He still felt the need to live up to something, he just didn't know what.

He sought solace in the arms of men who called him by other names as he tried to forget the one his mama gave him. One man took him to the Rockland Palace up in Harlem for the masquerade ball, where men dressed like women, and for the first time in his life he was surrounded by people he recognized. He wasn't interested in dressing up in a fancy gown and high heels, but still he found the freedom to be, the freedom to breathe.

But it wasn't never enough. Some folks always want more.

Tired of the chitlin circuit, he tried his hand at true theater, taking classes, joining performing companies, auditioning for shows like *A Trip to Coontown* and *The Octoroons*. When that didn't work out too good, he went back to college, but the second time wasn't the charm. Vaudeville was what he was good at, and vaudeville is where he returned.

An old queen told him things would go easier if he took a wife, settled down, had some children. So Aristotle proposed to a showgirl he worked with who knew the deal and just wanted a little security. His star was on the rise and he could provide her with that at least. To him it was just another part to play, but to her it turned into a challenge.

A charming man who treated her with kindness and care was too much to give up. Maybe he just hadn't met the right woman yet. Like so many other of these gals with hearts in their eyes and not enough sense, she was sure that what was between her legs would change him. When it didn't, she started drinking.

Watching her descend into the bottle drove some of the light out of him. He was packing his bags when she turned up pregnant. Aristotle didn't know or care who the daddy was, but he knew he couldn't up and leave. He thought about playing the role of father and started in on rehearsing. Nine long months later, the baby was stillborn and the marriage was just another cadaver.

And that elusive *more* was still calling for him.

That's when he met a Jamaican Chinese fortune-teller on 133rd Street who had a little shop wedged between a shoe store and a photography studio. She sold dream books and scented oils, candles and promises. Told him she could talk to spirits and he was fool enough to listen.

He asked her how he could become the best who ever lived. To disappear inside his roles so folks would only see the character—any character he wanted them to.

The old woman placed a bowl of water on the fabric-draped table between them. The surface of the water rippled and shook until a face poked out. Wet lips whispered to him of bright lights, of crowds applauding and screaming his name. No more cork and oversized shoes, no more darkie jokes and minstrel songs.

He said yes so fast he barely heard the Trick.

He wasn't even quite sure what it meant that he would always have to play a role or else be ignored? His whole life was an act. He never stopped, so that wouldn't make much of a difference. Besides, who was Aristotle Bishop anyways? The son of a washerwoman? A college dropout? A sad joke of a husband? Why be himself when he could be somebody better? Somebody bigger, somebody talented, successful, important. Always more.

His mama tried to reach out from Over There to stop him, but her spirit was tired and that boy was too hardheaded to listen anyway. Except he wasn't nearly a boy and was more than old enough to know better. Yet and still, that Enigma got his way and sank his claws into Aristotle.

For a while he was happy with the deal. Jumping for joy at the sight of his name up in lights, and in the papers, and on the lips of the folks across the country, singing his praises. Everywhere he went he was treated like a king. Negro royalty at least. He could convince anybody watching that he was someone different to who he was.

It was a long time before he found out what happened when he tried to be himself.

10

BOOTED AND SUITED

Miles's Pool Hall didn't see too many newcomers. It was a small neighborhood hangout and the regulars all lived within walking distance. The basement had been turned into a speakeasy several years before due to Prohibition and was accessed through the back alley. The metal door creaked and the dark stairs squeaked—Miles kept them that way as a deterrent. But once inside, the small space was cozy, homey even, like a juke joint down South that was part living room, part nightclub.

The stage in the corner was made of planks of wood laid across peach crates. The brick walls were streaked with lime deposits from over the years. An old rug had been thrown down on top of the cracked concrete and served as a dance floor, though Clara had never seen anyone dance on it.

It wasn't a popular spot because Miles's hooch was notoriously bad. He stayed under the notice of Bowlegged Mo and Crooked Knee Willy and instead served bathtub hooch made by somebody's grandmother out in Southwest. Everyone agreed it was vile stuff, but that didn't stop the regulars from knocking it back. And though Aristotle wasn't a regular, he threw the hooch down his throat with the rest of them.

They'd retreated to Miles's basement for a private place to talk. Aristotle had shifted from his African prince persona to someone a lot less conspicuous. This fellow was about sixty, Aristotle's own age if Clara wasn't mistaken, with salt-and-pepper hair and a neat mustache. There had been sort of a blurring of his features as he changed from one glamour to the next—taking off one mask to put on another. Zelda had said that she hadn't noticed it; she'd been standing next to Prince bin-Solomon one moment, and the next this rather nondescript man who Aristotle called Eddie had appeared in his place.

"Why give him another name?" Clara had asked.

"Every character needs a name."

Inside the speakeasy, they'd commandeered a corner table. The only other folks in the joint were a pair of old men at the makeshift bar and the bartender, Miles's brother Cole.

"So you say you have a way to help me?" he asked after swallowing down the fiery brew.

Clara pressed her palms down flat on the table, trying to ground herself. "I've been authorized by The Empress—the spirit who holds my debt—to offer a deal to anyone who helps me, anyone who owes an Enigma. She guarantees she'll clear the obligation once we retrieve a certain item that she wants." Aristotle's brows climbed. "As long as nobody owes The Man in Black," she hastened to add. "Apparently they're mortal enemies."

Clara didn't like looking at the incredulity on his false face, so she risked a glimpse through his glamour to the man beneath. Who, of course, wore the same disbelieving expression. "And you believe her?" He made her sound like a nincompoop.

"She made a vow. They can't break vows or speak false, you know that."

Now his brows climbed even higher. "That was a hell of a risk."

Clara shrugged. "She'll clear my debt as well."

He sat back in his seat, considering before turning to Zelda. "You owe one of these Enigmas too?"

She shook her head and jerked her thumb at Clara. "I'm her conscience."

Clara turned and glared. "What does that mean?"

"So what do we need to do?" Aristotle interrupted.

She decided to deal with Zelda later. "Steal a ring from the finger of Madame Josephine Lawrence. Some kind of magical ring."

He whistled slow and low.

"She's got bodyguards and doesn't let new people near her," Clara continued, "so I figured what you do would come in handy. Could you become someone she knows?"

"I could," he responded carefully.

Zelda leaned forward. "How does it work? Your Charm?"

"I embody the role and I change. My voice, face, clothes. I can be a man or a woman. White or Colored, though any role too different from myself is hard to keep on. A Colored man is far easier to play for long periods of time. Other folk see what I want them to see. Believe what I want them to believe."

"And your Enigma?" Clara asked.

"The Juggler. You think The Empress will really take my debt from him? Remove my Trick?"

"And your Charm. Her vow is binding. Far as I know, she and The Juggler don't have any beef. He'll have no choice but to deal with her."

Aristotle rolled the chipped glass between his palms, staring at the few drops left inside. He exhaled deeply. "Well, I guess I don't have anything to lose."

Clara froze. "I mean, none of us are professional criminals, and I personally have no idea what I'm doing. If we fail, Madame Josephine could retaliate. Bowlegged Mo's whole organization could come down on us. Not to mention whatever retribution The Empress might try to mete out herself."

Aristotle shrugged. "Like I said. Nothing to lose." He grinned sadly. "You have a way to get close to Josephine?"

Clara blinked, a little shocked he had agreed so easily. "Um, she's out on the town a lot. Not too difficult to find. We could get you in near her at an event to butter her up and make her feel comfortable."

Zelda got up from the table, brushing against Aristotle, to head to the bar for another bottle. Clara hadn't realized the two of them had finished the first one. Miles kept the bottles small to keep profits high, but still...Zelda was awfully sure-footed for someone who had drunk half a bottle of scrap iron.

"We get close to her and then what?" Aristotle asked.

"Zelda steals the ring."

The woman in question returned, thumping a full bottle of moonshine on the table.

"Right off her finger?" His tone was doubtful.

Zelda fell into her seat and held up a watch dangling between two fingers. Aristotle looked down at his empty wrist and then up, eyes widening, before his face split into a real grin. One tinged with admiration and hope.

Clara crossed her arms, leaning back in the chair. Zelda was going to give her an ulcer before she hit twenty-five. At least they'd finally found a good use for her skill set.

"We find an event where Josephine will be," she said, "and figure out a way to get in."

Aristotle poured himself another glass. "Well, *I* can get in anywhere, but you two with your shabby selves will need some help." Clara considered her borrowed dress with the mismatched shoes and Zelda's ill-fitting suit. He was probably right.

"Meet me tomorrow and we'll get you booted and suited."

The next afternoon Clara stood outside the New Rochelle apartment house at 16th and U when Aristotle, as Eddie, appeared through the front doors. He was sharply dressed in a double-breasted white linen suit and straw hat. His two-tone shoes shone with fresh polish. Clara saw through the glamour that the clothes were actually his own. He whistled as he approached, nodding to her in greeting while managing to give her drab gray day dress the evil eye.

They headed down W Street to a shop with a sign over the door reading "Henry's." It looked to be part tailor, part costume shop, with seventeenth-century dresses, complete with hoops, on display next to an assortment of sparkling modern evening gowns featuring more beading, fringes, and sequins than she could stand to look at. The bell over the door offered a pleasant ring, announcing their presence.

"Just a moment!" a voice called out from behind a curtain. Clara wandered over to a rack of shoes on display. Patent leather cutouts and lattice-strap pumps sparkled under the lights. She picked up a strap pump to find it was a size 16. She hadn't known women's shoes went up that high, then realization struck. The Fairy Ball attendees must get their footwear someplace. She must have found the spot.

"Will they have anything my size here?" Clara asked skeptically.

A figure emerged from behind the maroon velvet curtain separating the store, bringing with him the scent of apples and jasmine. Clara barely held in her gasp. He was perhaps the most beautiful man she'd ever seen. He looked to be in his forties, with a smattering of gray at the temples of hair that had been slicked down with a precise application of pomade. A crisp white shirt was visible beneath a violet silk kimono-style robe, embroidered with lilies and swans. A measuring tape was slung carelessly around his neck.

At some point between entering the shop and now, Aristotle had changed his role yet again. His clothing remained the same but his appearance was the closest to his real self that she'd seen yet. Though he'd shaven at least a decade off his true age, and close to ten pounds from his waistline.

"Eric," the robed man gushed, holding his arms open.

"Henry," Aristotle said with a bit less enthusiasm, returning the embrace. Their greeting was brief, but in "Eric's" face, Clara saw a well of deep longing. She swallowed.

The two pulled apart and Henry held out his hand, palm up, and made grabby fingers. "I believe we had a bet?"

Aristotle cracked a half smile and reached into his jacket pocket. He pulled out a red-and-yellow box of candy, Bit-O-Honeys, and placed them into Henry's outstretched hand.

"I was beginning to think you would never show and pay up," Henry said, teasing.

"I'm a man of my word. And you fared far better in that dance contest than I would have ever expected. I was a fool to doubt you."

Henry's chin rose magnanimously, then he spun to regard Clara. "What have you brought me?" He scanned her frankly, with an expression that wasn't unkind but deeply assessing.

"This child here needs a scrub-up. Cinderella's got a ball to go to."

The tailor's eyes were a rich, glittering chocolate, and though she now suspected his preferences lay elsewhere, she couldn't help but flush under the perusal of a man so attractive. "Turn around, dear, let me get a look at you."

She spun obediently, more conscious than ever of her ugly dress and plain shoes.

"A winter rose," he murmured. She faced him again and he squinted at her hair with his lips downturned. "You know, a Poro hair treatment wouldn't go amiss."

Clara patted her hair, which was a little dry, and found herself unable to speak. Henry tilted his head to the side, taking her in before smiling such a vivid smile, she had to half close her eyes. "I think I have just the thing. Wait here."

Then he disappeared behind the curtain. Aristotle stared after him and Clara couldn't keep her mouth shut. "What happens if you try to be yourself with him?" she whispered.

Faint surprise crossed his face, followed by chagrin. He took a deep breath. "I'll show you." His glamour faded, leaving just the man, gray-haired and clean-shaven. Clara sighed in relief. Something about his "roles" left her deeply uneasy.

Henry reemerged with three gowns all in shades of purple. Two were ankle length in filmy layers of chiffon with clusters of sparkly crystals decorating them. The third was daringly short with a tiered ruffle skirt and flower embroidery. All were far too beautiful and bright for Clara to ever consider wearing.

Henry walked right past Aristotle to hang the dresses on a nearby rack. "Did Eric step out?"

Clara's gaze shot back and forth between them, her heart sinking at the stricken expression on Aristotle's face. "J-just for a moment. He'll be back directly."

Henry nodded absentmindedly and began fluffing and messing with the skirts. She'd known that Aristotle's Trick was bad, but she finally understood what it was costing him.

She turned back to Henry. "Those are all quite a bit brighter than what I usually wear."

"I know," he said dryly. "But you need color, my dear. Brings out the richness of your skin, such a pretty chocolate. This orchid will make you glow." He pointed to what was probably her favorite dress even with the garish shade. "But I think the periwinkle will bring out your eyes."

Uncertainty roiled within her. She couldn't wear anything like that.

This entire plan was starting to look more and more ridiculous. Yes, she needed a proper dress to be able to get into any event that Madame Josephine would attend, otherwise she'd be laughed out the door, but there had to be other options.

The bell chimed and Zelda rushed in, breathless. "Am I late? Did I miss it?"

Henry turned to regard her, unwrapping a candy at the same time. Clara held her breath. His taste in formalwear aside, she was starting to like him and didn't want that to change.

"Henry, this is Zelda. She'll need a dress as well."

There was a long, pregnant pause before Henry popped the bit of taffy into his mouth and clapped his hands together. "Now, you don't see that every day." Clara stiffened. "That bone structure! Who do I have to murder for those cheekbones, sweetheart?"

Zelda's eyes widened, and she gave Clara an incredulous expression.

"I think maybe this dress would look better on her," Clara said, pointing to the gown he'd called periwinkle.

"Oh, no no no. She's a summer. We're doing ruby or a soft blush." He chewed for a few moments, thoughtful, then swallowed the candy before reaching into his pocket to unwrap another. He must be swallowing them nearly whole because it took her at least five minutes to finish just one Bit-O-Honey.

Henry snapped his fingers and radiated another blinding smile. "Teal!" And then he was gone into the back room again.

Zelda picked her way across the floor as if she was afraid it would cave in. "What happened to Aristotle?"

The man in question changed roles again right next to her, causing Zelda to jump. "You been there the whole time?"

He smiled sadly, his "Eric" glamour back in place. Clara's heart broke into a thousand pieces.

When Henry returned, the dress he held out for Zelda was a pale bluish-green creation with a gauzy skirt and a tight bodice. Unlike Clara, she jumped at the chance to try it on. When she emerged from the fitting room, she was greeted by a hushed silence.

"What? What is it?" Her face reddened as the moment stretched on.

"You look amazing. It's perfect," Clara finally said. The dress fit her like a dream and the color made even her pale skin glow.

The men agreed. "I am good at what I do," Henry exclaimed, beaming. "Now, Miss Clara, are you going to try on one of these dresses or what?"

Clara's genuine delight for her roommate was followed by a brief moment of regret. Zelda's brash confidence and swagger let her pull off any look, but unless Henry had a Charm of his own, nothing he did would make Clara look that good. And even if by some miracle, it did, it would all be a lie—a pretty glamour like Aristotle's that masked a bitter truth.

Her mouth moved, trying to form words, but she could find nothing to say. She held up a finger to Henry and pulled Aristotle away to whisper in his ear. "I think I should go in as a waitress or maybe a maid. I should be able to get on with a catering crew. There's no reason for me to be a guest. Zelda will need to mingle more with the crowd to actually get close enough to do the pull, but I can just be on the sidelines with a tray. That's a better plan." She nodded, convincing herself.

Aristotle frowned. "What's the real problem here, child?"

"Nothing. There's no problem," she said quickly. "I just thought about things from another angle, that's all."

She swallowed the lump in her throat. She couldn't articulate the dread forming at the thought of putting on one of those dresses and mingling with the class of people who would be at the type of event Madame Josephine frequented.

Addie Savoy's face raced across her mind. Dr. Harley's jabs pummeled at her. The sneers and the cuts amplified themselves and caused a ringing in her ears. "I'll stand out like a sore thumb."

"And you think Zelda won't?"

"She knows how to blend into a crowd. All folks will see is pale skin. They see me, they expect a maid."

Aristotle's brow creased.

"Listen, the rest of the plan stays the same. I'll still be there. I'll get everything we'll need. You distract, Zelda pulls the ring, and we all hie out of there like the Klan is chasing us. This don't change any of that."

His nostrils flared and she could tell he wanted to argue, but after a moment he simply shrugged. "All right. Whatever you want."

Clara's heart raced. She tried to slow it down but she needed some air. The atmosphere in the shop was stifling. "Okay. Now, how we gonna pay for that dress?"

"Don't worry about that. Henry owes Eric a favor or two. He'll loan the dress as long as we promise to bring it back clean."

As she headed out the door to wait on the sidewalk, Clara took a look back at Zelda, standing on the stool with Henry at her feet fussing with the hemline. The three-panel mirror in front of her entranced her. Clara had to admit, Zelda looked like a princess. There was no need for two Cinderellas. One was enough. Someone had to be the mouse.

11

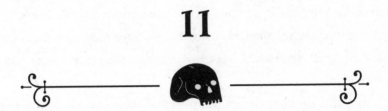

THE LUMINOUS FOUR HUNDRED

Clara stood at attention, buttoned into a waitress uniform that was a bit too snug. Getting hired on at the last minute by the catering company that served the Lincoln Theatre had been largely due to Aristotle, who, in character, had convinced one of the regulars, an aspiring actress, that she had won a role in a play. When Clara complained that the poor girl would lose a good job, he'd assured her that she actually had won the role, another favor from another friend of one of his aliases. So here Clara stood in front of the giant movie screen, a heavy tray of champagne in her hands.

She hadn't done much service work. Before Dr. Woodson had hired her, she'd been a janitor for a few months, cleaning offices in a building downtown alone. She'd never worked in a room full of fancily dressed people all smiling and drinking and eating without a care in the world.

The VIP reception was being held after the Washington premiere of the newest Oscar Micheaux picture, *Body and Soul*. Mr. Paul Robeson himself, the film's star, was here. His booming laugh filled the theater, vibrating the floorboards. When he'd taken a glass of champagne from her earlier, Clara's heart rate had sped.

Live music out in the lobby filtered to her ears. The five-piece band played the sort of tune that was supposed to fade into the background. So why was it boring into her head like a drill? Something about the notes and tones was slowly building into a thunderstorm inside her skull. She closed her eyes and took deep breaths as nausea threatened.

Thankfully, the song ended and the band took a break. Clara sagged with relief and made her way down the aisle and out into the lobby, staying out of the way but also keeping a watch. She'd lost sight of Zelda and Aristotle and hoped they had eyes on Madame Josephine. The woman shouldn't be too difficult to spot, she'd likely be holding court amid a throng of admirers.

No one paid Clara any attention. To the highfalutin Negroes gathered here tonight, she was just the help. Elegant fingers grabbed the flutes of champagne from her tray until only one remained. She'd have to go upstairs for a refill soon. Maybe she'd find Madame Josephine and the others there.

She was moving toward the side staircase when a hand shot out to grab the last flute. The sudden movement shocked her and she wobbled slightly. Something warm pressed into her back, steadying her.

"Sorry about that, lioness."

She recognized that voice. And that charming grin. And the wink he gave her before downing a healthy swallow of champagne. And he, apparently, recognized her.

"Not a problem." Her voice came out gravelly, and she cleared her throat. His hand was still pressed against her, so she took a step forward, breaking the contact.

Israel Lee was just as handsome as she remembered. Tonight he wore a crisp black dinner jacket with a cream-colored vest. Sweat beaded his forehead and he took another swallow of the champagne, draining the glass. He must have been playing with the band.

"That's not Adam's ale, you know," she said, then mentally kicked herself. She needed to keep her mouth shut and be on her way. Staring at the strong column of his throat was not what she was here to do.

"Not trying to quench my thirst. Just wanted a taste before this place gets raided."

She snorted. "You think the police gonna come in here over some champagne? With a former congressman, a bank owner, a half dozen ministers, and two former city commissioners?"

"All Negroes. You think they won't?"

His brow was raised. The shape of his lips mocked her in more ways than one, but there was no bite behind his skepticism. His question seemed sincere.

"I think the Luminous Four Hundred of Washington line their pockets. No flatfoot's coming within a mile of this place."

"The 'Luminous Four Hundred.' They'd like that." He grinned again and placed the empty flute on her tray and leaned to whisper conspiratorially. "The 'best specimens of the race' do tend to glow with their own self-importance."

He said this like he didn't roll in the same circles they did—the Colored elites. The government workers, doctors, lawyers, dentists, ministers, professors, and other professionals milling around them now. As if he could read her thoughts, he said, "I'm just a lowly musician who jooks in gutbuckets."

Her retort—the swanky lobby of the Lincoln was hardly a gutbucket—died when a voice called his name, breaking into the bubble that had seemed to surround them during their brief exchange. The sounds of the event crashed into her, people talking and laughing. She took another step away, and when he turned to see who had hailed him, she fled up the stairs.

Once at the top, she glanced down to find him looking up at her with a curious expression. But then a shorter man, underdressed in a brown herringbone suit, grabbed his arm insistently. A look of annoyance flared on Israel's face and he turned away.

Up on the second level, the crowd was a bit thinner and Clara took a moment to catch her breath. Talking with Israel had flustered her; she worked to bring her head back in the game. At least now that the music had ended she could think clearly without the headache. She quickly spotted Aristotle holding court, making wild gesticulations while entertaining a small group of people clustered around him.

This character, Josiah, was in his seventies, high brown with an elaborate curled mustache and dressed in a tuxedo with a billowing cloak. He wielded a dragon-headed cane with jeweled eyes more for effect than for assistance walking. He was a vaudevillian who'd gotten his start in the minstrel show days and could regale an audience with humorous tales of the folly of white folks.

On the other side of the room, Madame Josephine's sparkling figure emerged from what must be her box above the theater. Tonight two bodyguards flanked her. The enormous one she'd had at the Howard Theatre the other night and a slightly smaller man, which still meant he was larger than most.

As the woman and her entourage crossed the second-floor lobby, they were stopped by the approach of a short, graying high-yellow man leaning heavily on a cane. He was impeccably dressed, if a bit old-fashioned, in a tuxedo with full-length tails. White gloves graced his hands and a tall top hat sat jauntily canted on his head.

Clara had seen Crooked Knee Willy around town plenty of times, but from afar. Tonight he was accompanied by no bodyguards and showed no fear as he greeted a well-protected Madame Josephine with a bow. Clara edged to a nearby cocktail table and began clearing off used glasses and dishes, piling them on her tray, so she could stay nearby and listen.

"Josephine, you're looking lovely as ever this evening."

The former singer's beaded red dress shimmered in the light. The tasseled skirt showed quite an expanse of leg, and a fortune's worth of diamonds graced her neck, ears, and wrists, with a tiara perched on her head. She smiled prettily and produced a hand fan, flipping it open and waving it before her face. "William, always a pleasure."

"We're going to need to have a chat, you and I," he said, voice brittle and unyielding.

"Oh?"

Willy lowered his volume to the point where Clara had to strain to hear him. "Without Mo, that operation you're barely holding together is gonna dissolve like salt on a slug."

"Enchanting imagery, William. You have the soul of a poet. But I don't think there is anything for us to talk about. Maurice's *operation* is in good hands. Perhaps worry a bit more about what's happening in your own house."

The fan disappeared again and she waved goodbye to him. Each of her fingers was bedecked with a ring and most of them flashed or sparkled. However, the pointer finger of her right hand bore a ring different to the others. It was dull and scuffed, like the cheap brass trinkets you'd find at a carnival.

Madame Josephine directed a final smile at Willy, then moved around him. He stepped to the side, doffing his hat politely, but eyeing her with a narrowed gaze. Clara swallowed and, as the woman passed her, girded herself to use her second sight to confirm what she suspected—this plain ring was the one they sought. She looked through the veil, peering Over There in what she intended to be just a quick glimpse. But shock held her in place for far longer than she'd planned.

The ring was indeed magical. Its power shone through Madame Josephine's red-tinted aura like a prism refracting light. Dozens of rainbow threads shot out from it, disappearing into the far distance, connecting the ring to something else—some other energy. She couldn't tell what the jewelry's purpose was but sensed its power and also that it was well protected. That multicolored light contained powerful wards; they emitted a sense of danger that made her breath catch.

She knew she'd looked too long when she began to sense spirits racing toward her. She dropped her other sight at the same time she dropped her tray. Fortunately, it fell only to the table, clattering, but not so loud as to break anything or draw more than a surprised glance from those a few steps away. Crooked Knee Willy was nowhere to be seen.

Clara's breath stuttered in her chest. She had to warn them. They had to call this off.

Zelda was at Aristotle's side, stunning in the teal gown. Ruth Anne had painstakingly coiled her blonde hair into ringlets and clipped them to the side with a pearl-encrusted comb Henry had produced. Zelda was a curiosity, and Aristotle had said he would work her into his act, using her backstory as a springboard. She was playing a former circus freak he had taken under his wing and transformed into a stage performer now in high demand all across Europe.

The plan was to introduce her to Madame Josephine in the midst of a crowd, jostle them together, and let Zelda do her work. They had procured a numbing spray from the druggist, which would help Zelda pull the ring in case it was on tight.

Josephine parted the crowd like the Red Sea, demanding to be the center of attention. Aristotle's false face smiled and bowed before her. The opera singer appeared amused.

Though her guards still flanked her, Clara spotted the moment Zelda wobbled drunkenly into a young man beside her, causing him to splash his champagne onto Madame Josephine's shoes. While the woman's gaze was lowered, Zelda took the opportunity to spray the numbing oil on the woman's right hand. It came out in such a fine mist and would work so quickly she'd never feel it.

As the young man apologized profusely to a disgusted Madame Josephine, Zelda prepared to do the pull. Clara could not catch her eye.

Aristotle was concentrating on keeping Madame Josephine's attention diverted. And Clara's pulse was racing.

She could not allow Zelda to touch that ring.

She looked down at the full tray before her and took a deep breath. The she heaved it into her grip and stepped forward, purposefully tripping. Plates and glasses went crashing to the floor. Everyone turned to her and stared, mouths agape. Everyone, of course, but Zelda, whose gaze was centered on the back of Madame Josephine's head. Trust her not to be startled by anything, she probably thought the diversion was the perfect chance and was planning to take advantage of Josephine's inattention.

But Aristotle looked uneasy and caught Clara's eye. Sprawling on the ground, she frantically shook her head; his eyes widened. She prayed he'd gotten the message, and when he wrapped an arm around Zelda and pulled her back, she finally closed her eyes.

Shock and hostility radiated from the attendees. Normally, Clara would feel the humiliation acutely, but now only relief coursed through her. She climbed to her knees and began picking up the shards of glass and crockery. Not even the other servers helped her. Once the mess was cleared away she stood with the tray. Aristotle and Zelda were gone and she breathed deeply for the first time since using her second sight.

She'd hit her knee pretty hard in the fall and limped toward the stairs, needing to head down to the basement level to discard the broken dishes. Their ambitious plan might actually have worked if not for the ring's heavy protections. Her first order of business after getting out of there was to contact The Empress to ask about the wards on the ring. It would have been nice for the spirit to mention them.

Madame Josephine breezed by, bodyguards in tow, and floated

down the steps. Clara's pace was slow, injured and laden with dishware as she was, so she had a bird's-eye view of what happened next. At the bottom of the steps, Israel Lee stepped up to greet Madame Josephine with a warm smile. She offered him her hand, which he raised to his lips in a gentlemanly way.

He smiled and winked, and Clara narrowed her eyes. It seemed to her he was laying it on a little thick, but Josephine was eating it up. She threw back her head and laughed at something he said.

Israel being young enough to be her son obviously didn't matter to her. And maybe for him her wealth and prestige was enough. Or maybe he just couldn't help himself. He was obviously an incorrigible flirt, every phrase uttered with innuendo of some kind. Clara thought back to their brief exchange and kicked herself. For a moment she'd thought...

She shook herself and continued limping down the stairs. The crowd was still thick, but before she'd taken more than two more steps she noticed that the man who had hailed Israel before was standing close to him, staring. He stuck out a bit because of his brown suit and some other quality she couldn't quite put her finger on. He was neatly groomed, standing straight as a rail, but it was still obvious that he didn't belong. Israel's back was to him, but the man appeared to hang on his every word.

Clara spotted a small vial in his hand. One she recognized because she'd given an identical one to Zelda earlier that day. Was he...? No, it couldn't be.

But sure enough, the man stepped to Israel's side and surreptitiously sprayed Josephine's hand with mist. Israel laughed, bumping into him and pushing him into Madame Josephine.

Clara's jaw dropped. The man touched Josephine's hand and Clara's vision whited out. A sharp pain pierced her skull like an ice pick being shoved into her brain. The strength of the powerful spell forced her second sight to engage—it was like she was a child again, before she'd learned to block it all out and shut down that part of her senses.

The rainbow-colored beam surrounding the ring and splintering off into parts unknown intensified before shattering into a thousand pieces. Dark plumes of smoke poured from it, directly into the would-be thief. His aura, now clouded and murky, began to dim. All light drained away from him as the protection spell engaged.

Clara kept her footing on the steps—just barely—as she wrangled her sight under control, shuttering it once again. The last thing she'd seen was the rainbow light, now restored, an effective guardrail around the ring.

On the floor of the lobby, the thief gasped and fell to the ground. Clara didn't even need to look at him to know he was dead.

Madame Josephine's guards raced into action, hustling her away from the scene. Clara descended the steps quickly, ignoring the pain in her knee as a scream ripped through the crowd. She needed to get out of here quick, fast, and in a hurry.

She placed her tray on the ground and headed for the doors as the party quickly descended into chaos when folks noticed the fallen man. A quick glance over her shoulder revealed that Israel Lee had disappeared as well.

She ran the two blocks home and stopped inside the first-floor vestibule to catch her breath. There were quite a few things The Empress had neglected to tell her. Not only was the ring vigorously protected, but someone else wanted it too.

THE MUSICIAN

Israel Moses Lee came into this world by the full, bright light of a harvest moon. Took his mama three nights of laboring under that unblinking eye in the sky, and after she'd done her duty, she swore to never do it again. Her husband wasn't none too happy about it, since that meant she was to spurn his advances from now on, but as one of thirteen children whose own mama had never gotten a moment's rest or lost that crease between her eyes, Ernestine Stewart Lee knew she was done with birthing.

Her husband's father, Macon Lee, had been a slave on one Lee plantation or another—folks said it was some kin to old Robert E., if not the man himself. After the war, Macon had settled in Leetown, Virginia, which wasn't the name anyone wrote on the envelopes, but it was what they all called the town on account of everybody there being related to everybody else.

Ernestine fussed with that colicky baby for nine nights in a row. On the tenth, once she'd gotten him to quiet for more than a minute, she stuffed her things into a cotton sack and tiptoed out the house.

Tiptoed right into Macon Lee, setting there on the porch, smoking his pipe. She froze up, sure he was going to get to hollerin' at her for sneaking off on his son and grandson, but he didn't so much as fix his lips to chastise. Just peered up at her with eyes gone rheumy, the dark brown already tinting to blue in his old age, and leaned out of her way.

"If you're going, git." And she got. It would be fourteen years before she returned, and growing up, Israel felt each one like a plague on his soul.

Daddy Macon was a good man. Had withstood the death of several children and a wife. Israel's own daddy was there but not. The parts of him that weren't broken when his wife left were shattered by a blow to the head from a white man who accused him of stealing clean shirts off the drying line. He would sit in the rocking chair all day, eyes gone vacant, staring out the window into nothing, whispering Ernestine's name.

When she came back, it was in the fall, near enough to Israel's birthday that it could have been considered a present. She wore a green silk dress and drove down the gravel road in a brand-new roadster.

Daddy Macon had just been put in the ground, body not even cold yet, and young Israel had been about to pack himself and his father up to go stay with his great-aunt when the knock on the door came.

"Israel?" the woman had said, staring up at the tall teenager in wonder. "Didn't you turn out dark. Is that just from being in the sun for so long? I sure hope so."

He didn't know who this woman was spouting such foolishness—all his life his dark brown kinfolk had teased him for being so yellow. But the sound of her voice made his father perk up in his chair in the corner, eyes lighting up for the first time in years.

"Ernestine?" he called out. She looked over at him and frowned.

"Ernestine Lee?" Israel's daddy had asked again, rising to stand on wobbly legs.

"My name is Ernestine Pritchard now." She held up a hand with a shiny ring and waved it around, catching the light. "And I come for my son."

"You're my mama?" Israel asked, looking the woman up and down. She had some nerve to talk about his coloring; she was only a shade or two lighter herself. But he would soon find out that the scant hue dividing them made a big difference to some.

For now, he stood by as she became a whirlwind racing through their one-room cabin. Looking at everything with disdain. Not knowing how she could have ever lived like this. Never mind that she had grown up in an even more broken-down shack with far more people in it.

She instructed Israel to get his things, he was coming with her. "I got a new husband and he's all about family. So I told him that I was gonna bring my son up from the country." She tapped her foot, urging him to hurry.

"What about Daddy?" he asked. "He cain't live on his own."

She'd sighed and looked again at the man she'd fallen in love with at age fifteen, before she'd known any better. Before she'd known any-thing about the world at all.

"Where were *you* going to take him?"

And so they dropped his father off at his aunt's house and Israel rode in the roadster all the way to Washington. Their destination: a house in LeDroit Park—one with Colored servants and two cars in the garage out back. There were five bedrooms with only two people living there. Waste and excess were new concepts to him.

His mama's new husband, Archibald Pritchard, was a lawyer from one of the city's im-por-tant families. He didn't help folks accused of crimes, no, Mr. Pritchard was not that type of lawyer. Not being able to have children of his own, he took one look at Israel and deemed him an acceptable legacy. They starched him into a suit and enrolled him at M Street High School.

It was a far cry from Leetown's one-room schoolhouse. The other students were ruthless in mocking his countrified ways until he learned to walk like his arms and legs were bound with rope like they did. Speak with clipped syllables. Use the proper forks. Button his shirt up the right way and part his hair just so.

He often thought about what Daddy Macon would say if he could see him now, encased in the papier-mâché mask of a respectable Negro. One thing his grandaddy would still be proud of him for was his music. As a little boy, when he'd had nothing else, he'd beat his hands on the ground to make a cadence. Daddy Macon had scrounged him up a real drum, just some five-cent thing a traveling peddler was selling, but Israel soon mastered it. And the harmonica. And the fiddle. And the flute and the piano at the church and any other instrument that came within two feet of him.

Music was the stitching holding his life together. At school, he joined the band, a patchwork quilt of misfits all wearing their own masks. At home, he threaded the needle when his mama and stepfather would get to arguing. Once he sat down at that piano and played something sweet and calming, Archibald would forget he'd married a pretty little country girl with no education, and Ernestine could overlook the fact she'd left love behind when she snuck out of Leetown in the middle of the night. Loop and tuck, adagio and pianissimo. The spaces between the notes were empty, like the silences in that big old house.

By the time he enrolled at Howard University, Israel told himself he was a master at keeping the threads together. Class by day, gigs at night, playing with a band he'd formed with his high school friends. The syncopated melodies of ragtime had blended into the bold improvisation of jazz, but they would have to water it down sometimes and spice it up at others, playing anywhere from dance halls to poolrooms to cotillions and galas, changing the set list as the venue demanded. Whatever made the crowds cheer with delight, their raucous applause filling those empty spaces.

But his grades couldn't withstand the late nights. His mama wanted a doctor for a son and his stepfather didn't care what he became as long as it was respectable and he stopped playing that devil music. The spaces between the notes were soon filled with raised voices and slamming doors.

And what did Israel want?

The joy and jubilation of sweaty-faced, hair-mussed dancers who'd just spent hours stomping to rags he played. The elation and exhilaration from working men and women laying their heavy burdens down for the evening to eat and drink and laugh, clap their hands, tap their toes, and snap their fingers. Even the polite applause from high-toned gala attendees was preferable to the vacuous void of silence.

Then one night, after a gig at the country house of an im-por-tant Negro up in Montgomery County, twenty miles north of the city, his ride home had gone off with a girl, leaving him to walk down to the train station alone, guitar case in hand.

Above his head shone the same harvest moon he'd been born under. And unbeknownst to him, the barrier between here and Over There was thin as mist. Walking down that lonely road, he came to a fork, a crossroads. Out the corner of his eye, he spied a man walking his way, keeping to the shadows like a haint.

"What do you want, Israel Lee?" the voice called out deep and mellow.

Israel knew better than to talk to shadows at night, especially ones who knew his name, but the fact was he didn't want to be a doctor or a lawyer or an engineer. Behind the mask, when he wasn't pretending for the benefit of everybody except himself, he could finally admit that the wound left on his soul when he was just a few days old had never quite healed properly. What he wanted more than anything else was to be loved. If not by one, then by all.

So he listened to what the voice said, and when the time came, he agreed to the deal.

12

A GARDEN IN THE CITY

I'm not going to say 'I told you so,'" Mama Octavia said as Clara entered her apartment. She was positioned near the window, looking down at the street.

"Might as well." Defeated and angry, Clara pulled her shoes off, then went into her bedroom to change out of the ill-fitting waitress uniform.

"No, I understand why you feel you have to do this." Her grandmother appeared beside her as she slipped on her nightclothes. "Somebody has to try and stop this thing. And you're not the type to sit around and watch folks suffer without speaking up."

Clara paused, surprised. "I like to mind my business."

The ghostly woman snorted. "You mind your business about as well as I cooked."

Clara fought a grimace, remembering the taste of charred chicken and crunchy, thin biscuits from her childhood. Her granny was a lot of things, but a great cook was not among them.

"At least I knew I wasn't throwing down in the kitchen. You need to face the facts that you're a meddler." She crossed her arms. "And I do too."

"I was grateful for every meal," Clara said diplomatically. This was the olive branch being extended. Mama Octavia had never really apologized for anything as far as Clara could remember. Her temper would flare as hot as her granddaughter's, and then, after some reflection, the embers would cool and things would go back to normal with an acknowledgment of the disagreement and then a push to move past it.

"You gonna ask The Empress what happened?"

Clara stood in the bedroom doorway as the closed closet door called to her. "I have to. You *were* right. You told me not to trust her."

"We were both right, child. Now do what you gotta do."

Minutes later, The Empress's smoky visage emerged from the white smoke of the thick candle. Clara sat before it, wrangling all of her anger into a ball inside her chest, a mass of vibrant rage waiting for a chance to emerge—dangerous when dealing with a volatile spirit.

When the suggestion of otherworldly eyes looked down at her with a questioning glance, Clara made no preamble, growling through clenched teeth, "The ring is warded."

The Empress tilted her smoky head. "Warded? How?"

"Anyone who touches it drops down dead." Her bare foot began an agitated tapping against the wood floorboards. "Want to know how I know? Someone else tried to steal it tonight and died."

The piano music ended downstairs at Miles's, allowing the indistinct mingling of voices to filter up. Images of the man in the brown suit came unbidden, his aura filling with darkness, him falling to the ground. Clara shivered.

"Did you know?" she gritted out.

The Empress's face grew in size, ballooning taller and wider and growing more distinct, her expression twisting in a fair approximation of what Clara felt on the inside. She leaned back so the smoke didn't pass through her head.

The spirit hissed like an alley cat. "Do you think that I would send you to your death, Clara? I *need* you. How would your demise benefit me?"

"Well, seems like you're leaving out some key details. My associate could have gotten herself killed if she'd touched that thing."

"I didn't ask your *associate* to get the ring, I asked you. Her death would have been your own fault and none of my own." The face hovered in its enlarged state before affecting a more placid expression and shrinking once again.

Clara pressed her lips together to hold back her retort before choosing her words carefully. "This is not something I can do alone."

Accepting that had been difficult enough, but the idea of anyone helping her being in mortal danger...If that had been Zelda on the ground, lifeless eyes staring up at nothing, Clara didn't know what she would have done. Her anger ignited again; she just wished she had somewhere to funnel it.

"Who else was trying to get the ring?" The Empress asked.

"A local musician and the man who died—I didn't know him."

The Enigma's face flickered for a moment, then grew clear once again. "This task is not as impossible as you claim. If you were to use your Charm, the one I gifted to you, it would be child's play for you to get the ring."

A sour taste coated Clara's tongue. The Empress was proud of her "gift," but the thought of it drained Clara's wrath, leaving her feeling spent. "You know I'll never use it again. *Never.*"

"Not for your precious *freedom*? How is this different than the last time?"

Clara crossed her arms, clenching her jaw. She wasn't getting into a discussion about her Charm. Enigmas considered their offerings— the Charms and the Tricks—valuable and highly prized and couldn't understand why humans who received them were less than enthused. Even if her Charm could pull this off with ease—and that was a big "if"—the danger of doing so, the repercussions were far worse than whatever the ring was doing.

"What else can you tell me about the ring?" she asked. "How can I get it if I can't touch it?"

"You'll have to have Madame Josephine Lawrence remove it and give it to you, won't you?"

"That's about as likely to happen as hell is of freezing over."

"There's no such thing as hell," the Enigma snapped before letting out a long-suffering sigh. Was Clara imagining it or was the spirit taking on more human affectations? Years ago, she'd seemed much more remote and unemotional.

"If it is indeed warded against touch, gloves sewed with thread from a caul-born woman's burial clothes will protect the wearer."

Clara recoiled at the notion of obtaining such thread.

The Empress continued, "Use the glove and place the ring in a pinewood box lined with goofer dust and High John to keep the power neutralized."

While perhaps unsavory, none of those items were too difficult to obtain if she talked to the right people. "And how will I get it to you? You refused to tell me before, but I need to know everything before I even think about trying again. No more surprises."

The Enigma smiled, the expression eerie on her murky, opaque face. "Once the ring is inside the box, draw a crossmark on the ground at midnight that same day. Put the box in the center of the cross, hold a glass of water mixed with rose and lemon oil in your hands as you walk around the crossmark three times."

Clara tilted her head to the side. "*That's* how I get it to you?"

"That is what you need to do." Impatience colored her tone. "And get it done quickly. There is no way to know how many others are seeking the ring—there would be disastrous consequences if any Enigma but myself were to get it."

"But why? Who else wants it?"

"Don't be impertinent, Clara. Matters are at play here beyond mortal comprehension. You want your freedom? The longer you wait to get me that ring, the more chance it has of falling into the wrong hands. And if you insist on not using your Charm and obtaining outside assistance, remember I hold no sway with The Man in Black; all other debts but his I can get removed."

"I remember," Clara said.

And then The Empress was gone.

Unease prickled Clara's scalp, leaving a sensation like her skin didn't fit right over her skull. She still had so many questions—ones The Empress obviously had no intention of answering. But the ring was obviously dangerous. It had the potential to kill, in addition to whatever it was doing to Titus Monroe and others.

As for giving it to The Empress? She wasn't sure at all that the Enigma's insubstantial hands were the best for the ring to fall into...but what else could she do?

Once again, she was left with few good choices.

When Mama Octavia used to complain that Clara was working her last nerve, Clara always thought the woman must not have had too many to start with. Especially since Clara always managed to skip all the rest to land right on that last one. But now, standing out on the sidewalk in front of the Republic Gardens, the doorman continuing to eye her suspiciously, she understood how a person could burn right through every single nerve in her body to end up irritating the final one with only a little bit of effort.

The restaurant and nightclub had been converted from a row house and was just down the street from her apartment. Of course, she'd never been inside before. She'd arrived late, later than she'd like after being up half the night before—this mission was wreaking havoc on her sleep schedule. But her strategy had paid off at first. There was no line of patrons waiting outside to get in. She'd wanted to avoid both having to deal with a crowd at the popular nightspot and paying the cost of a ticket, but hadn't figured on actually having to stand out here until the place closed down for the night. The doorman and his strict adherence to a dress code was an obstacle she should have foreseen. Zelda certainly would have.

She crossed her arms and glared at him.

He sniffed, unruffled.

Two giggling flappers stumbled out of the club, tipsy as all get out, cigarette holders dangling from their fingers. Clara peered longingly at the open door, wondering if she made a run for it, could she leap the steps and sneak in before he caught her?

His eyes narrowed as if he could read her thoughts. Considering he was standing much closer to the door than she was, there was no way that plan could work.

"I just need to find someone," she said again through gritted teeth. "I'm not staying. What does it matter what I'm wearing?"

"You're staying right where you are. I ain't letting you in looking like you just crawled out from under some trash heap." Her navy-blue day dress and worn-down oxfords were perfectly acceptable at work, but apparently prohibited her from even stepping through the door of the small club. "Like I said before. No. Ragamuffins."

Her nostrils flared. She imagined steam pouring from them.

The large man folded his arms as if that would be the end of the discussion, but Clara wasn't having it. Intimidation—even from large, muscle-bound men—had never worked on her. She sucked in a breath, ready to read him the riot act, when one of the flappers tilted her head, blowing smoke out the side of her lips.

"Don't you know who this is, Charlie?"

The woman took another drag from her cigarette, pointing with her free hand. "It's the famous sniping negress. You got to let her inside, she's practically a celebrity."

Clara peered at the young woman closely. She didn't recognize her, but realized that under the few inches of thick makeup she wore, she was likely just a few years older than Clara.

Charlie *hmph*ed, unswayed by this revelation. "What's a sniping negress?" He must either be new to town or hadn't been paying attention to the papers after the riots back in '19.

"Just something some white man made up to sell newspapers," Clara grumbled.

"Come here, honey," the woman said, removing one of her long, dangling necklaces. It was probably crystal and paste, but glittered under the streetlights prettily. "Put this on and don't pay him no mind. Everybody in there's peeping through their liquor. Wouldn't know their nose from a doorknob. You looking for somebody who ain't where they supposed to be? Lot of that going around."

Clara's heart clenched as it did whenever she heard of yet another missing person. "No, I'm looking for Israel Lee."

The woman grinned lasciviously. "He sure is a fine piece of caramel. Shouldn't be too hard to find." The woman next to her dissolved into a fit of laughter.

"Thank you," Clara said, holding up the necklace.

The woman winked. "No, thank you. I sent in money to your defense fund—well, my mama did. We ain't never heard of a Colored girl like you before. Gave us all hope."

Clara nodded, uncomfortable with the attention, then raced up the steps and past a confused Charlie. It didn't happen as much as it used to, being recognized on the street, stopped, thanked. Everyone had known her name back then, but memories are short. And she was only in the news for a little while.

The inside of the nightclub smelled of sweat and liquor and smoke.

119

Cloth-covered tables lined the sides of the narrow room, with a stage set up against a wall and a dance floor in front of it. The band playing was a trio—not the District Rumblers, Israel's band. All around her, folks her age were living it up, dancing, shouting, eating—enjoying the music and the spirits and the company. Not the kind of spirits that visited her regularly either.

Just as the woman outside had said, Israel wasn't difficult to spot. He stood off to the side of the stage entertaining a dozen fans. Admirers both male and female clamored for his attention. He must have gotten done performing recently, since even from this distance, she could see the sweat dotting his forehead.

His smile seemed strained, but he accepted slaps on the back and hearty handshakes from the men. And more than one sultry, adoring glance from the women. Clara had no desire to insert herself into that crowd, so she waited, standing along the wall hoping the people would filter away.

Except they didn't.

More gathered around him. The piano player onstage gave him an exasperated glare, which Israel caught. More of the audience was trying to get Israel's attention than listening to the music. Israel ducked his head, bent to pick up his guitar, and began working his way through the crowd. It looked like he was heading out the back. Clara hadn't thought of that. She raced around the edges of the room to cut him off.

Speed walking through the darkened back hallway, she passed a few closed doors. The heavy door at the end led into a moonlit garden from which the place got its name. Neat rows of plants taking up the entire backyard gave the feeling of an oasis inside the city. She strolled through, transfixed for a moment by the beauty, and approached the fence, figuring Israel would make his escape into the alley.

Sure enough, he emerged a moment later, mercifully alone, and paused in the garden. He stood over a cluster of greenery Clara couldn't identify, pausing to inhale the subtle fragrance. Eyes closed and face limned by the silvery glow of the moon, he looked like a statue. A perfect specimen of male beauty carved by some ancient master. But also, a wearied man escaping all the craziness inside. She almost hated to break into his peace.

However, there were questions she needed answered.

She stepped forward out of the shadows and he turned sharply, startled. He squinted at her, then tilted his head.

"Lioness?"

"My name is Clara. Clara Johnson."

He frowned, but her name didn't cause any visible signs of recognition. He took in her dress and shoes and the out-of-place necklace. "Israel Lee," he said simply.

"Yes, I know. We need to talk about Madame Josephine."

13

A POSSIBLE ALLIANCE

The night wrapped velvet arms around them, while a breeze blew away the lingering heat. Clara and Israel walked in silence down to the park at the corner. She was glad he hadn't suggested they go back inside or to some shadowy dive—given what had happened last night, she wasn't quite sure it was safe to be alone with him, though Mama Octavia had shown up and was keeping a mistrustful eye turned his way. Clara had suggested the park, it was empty at this time of night but still out in the open, and he'd just nodded his head.

The urge was strong to pierce the veil and use her second sight on him . . . but she resisted. That could be even more dangerous. She was almost certain he held a debt to an Enigma, though. She hadn't viewed his aura before at the Lincoln, but The Empress's contention that others were after the ring made it a safe bet.

They settled on a bench looking out onto the tiny patch of moonlit grass. Israel shifted, getting ready to speak, but Clara cut him off. "Did you know the man who died last night?"

Her question startled him. He blinked a few times before crossing his leg and leaning back. Trying to look more comfortable than he felt, she guessed. "Not well. I'd seen him around. Gigged with him once or twice. His name was Montrose. Montrose Merriweather." His gaze turned solemn.

Clara's heart was heavy. Montrose's death should not have happened. "Who told you to steal the ring?"

Israel's eyes widened. "What do you know about it?"

"Please, answer my question. It must have been a spirit. Which one?"

He swallowed, wariness entering his expression. "You were after the ring as well?" he finally asked.

She nodded.

"And someone sent you?"

She nodded again.

"The Man in Black?"

She sucked in a breath. *Dammit.* "She won't like that." Clara caught Mama Octavia's eye. Her grandmother's expression was sad, knowing it to be true.

"Who won't like what?"

She turned back to him, taking his measure. He looked tired, much more so than he had the night before at the party. Circles ringed his eyes and his breathing seemed labored. Was Montrose's death affecting him more than he wanted to share?

"This is what I believe," she began. "You owe a debt to a spirit—an Enigma. The Man in Black often targets artists or musicians, promising them fame and fortune but leaving them with a nasty Trick. Something that probably didn't sound that bad when you signed on, but has made your life some kind of living hell. Am I right?"

As she spoke, his posture straightened. He blinked at her and his lips parted, but no sound came out.

"You want to ask me how I know all this? Take a guess."

Deep wells of sorrow and commiseration opened up in his eyes. "You owe a debt as well."

"Bingo. The Man in Black asked you to steal the ring?"

"He did. I refused."

Now it was Clara's turn to be shocked.

"Then Montrose came to me. He had a wife. A baby boy." Israel cleared his throat, his eyes shining with unshed tears. "He'd made his deal with The Man in Black a few months ago, trying to improve things for his family. Making a living as a musician is tough. Can't imagine doing it with a wife and child."

He shook his head and sat back again, staring forward into the distance. "Montrose said if I helped him get the ring, The Man in Black had promised him a national tour, a spot in a big show. Enough money to buy a house and take care of his family for life. I told him—" His fist tightened on his thigh. Clara closed her eyes. "I told him it was a bad idea. Hadn't he learned enough the first time? The only thing he should bargain for was his freedom."

When she opened her eyes again, a tear had slipped down Israel's cheek. "He said he'd do all the work. All I had to do was distract Josephine. He'd steal the ring and take care of everything else. I should have said no."

Unable to hold back, she grabbed his fist in her own, squeezing gently. "Wouldn't have made a difference. He would have gone ahead without you."

"I don't even know what happened. One minute he was right beside me, the next he just fell down dead." Israel looked over at her, the pain in his gaze arresting.

"It's protected—the ring. Warded with some powerful conjure. Anyone who tries to touch it will end up like Montrose."

Now he vibrated with anger. "He didn't warn us."

"Neither did she. The Empress. That's what my spirit calls herself. She claims she didn't know, maybe yours didn't either."

Israel blew out a breath and scrubbed at his face with his free hand. Clara realized she was still touching him and withdrew.

"What's your Charm?" she asked.

He smiled halfheartedly. "I'll show you."

He pulled a mouth organ from the inside of his jacket and held it to his lips, cupped in both hands. As he blew into it, a sad old bluesy tune twanged out into the air. The plaintive melody was full of pain, but that wasn't what created the headache which immediately began pulsing behind her eyes. Clara took a deep breath and placed her palm on her forehead.

It was the music. It was achingly beautiful to her ears, but it *hurt*. She recalled the sensations she'd felt when his band had been playing the night before. However, now she could sense that this wasn't a normal kind of pain. She breathed through it and dropped her protections, almost involuntarily activating her second sight. There was magic in the music. It floated out on the wave of his orange aura and wrapped around her. The magic wanted her to stand, to sway with the music and dance.

It was the most curious thing. Beside her, Israel watched her carefully, never ceasing his playing. Clara resisted the pull of the music though she sensed it acutely. She stiffened, realizing what this was. "You can make folks do what you want when they hear you play."

His playing stopped abruptly. "Usually I can. Everyone but you apparently."

"I feel it, I can just see through it better than most." She leaned away from him, jaw tightening. "You can make them do *anything* you want?"

"No. I can't make them steal something or kill somebody. Nothing like that. Not that I would. It's not mind control, just a sort of light hypnosis. A suggestion that makes folks lose their inhibitions. Respond favorably to the nudge I give them. Eat more, laugh more, drink more. Things they want to do, but maybe think they shouldn't."

She was slightly mollified, but his handsome face lost some of its pull on her. "No wonder you're a ladies' man," she muttered.

"I assure you, I've never had to use my Charm for *that*." The flirtatious grin was back, albeit set to a lower dial. She narrowed her eyes. He held up his hands then put away his harmonica.

"It just... makes things easier. Greases the wheels a little. Folks hear me play and leave thinking it's the best music they ever heard. I get more bookings, more popularity. Like I said, it's hard to make a living."

She cocked her head, eyeing him. "And the Trick?"

He let out a dry chuckle. "It's, ah, strange to be talking about this with someone. My Trick is that anyone who hears me play is in awe of my talent. Didn't sound so bad when he said it. Walking down a lonely road at night, wishing for a little awe."

"But?" Even as she asked, she sensed the mist of his Trick wafting over her. Pushing her to treat him not like a man, but like a marvel.

He met her eyes and just looked at her for a long time until she thought he wouldn't answer. The words came slowly. "How do you talk to someone you're in awe of? Someone you revere? Do you sit down to lunch with them? Toss a ball around on Saturday afternoons? Punch them in the shoulder when they make a bad joke?" He frowned, breaking eye contact. Clara hung on his words, a heaviness spreading inside her like she was sharing his emotions.

"No, with someone like that you try to get in good with them, curry favor, bring them things you think they'll like. You treat them like... like royalty. I know it sounds like a stupid thing to complain about, but—"

"But it means you don't have friends. You only have sycophants."

The corner of his mouth lifted in a wry smile. "Yeah."

"That's not stupid. That's a curse." She crossed her arms in front of her, tearing her gaze away. "I'm in the business of curses, and that's a doozy."

Clara had never been one for having a lot of friends—she didn't trust easily, so it was mostly her choice—but she wasn't immune to loneliness. She imagined Israel's life had been very solitary, even surrounded by people.

"Did he promise to take it away if you got the ring?" she asked.

"He did. Free and clear."

Clara felt weighted to the bench, sorrow for him like an anvil in her lap. Mama Octavia faded away, shaking her head sadly.

"Do you think it's possible to steal the ring?" Israel asked.

"Most things are possible. One way or another." She didn't yet trust him with the information The Empress had relayed. "Did The Man in Black tell you anything about the ring? What it does? Why he wants it?"

"Just said he needed it badly. He seemed desperate to have it."

"The Empress promised me that anyone who helps me get the ring will get a boon from her. She'll release debts from any spirit...except for one."

The brightening hope in his eyes shuttered. "And that one is..."

"I'll give you three guesses and the first two don't count."

His face blanked in understanding, the resignation in his expression so much like Dorothy Monroe's that Clara couldn't stand it. Her heart threatened to burst.

"You got some folks working with you?" he asked.

"Yeah." She tore her gaze from his face before she did something stupid.

"So you're going to try again?" Israel's voice rose with surprise.

"I believe so. It's not just about freedom from my Charm and my Trick—you heard about the folks gone missing around town?"

He tilted his hat back on his head and turned to face her fully. "I hired a new drummer, a kid who'd begged and begged me for a shot. He didn't show up tonight. And I been hearing folks talk about kin who seem to have up and run off. It does seem odd. More than usual."

"The ring's got something to do with it. The Empress said Josephine isn't the one wielding it, someone else is pulling the strings, but it's all connected. Even if we don't get free, getting the ring may mean finding those who've gone missing."

Israel was lost in thought. He tapped his finger to his lips in a rhythm, unconsciously, but tiny tendrils of power snaked out from it. She couldn't sense their intent, maybe they had none. But she focused on the thread of power so she wouldn't stare at his lips.

"You got a plan worked out?" he finally asked.

"Not yet."

"Well, The Man in Black and The Empress are enemies, but that doesn't mean we have to be."

She raised her brows as he continued. "I can get close to Josephine." He pulled a face that was just short of disgusted. "She's taken a particular liking to me that I encouraged for the sake of this… It's not something I want to sustain, but it could help."

"You want to help me get the ring? Why, so you can steal it and take it to The Man in Black?" Her eyes narrowed in suspicion.

He held up his hands. "Listen, if what you say is true, it's more than us at stake here. Colored folks are going missing, the ones I've heard about have all been poor. Folks no one really cares about. If getting that ring somehow helps us find them, then as I see it we have to try. Could be the only hope they have. And working together we have a better shot at succeeding."

His words made her soften toward him again. She was still wary of his natural God-given charm, almost as much as his Enigma-given Charm. But he wasn't hypnotizing her—he was sincere.

Her jaw worked as she considered his offer. After long moments, the rumble of his voice broke the silence, sending chills up her arm. "What's your Charm anyway? You're unaffected by mine—is it immunity?"

"No. I was born like that. Born with the caul, so I can sense magic, see spirits. My Charm is something else. I don't use it. Won't ever again." She hoped he'd let it drop, and fortunately he did.

"And your team?"

"One is a master of disguise. And I have a friend with no Enigma debt but who could pick your pocket clean without you ever knowing." *She already has*, Clara thought, recalling their first meeting.

His brows rose. "Well, I know someone else—someone with a Charm that would be useful. If we can bring him in, and guarantee that both Enigmas will free him too if we get the ring—no matter which one ends up with it—then I'm in. You and I can duke it out when it's all over."

When he turned to her this time, he no longer looked like a man who had accepted defeat. A gleam lit his dark eyes, filling Clara with hope and a sensation that felt suspiciously like butterflies beating their wings in her chest.

She swallowed, then cleared her throat. "Maybe we flip a coin or something."

The smile he gave her was sad, but she almost had to squint her eyes against its light.

When she'd sought him out tonight it hadn't been with this intention in mind. But as she'd seen his sincerity, listened to him speak, and watched his grief over Montrose, a man he barely knew, she felt strongly that he was someone she wanted on her side. And he did have the most access to Josephine.

"We'll all have to meet up first," she said reluctantly. "See if we get along and can figure out a way to do this."

"Sounds good to me." He held out his hand. "Deal?"

"I'm only agreeing to consider it, you understand?"

He grinned, and she stared at his hand for a long moment before stretching out her own to cross the short distance. Their palms touched. The tips of his callused fingers grazed her wrist. He squeezed her hand lightly, gently, and her bones began to rattle and vibrate. Her mouth went dry as the handshake seemed to last for eternity.

In reality, it was no longer than it needed to be and Israel didn't appear shaken at all by the contact. But when Clara retrieved her hand, it was tingly.

They were on the same side... for now. And the rest? Warm umber eyes regarded at her from a perfect face. The rest would work itself out, she supposed. One way or another.

14

THE PULLMAN PORTER

The glossy floors of Union Station smelled like wax. That scent, mingled with the pungent odor of shoe polish, made Clara crinkle her nose. She nodded at the old man working the shoeshine stand, tending to the brogans of a white man whose face was covered by a newspaper, and received a gap-toothed grin in response.

Israel's long stride ate up the distance of the lobby. People milled around the shops, ate at the restaurants, and sat clustered on the benches awaiting their trains or the arrival of loved ones. The glorious aroma of coffee wafted to her from a nearby café, clearing the other scents from her nose. She longed for it—she'd worked all day then caught the streetcar down to the train station to meet Israel—but he was on a mission, and she had no desire to give in to her caffeine addiction and fall behind.

They headed down the steps to the tracks where the Forty-Two from Chicago was resting. Passengers emerged from the green sleeping cars onto the platform. Halfway down, a policeman leaned against a support beam languidly. Clara tensed, but he didn't seem to be paying anyone any mind. In fact, it looked like he was dozing off.

A gaggle of teenage boys waited near the Colored car, greeting the weary passengers who disembarked. Clara edged closer to them, while Israel stayed put, scanning the white folks getting off the train.

An older Negro woman gripped her bag tight to her as a teen helped her descend the steps. "Do you need help, ma'am?" he asked. "I'm from the Traveler's Aid Committee."

"Oh yes, child. What have you got there?"

The boy held out a pamphlet the committee had put together with a listing of establishments around the city where a Negro would be welcome. The other boys fanned out, greeting folks, passing out pamphlets, and answering questions about local transportation and lodging.

Clara's attention turned back to Israel, standing rigidly while Pullman porters clad in their navy-blue uniforms and caps assisted white passengers with their luggage. One well-built, dark-skinned young man stacked suitcases onto a cart while a middle-aged white couple stood nearby, bickering. Israel's gaze had locked on them and Clara ambled closer.

"Be careful with that, George," the white man told the porter, who looked at him with barely veiled hostility.

"As I told you before, sir, my name is Jesse Lee. Feel free to use it, or call me 'porter,' but I am not George."

The man scoffed while his wife tittered wordlessly and gave an apologetic wave of her hand. When Jesse Lee was done arranging the bags on the cart, a station employee came up to take over. The two Negroes shared a look and the station employee pushed the cart away.

The white man reached into his pocket and tossed a dime at the porter—a paltry tip no matter how you looked at it. Jesse Lee caught the coin right out of the air, but when the man turned, he called out, "Wait."

The man spun back, affronted.

"This isn't the tip you wanted to give me."

Clara blinked, shock freezing her in place at the young man's audacity.

"It most certainly is," the man sputtered.

"No, you intended to give me ten dollars, not ten cents."

Clara's jaw dropped. The white man's face turned purple and his wife's eyes widened, but then, as one, both of their faces went slack. They stood still as stone while Jesse Lee glanced around to make sure no one was watching—no one white, she guessed, since she and Israel were staring straight at him. Then he slipped a hand into the man's jacket pocket and retrieved his wallet. The white man didn't move a muscle. His gaze was soft, staring ahead at nothing.

Jesse Lee pulled a crisp ten-dollar bill from the wallet, then replaced it in the man's coat and stepped back. The couple blinked, released from their stupor, and looked at each other.

"You all have a nice time in Washington," Jesse Lee called out.

The man nodded brusquely, then took his wife's hand and turned away. Both stumbled at first, as if dizzy, before disappearing up the steps. As soon as the couple was out of view, Jesse Lee turned to them, a wide grin on his face.

"Long time no see, cousin," he said, embracing Israel.

"Still up to no good?" Israel laughed.

Clara glanced back at the policeman, who was too far away to see what had happened and still dozing on the job.

"This is Clara Johnson." Israel motioned to her.

"Jesse Lee Stewart." He stepped forward and shook her hand.

"Nice to meet you," she said, but with a question in her voice. "What did you do to that man?"

"What makes you think I done something to him?" His grin was sly.

"She has the sight," Israel advised. "And a spirit debt of her own."

Jesse Lee's brows rose. He looked at her with new eyes and she peered back, unflinching. Then a slow smile spread across his face. He was easily as handsome as his cousin, with a neat mustache and a mischievous gleam in his eye. But on Jesse Lee it didn't come across flirtatious, just friendly. The subtle difference intrigued Clara.

"I just made him a little forgetful, that's all." He stuffed his hands in his pockets.

"You took his money," Clara countered.

"I earned that tip. That ofay has been treading my nerves since Detroit."

"And then you made him forget it?"

"That I did."

"And before, when he was just staring out at nothing?"

He shot a glance at Israel, who nodded. "Made him forget everything, just for a few seconds. How to walk, how to talk." He shrugged.

"So that's your Charm," she muttered. "And your Trick..." He tensed, uneasiness replacing his unbothered demeanor. "You don't have to tell me if you don't want. A Trick is a Trick. They're all bad."

He nodded, appearing relieved, then turned back to his cousin. "Your telegram was short on details. 'Meet me in DC soon as'?"

"It was a telegram, it said all it needed to get you here, right? I'll fill you in on the way home."

"Let me get my bag." Jesse Lee raced off back into the train and reemerged a moment later with a small duffel slung over his shoulder.

They went back up the steps and crossed into the lobby, which was much busier than it had been minutes before. Israel had vouched for his kin, and having seen Jesse Lee's Charm firsthand, Clara knew he'd be an asset, but he won a place on her good side when he insisted they stop for a cup of coffee before leaving.

Jesse Lee whistled low as Israel stepped up to the pristine Model T. "You got yourself a new tin lizzie, cousin? Maybe I need to spend more time down here in Washington."

Israel looked more embarrassed than proud as his cousin walked around the car, admiring. Then, with a flourish, Jesse Lee opened the passenger door and swept an arm toward Clara. "Ladies first."

She slid into the middle of the single seat with the men on either side of her. She wasn't certain when she'd been so close to two such handsome men, and tried to keep her focus. The electric starter rumbled the engine to life and Israel pulled into traffic on H Street.

Beside her, she could feel Jesse Lee's attention focused on her. He was an interesting mix of playful and solemn, a little manic in his switch from one to the other.

"So the reason I'm here has to do with you," he said in a low voice. While Israel navigated the traffic, Clara filled Jesse Lee in on the details of their task and what had happened up until then. He rubbed his chin in thought when she was done.

"I need to go to the barbershop," he finally announced. Clara blinked in surprise. Israel tilted his head.

"Your hair is fine," Clara said. He looked to be maybe just a week out from a previous cut.

"Why, thank you. But if you want to know what's going on in any Negro city, head to the barbershop, right? Those niggas gossip more than any hen sitting on a the front stoop. Folks going missing? They're gonna know about it. I got a brother from the 321st who cuts heads on 13th Street. I can get cleaned up and gather intel at the same time."

Clara sat back, surprised she hadn't thought of that herself. When she looked at Israel, he was grinning. "Told you he'd be good to have on board, and not just for his Charm."

Jesse Lee chuckled. "I am a charming motherfucker. Not just a pretty face."

"Who called you pretty?" Israel scoffed.

"Etheline Baker, fifth grade. Didn't you have a crush on her? But as I recall, she waited on me after school, always asking me to walk her home."

"I recall no such thing."

"You need help replacing that particular memory?" Jesse Lee said on a laugh. "I'm here for you, cuz."

Israel snorted. "Etheline Baker had two magnifying glasses strapped to her face. She ain't know what you looked like, she just thought you talked nice."

Jesse Lee scowled in mock affront, while Clara grumbled, "If either of you gets any prettier, this car might lift off the ground from all the air in your big heads."

"You think you're exempt, Miss Clara?" Jesse Lee's brow rose.

"I'm the brains of the operation."

"Beauty and brains." He smacked his chest dramatically. "I'm going to have to sweep up the shards of my cousin's broken heart before all this is done."

She glanced at him sharply, but his gaze was on his cousin. When she turned, Israel was staring straight ahead, his jaw clenched. Jesse Lee sat back, laughing to himself. Clara wasn't sure what was going on, but the narrow bench seat seemed to shrink.

"Don't worry, Iz. You know I didn't come to edge in on your territory."

Israel didn't respond. Clara stayed silent as well, unsure what to say. She could clarify that she wasn't any kind of territory, and if she was, Israel had staked no claim, nor was he likely to. But the tightening of his knuckles on the steering wheel and the tension thickening the air made her keep her lips sealed for once.

THE THIEF

The folks in Leetown who remember the day Jesse Lee Stewart was born always called him Hawk, on account of him being born screeching up a storm. Ain't nobody ever heard a baby sound like that, carrying on with lungs stronger than iron. His four older brothers and sisters had been quiet as mice when they was born, but not a one of them lived to see their first birthday, so it was just as well that he came into the world noisy.

He didn't stop being noisy, not when he raced through the fields as a toddler, or when he sang solos in the choir at church in a clear, high child's voice. Not even when, walking home from the fishing hole with his daddy one afternoon, the county sheriff and his deputy stopped them to ask what they knew about a chicken thief plying his trade thereabouts.

Deacon Stewart was a quiet and measured man, and one dedicated to the survival of himself and his family. He answered the questions calmly, and just as calmly put his hands behind his back and accepted the handcuffs when the sheriff asked him to. Jesse Lee refused to do any such thing.

'Course they wasn't planning to arrest the boy until he started running that loud mouth of his. Deacon told his son to hush, but Jesse Lee just hollered louder and louder, until the strike of a billy club across his head finally shut him up.

Fortunately, the police caught the chicken thief with the feathers still in his hair a week later, and the Stewart boys were released, but Jesse Lee's experience hadn't quieted him any.

The day he announced to his mama and daddy that he was going to sign up for the white man's army and fight the krauts over in Europe, the shouts rising out the windows weren't even his—at first. His mama started wailing, asking Jesus for help, and the rare boom of his daddy's voice nearly lifted the roof off the building. But Jesse Lee yelled louder than all of them that he was going and that was that.

The only one who could ever quiet him down was Daisy.

Daisy Schraeder was tall and dark with long legs and a long face. She had teeth white as the moon and a tough head of kinky hair that broke the teeth off more than one comb. She had a sweet voice and an even sweeter disposition and she was everything to Jesse Lee.

They would meet up out at her daddy's moonshine still which she watched over while he slept off the hooch he sucked down like it was Adam's ale. And when the bug crawled up Jesse Lee's behind to volunteer for the army, she'd been the first person he told.

She didn't scream like his mama or shout like his daddy. She understood what it meant to him, how he had the desire to prove himself, to stand up for something and declare that his manhood and patriotism had nothing to do with his skin color. All she did was make him promise to come back to her. "I'll wait for you, Jesse Lee," she whispered. "I'll be here when you come back."

And so he went off to Camp Jackson and soon found himself buttoned into a uniform and on a boat headed for France. But his dreams of fighting for his country were dashed. The white man's army didn't want Negroes to fight, it wanted them to clean. And cook. And unload the cargo from the depths of the ships crossing the Atlantic. Dig trenches, lay railroad tracks, butcher cattle.

As a part of Company A of the 321st Labor Battalion, Jesse Lee found himself a member of a skirmish line, walking two by two across a smoking battlefield, a folded wooden stretcher slung across his shoulder awaiting the body of one of many dead soldiers he would retrieve.

He carried corpses and dug graves, over and over in fields across France. He hadn't watched these men die, but he smelled the stench. Saw the horror etched into their frozen faces. Swatted the flies away from them, picked up the pieces that were left of them, and carried them to their rest.

The dead were emblazoned on his brain like a brand, images crying as loud as his voice on Sundays used to be. They wouldn't leave, not after armistice and peace and the boat back to Virginia. He didn't go home at first, he wanted to clear his head so he wouldn't go back to Daisy with these pictures still running in his mind like a photoplay, so he traveled. Rode the rails, took odd jobs, ran from whites—better understanding now his father's drive to survive.

In Louisiana, he met an old man who said he could make the nightmares stop. He was toothless and wrinkled up like old parchment paper and had dusted off some chicken bones, thrown them on the ground, and started speaking in tongues. He'd scared Jesse Lee half to death.

But the voice of the Enigma had come through those bones or up from the ground or from the pits of hell, Jesse Lee wasn't ever quite sure, and spoken to him. Asked him what he wanted. To forget the faces of the dead, he'd said. The stench of their deaths, the screams echoing in his mind—some he hadn't even heard with his ears yet they still haunted him. He wanted them gone. Couldn't see how having them rolling around in his head would ever do him any good.

The bones vibrating in the dirt had spoken. "Your Charm will be the ability to manipulate any memory you wish, to take and return them both for yourself and anyone you meet." A subtle tremor shook the ground, making way for the eventual earthquake.

The old man grinned his gummy smile and Jesse Lee waited for the rest. He wasn't so naïve as to believe that this gift wouldn't come with a price.

"The Trick is that you will be doomed to be forgotten by the woman you love."

Now, some would call Jesse Lee's thought process at that moment hubris. It certainly was a form of pride that rang through him. He didn't think it possible for Daisy to forget him. They'd known each other since they was children. She was his girl and she had promised to wait for him. And he wasn't no good to her with these memories rattling around in his skull. So he took the deal.

He made his way back to Leetown and to Daisy's porch. Relief made his whole body sag when she remembered him just fine. They kissed in the middle of the one-room cabin she'd grown up in, her daddy snoring away in the corner like always.

He filled the holes in his mind with dreams of the future instead of nightmares from the past. Told Daisy he was going to get a job and take her to the preacher and marry her. They would build a house at the edge of town and make moonshine or raise chickens and children and whatever else she wanted. She smiled her moonlit smile and he'd never been happier.

The next day he came back and knocked on her door again and she stared at him blankly. "Daisy? You all right?"

"How you know my name?" she asked, drawing back, suspicion cutting lines in her forehead.

"It's me. Jesse Lee. You know me. I've known you since we were little ones racing around your grandmammy's skirts."

But the frown on her face and the fear in her eyes made him crumple inside. And replacing her memories of him just wouldn't work. The spirits were indeed powerful and they couldn't be fooled. Not even by a fast, smooth talker like Jesse Lee.

After three months of trying in vain to get her to remember him and nearly being shot by her daddy more than once—thank the Lord he was too drunk to ever shoot straight—Jesse Lee was desperate. He went back to Louisiana to find that toothless old man and make him reverse the deal. He never did find him and sought out other hoodoo doctors, root women, folks born with the sight—anyone he thought might be able to help—but they all told him the same thing. The deal was done and he had to live with the consequences.

The next time he went home, a new idea popped into his head—if she didn't remember the old him, he would introduce her to the new him. He bumped into her at the feed store and acted like they'd never met. Asked her to walk out with him real respectful, and she, having no recollection of admiration from any man, not the least one as handsome as Jesse Lee with his dark skin and generous smile, eagerly accepted.

They'd gone down to the sandwich shop and then on a stroll along the river. Watched the dusk fall and listened to the crickets singing a melody with the frogs. She'd never had a better day in all her life. At her doorstep she even allowed him a kiss and hoped he would call on her again.

The next day she answered the door to find a strange man she'd never seen before. A handsome, chocolate man smiling at her like she'd painted the stars. He was sweet and kind and a little bit sad when she asked him his name. When he asked if she'd walk out with him, she said she'd like to go to the sandwich shop. He winced, just a little, but recovered quickly—maybe he didn't like sandwiches.

From then on, every few weeks, a man would stop her after church or shoot her a grin at the five-and-dime or cross her path at the riverside, and each time surprise would shower down on her that a man so fine would be interested in her. Jesse Lee and Daisy had a hundred first dates that she never remembered, and she never saw the tears on his face as he left her each and every time.

15

THE SPEAKEASY

Clara fought a yawn as she nearly tripped down the steps into Miles's basement speakeasy. It was late, ten o'clock, and normally she'd be in bed. She had to be at the journal offices early the next morning to open up as Mrs. Shuttlesworth was visiting her sister in Philadelphia, but tonight's meeting took precedence over much-needed sleep, especially since a heavy foreboding had swamped her since that afternoon.

She entered the low-ceilinged space to find that she was the last to arrive. Aristotle was seated in the corner, facing the room. Tonight he was playing someone new—an older and distinguished man, haughtily handsome and brown-skinned with conked hair silvering at the temples. Again his suit was impeccable.

Next to him sat Israel and Jesse Lee, both with fresh haircuts. Jesse Lee had changed from his porter's uniform into a salmon-colored wool summer suit that somehow managed not to be ostentatious. Israel was more conservative in a white shirt and brown vest, his jacket draped over the side of a nearby chair. Clara settled in next to Zelda, who wore her favorite sport trousers. Though Clara was the youngest present, she felt frumpy and awkward. She tugged at the ragged hem of her dress, her face hot.

"I take it you all made the introductions?" she asked.

Affirmative murmurs went up.

"Well, we need to figure out if it makes sense to work together on this." She eyed Israel cautiously, but his demeanor gave nothing away of his feelings. She hadn't confessed to Aristotle or Zelda the peculiar bind she and Israel found themselves in.

Since both The Empress and The Man in Black had agreed to release the debts of anyone who helped retrieve the ring, telling the others that the agreement didn't extend to either Clara or Israel if their Enigma didn't win hadn't seemed helpful. Aristotle would be fine either way and Zelda didn't even have a debt in the first place, she was only here out of some misguided idea of friendship. Clara didn't need friends. She was helping Zelda, that was all. Giving her a place to stay and keeping her out of trouble as best she could. She should probably do more to remind the woman that they were not, in fact, bosom buddies.

What Israel had told his cousin was a mystery. He might not have had the same compunction for keeping the truth close to his chest. Clara had to assume Jesse Lee knew their situation and had aligned with Israel. It would only make sense, them being kin and all.

"Why wouldn't it?" Zelda asked. At Clara's questioning expression, she clarified. "Make sense to work together?"

"They're strangers." She shrugged.

Zelda rested her chin on her fist. "Everyone's a stranger at first."

Clara didn't appreciate the speculative gaze in the woman's eyes and got back to the matter at hand. "After the last attempt, Josephine will probably be even more on her guard. So this will be even harder."

"Seems like we need to know more about the ring," Aristotle said. "Like where did it come from? How did Josephine get it?"

"You mind if I ask what your Charm is?" Jesse Lee broke in, leaning forward. "And yours?" He motioned to Zelda, who grinned.

"No Charm. I'm just here to keep this one out of trouble." She jerked her thumb at Clara, whose eyes widened.

Aristotle spoke up before Clara could respond. "It would be easier for me to show you."

His form blurred before taking on the visage of Prince Abdul Menelik bin-Solomon—purple caftan, feathered hat and all. Then he changed back to the sophisticated character.

"Who are you tonight?" Clara asked while Israel and Jesse Lee picked their jaws up off the floor.

"I call him Clarence. He owns an engineering firm and lives in a house in LeDroit Park." He made a dramatic flourish with his hands and smiled brilliantly with glowing white teeth. Clara blinked in response.

"Well, I steal memories," Jesse Lee said when Zelda looked at him expectantly. "Can make you forget I was ever here."

She looked impressed, but Clara frowned. "You got to promise not to use your Charm on any of us."

A wide grin spread across Jesse Lee's face. "Not unless you ask. Cross my heart." Clara rolled her eyes while Zelda continued her questioning.

"And you?" she asked Israel.

His mouth twisted before he took a deep breath. "My music makes people do and think and feel what I want. It's a light hypnotism. I'd rather not show you."

Zelda bit her lip and nodded.

"We'll need a way to protect everyone from falling under his spell," Clara said. "And his Trick. That is, if we decide to work together on this."

Israel's expression was solemn; the severity seemed out of character to Clara, though she barely knew the man. "And Clara's Charm remains a mystery," he added, a little sadly. "Though she's immune to mine."

She met the expectant eyes of the rest of the group. "I don't use my Charm. Ever. And I'm not immune to all of yours, but I can sense them, avoid being taken in. It's part of the gift I was born with, which can help us, but can also cause trouble, so I use it sparingly. When Madame Josephine passed by, I peered through the veil, but all I could tell about the ring is that it's powerful and well protected."

Israel sat back in his chair. "I've been up close to it—the ring is old. It's bronze-colored but I don't know what metal it's made from. And The Man in Black wouldn't say anything about where it came from or what it really does."

Zelda shot a glance her way. Had she overheard The Empress talking about The Man in Black? Clara didn't return the look, keeping her gaze stubbornly focused on Israel. "The Empress wouldn't tell me anything else either. We'll have to figure out a way to learn more about it."

"So we're back at square one," he said.

"Not necessarily." Zelda had a gleam in her eye. "If it's old, then an ancestor should know something, right?"

Clara squinted in thought. "It's just a matter of finding the right ancestor. I'll ask Mama Octavia to make some inquiries, but if the ring is ancient then that will be hard. The older spirits can be...difficult." She shivered. The old ones were ornery and unpredictable. Even Mama Octavia would have to tread carefully around them.

"Well, until then, I have another idea," Jesse Lee announced. "Down at the barbershop, I talked to my buddy from the 321st. He has a brother who was in the Harlem Hellfighters. Settled down here after the war and took on work as a bodyguard. Name's Thaniel Dawson, one of the biggest niggas I ever seen. Apparently he works for Madame Josephine." Sparks of excitement practically shot from Jesse Lee's skin. "Since Bowlegged Mo went down, she's been tightening security."

"Why's that?" Aristotle asked.

"Crooked Knee Willy. Mo thinks Willy set him up as a way of trying to move in on the territory. Don't nobody want to see a war between bootleggers."

"Willy confronted Madame Josephine at the Lincoln the other night," Clara said. "There's definitely some tension there."

"Well, Josephine is hiring more bodyguards, and I think I can get in with them," Jesse Lee said. "I get hired, I can be the inside man." He looked very proud of himself. Israel chuckled, and Aristotle nodded in approval.

Clara had to admit that Jesse Lee had swept into town and gotten a lot done in a single afternoon. But the look he shared with his cousin raised her hackles. "I'm not sure," she began, once again making herself the center of attention. "You really want to be getting into bed with gangsters?"

He shot her a hard look. "It's not getting in bed with them, it's going undercover. Besides, I can snoop around and take the memories of anyone who gets suspicious. Do you have any better ideas?"

Over at the bar, Cole polished the scarred surface. He was mostly deaf and Clara was sure he couldn't hear them, but her anxiety grew. Normally she knew to trust her senses, but tonight she feared paranoia was clouding her judgment.

"Let's get something to wet our whistles." Zelda rose and pulled Clara up with her, giving her a meaningful look. Clara sighed and allowed herself to be dragged over to the bartender. When Cole turned away, Zelda whispered, "What's wrong? You look strange."

"Gee, thanks."

"I'm serious. Why don't you like the idea of Jesse Lee going in as one of Josephine's guards?"

Clara struggled to put it into words. The ghost of the white policeman popped into existence in the opposite corner, standing on the empty makeshift stage. He smirked at her knowingly, and Clara shut her eyes tight. When she opened them, Israel and Jesse Lee were whispering.

Were they talking about her? Planning on how to make sure Israel's Trick was removed and not hers? This wasn't going to work. She couldn't team up with people who had a vested interest in her failure.

Whispers from the past assailed her. *If it ain't the Little Sniper. You shoot every man who comes in your bedroom? You think those bars will keep you safe? There's a rope right here with your name on it.*

Phantom pain ripped through her thigh. She tightened her hands into fists and gritted her teeth. She was never sure if the shrapnel lodged there was making itself known or if she was just experiencing the ghost of the pain from when she'd been shot. It would settle down in a minute, she just had to breathe through it.

The *thunk* of the bottle of hooch Cole slammed down in front of them made her bones rattle. She wrestled the old thoughts back where they belonged, stoppered up tight in her memory. The pain faded away with it. Zelda was looking at her with concern. She'd asked a question; Clara struggled to remember what they were talking about.

"What do we know about him?" she offered lamely. "How do we know we can trust him?" Was she talking about Jesse Lee or Israel? She wasn't even sure.

"He's got a Trick, don't he? If it's as bad as they all are, then why *wouldn't* you trust him? We work together and everybody wins, right? Including the people in the neighborhood."

Clara swallowed. The dead policeman grinned and faded away. Had he even been there at all or was she cracking up?

"What are you not telling me?" Zelda prodded.

Clara closed her eyes for a long blink before opening them again. Clearing her mind. "Nothing. It's nothing."

With a suspicious glance, Zelda snatched up the bottle and took it back to the table, with Clara following slowly behind.

"Once you get in good with her," Zelda was saying to Jesse Lee, "we need to figure out a way to pass information. If they're worried about Crooked Knee Willy, then they may be watching their guards closely."

"We haven't even decided to work together," Clara said, her voice trembling for some reason. She cleared her throat.

"You're the only one who hasn't decided, child," Aristotle drawled, his character's voice languid. "It makes a lot of sense to me. Why wouldn't we partner up?"

She wrung her hands together under the table, her mind searching for a valid reason to share.

Jesse Lee slung an arm over the back of his chair, looking smug. "Seems like you're outvoted, sweetheart."

She cut her eyes at him. "I'm not your sweetheart."

"No, you're not." A flash of grief crossed his face before it was replaced by his carefree grin. "You're just an ornery chicken who likes to squawk."

She stood up suddenly, her chair flying out behind her. "Now listen here, you gator-faced bamma—"

Israel rose and placed an arm around her shoulders, turning her to face the empty room. She shook him off and stepped away, not caring for how much she liked his touch, even through her anger.

Behind her, Zelda was fussing at Jesse Lee, whose voice never rose. Israel got right up in Clara's face, bending to peer into her eyes.

"Listen, I'll talk to him, but I need to know where you're at."

"I'm right here." She crossed her arms, avoiding his gaze as best she could.

"You're not where the rest of us are. Why don't you want to team up on this? Really?"

Her foot tapped a rapid beat; she held her breath for as long as she could before exhaling loudly. Israel's eyes searched hers. Frown lines marred his forehead.

"I just don't...I just don't like it," she mumbled.

"She's the brains of the operation," Jesse Lee said sarcastically. "Don't like any idea she didn't come up with herself, right?"

She spun around to find four pairs of eyes staring holes in her.

"I knew men like you in the service," Jesse Lee continued. "Couldn't stand not being in charge of everything. You want to be the general, fine. I don't care." He gave her a mock salute. "But you have to lead us somewhere, and right now you don't have nowhere to go. We work together and everybody gets what they want—our Tricks gone, the missing people found...Isn't that what you're after?"

The scrutiny was unbearable, and she had no words. She pressed her lips tighter, feeling mulish. Israel's gaze was palpable, crossing her skin and seeking a way inside her mind.

"Fine," she said through clenched teeth. "We work together."

After a beat of silence, the others began talking again. Planning. Cutting through the thick tension in the room.

She took her seat and listened in, cooling the fire in her veins. Teaming up was a risk whether the others believed it or not. And whether she had true cause for concern or was just being paranoid, she was definitely losing control—of herself, if not the situation.

There was something worse than failure—hopelessness. She didn't want to believe that the hope burgeoning deep in her breast would be for naught. The taste of possible freedom was addictive, but now she wasn't certain it hadn't been poison.

16

SOUL FOOD

On Thursday afternoon, Clara walked out the door of the journal offices to find a swarm of women, including the other typists and stenographers, buzzing around the sidewalk. They orbited a tall figure, but all she could see was a jauntily tilted hat. She peered through the bodies for a better look, when the sound of a whistled tune rang out.

The melody punctured her skull like a drill, making her brain ache. As one, the women all moved away to scatter down the street, revealing a man leaning against the door of his Ford, long legs crossed at the ankles, hands in his pockets. His full lips were pursed mid-whistle, and Clara forcibly drew her gaze away from them. She dredged up a scowl.

"Israel."

His response was an ice-melting smile, which had the benefit of forcing him to stop whistling. She glanced up and down the sidewalk before stepping up to him. "Handy. Being able to make them leave you alone like that."

He merely shrugged.

"What do you want?" She crossed her arms, trying to build a wall of protection between them.

"We need to talk." His expression gave nothing away. He was back to his amiable self, his light demeanor more natural than the melancholy that had clung to him the last time she'd seen him.

"What I need is a hot and my cot. I been playing office manager all day, and I'm too tired to talk to you."

His grin was meant to disarm and was doing a good job of it too, but Clara held fast. Israel pushed away from the car, taking a step forward, which brought him closer to her, then turned and opened the passenger door. "I'll buy you dinner, how's that?"

She narrowed her eyes. The interior of his car smelled too much like him. The cologne he wore that managed to be sweet and spicy at the same time mixed with his natural scent. She didn't want to breathe all of that in, nor did she want to sit across from him at a dinner table trying to pretend he wasn't scrambling her up inside.

He stood patiently, waiting for her to decide. Something skated across her backside and she turned sharply, ready to lay into whoever had dared touch her, only to find Mama Octavia standing behind her, brows raised.

Surprise widened Clara's eyes. She didn't speak, not wanting to alarm Israel. Her grandmother smirked and shooed her toward the car. Spirits like hers, the dead who had been around for a while, could muster up enough energy to interact with the material world. Others could too, the angry or disturbed intent on haunting the living. But Mama Octavia usually spent her energy on other things, like traveling back and forth between here and Over There. Occasionally, though, she took it upon herself to swat Clara's bottom like she used to when she was alive. Thankfully, as a ghost, her strikes didn't hurt anywhere near as much as they used to.

Israel was still looking at her expectantly, but uncertainty had crept into his expression. That, plus her growling stomach, made her inch closer to the car and finally settle herself inside. The hint of his vulnerability did more to make her risk being alone with him for the next hour or so than Mama Octavia's "encouragement."

With just the two of them in the car, she didn't have to sit pressed up against him like before. She stared out the window on the short drive over to the Southern Dining Room. When he parked on 7th Street, she snorted. "We could have walked." They'd only driven two blocks.

Israel grinned. "Thought I'd give your feet a break, you been working all day."

She bit her lip to keep a smile from breaking through and waited for him to round the car and open the door for her. If she didn't know better, she'd think he was using his Charm to soften her up, but he wasn't making any type of melody and she didn't have a headache.

Inside the eatery, red-and-white-checkered tablecloths covered the tables. A clientele of mostly working people sat over steaming plates of fried chicken, collard greens, okra, and corn bread. This wasn't a high-toned place with fine people turning their noses up, this was a honey-homey spot she could be comfortable in. She glanced up at Israel, whose eyes were closed as he breathed in the aroma of good cooking.

Miss Hettie, the proprietress, offered them a warm greeting and led them to a booth in the back, near enough to the kitchen that Clara's mouth was actually watering. They put their orders in with the waitress and sat in silence as she poured them each a sweet tea before retreating. Sitting across from him, Clara was determined not to stare, so she peered around the restaurant.

"We got a problem, Clara?"

He spoke so bluntly it surprised her. She wasn't used to folks speaking their mind. When she did it, people had a tendency to complain.

She sucked in a deep breath and finally looked him in the eye, even more surprised to find hurt lurking there. She frowned, pausing. "I don't know."

Best be honest, it didn't make no sense to lie. "I just don't know. I'm not sure this is a good idea—us working together. I know neither of us can do this alone, but I can't stop thinking about only one of us getting free at the end."

His gaze dropped to the table before them. "Yeah, I thought that might be the case. Thought we was gonna cross that bridge when we came to it."

"It's a long bridge."

He chuckled, then drew the salt and pepper shakers closer to him. Long fingers fidgeted with them and she dragged her gaze up to his shirt collar.

"Well, we can't do anything about that right now," he said. "My granddaddy used to always tell me, don't worry about what you can't control. I been out of control of my life for a while. But I should have listened to him more. If I hadn't tried to make everything go the way I wanted it to, if I'd have had a little more grace, then I wouldn't be in this situation."

That's something they had in common. "Hard to let go when it means giving in to what others want you to do and be."

He nodded slowly. "I meant it when I said that we will figure it out. If I can't be free of this curse, then I'll be happy for you to be. And Jesse Lee. He had a hard time after the war. Things haven't been great."

Clara's brows shot up. "He's a porter. Folks would give a lot for a job like that. See the country, get a good paycheck."

"Yeah, he settled into it but... his Trick cost him."

The sorrow in his expression made her swallow further questions. She didn't know what Jesse Lee's Trick was, but it didn't matter. It caused pain, heartache, and chaos the way the Enigmas wanted.

"You told him? That only one of us can get free?"

He shook his head slowly. "No. That's what you're afraid of?"

She stayed silent, feeling guilty.

"You tell the others?" he asked.

"Didn't think it was their business."

"So we're agreed, then."

Clara took a shaky breath. She was off balance and could no longer distinguish between a true warning from her connection to the spirit world and her own fears and insecurities. The policeman hadn't shown up again, but the fact that he'd appeared twice in as many weeks was odd. Nothing good would come of it. And she'd been using her sight more, opening herself up to mischief and worse. It couldn't be helped, but left her unsettled.

At any rate, Israel was right. "I been helping to curse people so long that getting even a few folks free is worth it, regardless of which of us wins." She held out her hand. "I'm sorry for how I was acting. Truce?"

Israel looked relieved as they shook on it. Clara tried to hide her reaction to the feel of his hand engulfing her. The calluses on his fingers gently abraded her skin. She pulled out of his grasp quickly and tucked her hand under her thigh just as their food came.

They ate in companionable quiet. There wasn't much small talk, which she was grateful for. She both wanted to know more about him and didn't. Best to stick to the job at hand, focus on what was important. Not get distracted.

The food melted in her mouth, and she cleaned her plate. Both she and Israel sang the praises of Miss Hettie's near-magical mastery of Southern cooking when she came by to check on them.

Israel paid, as promised. Under other circumstances this could have been considered a date. Clara chuckled to herself as he held the door open for her.

"What?" he asked.

She waved him off. "Nothing." This man literally had hordes of women following him around. Stepping out with Clara Johnson was a ridiculous proposition. Eager to change the subject, she tilted her head, listening to the faint sound of a wailing trumpet in the air. "You hear that?"

Israel closed his eyes and smiled. "Sounds like old Hip Slim is at it. He's playing down at the Oriental Gardens tonight. Man, can that cat blow!"

They turned the corner, walking back to where he'd parked, and she was about to ask if he was going to head over to the nightclub to listen when something in the corner of her eye caught her attention.

A large delivery truck idled in the alley and two rough-looking men were practically dragging a young woman into the back. Clara grabbed Israel's arm and jerked him to a stop.

Inside the back of the truck, at least a half dozen other people sat, motionless. The young woman being manhandled didn't utter so much as a word of protest. One fellow hoisted her limp form up easily, then she simply sat on the bench seat.

"Hey!" Clara called out, causing one of the toughs to look up. He glared, slammed the door of the truck, and strode toward the cab. The other man disappeared around the other side of the vehicle, headed to the passenger seat.

Clara moved forward, dragging Israel along. The truck shifted into gear and moved forward down the alley away from her, knocking a trash can out of the way, making it topple over. Clara gave chase, jogging to keep up until the truck turned onto Q Street and sped away.

Israel was right on her heels staring after it. Clara cursed. "Those were Afflicted people. Those men were kidnapping them!"

"That's why they were going along easy as pie?"

"They're addled. Not in their right minds. Dammit! We need to know where that truck is going."

"Looks like they tried to paint over the labeling on the side, but it was done shoddy."

Clara whipped her head to the side. "You made it out?"

"Just the first few letters. 'AGB.' But based on the lettering style, I'm pretty sure it said Agbrooke Stables & Garage. Could be where they got the truck at least."

She scanned her memory. "That's over on 17th and V, right? Closed down a couple of years back?"

"Yep. My stepfather used to take his cars there, before the owner died."

Clara looked out onto busy Q Street. "Want to check it out?"

"Now?"

"No time like the present, Mr. Lee."

He tilted his hat back and scratched his head. "I reckon so. After you." He swooped his arm in a gentlemanly gesture back to the alley they'd emerged from.

They drove to the other side of the neighborhood and parked in front of an empty, grassy lot on V Street, a few blocks away from the garage. The truck they'd seen was nowhere in sight, but a Model T with a pickup body emerged from a driveway midway down the block.

"That looks like the car I first saw picking up the Afflicted," Clara said, stepping out of Israel's Ford.

Once the vehicle disappeared around the corner, she and Israel approached the place it had emerged from. The narrow lane was dark and emptied onto a sort of shared courtyard in the center of the block where the backs of all the buildings met. A few lamps were lit back here; the structures were large and industrial.

A wooden sign with the words "Agbrooke Stables" painted on it was affixed to a nondescript brick structure just above the wide stable doors. Since old Henry Ford changed the world, stables in the city were less and less common, most transitioning to garages. This block held several such garages along with a city utility building, a few apartment buildings, and row homes.

If she wasn't mistaken, Aristotle's apartment building was just behind them, facing U Street. The former stable stood in the opposite corner. The doors to the surrounding buildings were all padlocked, but not this one. However, the handles had been removed. Conspicuous holes remained where the hardware used to be.

Clara nudged Israel, bringing his attention to it. "Looks like they don't want nobody coming in from the outside." He nodded, his expression grim.

The windows were all boarded shut and no light escaped from inside, but Clara smelled exhaust fumes, proof that one or more vehicles had just entered or exited.

"We need to see what's inside there," she said, rushing forward, only to have Israel grab her around the waist.

"Hold on there, lioness. We have no idea who or what is in that building, how many there are, and what state of mind they're in. Whoever's in there can't see us where we are now. What happens if that changes and they don't like what they see? Do you always go running into places half-cocked, girl?"

She wanted to answer yes but kept her lips sealed. She struggled against him for a moment longer, pulling against a grip of gentle iron. When she finally stopped, Israel's arms tightened around her. Which was wise of him because she sure would have darted away again if he'd let go. The fading sensation of his breath on her ear siphoned away the rest of her frenzy and reason crept in.

"All right. I hear you. I wasn't thinking clear."

"How in the hell have you survived this long?" Humor and exasperation colored his voice.

She snorted, and he finally let her go. "Fine, Mr. Voice of Reason."

Ignoring the fact that her waist now felt cold where his hands had been, she turned to face him. "What do *you* suppose we do?"

"Figure out what this place is, who owns it, and what we're likely to find when we go inside. That way we don't get ourselves killed walking into who knows what."

She scowled, not liking how reasonable he sounded. "I'll bet money that truck took those Afflicted people in there. What if *all* the missing folks is in there? It certainly looks big enough."

"If all the missing folks is in there, who's keeping them there? And why? You want to run into those two roughnecks by yourself?"

She shook her head. "Those folks just *let* themselves be taken... What if someone has a Charm like yours and is hypnotizing them?"

"Yeah. I thought of that too," he admitted. "But if we're going to help anyone and not just run straight to our deaths, we need to put together a plan with the others."

Clara gritted her teeth but grudgingly agreed. "We call everyone together tomorrow. I don't want to leave it much longer. Samuel could be in there."

She stepped away to look over at the building again. He spoke sense, that much was true, but her intuition was firing, hard, and this time she knew the foreboding for what it was.

Samuel had been missing for nearly two weeks. They didn't have too much longer to figure things out and get him back, hopefully with his wits restored. Along with everyone else.

After squaring her shoulders and psyching herself up, she used her second sight on the building. She might be able to sense the auras of anyone close to the doors or sense if there was any magic at work inside.

But she got nothing.

No idea of who or what was inside, not even so much as a hint of danger. The entire building had a powerful ward around it blocking out everything. That was proof enough what was going on in there was out of the ordinary.

Israel watched the building with guarded eyes. Then he stuffed his hands in his pockets and started back the way they'd come. It tore Clara apart to leave, but she knew they'd be back. With reinforcements and a plan to figure out exactly what was happening in this city, and how the ring and Madame Josephine were connected to it.

17

THE GARAGE

A ll right, you're going to have to explain this to me again," Jesse
Lee said. He stood leaning against the wall in the small storage
room they'd commandeered in the back of Mr. Vasiliadis's butcher
shop. Zelda worked as a butcher sporadically, depending on whether
or not she was feuding with the owner's son. Apparently she was very
good with knives, so she was always hired back a few days or weeks
after a blowup.

Currently, she and the younger Vasiliadis were on speaking terms,
and since Miles's place was closed during the day on Fridays, Zelda
had opened up the back room for the crew to meet. Clara had claimed
illness at work after lunch, taking the afternoon off. She'd arrived
not long before and squeezed into the narrow space lined with shelv-
ing where long rolls of butcher paper were stacked neatly, along with
wooden crates and cardboard cartons of supplies.

"Because I think we need to stay focused on the ring," Jesse Lee
continued. "I know you said your Enigma told you it's connected to the
Affliction, but if we keep our efforts centered on taking the ring, we'll
be helping those folks automatically."

"And we don't even know if the missing are in there," Zelda added, crossing her arms over her blood-spattered apron.

"The whole point is to find out," Clara said. She turned to Jesse Lee. "On two separate occasions I saw folks who look Afflicted being put in trucks and driven off somewhere. If we're following the ring, that means we have to follow the Affliction too. And if we connect the stables to Madame Josephine, that's more proof that she must know something, even if she isn't directly responsible." She kept her voice even, doing her best to be polite after the row the other night. "Have you heard anything about this place from folks around her?"

"I know she's been buying up property," Jesse Lee said. "I haven't heard specifically about a garage, though I can do some digging. Thaniel mentioned her buying a clay mine because he thought it was peculiar." He cut a dashing figure in his gray suit. Though the shoulder holster peeking out from beneath his jacket was a little alarming. Because of his connections and military service, he'd found it incredibly easy to get hired on as one of Madame Josephine's guards. They'd given him a Smith & Wesson and put him to work immediately.

"A clay mine *is* peculiar," Zelda agreed. "Especially when just about everything else she owns is in the city. Where is it?"

"Out in Virginia somewhere."

Everyone shared looks of confusion before Israel spoke up. He sat on a crate with his elbows on his knees, spinning his harmonica on his fingertips. "Clara's right. The ring is the goal, but so are the missing people. It makes sense that they're connected, and a lead on one could help with the other. I'll check on the garage ownership down at the city records office. See if we can trace it to Josephine or even Mo."

Jesse Lee held up his palms. "All right. But no one else thinks this is getting a little out of hand?"

"What's wrong with getting out of hand?" Zelda asked, a disturbing gleam in her eye. "In hand is a mighty boring place to be." Jesse Lee took a step away from her with the same caution he'd use with an unfamiliar and potentially rabid dog.

"We all knew this was going to be hard," Clara said.

"If it ain't hard it ain't worth it, or so I've been told," Aristotle added, a little smile on his lips. He perched on a stool in a cream-colored suit. Today he was playing Clarence, the role he preferred when around the other men.

Jesse Lee huffed, looking for all the world like he'd prefer to be elsewhere, but seemed mollified. So far this was all going well; Clara's suspicious nature didn't want to believe it, but she was committed to playing nice.

Israel turned to her. "And you're planning to watch the building, but not go in?"

She narrowed her eyes. "I'm just going to watch. See who goes in and out. Try to verify they're taking the Afflicted people there."

"Promise you won't rush in half-cocked if you see something that don't sit right with you?" A flirtatious grin was in place, but tension ringed his eyes.

Clara took a deep breath, then let it out slow. "Promise." She didn't know why it took a lot out of her to make that pledge.

Turning to Aristotle, she asked, "Can you walk the block a few times, then change characters so nobody watching will suspect anything?"

"Sure can."

"Just see who goes and comes, whether they look like Afflicted or guards or somebody else."

Aristotle tipped his straw hat in agreement.

"I think I know another way to watch the place," Zelda announced. "There's another garage next door that's a bit taller, and some of the outbuildings at the storage yard have very promising roofs. I'll see if I can get a bird's-eye view of things."

Israel and Jesse Lee both looked incredulous, but Clara merely shrugged. "You can take the girl out of the circus…Fine. Just be careful."

Zelda's eyes lit up in a way that didn't put Clara's mind at ease, but her rooftop surveillance could be helpful.

"I'm going to stay out of sight down by the church on the next block," Clara said, looking at Israel.

He held up his hands as if he hadn't been doubting her. Not that he didn't have good reason to.

"I'm back with Josephine this afternoon." Jesse Lee buttoned his coat, straightening. "She's got supper with some bankers, then a meeting down on New York Avenue."

Clara stood. "All right. Let's see what we can find out."

The tiny church on the corner was fenced in with a patchy lawn of parched grass. Agbrooke Stables & Garage was two blocks away, out of sight, but Clara didn't need to get any closer. She had a perfect view of the alley, which was the only way a vehicle could access the stable doors.

She kept her eyes peeled for anyone around who didn't look quite right and seemed to be struggling with the strange affliction that had taken over Samuel and Titus Monroe and who knew how many others. But she didn't see anyone.

Every half hour or so, Aristotle would walk by disguised as someone else. An elderly woman. A dapper young man. A nondescript housewife. She would know it was him without using her second sight because he'd always nod at her and touch his nose.

Directly across from the church was another triangular patch of grass made by the intersection of three streets. It reminded her of the place down on 10th where she'd encountered the boys and their magazine—though this park was empty save for an old man seated on the far bench feeding the pigeons.

As she watched him toss bits of stale bread on the ground for the cooing band of birds, an idea struck. Why hadn't she thought of it before?

They were all scheduled to meet back at the Waffle Shoppe that evening and the time couldn't pass fast enough. She continued to pace the streets, keeping a wide berth around the area of the garage to avoid being spotted, but her eagerness was hard to contain—even though she witnessed no trucks enter or exit the entire time she was there.

At the meeting time, everyone but Jesse Lee arrived, since he was still on duty with Josephine.

"See anything good?" Zelda asked Aristotle, who shook his head.

"No one going or coming today. Maybe they only pick up folks in the evening."

"What'd you find?" Zelda turned to Israel.

"Maurice Douglass, a.k.a. Bowlegged Mo, purchased Agbrooke Stables & Garage about three months ago. There's no mortgage on file, so he must have paid in cash."

Aristotle whistled.

"I even got a lead on that clay mine Jesse Lee mentioned." Israel's eye sparkled. "It's actually in West Virginia. And it was being sold along with a brick plant that *wasn't* purchased. I put in a call to the records office in Morgantown and the place is in Josephine's name, not Mo's."

Zelda, the only one who'd ordered food, chewed her waffle thoughtfully. "So she bought the mine, but not the brick plant, so either she ran out of money or she's doing something else with the clay."

"Don't know anything about mining," Israel said. The others shrugged as well.

Clara could barely hold back her excitement. "Well, I have an idea." Everyone turned to her.

"We need to get inside that building and see what's going on. If we're right and the Afflicted are in there, then why don't we let them invite us in?"

"What are you saying?" Israel asked.

"We get ourselves picked up."

18

THE AFFLICTED

"This is a bad idea," Israel murmured under his breath.

"No it's not, it's brilliant." Energy buzzed through Clara's limbs.

"Are you sure I can't talk you out of this?"

"Don't even try." She was happy to be doing something. Happy to be taking action and not just sitting around wringing her hands like the helpless heroine in some penny novel.

"All right." He dropped his head, sounding resigned. Though he doubted the plan, he had been the first to volunteer to go with her on this crazy scheme. She'd argued that he was too recognizable, but Israel had been steadfast. If things went bad, he'd said, and they weren't back out by midnight, Aristotle would get help, and Zelda could monitor from up high.

Clara suspected that he was just being manly and didn't trust a sixty-year-old man or a hundred-thirty-pound woman to be able to protect her. But his eyes had told her he wasn't backing down, so she'd agreed. Both Mama Octavia and Mrs. Shuttlesworth were always telling her to pick her battles, so maybe, just maybe, having him along wasn't the worst thing in the world. Aristotle had provided a fake mustache and goatee in order to disguise him and they'd moved forward with the plan.

Night had fallen and the two of them stood at the little park at 10th and V, just where she'd seen the first Afflicted man and woman taken. She'd considered going back to the Q Street alley where they'd spotted the delivery truck, but Clara figured there must be pickup spaces all around the neighborhood and this one was closer, though more out in the open.

She and Israel shuffled and fidgeted, doing their best to look the part, to look the way Titus Monroe had, dispassionate and listless. As her feet moved around, the bottoms of her shoes felt unusually gritty. She was scraping her soles on the grass when what appeared to be the same Model T pickup arrived. A burly man, one Clara didn't recognize, lowered the back hatch and dragged them up. She played along even as she was manhandled, working to keep her gaze slack and jaw loose.

The woman already sitting in the back was nearly drooling in her stupor. Clara tried to mimic her as best she could. Israel sat next to her, playing his role too. So far the plan was working. The energy that had been running through her like electricity in a wire cranked even higher, blasting away any fear. Was this how Zelda felt up on a tightrope, or pulling one of her schemes?

The truck careened through the streets and made two more stops at corners on different sides of the neighborhood before the space was full of bodies. Clara pressed into Israel as the last passenger practically sat on top of her. The driver and the other man in the seats up front didn't speak to any of them, and she didn't hear them talking to each other either. No one they passed seemed to bat an eye at the sight of these folks squeezed up in the back of this truck like so much cargo.

Just as she'd suspected, the vehicle turned down V Street and into the driveway leading to the Agbrooke Stable. Someone inside opened one of the large carriage doors, admitting them.

The interior of the space was dim, lit only by the headlamps of the Ford. But then someone flipped the switch, blinding them all briefly. When her eyes adjusted, she saw that this area held two other vehicles of the same type, along with the larger delivery truck with the poorly painted-over lettering identifying the business.

The man who'd pushed them into the Ford opened the hatch and began grabbing at them, halfway dragging them out. She tried to minimize how much he touched her by scrambling out on her own, knowing her temper couldn't handle much more of that kind of treatment, mission or no mission.

The Afflicted were placed in a line and led, single file, through a doorway. Israel was right in front of her, back straight, broad shoulders somehow giving her comfort. *They could do this.* One thing was clear— this place was no longer a garage. The clanging of machinery, hissing of steam, and an increase in heat preceded their arrival in a large main room filled with metal vats of different sizes. Some were enormous, two stories high and wide enough for dozens people to bathe in comfortably. Some were smaller, her height and the width of a barrel. Actual wooden barrels were scattered around and a pungent smell filled the air.

"It's a distillery," she muttered. The guards were too far away to hear her, especially over the noise, but Israel nodded almost imperceptibly. The concrete floor beneath their feet was wet and filthy with a sandy grit. Thick metal pipes rose from the vats and rubber hoses seemed to have been tossed around haphazardly.

The room was the size of an auditorium; at the far end people filled barrels and bottles and sealed them shut. Others monitored the giant stills, carried crates and boxes, mopped the floor. Men and women, all appearing to be under thirty, worked here, though a significant number of them were just standing around, staring at nothing.

This was a big operation. She knew nothing about how liquor was made, but this place must have the capacity to supply all of Washington with alcohol.

A wiry, balding man in spectacles with his shirtsleeves rolled up approached. "Who told you to bring them here? We already have more than we need. From now on, take them to the other locations."

The guard grunted in response.

"Have them stand out of the way over there until we can deal with them. The new still will be up and running in a couple of days, maybe we can move some of them over there."

The guard shrugged and the bespectacled man lifted a whistle from around his neck. He blew two sharp bleats, piercing Clara's skull with pain. Everyone in their line turned and marched away, if not with military precision, then at least in shambling unison. Clara and Israel rushed to keep up; she hoped no one noticed they weren't quite in sync.

Whistles? Like for dogs? But the Afflicted were obedient. And since the group she was with was assumably new, how did they automatically know the commands?

All around them the people behaved like mindless automatons. Like the empty husks of folks after they'd been reinvigorated in those children's science fiction stories. Clara's pulse began to race, not with the exhilaration of taking action but with a creeping fury. These people likely had families, someone who was missing them right now, someone they belonged to.

As their group of newcomers was led to the side of the room to stand behind one of the larger stills, she kept her eyes open for signs of Samuel. The guard walked away, leaving them alone. Clara turned to the woman next to her, ebony-skinned and in her mid-twenties. "What's your name?" she whispered.

The woman didn't so much as blink.

"Where are you from?"

Further questions to the others yielded the same results.

"Israel, can you compel them to answer?"

His expression was uncertain, but he whistled low and slow, just a simple tune from childhood that they'd sung a nursery rhyme to. The young man next to him, thin and wiry, blinked slowly and focused his eyes on Israel.

"Ask him how he knew to wait for the truck."

Israel made the request and the man shrugged. "Voice in my head. Don't get no peace unless I follow."

Under Israel's compulsion, others said variations of the same thing. They heard a voice issuing commands. They couldn't identify it as male or female, old or young, but they felt the need to follow it. When the man blew the whistle, the voice returned, beating at them if they did anything other than follow.

The Afflicted couldn't put into words what was making them so lethargic and lifeless, they just stood obediently and would likely do so for days until they were commanded to do something else.

Keeping a careful eye on the guards, Clara grabbed Israel's hand and hunched down, leading him along the wall to where they could question one of the distillery workers.

"What's your name?" Israel asked the thin, cinnamon-colored woman after whistling the tune. She blinked at him before shaking her head. Israel frowned. *Did she not remember?*

"How long you been here?"

Her brow furrowed like she was trying to think about it, then her expression blanked again.

"What are you doing here?" He motioned to the piece of machinery that neither of them could identify, which emitted a hissing sound when she turned a wheel.

"What they say." Her voice was raspy from disuse. After breaking her silence, her attention went back to the equipment and her task.

"Whatever's controlling them is much stronger than my Charm,"

Israel said as they ducked back behind the nearest vat. "Must get more powerful the longer they're here."

For a brief moment Clara considered using her own Charm. She would be able to find out quite a lot if she did, but guilt swamped her immediately. *No.* No matter what, that wasn't the answer. She'd made a vow and intended to keep it—the potential disaster of using the Charm outweighed even the benefit of its help in finding and restoring all the missing people or getting the ring.

From their hiding place, Clara observed the operation. The man with the spectacles appeared to be in charge. He was the only one with a whistle. He marched over to a counter filled with empty bottles and spoke to two teenage boys who stood there—one of whom she realized with elation was Samuel. She was just within earshot to hear his commands.

"Rinse out those barrels in the corner." The manager pointed, then punctuated the command with a series of whistles which nearly made Clara convulse. Israel placed a steadying hand on her back.

Samuel, empty of the joy and life that usually filled his eyes, turned to comply. When the manager left, she hurried over to him, desperate to see if anything remained of her young friend.

"Samuel?" she said, leaning toward him. He gripped the hose and cranked the water on.

Clara repeated his name and waved a hand in front of his face but got no response. The hope that somehow the strength of his personality could have pushed through the force of this spell, whatever it was, died. The boy paused, holding the hose until she moved out of his way, and then began spraying the barrels.

Tears pricked the backs of Clara's eyes and her throat grew thick. How were they going to get these people free of whatever conjure was controlling them? Could they overpower the manager and use the whistle to undo the enchantment? Probably not. The way these things usually worked was that the original object that had bewitched these folks would need to be used to undo it, which meant they would need the ring. And probably whoever had created this spell in the first place.

They had what they'd come for—proof that the missing were here, at least some of them, anyway. She should start looking for an exit strategy... But Clara still had so many questions. Was the ring just creating a free source of labor for a moonshine operation? That couldn't be what The Empress was so concerned about. The wards around this building must be hiding something else, and she needed to figure out what it was.

The few times she'd used her second sight over the past weeks was still heaps more than she usually did. So far nothing bad had happened, but it was only a matter of time. Still, she had no other choice in this moment. She would do it quickly, just a peek so she could put the pieces together better and come up with a plan to save these folks.

The wards on the walls that prevented her from sensing anything from outside didn't affect her now that she was inside. She sank into her other vision and found that each and every Afflicted person here bore the heavy cloud on their auras she'd first identified on Titus Monroe. Hopefully his mama was still keeping him safe from all of this. She suspected Mrs. Monroe would chain her son to his bed rather than risk losing him.

In addition to clouded auras, all the Afflicted within her view had a tendril of that rainbow-colored light strand she'd seen with Titus. The tendrils disappeared through the wall, the wards preventing her from seeing even what direction they went.

Something else was going on with the Afflicted, something she couldn't identify, unused as she was to viewing things this way. Before she could ponder it more, a sensation coming from the other side of the far wall caught her attention. It felt peculiar. The unguarded wooden door looked normal enough, but beyond it the energy was... different. She couldn't say more than that and needed to get a closer look.

Her eyelids fluttered and she shuddered involuntarily as she shut off her extra sense. She needed to stop playing with fire; she did know better.

Leaning in to Israel, she whispered, "Come on. We need to see what's back there." He hesitated, brow furrowed, before following.

To stay out of sight, they crept along the ground on their hands and knees, keeping to the outside wall. That strange gritty substance and spilled liquid stinking of fermentation coated her hands and dress and was difficult to rub off. They made their way slowly to the door, which they found unlocked. Of course, if everyone was so easy to control, then why bother locking doors?

With a look at the busy floor of the distillery, Clara whipped the door open and raced in, Israel on her heels. Distantly, she heard the door snick shut behind her, but her entire focus was stolen by the sight before her.

The spacious room had another door along one side wide enough for a carriage or automobile. In the center of the space lay an enormous pile of grayish-red dirt. The scent was earthy and a little pungent.

"Guess we know where all that clay is going." Israel's tone was wry.

"But why?" she whispered.

Another room lay on the other side of the space.

"Stay here, will you?" Clara said. "Let me know if someone comes. I want to check in there." Israel nodded and leaned against the door, pressing his ear to the wood.

The presence of this pile of clay couldn't be what felt so off in her second sight, could it? Maybe what had triggered her was behind this door. Once again, she found it unlocked. She winced as the hinges creaked noisily.

She peeked into the dim interior, then risked the clamor of opening the door wider. The overhead lighting behind her creeped into the space and her heart lodged into her throat for a long moment when she caught sight of what occupied the room.

Lying in neat rows on the ground were motionless forms. Were these the rest of the missing? Were they dead?

She sucked in an agonized breath, then swung the door wider to get a better view.

They weren't human bodies, just mounds of clay, fashioned and shaped into roughly human proportions. Clara's breathing restarted normally. This clay looked like what she'd played with as a child. Though she had no desire to touch it, the surface looked moist. There was nothing here that could be used to fire it, if the clay had been shaped here.

"What in God's name *is* this?" she whispered.

Just then Israel whistled low, with no command in it to hurt her head—just a warning. Clara hurried out of the smaller room and back to the main door. "Someone's coming?"

"Not this way, but somebody just arrived out there. I heard a big commotion. Sounded like someone important."

Clara swallowed as Israel cracked the door open so they could peek through. None of the guards were looking their way—all were focused on the door leading to the parking area. Workers continued toiling, unaffected like the guards and manager were, so she and Israel slipped out to join a pair of young men standing in the corner.

Sharp commanding whistles rang out. Everyone stopped what they were doing and stood at attention like soldiers. Clara breathed through the pain behind her eyes as Thaniel Dawson entered with a leaner man right behind him. Jesse Lee.

Walking close behind him was Madame Josephine, who waltzed onto the distillery floor with a smile on her face.

19

THE GRAYS

Madame Josephine, this is unexpected." The manager's voice had lost its commanding tone and was now threaded through with fear as he approached the woman. In addition to Jesse Lee, three other guards, including Thaniel Dawson, surrounded her. Jesse Lee's gaze took everything in. Clara held her breath. They were pretty far away from him and he hadn't spotted them yet; she just hoped he could hold in his surprise when he did. Next to her, Israel had turned to stone.

They had to make sure Josephine didn't spot *him*. The fake mustache and goatee would certainly not be enough to fool someone who knew him well.

"I wanted an update on things." Josephine's sultry voice filled the space. "The profits are not what Maurice led me to believe they would be. We will not have these workers forever and I want to maximize this operation before I'm forced to get new laborers."

Clara frowned. What did that mean? And what would happen to these folks when she got new laborers?

"Is the new location ready?" Josephine asked.

"Why don't we talk about it in my office?" the manager said. The woman nodded regally and the two moved toward a staircase in the corner leading to an office with a large window overlooking the main production floor.

The manager blew his whistle on his way up and everyone smoothly went back to work. The two Afflicted men Clara stood next to remained motionless, and she was undecided about where to go. They needed an exit strategy and fast.

Jesse Lee and Thaniel stationed themselves at the bottom of the staircase. The other two guards stood near the doors to the parking area. Clara hadn't seen another way out of here; however, since they'd arrived via the alley, there must be a front door of some kind.

One of the distillery guards headed their way. Clara stiffened and put on her best impression of an Afflicted, staring into space and loosening her jaw. The guard patrolled near them, shrewd gaze taking in everything before he spun around and headed back the way he'd come.

A frenzied energy built up in her limbs with no escape. They had to get away from here now, before things got out of control. She scanned the area around them but still saw no exits. Finally, she whispered to Israel, "Maybe one of the Afflicted knows about another door?"

He looked as skeptical as she felt, but they were out of options. Her gaze fell upon Samuel still rinsing barrels with a hose. He stood about fifty feet away, eyes on his task, partially hidden from view by one of the medium-sized tanks.

When the coast seemed clear, they slowly moved between the machinery to where Samuel was. Clara held in a wince when Israel whistled his commanding tune. "You know where the front door is?" he asked the boy.

Samuel looked up and frowned. Then his face cleared and he went back to his washing.

Israel tried a few different variations of the question, but the teen didn't respond. Nerves rising, Clara looked around. Israel placed a hand on her arm. "You cold?"

She realized that goose bumps had formed on her exposed skin. A shiver vibrated through her, making her aware of the cooling temperatures. "Are you?"

"No." He shook his head. "Still feels like a steam bath in here to me."

True fear locked her into place. She didn't bother to look with her other sight, though it would soon become unnecessary—something had followed her back from Over There.

Now, "spirit" could mean a lot of things, it was a catch-all term that included ghosts, phantoms, hags, Enigmas, and everything in between—including entities without the personality of a ghost or the willpower of an Enigma. These beings were far more primitive. They didn't speak, couldn't form bodies or faces or mouths from smoke or water or anything else. They were presences, energies, sometimes malevolent, sometimes merely mischievous, and the effects of them permeating the world were unpredictable. Clara called them *Grays*.

When the Grays entered the world, the space around them grew cold and dark to Clara's senses, as if they were leaching out all warmth and light. Others couldn't tell the difference, couldn't feel the change unless they were targeted directly. And being in the crosshairs of the Grays was dangerous. Enigmas were bound to certain rules—they couldn't lie, their interference among humans was limited to the deals they made and people's willingness to become indebted to them or Embraced by them.

Ghosts could affect the world, becoming a nuisance and inspiring fear, but their ability to actually harm people was limited. Very rarely were the ghosts old and angry enough to be powerful enough to hurt someone. Grays had no such limitations. Clara believed these were the spirits that caused men to go insane, made women murder their own children, caused folks to slit their necks or run off the edge of cliffs babbling nonsense. Or simply destabilized someone, scrambled their thoughts, caused them to doubt everyone around them, including themselves. Based on personal experience, she knew they could leave a swath of madness, destruction, and violence in their wake.

Clara suspected it was because unlike ghosts and Enigmas, Grays had no souls. How they'd come into existence without souls was a mystery. She believed that God created all life and every living creature had a soul, even what many called demons, which were really just less powerful Enigmas. Had the Grays been something else once and lost or given up their soul? Or could their existence be evidence of a blind spot in creation? Either way, she had taken the risk of using her power, knowing it put a spotlight on her, knowing it could draw them to her as it had before, and now they were here.

Her pockets were empty and she cursed herself for not leaving home prepared to face a spiritual threat. Mama Octavia had been scarce in recent days, following up on leads on the ring, so Clara couldn't call to her for help. And she didn't dare try to summon any other friendly spirits. Looking Over There now would only make things worse. She'd have to face this alone.

"Do you have any matches?" she whispered to Israel.

He checked his pockets and produced a box. She lit one with shaking fingers and watched the tiny trail of smoke rise. She only had until the match burned down to do this. Using the smoke and flame to focus her gift, she began to hurriedly work a protection. Cold seeped into her bones and around her; the floor of the distillery darkened. Clara wove the energy around her into armor, creating her own ward. With more time and additional supplies she could have protected the entire space, but while she knew they targeted others indiscriminately, when she breached the veil, they usually came after her. And if she was compromised, then she couldn't help anyone else should the Grays turn their attention to others.

The Afflicted man just across the way, a handsome, stocky fellow, began to sniff. Clara paid him no mind, but part of her recognized that as unusual. The match was nearly burned down, but she needed every last bit of its flame to strengthen her personal ward. She crouched down, hiding it behind her palm, while the man sniffed again, then raised his hand and shouted, "Fire!"

Clara froze. Around the distillery floor, other Afflicted began to repeat the word, shouting "Fire!" in an eerie chant. No emotion colored their voices, they did not seem to be afraid, but they were an effective alarm. Perhaps they'd all been commanded to alert the guards to the presence of a flame in a room full of alcohol. Regardless, two of the distillery guards stalked down the main aisle between the machinery, directly to her. She had nowhere to hide and so straightened and strode forward, hoping to keep their gazes off Israel.

Except the noodle-headed man didn't seem to understand what she was doing and moved forward with her. The match was done. It singed her fingers and she dropped it, using the final trail of smoke to complete her barrier. The light was dim to her eyes and the temperature even cooler; her teeth were beginning to chatter so that when the guards grabbed her arms roughly, the heat they provided was almost welcome.

Israel was still moving, bound to draw attention to himself since all the other Afflicted were stock-still. Clara struggled, more for show and to keep the focus on her than out of any hope for getting free. The men's grips were bruising on her flesh.

Jesse Lee was staring at her, clenching his jaw and looking none too pleased. For his part, Thaniel Dawson, the giant beside him, appeared bemused, his brow furrowed. The sharp notes of a harmonica rang out, vibrating against Clara's skull. But the guards' grip loosened and she actually got an arm free.

When the men turned their heads to find the source of the sound, she let loose a wild punch, striking one man in the temple. Her hand blazed with pain, but she'd successfully diverted their attention again as the harmonica continued. If Israel didn't get himself out of sight, she would punch him too, knock him out and drag him under one of the tanks.

The two guards slackened suddenly, looking for a moment like Afflicted themselves. Then they blinked, looking around as if they'd forgotten why they were there and stumbling in place as if dizzy.

Thank you, Jesse Lee. He stood with his fingers plugging his ears, protecting himself from Israel's hypnotism as best he could. Clara ran to the side just as a dark figure dropped down from the ceiling.

The lithe form was dressed head to toe in black, with a full face mask, but Clara recognized Zelda immediately. She swung from a chain and landed right on top of the same guard Clara had punched. She was on his back and wrestling him to the ground using some kind of Asian martial art she'd learned in the circus.

But the distillery's other guards were running forward, along with two of Josephine's men. Between Israel and Jesse Lee, the men's forward motion came in fits and starts. Israel had said that his light hypnosis couldn't overcome strong will, and she didn't know what limitations Jesse Lee had on manipulating memories, but it did give her and Zelda enough time to disable the nearest two guards and dart away, squeezing between two giant tanks.

A sharp whistle rang out, and Clara nearly blacked out from the force of the command. After blinking her eyes to clear her swimming vision, she pushed forward. She and Zelda were rushing along the wall, clambering over pipes and hoses, but were stopped by the same group of Afflicted that Clara had come in with. They had been standing motionless and purposeless, but at the whistled command they turned to face her and Zelda.

Clara felt Israel run up behind them, then skid to a stop. The men and women provided a significant obstacle. Clara and her group had no choice but to go back into the main aisle.

A wall of guards was there to greet them. Israel put his harmonica to his lips again and played louder and faster than before. The guards blinked, stumbling forward, then losing their balance. Behind them, Jesse Lee stared straight ahead, fingers in ears, forehead sweating with effort. The effect both men were having on the guards was comical, but it caused enough confusion that she, Zelda, and Israel were able to run right through them.

Zelda pulled Clara's sleeve and led her in the opposite direction of the parking area, to a dim hallway that she hadn't noticed before. They ended up at a heavy door with half a dozen deadbolts in it. Zelda threw the locks while Israel kept playing. Clara clenched her jaw tight to keep her head from rattling from his music.

And then they were free, rushing out the front door into the humid night, a whoop of victory wanting to fly from Clara's throat but being strangled by the sight that greeted them.

Two dozen uniformed policemen, guns drawn and pointed right at them.

HAINTS

Now, while Clara was born ornery, she'd been a peaceful baby and an easy child. She wasn't picky about what she ate, stayed quiet when grown folks was talking, minded her parents and her granny. Most mothers would have gotten down on their knees to thank the Lord above that they'd given birth to her. But Aurora Johnson was not most women.

She'd been eager to leave what she called the backwoods of North Carolina. Benjamin had promised her they'd make their way to New York, that Washington was just a pit stop so he could work and save some money so they could live a little larger than they had been.

She did love Benjamin, his mama not so much, and the jury was still out on baby Clara. Seeing her come out with that birthing sac covering her had made Aurora's gorge rise, even through the misery of childbirth. Sometimes when she looked into the baby's smiling face, she still imagined it covered with that thin film, mucus and blood coating it, and had to go empty the contents of her stomach.

And not only had the little girl come out unfortunately dark—darker than either of her parents—she only got stranger as she grew older. She did just about everything earlier than other babies: walking, talking, using the toilet. And once she learned to talk in full sentences, she didn't never stop. Child yammered to herself constantly.

Well, not herself. Aurora had rather the child talk to herself than what that baby and Mama Octavia claimed the truth was. Talking to spirits? Haints and ghosts and the like? Her mother-in-law had always struck her as a few spoons short of a drawer. She'd been over forty when she gave birth to Benjamin and had a lot of old-fashioned ways about her. Or maybe she took one too many beatings on the old plantation, but she sure liked to fill Clara's head with hooey.

Aurora was always sweeping up salt and dirt the old woman sprinkled on the floorboards or under the windows. She'd caught her burning hair pulled out of combs and wrapping potatoes in socks for some purpose or another. A bunch of countrified foolishness that Aurora couldn't stand.

Then, one day when Clara was six years old, the little girl awoke in the middle of the night screaming bloody murder. Aurora was sure she'd find the child dismembered in her own bed with the way she was carrying on.

Benjamin leaped straight from his mattress out of the room and she was right on his heels. The girl was whole and physically healthy, but busy battling imaginary foes. Her eyes were open, but the more they tried to get her calm, the louder she wailed. Benjamin wrapped her in his arms and Aurora slapped her face, trying to bring her back to her senses.

The child's skin was icy cold and even her goose bumps had goose bumps though it was the middle of July and the notorious Washington humidity was in full effect. Sometimes being in this godforsaken city was like living inside the mouth of a giant, and the child had the nerve to be cold.

Nothing they did could quiet her fit until Mama Octavia rushed in with a bag of herbs and dirt and some candles. She did some kind of backward witchy nonsense, sprinkling this and burning that and reciting some devilish incantation, but miracle of miracles, the girl quieted down.

Clara claimed an impenetrable gray darkness had surrounded her and tried to kill her. Wrapped icy fingers around her, repeated her name over and over, and kept her from breathing. Aurora didn't know what to think—the child was addlepated, that was for sure, and she didn't know how much longer she could live like this.

She'd sat the girl down and told her that if the spirits attacked one more time, she was leaving. Her constitution just wasn't strong enough to handle that kind of disturbance.

The child had promised to do her best not to let the spirits come back. Aurora wasn't sure how far the word of a six-year-old could go; she had one foot out the door already.

Truth be told, she hadn't ever been happy in the little row house on G Street. Her husband worked long hours and came home smelling of sawdust and sweat—not that different to how it had been back home in Gastonia. Their life was larger here, but not by much.

That little stop in Washington had lasted years. Sure, Benjamin had found a good, stable job as a carpenter for one of the government buildings. He was moving up the ranks and could be a manager soon. But job or not, the District was not New York and he could cut wood any damn place, couldn't he?

Not one month later, Clara had another fit. Aurora had held on as long as she could, but with her husband ignoring her pleas and her daughter halfway possessed by some demon, she was done.

Done with her marriage and with mothering a child who talked to thin air all day and was beset by the spirits at night. Her nerves were frayed, her skin was prematurely wrinkling, and she needed to leave.

She found herself heading out from the brand-new train station they'd built not far from the row house, on a railcar headed north, her ticket purchased by a gentleman friend who had no children, smelled like expensive cologne, and wanted a bigger life in a bigger city just as much as she did.

When she left her family behind, she always intended to write...

Clara waited in the front hall staring out the windows every day for months. The Grays were to blame for Mama leaving, she knew it. She'd tried to keep her promise, tried to not let them in, only she wasn't sure exactly how to keep them away.

She hated when they creeped all over her, covering her from all sides, making it hard for her to breathe or think. Their raspy unvoices that only she could hear would call out her name and freeze her from the inside out.

Mama Octavia said that if she learned to control her gift, they would stop bothering her. Other spirits too. The ones who begged and pleaded, or laughed and watched her with spooky eyes, or warned her when she was about to step into the street and a carriage or automobile was coming.

If she could control her gift, Mama would come back home and Daddy would smile again and her granny would stop muttering curses under her breath about no-good, fast-tailed heifers.

Eventually, Clara did learn to block out the visions, to not drift Over There without meaning to, and eventually, not look Over There at all.

But it was already too late.

20

SOURCE OF LEGENDS

A burly police officer with a large belly and larger mustache squinted up at Clara and lowered his gun. "Let them through. These are the folks I had on the inside—the informants I told you about." His voice was gritty, but when he tapped his nose and winked at Clara, her eyes widened.

"Are you sure, Captain?" a young copper asked from next to him.

"Of course I'm sure," Aristotle barked. He nodded at the three Negroes who'd emerged from the distillery and shooed them away. Clara unstuck her feet from the concrete and walked slowly along the edge of the building. Police cars and paddy wagons filled the street before them. She led the others, keeping their pace measured until they turned the corner onto U Street and finally took a breath. They didn't stop walking until they arrived at Clara's and wordlessly made their way into the alley and down the creaking steps to Miles's speakeasy.

Cole brought over a bottle of hooch without even being asked. They must all look like they needed it. Zelda had removed her mask and earplugs, but was still dressed in what looked to be black pajamas.

A half hour after they'd settled in, Aristotle—in his Clarence persona—appeared in the doorway, grinning from ear to ear. The rest of them began peppering him with questions before he'd even sat down, but he ignored everyone until he'd thrown back a healthy shot of liquor.

"Calm down, children. I'll tell you everything," he said, a smile in his voice. "Yes, I called the cops once I saw Josephine and her entourage go in. Then I headed around the corner to the police station. It was just pure luck that the policeman I talked to first was on Crooked Knee Willy's payroll. Overheard him chopping it up about how much loot he was gonna pull in for busting up Bowlegged Mo's operation."

"But how did you get rid of the real captain?" Zelda asked, eyes wide.

Aristotle grinned and spread his arms out. "I am good at what I do."

The sounds of the busy speakeasy washed over Clara. The Grays fortunately hadn't followed her out of the distillery. The wards in place around the building might have kept the spirits from pursuing her. She only hoped they hadn't targeted anyone else; the thought of the Afflicted being further tormented made her sick. And Jesse Lee's safety came to mind as well. He'd saved their bacon working along with Israel.

"What do you think will happen to Madame Josephine and all the Afflicted?" Zelda asked.

"Josephine is slippery," Israel replied. "I'm sure she was headed out the back while the police were coming in the front. Nothing will stick to her, and I wouldn't be surprised if she gets all her workers released in the next few days."

"Think the police will find it strange all those workers are basically insensible?"

"To hear them tell it, that's the natural state of Negroes," Aristotle said. "They probably won't notice at all." He laughed humorlessly.

"They were talking about opening another distillery," Clara mused. "So even if this one stays closed, she'll be up and running again soon.

And the manager mentioned other locations where the Afflicted are being held. There were only a few dozen folks working there, could be missing people squirreled away all over town."

They all agreed they needed to figure out where these other locations were.

Just before one o'clock, Jesse Lee sauntered through the doors and tension Clara didn't realize she was holding released like steam from a pot. Israel rose and embraced his cousin, adding some manly thumps on the back, and Cole delivered another bottle.

"That was something else," Jesse Lee said, laughing and slapping his thigh. "When I caught sight of both of y'all standing there, I thought I'd gone and lost my damn mind. Y'all sneak in?"

"Got ourselves picked up by acting like we was Afflicted," Israel responded.

"Figured it was something like that. How'd she get you to agree?"

Israel shrugged. "She was going with or without me. Thought she had a better chance to make it out if someone kept an eye on her."

Clara stiffened as Zelda piped up. "I been telling her that for years."

"I'm sitting right here, you know." Clara gave the boys the stink eye before turning to Zelda. "Word is, Lainie Harris has a room to let on 16th Street."

Zelda scoffed. "Lainie Harris don't have heat or hot water."

"And when you dropped down from the ceiling, Zelda, woo-wee!" Jesse Lee continued. "Ain't never seen nothing like that before. How did you not break a leg?"

"It's all in the knees." She stood to demonstrate, bouncing lightly on her toes before jumping up and down. Jesse Lee joined her, mimicking her actions.

"Now, I don't think I've heard the entire story," Aristotle said, leaning forward. "How did you get into the ceiling?"

"Well, you see, there are ventilation shafts in the roof—"

"I think we're getting off track," Clara cut in testily. "Jesse Lee, Josephine and all her folks escaped arrest?"

He took his seat again, stretching his legs out. "The madame was hopping mad, that's for sure. But we got her out as the police were streaming in. She was acting real strange, though, running through the distillery shivering and swatting at the air like invisible bees were surrounding her." He shook his head. "Some folks just ain't good under pressure. The workers got taken. And she was not pleased about losing them. Went back to her office and slammed the door, then I heard a whole lot of crashing in there. I asked Thaniel what he thought would happen—he said she had more connections on the police force than Crooked Knee Willy, so if she wants the workers back, she'll get them. Then I had to wipe his memory 'cause I had the impression he was trying to figure out why I cared so much." Jesse Lee chuckled.

"Did anyone recognize Israel?"

"No. Nobody said anything about it."

Clara hoped Samuel and all the others would be okay. But maybe jail was the safest place for them right now. They were protected at least from the ring. Freeing them would be so much harder than she'd thought. She was flying blind on just about everything.

"The Empress said that Madame Josephine wasn't responsible for the Affliction. She can't lie, so I don't understand what's going on." No one else had any answers either. Clara had already drunk more hooch than was healthy, but was considering swilling down more to drown her sorrows, when Mama Octavia popped up beside her. She straightened, shoving her glass away.

Of course her grandmother's disapproving glance missed nothing. Still, all she said was, "I found something."

"What is it?"

The others peered at Clara strangely but quieted once Zelda explained she was likely talking to a spirit.

"Finally found somebody old enough to recognize that ring when I described it to them. Got 'em to come through and take a look at Madame Josephine's finger, though even we couldn't get too close because of that ward she's got around her like a dark cloud." Mama Octavia scowled.

"Anyways, this spirit is one of the old ones originally stolen from Africa. She says the ring is from her continent. She remembers her great-grandmother talking about such a ring—filled with power— though she can't recall now what the tales were. Scary, though. Stuff not to be messed with."

Clara nodded and thanked her grandmother. Then she turned to the others and relayed the new information.

"We need to find someone we can ask about this," Jesse Lee said.

"Someone who knows about old African rings? I don't know anyone like that," Clara replied.

Israel raked his hands through his hair. He still wore the fake mustache and beard, which now were sagging comically. "I do. And he's not far."

Howard University's campus was eerily quiet on a Saturday morning. Clara, Israel, and Jesse Lee climbed the hill leading to the large grassy area known as the Yard, where a handful of students could be spotted in the distance. The three of them ambled down one of the many sidewalks crisscrossing the lawn, heading for Douglass Hall. Aristotle had gone back to the police station to check on those arrested in the raid the night before, and Zelda had a shift at the butcher shop. They would all meet up later to review whatever they discovered today.

"Do you think he'll be here on a Saturday?" Clara asked.

"He's always here," Israel replied.

The building was open, the floors freshly polished and smelling of cleaning solution. They made their way to the history department where the professors had their offices. The clock tower bell above Founders Library chimed announcing the time. Ten o'clock on Saturday—despite Israel's certainty, Clara wasn't sure if the man they sought would be in.

They stopped outside an office, but before they could knock, a young, light-skinned man with closely cropped hair ambled up, then stopped, gaping at them.

"Israel Lee? Is that you?"

"Yes, sir," Israel said, and the two men shook hands. "It's good to see you, Professor."

Clara's jaw unhinged. The man looked more like a student than a professor. He was in a vest with his shirtsleeves rolled up and couldn't be that much older than them. His jovial manner was so different to the other learned men she was around at work.

"You know, I was supposed to see the District Rumblers at the Cimarron a few months ago," the man said. "But something came up and I missed it. Though I've heard that band you have is great, I still wish you hadn't left us before finishing your degree."

Clara's jaw was never closing again. "You *went* here?"

Israel ducked his head. "I used to." She stood staring until the introductions were made.

"Uh, this is my former professor, William Hansberry. This is my cousin Jesse Lee Stewart, and Miss Clara Johnson."

The professor's head whipped around to consider her more closely. "Clara Johnson? *The* Clara Johnson?" He looked her up and down as if he could find the answer to his question that way.

"Yes, sir, that's me."

"*The?*" Jesse Lee asked, plainly not understanding what would make Clara so special. Israel appeared equally confused.

"It's an honor to meet you in person," Professor Hansberry said, grasping her hand in an emphatic shake. "I followed your case closely and was so relieved when you were freed."

"Thank you, sir." Heat rose to her cheeks. She hoped she didn't look as embarrassed as she felt.

Jesse Lee tilted his head to the side and snapped his fingers. "Wait, I read about that. The riots of 1919. That was you? You shot and killed a white policeman."

"He shot me and my daddy too." Clara winced and the phantom pain in her thigh flared up for a brief moment. She didn't like to talk about that night and the two long years afterward.

"A Colored girl going free after killing a white policeman." Jesse Lee smiled, but Clara didn't. "How did that happen?"

She stared at him significantly, hoping he would get the message. "It's an *enigma*, isn't it?"

His smile fell, and he sobered quickly. Israel stared at her as if seeing her for the first time. She didn't share her past if she could help it; folks tended to look at her differently when they knew. Kind of like the way he was looking at her now.

"Were you all waiting for me?" Professor Hansberry asked, apparently unaffected by the sudden tension in the air.

"Yes, sir," Israel said, pulling his scrutiny away from Clara. "We had some questions for you about an artifact. Wondered if you could point us in the right direction."

"Well, step into my office," he said, grinning. They all followed him into a cluttered space. Shelves overflowing with books and papers lined the room. Stacks of files, pamphlets, newspapers, and other documents teetered on the desk and in piles on the floor. And on every other inch of wall space was some kind of African art or object. Masks, shields, spears, fabrics, bowls, jewelry, and other items Clara didn't know the names or functions for. His office was like a library and a museum, stuffed into a space that couldn't be more than forty square feet.

There was only one guest seat available, the other being used to hold a leaning tower of boxes. Professor Hansberry settled into his chair behind the desk; Clara perched on the edge of the empty wooden chair while the men stood.

She glanced back at Israel, something like resentment punching a hole in her chest. He'd gone here to *the* university, something she had long dreamed of doing, and had dropped out. Thrown it all away.

She fisted her hands and focused back in on what the professor was saying.

"So what type of artifact are we talking about?" Hansberry asked, pushing his spectacles up his nose.

"It's a ring, originally from Africa. Very ancient, and possibly the source of legends. It's brass-colored with markings on it." Israel looked to Clara, who produced a sketch from her purse. She and Mama Octavia had worked on it the night before based on what they'd both seen, plus notes from the ancestor Octavia had talked to.

She passed the paper over and the professor peered at it, then turned it around and upside down to look at the drawing from other directions. He held it up to his face, the page grazing his nose, scrutinizing it carefully. "You've seen this ring?"

Israel cleared his throat. "It's been described to us in detail."

Professor Hansberry nodded, never taking his gaze from the page. "These characters...they could be Semitic in origin, perhaps the language is a cousin of Arabic, Hebrew, or Amharic, though I'm no linguist. But there are a few symbols that seem vaguely familiar."

He finally set the paper down, looking up at them. "My initial guess is this could be the ring of Makeda."

Clara sat up straighter. "I really wish my grandmother were here now," she murmured. Mama Octavia popped into existence right next to Jesse Lee.

Hansberry gave her an odd look but continued, "You all are familiar with the biblical tale of King Solomon and his meeting with the Queen of Sheba?"

The boys nodded but Clara shook her head.

"The Queen of Sheba was a mysterious figure. She's unnamed in the Bible and the Quran, and there's some disagreement about where Sheba was actually located. Stories from Arabia name her Bilqis, and some tales describe her as descended from djinn, supernatural creatures in Arabian and Islamic tradition. But according to Ethiopian legend, Sheba was one of *their* kingdoms and its queen was named Makeda.

"The story goes that Makeda heard of the wisdom of King Solomon and set out on a long journey to meet him and learn from him. Solomon was taken with her great beauty and intelligence and wanted to make her his. But she, a virgin queen, would not submit. So he tricked her."

Clara's expression twisted with outrage, and Hansberry nodded gravely. "He fed her spicy food and then set out a bowl of water for her. When she drank it, he accused her of stealing the water from him and refused to let her leave until she slept with him."

Clara winced, revolted.

"Before she left to return to her kingdom," the professor continued, "Solomon gifted her a ring to give to any son born of their union. Makeda did give birth to a son, Menelik, who eventually took the ring and returned to Solomon, but according to some arcane tales, she bore twins and kept her daughter a secret.

"While the descendants of Menelik include Haile Selassi, the current king of Ethiopia, we don't know anything of her daughter, but the story goes that Makeda made another ring for her, one which was passed down through the generations."

"Is the ring supposed to be magical?" Clara asked.

"Well, Solomon is said to have worn a ring that allowed him to control the djinn and force them to build his great temple—some call them demons but that's not precisely accurate." Clara suspected that these creatures were really Enigmas and understood the desire to term them *demons*.

"The ring Solomon gave his son protected the boy from harm until the two were reunited," Hansberry continued. "We don't know much about Makeda's ring. But the legends say that the queen used the knowledge she'd gained from Solomon as well as her pain over his trickery to imbue the ring with a power that would protect her daughter. To ensure she was never victimized the way Makeda was."

Professor Hansberry rubbed a hand across his face then massaged the bridge of his nose. "A former student of mine wrote a paper on this topic and submitted it to the *Journal of Negro History* a few years ago, but as I recall, Dr. Woodson rejected it. I don't have a copy anymore, I've been organizing and purging old files for the past few months."

Clara couldn't help but scan his office for any evidence of such. If this place had been worse a few months ago, she couldn't imagine it.

"The paper was well researched and contains more detail on the ring and the legends about its supposed powers. But some scholars don't cotton with myths and that sort of oral history. What they term 'witchcraft' is a hard sell for many. It doesn't dampen my regard for Dr. Woodson or what he does, but it means that many interesting ideas are scuttled before they have a chance to be disseminated."

Israel turned to Clara. "Do you think the journal would still have this paper?"

"It was submitted perhaps three years ago," Professor Hansberry offered.

Clara nodded. "Dr. Woodson keeps everything, even the papers they reject. The basement over there looks a little bit like this office."

Hansberry grinned, unabashed. "My student was disappointed not to get his work published. He finished his degree and went back to Sudan, else I'd point you in his direction. Can I ask why you're interested in such a ring?"

Israel spoke up. "Your class was always my favorite, Professor. The history bug hit me hard. Came across a fellow selling a ring he claimed was from Africa. I suspected he was trying to scam some wealthy Negro and thought I'd check out the story."

"Well, we'd welcome you back here anytime, Israel. As talented as you are with music, I sense that you have a scholar's heart." The man's smile was warm and sincere. "And if you can prevent a scam, even better. Good luck!"

"Thank you, sir."

They filed out of the office, buoyed by the knowledge they'd gained. Once they were back out on the Yard, Jesse Lee spoke. "That ring controls people the same way that Solomon controlled those demons, or my name's Sam. That's some powerful juju."

"Certainly seems so." Waves of unease rippled through Clara. "And at least two powerful Enigmas want it for themselves." She glanced at Israel. Reflected in his gaze was the same thing she was thinking—if an Enigma *did* get control of the ring, it could be disastrous. They still didn't know who or what was controlling it now. It certainly seemed like Madame Josephine had bent its magic to her will, but The Empress had to have been telling the truth when denying it.

"Think we can get into the journal office and take a look at that research paper?" Israel asked.

"We have to. We need as much information as we can get."

"But aren't they closed on Saturdays?"

"I have the key," she announced. "I don't think there's time to waste."

21

THE SATURDAY NIGHTERS

It was still before noon when Clara turned the key in the lock to the office's front door. The interior was dim and quiet—the staff sometimes worked long hours, but rarely on the weekends. Still, she hesitated before flicking on the light switch. If anyone were here, she'd have to explain her presence as well as that of Israel and Jesse Lee. Quietly, she led them through the front rooms to the basement steps.

They descended into a whirlwind of paper and boxes. She'd thought Professor Hansberry's office was bad, but it was orderly as a graveyard compared to the chaos down here. Most of the papers and articles were stored in boxes, though pages stuck haphazardly out of some of the lids, and, to her dismay, many were missing labels.

Footsteps sounded above and a deep voice called out, "Hello? Who's there?"

Clara stiffened. She had not forgotten that Dr. Woodson lived on the third floor of the offices, she just hadn't expected him to be here.

"Dr. Woodson, it's me, Clara." She motioned for the men to stay silent while she went back up the steps. She found Dr. Carter G. Woodson in his shirtsleeves, holding an egg sandwich in one hand.

"I thought you were still out of town, sir. Please forgive me for scaring you."

"Oh, I wasn't scared. I figured it was some enterprising employee coming in on the weekend, just not you."

She blinked, unsure if the statement was an insult or not.

"Not that you're not an industrious young woman," he continued.

"This is more of a personal mission, sir. I was looking for a research paper, one that was rejected from the journal a few years ago. However, the organization system seems to be in disarray."

He pressed his lips together. If she'd ever seen him smile, she might have thought he was holding one back, but maybe this was actually a grimace. "Langston." He said the name with great aggravation. "That boy never quite knows how to finish a job. I had him in the middle of reorganizing the files down there, but that was weeks ago, and I shouldn't be surprised he hasn't finished. He was supposed to relabel everything, many of the old ones had faded or were illegible. He told me he had some system of his own that he was using to catalog the files; wrote it all in a notebook that he keeps the Lord only knows where."

Clara's heart fell. "So he might be the only one who knows how to find what I'm looking for."

"If you're lucky." Dr. Woodson's voice was wry. He shook his head. "Just don't count on it."

"I'm sorry he's not working out."

"Last time I do a favor for a friend and hire someone."

Clara dropped her head. Hiring her had been as a favor for one of his friends, Mr. Hart, one of the lawyers from her court case.

"Oh, you worked out just fine, Clara. I suppose I shouldn't make blanket statements." He took a bite of his sandwich. Then his dark gaze turned on her speculatively. "You've been with us for a couple of years now. I get excellent reports from Mrs. Shuttlesworth about you."

Her eyes widened. She was never quite sure how Mrs. S. felt about her performance. "That's very good to hear."

"We often lose typists to better-paying jobs, so I feel lucky that you're still with us."

"I like being a part of the work you do for the race, sir."

His severe face softened somewhat, still not what anyone would call a smile. "But are you merely satisfied here? Or are you happy?"

The question took her so off guard she actually took a step backward. "W-what do you mean?"

"Do you want to know why I began studying Negro history? Why I've been driven to pursue the Cause, celebrate the race, and educate our people about the truth of their history?"

She blinked at him, entranced.

"The Emancipation Proclamation freed our bodies, the end of the Civil War liberated us from bondage, but it is up to us to free our minds. Part of that freedom includes finally participating in the ideals of this country, ensuring they apply to us: life, liberty, and the pursuit of happiness. Are you pursuing happiness, Clara?"

She felt blown back by a strong wind. Not once in her twenty-three years had someone ever asked about her happiness. The question stymied her. Fortunately, he didn't seem to expect an answer. By the time she'd recovered from the shock, he was already shuffling back up the steps to his apartment.

"Think about it. And remember to lock up when you leave, Clara."

"Yes, I will. Thank you, Dr. Woodson."

Her steps were unsteady as she went back to the basement where a dust-covered Jesse Lee was elbow deep in a water-damaged box of papers.

"Don't bother," she said, still shaking the cobwebs from her brain. "Apparently Langston has been reorganizing and he's the only one who knows how to find anything down here."

"You know where we can find this Langston character?" Jesse Lee asked, scowling and brushing off his pants.

"I think I know him," Israel said. He'd wisely been standing against the wall, his clothing still pristine. "Hangs with the crowd that gathers at Mrs. Johnson's house on Saturday nights."

"Who is that, one of his lady friends?" Clara asked dully.

Israel chuckled. "No. Mrs. Georgia Douglas Johnson, her husband was part of President Taft's Black Cabinet—used to be the Recorder of Deeds. She's a poet and hosts a salon for writers on Saturday nights. Langston fancies himself a poet too, as I recall. He should be there tonight."

Clara's shoulders slumped; that didn't sound at all like something she'd want to attend.

"I'm working with Madame Josephine tonight," Jesse Lee announced. "I'll try and get more information on the new distillery and these other locations they might be storing people at."

Israel looked at Clara expectantly. "We'll go to the salon and find Langston, then meet up with everyone tomorrow and see what's what."

It was a solid plan and she wanted to protest for no good reason other than she was feeling ornery. But she sealed her lips shut and led them back up the stairs, feet heavy like she was going to the gallows instead of a social event.

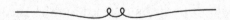

The rose-lined walkway leading to Mrs. Johnson's S Street house seemed to laugh at Clara. She stopped walking before they'd gotten to the front steps. "Maybe you should do this alone," she said to Israel. "I mean, you're more a part of this world than me."

"And you work with Langston. I know him in passing, but you

should be the one to talk to him." He gazed at her with a frown; she hated that he was making sense.

Her nerves were starting to fly away from her. She ran her hands down the skirt of her best dress, which was still sadly faded and bland, and gripped her purse with bloodless fingers as they climbed the steps and Israel rang the bell.

When the door opened, they were greeted, not by a maid as Clara had expected, but by a pale, elegant woman in her forties, her graying hair in an elaborate updo. Her dress was gold silk, fashionably drop waisted with bell sleeves.

"Israel Lee!" she exclaimed, smiling up at him. Her hands grazed his shoulders as she leaned in to brush her lips over each of his cheeks. When she turned to Clara, her expression froze. "And what do we have here?" Icy politeness chilled her tone.

"This is Miss Clara Johnson," Israel said.

"Pleased to meet you, Mrs. Johnson. I suppose it's too much to hope that we're distant relations," Clara quipped, but the woman just stared down at her for another moment.

Mrs. Johnson's lips curved in the barest imitation of a smile before she turned back to Israel. "How droll. Tonight's gathering will certainly have more…character than usual." Fortunately, she stepped to the side to let them enter, though she continued to stare appraisingly at the ragamuffin Israel had brought with him.

The interior of the home was just as lovely as Clara had imagined. Highly polished floors in the hallway led to thick carpeting in the parlor. The walls were covered in richly textured wallpaper. The expected maid in a black-and-white uniform walked by with a tray of appetizers. Clara felt a kinship with the woman—she would once again have been more comfortable in the role of servant than guest. She suspected Mrs. Johnson felt the same.

The front parlor led to a dining room; both were filled with guests who appeared far more at ease than Clara. Though now that she looked more carefully, it was obvious that at least some of it was an act. Several people clutched notebooks in tense hands. Many of the laughs sounded forced and a bit too loud. Educated men and women filled the available spaces, wearing their smart hats and smarter dresses and suits, and while on the surface they looked to be at ease, Clara was beginning to sense their nerves. Having never been to a literary salon, she could only assume the anxiety was due to having to share their work later on.

A familiar, caustic voice assaulted her ears from the dining room. She closed her eyes and breathed deeply to calm the rising panic and ire. Israel led her farther into the room where the Jackass, Dr. Harley, along with his equally distasteful fiancée, Addie Savoy, stood chattering with a small group of attendees.

Clara recognized a few from Addie's clique. Folks she knew by sight from growing up in the city. Her high school, Armstrong, and the more elite Colored school, Dunbar, had held a friendly-ish rivalry in everything from sports to cadet drills. Though her education had been cut short by her arrest, she still felt the blatant disregard from the Dunbar girls, who later, as young women, had proven they were just as disreputable as she'd always known. The run-in with Addie from a couple of weeks ago fresh in her mind, she planted her feet, refusing to move forward. Israel turned to her, brows raised.

But then he was recognized. Clara was soon pushed into the corner by fans and admirers who all clamored for a moment of his time.

"Israel, when is your next show?"

"Oh, Israel, I can't believe you came tonight!"

Titters and giggles from the women, bright-eyed fervency bordering on mania from the men. He took it all with grace, but for the first time Clara was able to truly observe the cost of his Trick. You had to focus to see it, really pay attention to more than just the words coming from their lips. Even without using her second sight, she sensed the distance between him and everyone else.

Mrs. Johnson joined the crowd to coo over him, introducing him to this and that person, something like the pride of ownership in her eyes. The women who fawned did so breathily, batting their lashes and fanning themselves, working themselves up into a froth. She'd seen women preen for attractive men before, hoping to catch their eye, but this was different. Subtly so, in a way that was difficult to put into words, but it seemed as if Israel was a mere object to be collected. Something to be acquired and displayed proudly for no other reason than to show it off.

People talked at him, gushed about his music and his talent in a way that made it seem like they were talking about a player piano or a phonograph and not a man. No one inquired about him as a person or even talked about anything other than how fantastic this or that show was, and how much they loved some song or another. He smiled and chatted, beating his gums about nonsense, but his isolation amid the crowd pulled at her.

Not being able to do anything about it, and not wanting to think on the pit of sympathy opening up in her stomach, she began searching for Langston. Unfortunately, he had parked his happy-go-lucky self in the group where Dr. Harley was holding court.

She gritted her teeth and forced her feet forward, standing at the back of the coterie of hangers-on. An internal timer counted down the seconds until she was spotted by those she'd rather avoid.

"Clara Johnson? Well, who let you in here?" Addie's voice grated. Everyone turned to stare, causing Clara's cheeks to heat. Dr. Harley scowled as if scenting something foul.

Langston was the only one with a smile on his face. "Clara! I didn't know you came to these shindigs."

"First time. Can I talk to you?" Her own smile was tight. She ignored the onlookers with steely determination.

"Sure, sure," he said amiably. That was the thing about him, he was always amiable. On the surface, nothing seemed to get him down. He was incessantly friendly and jocular. If he would just get his work done and come in on time, he would be easy to like.

He sauntered with her over to another corner out of earshot of the others, though their stares cut into her back like shards of glass.

"I need to find a research paper in the basement of the journal offices. Dr. Woodson said you were reorganizing things?"

Langston's expression turned quizzical. "It's Saturday night, Clara, and you want to talk about work?" A deep chuckle sprang from his chest. "Why don't you have some wine and get a plate of food—Miss Georgia's offerings are divine. Let's just leave work for Monday." He turned away, still laughing, and Clara rolled her eyes.

Then Israel was there as if he'd performed some magic trick of his own. Langston took a step back. "Israel Lee! Man, I saw the Rumblers at Café De Luxe the other week and you cats were on fire!" He looked back and forth between Israel and Clara. "You two know each other?"

"We're acquainted." Israel sidled up a little too close to her and bumped her shoulder playfully.

Langston did a double take. "Well, good to see you, man. Glad you could come out."

"I was just telling him how we're looking for that paper," Clara said through clenched teeth.

Langston shook his head in a pitying manner. "This one never stops, does she? She's trying to be Dr. Woodson's favorite. Leave some work for the rest of us."

Clara bit back her ire at the fact that the whole office was picking up the slack for the fun-loving Langston Hughes.

Israel's charming grin was in place. "It would really be a favor to me if we could find that paper. It's a bit urgent, you understand?" He didn't sing or whistle or blow his harmonica. Nothing anywhere near musical came out of him, but Langston was still starstruck.

"Sure, I can do that. I have everything organized up here." He tapped his temple. "My notes are a little jumbled, but my mind is a steel trap."

Clara held back a skeptical snort.

"I can meet you over there in the morning if you like."

"Thanks, man. I appreciate it." Israel pumped Langston's hand a few times just as a bell tinkled prettily in the parlor.

Mrs. Johnson's voice rose above the din. "Gather round. We're ready to begin."

Clara wanted to push, to insist they not wait until morning and drag Langston back to the journal offices tonight and find that paper. Her thoughts must have been written across her face, because Israel caught her hand and bent to whisper in her ear. "Another few hours won't make much difference. And no, we can't leave now, it would be rude."

She huffed, a little offended that she was so easy to read.

"Let's sit through at least a few of the readings. I see Miss Fauset and Jean Toomer over there, don't you want to hear what they're working on next? Zelda told me you'd loved *There Is Confusion* and had quite a lot to say about Jean's book *Cane*."

"Zelda should keep her mouth shut," Clara grumbled. Though she looked over at the writers with some curiosity. She'd been entranced by Jessie Fauset's first novel, which had come out the year before to much acclaim. And her legs nearly buckled when Israel marched her right over and introduced her to Jean Toomer. The elegant man gave a wry half smile as she stammered over her admiration of his work.

When she turned around, Addie Savoy was there along with her own personal Greek chorus of sycophants. These were the same girls who'd witnessed the dustup outside the Casbah. Clara was determined to keep a hold on her temper, especially since Israel's attention had been captured by the young man next to him who was waxing poetic about the chord progression in some tune or another he'd heard the band play.

"I'm surprised to see you here, Clara. I didn't realize you enjoyed literature." Addie enunciated the last word slowly, as if unsure whether Clara was familiar with the term.

The words *play nice* repeated in Clara's head over and over. Not only could she not start a fight in this fancy home around all this expensive furniture and art, she couldn't even cuss this heifer out.

"Of course. I'm down at the Carnegie Library just about every week."

She wanted to tell Addie how she could tear through a stack of books faster than a hungry teenage boy could get through a stack of pancakes, but she was afraid if she opened her mouth again, nothing but pure venom would come out.

Addie tittered in response. "Hmm. I suppose I figured you to be more of an Old Negro, off somewhere singing spirituals in the woods. Nice to know you have developed the necessary discernment to appreciate a more elevated level of artistry. Oh, not *old* as in age, of course." She giggled.

Israel must have felt the storm brewing, for he turned toward Clara and placed a steadying hand on her back. The firm touch and the warmth of his hand through the fabric of her dress siphoned off some of the gasoline that was racing its way in the direction of the nearest spark.

Clara took a deep, clarifying breath and smiled her fakest smile. "Oh, I'm familiar with Dr. Locke's work on the New Negro. I enjoyed his anthology a great deal. And as for spirituals, even if I were singing them at home or in the woods, that's nothing to be ashamed of. Dr. Locke himself talks about how they're an important part of our culture and the bedrock of what is now folk music. Or did you not read that part?"

Mrs. Johnson's voice rose again above the low murmurs in the room, stealing everyone's attention. The last Clara saw of Addie before turning away and putting the woman out of her mind was her mouth opening and closing like a fish. A deep sense of satisfaction filled Clara—she'd actually done it. She'd held her temper. She chuckled to herself, while next to her, Israel raised his brows, looking impressed.

The event had turned into something of a squeeze. There were not nearly enough chairs for everyone in attendance, and Israel was a solid presence at her side. She became more aware of him during the course of the evening as guests continued to arrive, causing him to stand even closer.

All hopes for a speedy getaway were long dead, but she found she didn't mind. The poems, short fiction, and essays recited aloud were quite good. There were more women than men in attendance and Clara reveled in the atmosphere of creativity and mutual support. Soon a lively discussion rose on the failures of the anti-lynching legislation to pass Congress and on the proper role for Colored women in politics.

Langston read two of his poems, and Clara's esteem for him grew. She was quite blown away. His words were like jazz music flowing through the room as folks listened with bated breath.

All in all, she ended up enjoying the evening, much to her surprise. As Israel walked her back to her apartment, her mind buzzed, full as it was with so much conversation and art and inspiration.

She had never thought of herself as someone who could belong at a place like this. Then again, she had also never considered what it would mean for her to be happy. Life was about surviving, putting one foot in front of the other to make it from day to day. She well knew it could also be about poetry and creativity and purpose. Camaraderie and friendship and love. But those had always seemed like lofty ideas for other people.

In some other life, if she wasn't who she was, could she have been one of the Saturday Nighters? Could she even have penned a poem or two or perhaps a short story? Shared it with an eager audience? And if it could happen in another life, what was stopping it from happening in this one?

Maybe the biggest thing holding her back now was the limits of her own imagination. Maybe the problem was her.

22

THE QUEEN OF SHEBA

Garang Geteneh wasn't born with the sight. Neither his mama or his daddy passed down any particular skills that let him talk with spirits or see past the veil. He trekked from a village outside Khartoum in eastern Africa to Monrovia on the western coast, then took a steamer ship to Washington, DC, to study at Howard University. He knew the journey would change his life, but it didn't happen the way he expected.

That ship he sailed on traveled the same route his ancestors did. Well, not his particular ancestors—his daddy was an Ethiopian soldier who fled after the Egyptians invaded once again. His mama was Nubian and none of his foreparents had ever been sold in chains to white men and carted across the sea. But the plight of those who shared his skin color both interested and confounded him and led him to the United States to study with their descendants.

It was on the deck of that ship, late one night with the snores of the men and women packed into berths below vibrating in his skull, that he peered out onto the moonlit waters and heard the singing. Late summer in the middle of the Atlantic Ocean and the nights were warm, but that evening a biting cold stuck to his bones, a thick smoke surrounded him, and he heard the wailing songs of those who had come before.

He didn't ask how—those questions would come later—but he managed to quiet his beating heart long enough to listen. Before that night, he'd planned to study medicine. Wanted to bring back doctoring skills to his home, his mother's village, and maybe teach at the college in Khartoum where folks was raising money to open a medical school. But soon enough he switched his focus to history, a change which plumb flummoxed his family and friends. But what Garang learned out on the deck of that ship that night was that while men's bodies were fragile and easily broken, the stories that went lost and unremembered could do just as much damage as any stick or disease.

There ain't too much true about history that survives the telling. Once your time is done and you head Over There, you get to watch the rumors about your life and times turn into lies that turn into myths. It's just the way of things, and by that time you ain't got too much to complain over. If you lived righteous, then you hope those who knew you remember the truth, but whether or not that truth can last for more than a generation...well, maybe it weren't meant to. So, the ancestors—one in particular—chose him to tell her story to, and fortunately (for some) he listened.

She had been a seeker of knowledge, just like him. Had traveled a great distance for it, just like him, hoping to take what she learned back home and help her people. Maybe that's why she chose him—or maybe he was the only one who would settle long enough to hear.

Either way, thousands of years is a long time, even for someone Over There, and as the ties that bind a mind to the world fray and sever, pieces of that mind do too. We wasn't meant to hang around forever in that place and those who linger there too long pay a steep price. But she paid it, that ancestor, 'cause she wasn't never content to let the story go untold.

To understand what had been vexing her, though, you got to know some things. Things that may not be writ down in the Bible, and the preacher may have never sermonized about them, but folks have been knowing them for longer than the good book has been around.

God made us all in four parts: soul, body, spirit, and destiny. The soul is the divine spark; every creature She created has one. The body is the soul's home, the animated clay, some might say. The spirit is the independent essence—if the soul is the part of you that's connected to God, the spirit is the part of you that's all your own. And finally, the destiny—God's expectation. While everything that breathes and eats and shits gets the first three, the last is only for humans. No rat, dog, bird, or even Enigma gets a destiny; it's what sets men apart.

You're thinking it's fate, and that's part of it, but a destiny ain't just a book written by some divine hand up on high telling everything that's going to happen in your life. It's *possibility*, the beginning of a path each man walks, separate but not alone, because our destinies are all linked together.

That ocean that Garang crossed is a graveyard that holds the bodies of ancestors dumped overboard during the Middle Passage. It flows with the tears of our foreparents and carries the echoes of their sorrow. Any man who's born and dies a slave has had their destiny damaged irreparably, and that injury is a scar passed on down to their children and their children's children.

Wasn't only slavers who harmed destinies neither. Evil men and women have done it, good men too, from time to time, either on purpose or on accident. Which brings us to *her*, Makeda. The Queen of Sheba herself. A beautiful woman, a little spoiled some might say, but sheltered the way women like that used to be. She took a journey to find knowledge and met a king who gave her more than she bargained for.

Old Solomon expected her to bend to his whims with no complaint, probably since that was all he'd ever known—blind acceptance and accolades—but Makeda wasn't like the other women he chased or chased after him. She remembered everything she learned and she was able to use the knowledge like a weapon.

See, the king hadn't taught her how to craft a ring like the one he wore, one given to him straight from heaven as a reward for his good deeds. And Solomon hadn't intended to share the secrets of how he controlled the spirits who built his temple and toiled under his rule, slaves from Over There brought to life in bodies of his creation who laid the foundation of his kingdom and legacy. But Makeda was clever and she figured it out anyway. Learned well enough that when she was back on the road, traveling to her kingdom, belly growing bigger with the evidence of his treachery, she made her own ring. She didn't have no use for controlling spirits, she wanted to control men—and not just men, the destinies of men.

Her future, all her possibilities had changed the night she was bent and tricked and betrayed, but never again. Not for her, nor her daughter, nor her daughter's daughter.

Taking a hold of a man's destiny is easiest when he's already weakened: isolated, imprisoned, dejected, poor, or separated from his purpose. A rich and powerful man's destiny is harder to take, though all the more satisfying when it's done. Those're the men who make the most mischief and cause the most pain.

The spirits, long free of Solomon's control, those Enigmas who'd watched mankind live out their futures in a way they couldn't ever, took note. They'd been easy to enslave, seeing as they had no destinies of their own. Solomon's ring had stolen their pride and taught them a powerful lesson.

And while Makeda was busy securing her daughter's legacy and ensuring that her own betrayal would never be repeated, the Enigmas were keeping a close eye.

And biding their time.

"So, the ring steals *destinies*?" Zelda asked, mouth downturned.

The crew was once again gathered in Mr. Vasiliadis's back room since the idea of heading to a speakeasy on a Sunday morning had made Mama Octavia give Clara the most withering of glares.

As promised, Langston had met Clara and Israel at the journal offices that morning and, after consulting with his notebook and briefly searching several boxes, produced the research paper entitled "Solomon and the Queen of Sheba: Exploring the Origins of African Myth," by Garang Geteneh.

Clara had read while Israel drove them to the butcher shop. Once they were all together, Israel read the article aloud in his sonorous tenor. Once he'd finished, silence echoed in the small space until Zelda pierced it. "Go over it again?" she whispered, meeting each of their perplexed gazes.

Clara complied, reviewing what they'd learned. "The ring separates a person from his destiny, slowly pulling it away from the soul it resides in like a rubber band being stretched until it snaps. That process drains the life from a person, Afflicting them with the malaise that makes them lose themselves."

Israel frowned, leaning forward to rest his arms on his knees. "And according to the paper, when the rubber band snaps, the destiny is fully detached, the person left behind is just an empty shell. Not even a person anymore."

Clara whispered, "Then the soul fades and the spirit leaves the body."

She shivered. She'd seen spirits pushed out of their bodies by force a time or two, and it wasn't pretty—this would be a very similar thing. While ghosts like Mama Octavia stayed around for their own reasons, they could always go deeper Over There and into the Next Place if they chose. But those who were forced against their will could never seem to get their bearings. They were volatile and bewildered, emotional and dangerous. Encountering spirits like those was a heartbreaking experience.

"But the body lives on?" Jesse Lee asked from his spot leaning against the wall.

"How long you think a body can last without a spirit? Without a soul? They don't die fast, but what they're doing ain't living, and after they're gone, they don't find peace." Clara rubbed her arms, the chill pervading down to her bones. She was so cold she halfway thought the Grays had found her again.

Aristotle took the typewritten pages from Israel and flipped through them. "So the ring lets Madame Josephine separate people from their destinies and then control them."

Israel nodded. "With the destiny being weakened, they have no free will, and no purpose but the one they're given by her. It's a fancy form of slavery."

"And eventually, the destiny is snipped away and the spirit flees the body." Aristotle caught Clara's eye.

"Right."

"But Clara, didn't The Empress tell you Madame Josephine wasn't the one doing this?"

She spread her arms. "She insists Josephine *isn't* responsible. I can't understand it."

"And she doesn't know or won't say how Josephine got the ring in the first place? Or who *is* responsible?" Israel scratched his brow.

"No."

Israel turned to his cousin. "Nobody around her has mentioned anything about the ring?"

"Naw, nothing I've heard. They don't talk much about all them folks she's got working for her acting like walking corpses either. I done asked some of the fellas, wiped their memories after, but they don't know anything. Most of them believe she's got something going with Uncle Nazareth and they're afraid to even think too much about it."

Clara snorted at the idea of Uncle Nazareth being powerful enough to cause the Affliction. "How does she act?" she asked, leaning forward. "Has she seemed strange, doing or saying unusual things?"

Jesse Lee squinted in thought. "She got what my mama would call an artist's temperament. Most days she's sweet as punch, quick with a 'please' or a 'thank you.' Batting her lashes and trying to kill us with kindness. But every once in a while, she's a right harridan. Getting into a lather at the smallest thing. Screaming for us to jump and expecting us to already know how high." He shook his head, eyes wide, as if the thought exhausted him.

"When we come on shift, we always ask the fellas leaving which one she'll be: the princess or the witch."

"And you haven't talked to her directly yet about any of this?"

Jesse Lee's brows rose. "You nearly chopped my head off when I went to work with her in the first place. But no, not yet. I can't always get a good hold of her memories. Sometimes I can sense them right there like everyone else's, but other times..." He gave a frustrated shrug. "Could be the wards on the ring. Besides, Thaniel's the closest to her. He's got the most access. I'm too new to even bring her coffee. And what I'm supposed to ask her—'Please take that ring off, ma'am'?"

Zelda snickered, and Clara rolled her eyes. "She must know who's doing this—she gotta be working for or with them."

"Maybe it's Bowlegged Mo?" Aristotle offered. He looked almost regal in his Clarence persona, holding court over the dingy storage room that smelled of old meat. "When he was arrested, a lot of his crew was taken down as well. His entire operation was hamstrung, assets seized, facilities closed down. Crooked Knee Willy probably thought he'd wiped out the competition and was going to swoop in like a savior."

Israel straightened. "Then here comes the Agbrooke distillery pumping out more liquor than a river. And Josephine doesn't even have to pay for labor."

Clara considered. "Makes sense. He's inside, but he's got her on the outside with some magical way of controlling folks."

"Enslaving folks," Zelda corrected, jaw tight.

"Right. Free labor, increased production, plenty of profits." She looked around at everyone. "Greed. Simple as that?" It was as good a reason as any.

"There's a dozen ways to get cheap labor," Zelda said. "Just look at the sharecroppers down South, working harder and harder but ending up more in debt every year. Stealing destinies just for workers can't be the end of the story."

She stood and began pacing the short length of the room. "Jesse Lee, could you erase everyone's memories and sneak in to talk to her?"

Jesse Lee shook his head. "With one or two people at a time, I can take hours or even days of their memories—give them back too, afterward. But with more folks, especially if they're spread out, I can only take short bursts. At the distillery, with all those guards, I removed their last few seconds, enough to confuse them and for y'all to slip away. But at Josephine's, we're always in pairs. For me to get away from my partner and talk to her, I'd have to wipe her—if I could—*and* him, and everyone I encountered along the way. Lot of ways that could backfire. I'll do it if we absolutely need to, if I want to burn the bridge and if that's the only option we have. But there's no guarantee she'll answer my questions even if I do get to her."

"What are you thinking, Z?" Clara studied her carefully.

"Sometimes you need to go to the horse's mouth. We know the ring must be the key to freeing those missing people she's got ensorcelled. But we can't touch it. Stands to reason we should ask the only person who can."

"But what would make her answer?" Jesse Lee asked.

"Him." She pointed and everyone turned to Israel. "Can you make her tell you how she got the ring? How she's able to wear it? Who might be operating it?"

He swallowed, looking uneasy.

Zelda continued, "Can you make her take it off?"

He gave a sad smile. "It's a light hypnotism. If she's of a mind to tell me, I can compel her. But if she's not, or if she's got some kind of ward or spell preventing her..." He shrugged.

"It might be worth a try," Zelda said. "Especially if Jesse Lee can sense her memories and she won't remember talking to you about it. Otherwise we're still flying blind."

"And someone else is bound to end up like Montrose Merriweather," Aristotle added darkly.

Israel's lips compressed into a thin line at the mention of the dead musician.

"But what's to stop her—or whoever—using it on him if he gets too close?" Clara asked, uneasiness spreading through her like an ache. "She could take his destiny if she felt threatened."

"Could be," Aristotle said slowly, tapping his chin. "But look at the folks who been targeted so far. Alley dwellers, washerwomen, working folks. Young people, *poor* young people. Nobody working in that distillery looked like they were from Strivers' Section or LeDroit Park, right?" He gazed at them for confirmation. "The ring is being used to target the lower classes. Afflicting someone as well-known and connected as Israel Lee wouldn't be smart, no matter who's doing it."

Clara shook her head. "The risk is too big and we don't even know how the power works. Putting Israel in that kind of jeopardy is a bad idea. If it goes wrong..." Her words hung in the air.

"I'm with Clara," Jesse Lee said, pulling a gasp of shock from her.

He shrugged. "The thing with Josephine's memories is intermittent.

If it's a ward, maybe it runs out and needs to be renewed. But if I can't get hold of her memories when Israel shows up, then he's not going to get too far."

Clara crossed her arms, surprised but vindicated at Jesse Lee's support. Israel met her eye and held it for a long moment. Something passed between them, but she wasn't sure what his conflicted expression meant.

"It's still the best shot we've got right now," he said. "I'm the one who knows her best. And I can get close to her without Jesse Lee having to risk his position. I think it's worth the risk."

"Well, I don't." Clara stood, pushing the crate she'd been sitting on backward with a screech. "You go and get yourself Afflicted and then what? Where will we be? No, I'll talk to The Empress again, see if I can't get some real answers this time. Jesse Lee, do what you're doing, keep listening and let us know who she's meeting with. This operation is too big for her to be running it alone. Someone close to her knows something. What about that manager at the distillery?"

"Mr. Walters," Jesse Lee said. "Yeah, we could go and talk to him."

Clara turned to Aristotle. "I think we need to get face-to-face with Bowlegged Mo to test your theory, try to figure out if he's still running things. If he's controlling the ring. You think your policeman persona can get in to see him?"

"I believe so."

"If he does control the ring," Zelda said in a low voice, "won't talking to him be dangerous? Couldn't he Afflict anyone snooping around?"

Clara's mind raced. "You don't have to ask him directly about the ring. I can tell if there's anything magical about him if I go too. If I look through the veil." Though the thought made her shiver, it had to be done. "No one talks to Josephine." She slashed her hands apart to punctuate her statement.

But Israel straightened slowly, mouth turned down. "If we're gonna risk talking to Mo, we need to talk to Josephine as well. And we have more reason to believe that she's *not* directly using the ring."

Clara crossed her arms, ready to dig in, but Aristotle's soft voice cut in. "There's nothing safe or guaranteed about what we're doing here, child. But we all agreed to this crazy scheme. It's not just about our freedom anymore, it's about the freedom of the people in our community. We're willing to take the chance."

Zelda nodded at her, holding her gaze. Clara broke away to peer at Jesse Lee, who just shook his head and shrugged. So much for support.

Finally, she looked to Israel, whose grim smile was firmly in place.

"We have a lot to do and not much time," he said. "It's already been three weeks or more that some of these folks have been missing. We don't know how long it takes for a destiny to fully detach, but Josephine said she wouldn't have the workers forever. Sounded like she was already making plans to replace them. These people, our neighbors and our friends, are on borrowed time."

Clara dropped her head, not ready to admit defeat, but knowing she was outvoted. Putting herself in jeopardy was one thing—falling victim to the Grays or any other danger was not something she was going to shy away from—but the rest of them?

This was why she preferred to do things alone.

"Looks like y'all done decided anyway," she said, standing up in a huff. "Do what you want to, then. See if I care if everybody turns up dead."

She stomped out of the room and slammed the door, but the rattling of the hinges did not produce the sense of satisfaction they usually did. Instead she felt empty and oddly alone.

23

BREAKFAST FOR HEATHENS

Israel caught up with Clara three blocks away from the butcher shop, his long strides devouring the distance between them. A hot wind blew like a bellows, forcing muggy air across their skin as they walked in silence for a few minutes.

"Still don't trust me, lioness?" he finally asked.

"That's what you think this is about?" she snapped. "Getting you Afflicted doesn't help any of us. You think I'm worried you'll just Charm Josephine into taking that ring off and then run back to The Man in Black?"

The thought hadn't actually crossed her mind, but now it made her pulse race. She searched his expression for signs that he would consider something like that. And he looked back at her, guileless, until she had to turn away.

Israel blew out a breath and tilted his head back to stare at the sky, revealing the long, strong column of his throat. His Adam's apple bobbed as he swallowed, drawing her gaze back like a magnet. That's when her stomach growled, seeming to echo off the sidewalk. Israel chuckled. "I think we need to get you fed."

"Feeding me won't get you off the hook. Besides, it's Sunday morning. Can't think of too many places open."

"I know a few spots."

She told herself that her desire for a free meal overrode her irritation with him—and almost believed it. Fifteen minutes later they sat wedged into a corner table at a packed basement eatery Clara had never been to before. "So this is where the heathens eat breakfast?"

Israel threw back his head and laughed. "I suppose so."

They placed their orders with the harried waitress and Clara leaned her chair back against the wall.

"You know, you never told me your story," he said.

"What story?"

"How it was you got hooked up with The Empress in the first place." Israel's dark eyes were cautious, as if he wasn't sure if this was a topic that should be broached.

"She got me out of jail."

"That's not a story." Laughter glittered in his eyes.

She didn't talk about it much; then again there wasn't usually anybody to talk about it with. Zelda knew, 'cause that girl was nosier than an elephant, but she found she didn't mind sharing with him. She settled into her chair and stretched her legs out. "You were here during the rioting?"

He nodded slow. "I was still at Howard. The ROTC passed out rifles and ammunition and we helped hold off the white mob coming up 7th Street."

She took a deep breath. "What I remember from that night is the sound of the door busting open downstairs and how the fear tasted in my mouth. Bitter, so sharp it almost made me gag. There was already so much noise. Gunshots outside, shouting and screaming."

She blinked as the memories assailed her. Israel's expression was serious, but his presence—just the fact that he wanted to know—helped her continue. "Daddy was in the hallway when the men burst through the door, yelling about a sniper. We didn't even know they were police, thought they were just some crazy white men. Daddy ran into my room, handed me his Colt, and he had his shotgun. We hid under the bed." Her voice began to waver. Israel slid his chair closer until he could wrap an arm around her shoulder, pulling her in to him.

"Then they were at my bedroom door. Kicked it in. I don't even remember pulling the trigger. I just heard my daddy's voice in my head telling me like he had ever since I was a little girl, 'White man comes toward you with evil in his eyes, you shoot first. Ask questions later.' And that's what I did."

The noise of the dining room faded, replaced by the echoing sounds of the jail—footsteps and barred door slams vibrating against the concrete. "Ever been to jail, Israel Lee?"

"Can't say that I have."

"The first few weeks I was still recovering from being shot. Scared every day that a lynch mob would turn up outside and drag me out of that cell. The guards would stand outside my door and taunt me. Threaten me. I killed a white man. A white policeman. Wasn't no question in my mind I was never going home again. And I was in so much pain I cried myself to sleep every night. Then the lawyers and the ministers started coming. They showed me the newspapers, the letters folks had written. Told me I was a celebrity." She snorted.

"Famous or not, it didn't help me much. Month after month in that cell waiting for the trial. Mama Octavia was there, though. She'd passed the year before and hadn't been coming around at first, but she brought herself back from Over There to keep me company. She'd sing to me, tell me stories. Try to keep my spirits up. And then the trial and the verdict—guilty, just like I'd thought. Just like I knew. Wouldn't even let me plead self-defense. Thought I was gonna hang." His arm around her stiffened.

"All those folks who died over those days of rioting? I was the only one convicted of killing someone. Didn't think I had anything more to lose." Her breathing evened out and the threatening tears receded.

"I'd gotten a hold of some matches, hid them in my shoe 'cause I wasn't supposed to have them. One night, I lit a match and called a spirit to me. Mama Octavia didn't even try to stop me." She gave a humorless chuckle.

"And The Empress was only too happy to help. Told me not only could she spare me the noose, she could get me free. I'd been there a year and a half. So I agreed." She swallowed the old guilt down.

"A few days later, the judge who heard my case lay on his death-bed. He said one of his regrets was that he should've let me plead self-defense. Told his friend, another judge, and he gave me a new trial. District attorney knew he couldn't win again, not if the jury heard what actually happened, and dropped the charges. Just like that." She snapped her fingers.

Israel searched her gaze. "Your Charm did that?"

She was leaving out part of the story, the part she hated to even think about. Exactly how the "gift" The Empress had given her paved the way for her freedom. "My Charm..." She cleared her throat. "No one should have it. I used it then, but never again. No matter what." She pinned him in place with her gaze, willing him to see her determination. He squeezed her shoulder, then withdrew his arm as the waitress approached with their plates.

As they dug into their eggs, bacon, and biscuits, Israel thankfully changed the subject. "So how did you start working for Dr. Woodson?"

Clara smiled this time. "One of my lawyers, Mr. Hart, is good friends with Dr. Woodson. When I got out of jail, things were tough for a while. I wasn't in the right frame of mind to go back to school and I worked some odd jobs while I got myself together. Mr. Hart would check in on me and finally convinced Dr. Woodson that I was a good enough typist to give me a shot. After what the Pollyannas did, I needed a better job than what I had."

His brows descended. "The Pollyannas? The social club?"

She nodded. "Were you in one of those highfalutin high-yellow clubs? Bet you were. Probably in the Bluebirds or the Guardsmen or something."

His guilty expression said it all. "My mother put me in Jack and Jill."

She laughed and shook her head. "Well, the Pollyannas say they're a charity group. Raise money for orphans and whatnot. They held this big fashion show to get donations for my defense fund while I was locked up. Folks from all over the city donated time and services. Only after the show, they never gave me any of the money." She smiled cheerlessly, and Israel scowled. "Daddy went bankrupt paying for my defense, even with the other donations. He moved back to North Carolina not long after my release."

"Wait, isn't Addie Savoy a Pollyanna?"

Clara nodded slowly. "Never met a bigger snake in the grass. Smile in your face one moment then take food out of your mouth the next." The pain of the betrayal had faded over the years into nothing but a dull ache. Of course the sight of Addie's smug face would bring it back in no time at all.

Quiet descended while they cleaned their plates. When Israel sat back, she felt his eyes on her like a caress, but didn't lift her head.

"You think I'm like that too?"

She set her fork down, still staring at the table. She didn't, not anymore. But for some reason she didn't want to tell him that. She'd already opened up far more than she usually did. Being around him felt comfortable, safe in a way she wasn't used to. Offering him any more right now would be a step too far.

But his deep voice stroked her exposed skin. "I didn't meet my mother until I was fourteen." At that, she looked up, but he was gazing off, unseeing. "Knowing she'd run off when I was just a few days old, it did something to me. Left a hole that, even after she came back, I couldn't fill. She took me away from my home and brought me into a world I didn't belong in, and I twisted myself every which way to fit."

His gaze focused, and he turned to her. "That's what I admire about you, Clara. You don't ever try to fit your square self into a round hole. I can't seem to stop." His smile was rueful. "The deal I struck with The Man in Black made it so I'd never fit again. It looks like I do, from the outside. Folks all around, wanting to be near me. But on the inside…" He twisted his lips. "I haven't had a real conversation like this with anybody in years, since I gave my soul away. Ain't had anybody really see me in a long time."

She stared him full in the face. The true understanding of his words sinking in.

When she couldn't stand it anymore, she looked away. *Coward*, a voice inside screamed.

"Your mama came back, at least. Wanted you enough to return and give you everything a little motherless child could want. Wish I could say the same."

"She came back," Israel acknowledged. "But what I wanted she didn't have in her anymore."

Clara played with the edge of her napkin, all bravery gone. "But you had chances. College. *Howard*. Why throw it away? I'd have given any-thing…" She couldn't finish that statement because it wasn't precisely true. She supposed she could have used her Charm to get into school. Maybe even pass all her classes with ease. But that thought had never even crossed her mind.

"I don't think I threw it away, I just chose another path. Maybe my destiny was leading me somewhere else…"

The waitress approached with the check, cutting off whatever he was about to say. Israel paid and they were out on the street again before she knew it, Sunday-morning church bells ringing from towers across the city.

They walked in silence toward her apartment, Clara not knowing what to say and Israel apparently caught in his own thoughts. Her street was quiet and Miles's place was subdued, with only the diehards there at this hour on the Lord's day. She slid her key into the lock, her back to Israel, not wanting to leave it like this.

She pushed the heavy door open and spun to face him, just as he was turning to leave. His eyes widened when she dragged him into the vestibule of the building. The air was close and stuffy; his brows were nearly to his hairline.

"I see you, Israel Lee," she said, then raised on her tiptoes and pressed her lips to his.

His shock melted almost instantly as she practically dissolved into his arms. His hands spread across her back, holding her tight, branding her through the fabric of her dress. She looped her arms around his neck and liquefied into a puddle of who she used to be.

The kiss pulsed through her from the ends of her hair all the way to her toenails. She pulled away, mostly because she didn't want it to end. Her vision swam for a moment before he came into focus, eyes soft, still staring at her mouth.

He stroked the side of her face with a single finger. "You're so lovely." His voice gave her chills now too, the vibrations of it moving inside her. This was a different kind of hypnotism, one he couldn't control—not on purpose. She felt its pull and wanted desperately to give in.

But because she wanted to step into his arms again, she instead moved back, then up onto the first step of the staircase. He tracked her movements, a calm but sultry expression still on his face. He had the nerve to be calm after a kiss like that.

She backed up the stairs like a scared animal, wanting to get away, even though his scent still permeated her nostrils and her fingers tingled from the desire to be against his skin again.

He grinned at her, watching her retreat with knowing eyes. She turned and raced up the steps. As she fit her key into her apartment door, she swore she heard him say, "Miss Clara, I do believe I'm smitten." But she ducked into her apartment and stood with her back against the door to block out the words.

24

AN UNEXPECTED VISIT

Clara was sitting on the couch, eyes staring at the same page of *The Conjure Woman* she'd had open for the past hour, when Zelda waltzed through the door. It was a shame, Mr. Chestnutt's short stories were favorites of hers, usually guaranteed to take her mind off her troubles, but not today.

Her roommate took one look at her and frowned. "What, you still upset?"

Clara slammed the book shut. "No. Why should I be upset?"

"You sure were in a tizzy when you left the butcher shop."

"I wasn't in a tizzy. And if the rest of you knuckleheads want to get yourselves dead, it don't have nothing to do with me." She slid the book off her lap and turned to stare out the window to the quiet street below.

"You didn't seem to have a problem with Aristotle going to see Mo in jail. So why are you so upset about Israel and Josephine?" Zelda asked.

Clara kept her lips sealed, monitoring the progress of a pigeon crossing the sidewalk toward a crust of bread sitting next to a trash bin.

"It have something to do with the way Israel Lee was looking at you today? The way he looks at you every day?"

Clara's neck almost cracked, she whipped it around so fast. "Israel Lee don't look at me no kind of way, Zelda Claudine."

Zelda burst into laughter and stumbled over to the kitchen to start banging around in the cabinets, putting on a pot of tea. The girl drank so many hot liquids during the dog days of summertime it was a wonder she didn't evaporate in a pool of her own sweat.

"That man can never take his eyes off you, girl. I think he just might be sweet on you."

The memory of Israel's kiss had not strayed far from Clara's mind. Her system was still in a state of shock in the aftermath and the image and associated sensations played over and over on a loop. *She'd* kissed *him*, in fact, which had to mean he *couldn't* be sweet on her, right? If he was, it would have been the other way around.

She didn't know much about flirting and womanly wiles and all of that, hadn't had any type of beau since she was sixteen years old, and back then her daddy, large and strong as he was, had struck fear into the hearts of most of the boys who would have come calling. After that she was too damaged and broken to even consider walking out with someone. Brave and curious young men sometimes approached, but her sharp tongue and short temper usually sent them packing before too long.

"If Israel Lee thinks I'm going to fall at his feet like those empty-headed flappers who hang off him like ivy, he has another think coming." She would die before admitting to Zelda how she'd come perilously close to doing just that not too long ago.

"Would it be such a bad thing, Clara?" Zelda asked, settling into the armchair.

A car passed by on the street outside, its occupants shouting at one another. The pigeon had claimed its prize and was now waddling away. Clara remained quiet for long moments while Zelda sipped her tea.

Finally, she twisted back around to face the room. "Why would he be sweet on someone like me?"

Zelda began ticking things off on her fingers. "Someone brave and smart who doesn't take any bullshit and gives as good as she gets? Someone strong and beautiful who's always helping people? Gee, why would he like someone like that? Why would anyone?" She picked up her cup and slurped her tea loudly.

"That ain't what men are interested in," Clara grumbled. "They want pretty smiles and dainty handshakes. Eyelash fluttering and all that sort of nonsense."

"Men who don't have any sense *only* want that sort of thing."

Clara rolled her eyes. She'd seen too many men's attention grabbed by a high hemline or low bodice, or a fair complexion and fine grade of hair, to completely believe it. "If he was looking at me at all, it's only because we're working together for a short period of time. I'm a means to an end, just like he is. He wasn't seeing me for real."

Zelda sank into the armchair, studying her. "I think he sees you just fine, Clara Johnson."

The words were a repeat of what she'd told Israel. The memory of his lips pressed to hers made her throat dry. Zelda's gaze was a little too perceptive.

"You go on outta here with all that hogwash," Clara said, tilting her head back and sliding down the couch in as unladylike a posture as she could manage. "What you still doing here anyway? Thought you was moving out."

"I'll be out of here tomorrow," Zelda said with a smile in her voice. "You really want me gone."

"What we need to be talking about is how we're gonna pull off this caper without any of us waking up dead or Afflicted," Clara said testily. "This was supposed to be about getting free of the spirits. Now we got bootlegging gangsters and ancient Africans and Lord only knows what else to worry about. Ain't none of us really cut out for this."

"We're not doing that bad," Zelda replied. "Haven't been shot, stabbed, or arrested yet. Got out of a pretty righteous scrape down at the garage. Honestly, I ain't had that much fun in years."

"That's all well and good for you, but all of us didn't grow up in the circus."

Zelda leaned forward and set her teacup down with a loud clatter. "No, some folks is normal. Got the right kind of skin, the right height, the right weight, a regular amount of hair in the expected places. Don't get sold off to a sideshow by their mamas. Still manage to find things to complain about, though."

Her piercing gaze pinned Clara, who grimaced, regret knotting her belly. She looked away and opened her mouth to apologize, but Zelda continued, still hunched over, arms on her thighs. "You ever seen the Queen of Coins?"

Clara swallowed, jarred at the change of subject. "Who's that?"

"Magician who toured with us, just for a summer. She was a gypsy, from a family of circus people. Started out reading palms, telling fortunes. By the time I met her, she was doing coin magic. I never met someone so dedicated."

Zelda sat up and held her hands out, flipping them over as if to prove they were empty. Then with a snap of her wrist, a silver dollar appeared between her fingertips. With another flourish, it changed to a Buffalo nickel. Clara huffed in surprise.

"She wasn't quite famous yet, not when I knew her, but she told me she was gonna be. Told me exactly what was going to happen like she really could read the future. How in two years she'd be off the sideshow circuit and traveling the world, awing the audiences with her illusions." The nickel transformed back into the silver dollar, which then rose straight into the air from one palm to the other, hovering above it. Clara jerked in surprise.

"Turned herself into the Queen of Coins, descendant of the ancient magi, the ones who gave gifts at Christ's birth, you know. Story was that in return, her family line had been blessed with otherworldly powers. She could make coins fly straight across the room. Pull change out of folks' pockets. Levitate herself and a table full of gold ducats."

Holding up the dollar, Zelda snapped her fingers and it disappeared. She flashed two empty hands. "In just a few years, she'd turned herself from a penniless immigrant hawking two-cent fortunes to a rich and feared woman, who grown, educated people truly believed had real magic."

"Maybe she did," Clara said. "Could have had a Charm."

Zelda gave a sardonic scoff. "Charms don't need years of practice or finger stretches and hand weights. No, she looked me in the eye and wrote her own story. Then went out and lived it. So the way I figure, if you want somebody else to buy what you're selling them, you gotta believe it too. You can't show any doubts or the audience will feel it. Deep in their bones. You show fear or waver in any way, then that's what they focus on. You believe your own story, that you're the greatest coin illusionist that ever lived?" She shrugged and grabbed her teacup again. "You make them all believe what you want them to."

Clara sighed, finally understanding the point of the story. Trust had never come easily to her, not in others, and not in herself. She disappointed herself about as often as other people did. Shooting first and asking questions later was the only way she knew how to be. That kind of mentality didn't lend itself easily to thinking too far into the future. What would it take for that to change? She'd been trying to imagine herself differently but was still struggling.

"And you may not have grown up among the freaks, Miss Clara, but you got something more powerful than stagecraft and illusion. You got a gift, a group of folks willing to help you, and a task worth doing. More than I can say for most."

Clara nodded. Trusting the team was the only way this could work. She'd have to try harder.

"Anyway." Zelda stood, stretching her back. "Can I get my dollar back? I'm gonna go down to the sweet shop, get me some ice cream."

"I didn't give you no dollar," Clara said, scowling.

"In your pocket?" Zelda's brows rose.

Clara fished into her skirt pocket and pulled out a shiny silver dollar that she was sure hadn't been there before. Zelda broke into a cackle before reaching over to take it.

Later that evening, alone thanks to the temptation of a backroom poker game on Florida Avenue that had made Zelda's eyes go round with anticipation, Clara sat in her altar closet. The Empress had a lot of explaining to do.

An unlit match hovered in Clara's hand for long moments until she struck it and the scent of sulfur filled her nostrils. She lit a fat white candle, closed her eyes, and focused her mind. The crackle of the flame on the wick, the faint heat and glow behind her eyelids drew her attention, creating the lens she could use to see Over There without opening herself up to any unwanted intruders.

Other spirits reached for her, wanting her attention, but she ignored them in favor of seeking The Empress. She was surprised it was taking the Enigma this long to appear. Usually she was eager for a status update on the mission she'd given.

Clara opened her eyes, staring into the flame. She breathed slowly, pouring more of her energy into the task at hand. The dim closet, lit only by the single candle, grew even darker. Shadows danced merrily on the three walls surrounding her. Clara shivered though the August temperatures had not relented. Stale air sat heavy in the apartment. No breeze interrupted the oven-like heat.

The flame flickered and lowered. This was not how The Empress usually arrived.

Soon, the wisp of fire was down to practically nothing. Just a soft blue glow hovering around the wick. Shadows writhed all around her, snaking along the walls, climbing them like vines until they began to coalesce.

A new figure emerged from the darkness, one she had never dealt with directly before.

The suggestion of a face, a top hat above it, glittering eyes shining at her made of something sparkly—*starlight* was the word that came to mind.

"The Man in Black?" Clara whispered, awe warring with confusion.

"You court chaos, young seer." His voice was more a suggestion of words than a sound. Yet it rumbled up her spine like an earthquake.

"I—I seek an audience with The Empress," she replied slowly.

"And yet you speak with me."

She had to tread carefully, Enigmas were mercurial and easily offended. She bowed her head. "To what do I owe the honor of this unexpected visit?"

He laughed, a deep chuckle that vibrated underfoot. "I come with something of value, young seer. Information."

She tensed. "And what do you wish to trade?"

There was never something for nothing with the spirits. An offering of some kind was always needed. The Man in Black sobered, the shadows he was made of stilled. "The information is freely given for now, but I may seek a favor in the future."

Clara shook her head. "That is too open-ended. I cannot possibly agree to an unknown, future price. I have no way of knowing if it will match the value of the information."

The shadows shifted and hung before her before swirling riotously, growing closer to her face. She blinked, holding herself rigid as the inspection from the Enigma continued.

"You have dealt with us for a long time, seer, and are wise to our ploys. Very well, in payment I request a song."

"A s-song?" She flattened her hands on her thighs. "But I don't sing."

"You have a voice don't you?" He sounded amused, not annoyed, fortunately.

"I do not have a singing voice fit to hear."

"That is my price." The shadows retreated somewhat.

This was a strange request, though she supposed it's what church-going folks did every Sunday. Sang and clapped and danced and sent praise to their Lord. Other folks—some godly, some not—left offerings of food and libations, clothing, string, shoes, hair, and more to the spirits as part of their pleas and reverence, so why not a song? Singing aloud would certainly be humiliating enough to be a fair price.

"What song?"

"Whatever you wish. I guarantee my information is worth it."

She swallowed, her mind suddenly blank of every tune she'd ever heard. A few popular blues songs slowly swam up through the cloudy waters of her brain.

The first appropriate song that emerged was one her mama had sung to her, just once. Mama Octavia was usually the one tucking her in at night, her own mother being often out on the town with friends, leaving her husband and daughter to fend for themselves. But that one afternoon, when Clara was maybe four years old, was emblazoned on her memory. She'd had a fever, she'd been miserable but suffering as silent as she could.

Mama Octavia had been visiting some kin in West Virginia after a funeral. Daddy was still at work. Mama had sat next to Clara on her bed and sang with a beautiful alto that the little girl never forgot. Sometimes she still heard the notes vibrating in her dreams.

Baby mine, don't you cry
Rock a bye, sleep to find

Mammy's here, don't you fear
Sweet as pie, baby mine
Papa may go away
Sister, brother, gone to stay
Lay your head on the bed
And dream, baby mine

Tears streamed down her face by the time she finished the first verse. Tears she didn't know she needed to cry. More lyrics to the simple lullaby forced themselves from the depth of her memory and she kept singing, her voice tremorous and off-key.

The last notes of the final verse faded into the woodwork. Clara breathed deeply, regaining her composure. She made it a point to never think about her mother. If the purpose of the payment was to charge something painful, then the price had been dear indeed. She hoped the information was worth it.

"Thank you, Clara," The Man in Black said when silence had reigned for long moments. "Your offering is accepted. What I came to tell you is if you give that ring over to The Empress, she will rain down destruction on both our worlds."

Surprise knocked her back on her stool. "W-what do you mean?"

"Long as that ring exists, it will be fought over by those of us Over Here. It's the only thing that can make us as you are, that can give us a divine purpose."

"Give you one, or allow you to steal someone else's?"

A shadowy hand appeared and waved off the sentiment. "Whoever possesses that ring will be able to control every spirit willing to place themselves into debt for a chance at a destiny. For a chance to walk a path of fulfillment, even if we never actually find it. Footsteps are powerful. They can be directed, they can be stolen, they can be changed. But the path is the path, and having one is better than having none, even if you never locate it. That ring can give our footsteps a purpose, or take one away."

The shadows around him, forming him, swelled even more, leaving the tiny closet almost in pitch-darkness except for the sparks from his eyes. "Many would give everything they have for what humans take for granted."

Clara swallowed, unable to look away. She ran his words over again. "Is that what the ring is being used for? Stealing human destinies and then giving them to spirits? And whoever is controlling the ring is charging them for it?"

The glittering points of his starlit eyes grew brighter. Shadows parted to reveal a moon-white smile. "Those in debt are rarely satisfied with the terms of their deals. And those who think they can control the ones who owe them are often surprised."

His words were cryptic, but the meaning was clear. Selling destinies to Enigmas was stirring up some trouble. "Who's responsible? Who is stealing and selling our destinies?"

The Enigma did not answer.

"Why are you telling me any of this at all if you won't name the one responsible?"

"We can speak no lies, but we are also, at times, prohibited from speaking the truth," he purred.

Clara frowned, unsettled by both his words and his nearness. The shadows pulsed, brushing against the tip of her nose before retreating again. The barely-there contact repulsed her. It was both oddly intimate and terrifyingly enticing.

"Something is stopping you from telling me who's responsible?" Clara guessed. "A ward?"

The glittering smile shined again through the darkness. All the answer she would get.

"You have Israel trying to get the ring from whoever has it now—are you saying you're planning to do something more altruistic with it?" Much as she wanted to remain polite and respectful, she couldn't keep the skepticism from her tone.

"I would like to prevent the war that will happen if I do not get the ring."

Did that mean The Empress would start a war? But he wouldn't? Clara's mind was racing.

"Why come to me and not Israel? He's yours, I'm not." She tried to edge out of the way of the shadows but there was no use, they were clinging to her now.

"I wanted to meet you in person," The Man in Black replied. "This human spoken of in such reverent tones. Clara Johnson. The seer. I needed to see who you are for myself."

Spoken of by whom? She scanned what she could make out of his features. It wasn't much. The smile had thankfully dimmed, and so had the eyes, somewhat. But the shadow touch was still upon on her, like soft spiders crawling up her face.

"Even if I could trust what you're telling me, if I do get the ring and give it to you, I won't get free. I'll still be indebted to The Empress."

"It is true I cannot free you from her bonds. But are you certain that she will?"

Her chest grew suddenly tight. "She said she would. Your kind cannot lie."

"There are many ways to tell the truth, young seer."

He coalesced into the most solid form she'd seen of him yet, the most man-like, with broad shoulders and a long torso. "Thank you for your song and think on what I've said." The spirit sketched a low bow, and then was gone.

The glow of the single flickering candle returned to normal, illuminating the closet and making it seem bright after the period of near pitch-darkness. Clara was left discombobulated by the visit—a shakiness had invaded her muscles. She stood on wobbling legs, nearly forgetting to blow out the candle first.

Was The Man in Black trying to manipulate her, to work against The Empress through her? She had no desire to get embroiled in a war between powerful spirits, but in a way, she already had as soon as she agreed to steal the ring.

And if what he'd said was true, how could they let any of the Enigmas get the ring now?

25

THE SCRYING JAR

Clara left work the next afternoon, mind clouded in the same haze she'd been attempting to think through all day. Focusing was difficult. Her fingers had been like mallets on the keyboard and she'd had to retype one article three times to get it right. Mrs. Shuttlesworth had eyed her curiously from the next desk, but hadn't voiced any questions, for which Clara was grateful. She had no answers.

Out on the street, wading through the fog-like humidity of the evening was little better. She hoped she could get herself home in one piece, when Mama Octavia popped up beside her.

"Do you know what that scallywag is up to right now?" she asked, hands on her ample hips.

"Which scallywag are we talking about?"

"Your Israel Lee."

She stiffened. "He's not mine. And I'm not his personal secretary." Her grandmother raised her brows at Clara's sharp tone, and Clara closed her eyes. After a deep, calming breath, she gave an apologetic expression and was silently grateful she hadn't gotten a swat on her backside.

"He's headed over to Bowlegged Mo's office at Club Bengasi."

"But Mo's in jail. He get out?" She squinted in confusion. Mama Octavia's glare spoke volumes. "Israel went to see Madame Josephine?"

The woman nodded grimly.

"Now?" She blinked, looking around her as her heart raced. "Dammit."

She hadn't known he'd go so soon. Though there really wasn't time to waste.

She turned in the direction of Club Bengasi before Mama Octavia popped up in front of her, blocking her path. "Now wait a minute there, gal. What you're not going to do is march into a gangster's office after that boy."

Clara clenched her jaw as her fists tightened. "He's going to get himself killed or worse."

Passersby on the sidewalk gave a wide berth around the young woman apparently talking to herself. The strange glances just made her irritation grow.

"So what you gonna do about it?" Mama Octavia asked. "Between him and Jesse Lee, they have a better chance of getting out unscathed than if you waltz in there all willy-nilly."

Clara crossed her arms obstinately. Concern for Israel warred with the lingering fear that he really was going to try and take the ring for himself. "I need to know what's going on in that office."

Mama Octavia's frown deepened. "You gonna risk a look Over There?"

When she was a young child, before she'd learned control over her abilities, she would sometimes get uncontrolled visions of things happening in other places. Her grandmother scrubbing a floor at the hotel where she worked. Her daddy fitting together intricate pieces of wood at his carpentry job. Her mother tangled in a pair of unfamiliar bedsheets with a light-skinned man.

It was called scrying, and once she was able to stop doing it unwillingly, she'd never delved into other folks' business again. "I wouldn't even know how to anymore," she admitted to her grandmother. "Not on my own."

Mama Octavia pursed her lips.

"Israel is headed there now?" Clara asked.

"Driving over in his shiny Ford. Where you going?" Her voice rose as Clara took off down R Street.

"To find someone who can help."

There wasn't much she could do to save Israel if Josephine or whoever else took his destiny. She'd tried to prevent him from even being in this situation, but the next best thing was to know what was happening. To satisfy the gnawing curiosity within that was gorging itself on the threat of being stabbed in the back.

Three blocks later, she turned up 14th Street and quickly found herself standing before a little shop wedged between a tailor and an insurance company. Fading gold paint on the window announced *Mystic Wonders of the Spirit World. Fortunes Told.* She rolled her eyes and entered.

The interior was dark and smelled strongly of incense. On the shelves, candles of all colors, heights, and thicknesses stood in neat rows. Other items for sale included a wide variety of dried herbs, charms and trinkets, shells, beads, glass balls, and multicolored gemstones. Near the cash register stood a display of dream books, including an entire row of one with Uncle Nazareth's name emblazoned proudly on the front. Twelfth edition.

A beaded curtain separated the front from the back, and the old man himself appeared a few moments after Clara's entry. The ready smile on his face morphed into a scowl when he caught sight of her. "What you want?"

"Good afternoon to you too. Is that how you treat a customer?"

"You a customer now? You not here to put me out of business?"

"I'm here to *do* business."

"Well, what is it, then?" He glanced at the space Mama Octavia occupied, then back to Clara.

"I need to scry someone. Quickly. Can you do that?"

Uncle Nazareth's forehead creased. Clara pulled out her wallet and waved a few bills in his face. He pressed his lips together and turned on his heel. "Follow me." Then he slipped behind the curtain.

She trailed him down a short hallway to a room with a small round table in the center and two plush, comfy-looking chairs on either side. This must be where he did his consultations.

There was a longer table pressed against the wall. This one held an altar of sorts, with well-used candles, small wooden figurines, a scattering of bones and cowrie shells, and a large copper cooking pot filled with water sitting on a hot plate.

"The great Clara Johnson can't divine on her own?" Uncle Nazareth asked saucily, crossing the room.

"I don't do things this way, and I don't want to open myself up to whatever's Over There just now. Things are...tense."

He frowned, scratching his ear. "I've felt that too."

"You been seeing the folks Afflicted with that...malaise?"

His lips twisted. "Can't do nothing for them. Something heavy and dark is controlling things. Don't need to draw their attention my way."

His gaze turned assessing. "That's what I was doing last time I seen you. On a house call seeing to a man whose wife had lost all her faculties. Stopped going to work or caring for the baby. I've seen a half dozen cases all the same."

"Those folks are disappearing after a while?"

He nodded sadly. "If they're not tied down, they wander off and don't come back. Never seen anything like it in all my years."

Clara blew out a slow breath. "I haven't been able to help them either."

The regret obvious in the slump of the man's thin shoulders knotted in her belly. If they hadn't been at odds these past years, she might have come to him for information. Maybe they could have worked together. Whatever else he was, charlatan or huckster, he must have some kind of real connection to the spirit world to sense what he had. And he obviously cared for the people in the community.

"I'm looking into it too," she said, "trying to figure a way to stop it."

He looked at her with begrudging respect. His demeanor shifted, some of the hostility melting away. "Sit down there." He pointed to the round table.

Uncle Nazareth brought out a large mason jar from a cabinet against the wall and placed it next to the copper pot. He filled the clear jar with water from the pot, then brought a white handkerchief over, laid it down in front of Clara, and carefully smoothed it out. Next came four tea candles set at the corners of the handkerchief, forming a sort of cross. Then he placed the jar in the center of the cross.

From his pocket, he produced a slim vial and added three drops of a blue liquid into the jar, then stirred it with the blade of a knife pulled from a sheath at his belt. The clear water turned a vibrant blue. Into this, he sprinkled powder from another small vial concealed on his person, all while whispering a string of words too low for her to hear.

Finally he stood across the table from her and motioned for her to stand as well. "Who is it you want to see?" His voice was thick and full, much different to its usual reedy tone.

"Israel Lee."

He made no reaction to her request, just focused on the water in the jar. He bent over the table, placing his palms flat, just next to the candles.

Slowly the surface of the water in the jar began to ripple and a blurry image of a man's hands took shape. Clara sucked in a breath.

"You can see it too?" Surprise colored his voice.

She nodded. Uncle Nazareth grunted. "It's 'cause you have the sight. Usually I have to narrate for folks."

"Is that him?"

"You'll see through his eyes."

Israel was seated inside an empty nightclub. Clara had never been to Club Bengasi, but this must be it. The place was dimly lit, tables bare of their tablecloths. He drummed his long fingers against the scarred wood, tapping out a subtle melody. The only person in view was a woman mopping the floors.

A guard approached. Clara recognized him from the distillery, but it was not the enormous Thaniel Dawson. The guard's lips moved, but no sound came out.

"Can we hear?" she whispered, looking up.

Uncle Nazareth tapped his ear three times, then sprinkled something else into the jar, causing the image to scatter. Sure enough, tinny sound emerged from the blue water. She watched the events unfold as if they were happening in a photoplay at a movie house.

Israel stood, his footsteps echoing through the empty room as he followed the broad-shouldered man through a doorway and up a set of dark stairs. They emerged at a landing where Jesse Lee stood guard outside the only door. Jesse Lee gave his cousin a nod that seemed to communicate something, before opening the door and following Israel inside.

Madame Josephine sat behind a large, messy desk in a flowing ruby-red caftan. Diamonds ringed her neck and flashed in her earlobes and on her fingers. This close, Clara realized the woman was a bit older than she'd thought. Her face was covered in thick layers of makeup and her hair wrapped in a turban which matched her gown. She rose to greet Israel with a kiss on both cheeks, European-style.

"Israel Lee, how is my favorite musician today? And what is this business proposition that brings you to me? Of course, you know you don't need an excuse to come and see me." She looked him up and down lasciviously, then fluttered her lashes. Clara clenched her fists.

"Please sit. Would you like a drink?" she asked, already turning toward the bureau with a variety of bottles on display.

"Thank you," Israel said as she poured them both scotches. She handed him the glass, then perched herself at the edge of her desk, crossing her legs so that a high slit in the side of the caftan revealed a long, shapely leg.

Israel cleared his throat, took a sip of his scotch, and then began to whistle. Josephine's brow furrowed with confusion at first, but soon smoothed out. She blinked several times and then smiled vacantly. Through the magic of the divination, his song neither hypnotized Uncle Nazareth nor gave Clara a headache. But Madame Josephine's eyes became droopy, and she slumped until she was practically lying on the desk, the glass dangling from her fingertips.

Israel rescued the woman's scotch and set it on the table. He looked behind him to find Jesse Lee focused intently on the woman, apparently immune to the Charm. Israel gave a hand signal and Jesse Lee removed a pair of earplugs from his ears. Clara smiled.

Israel turned back to Madame Josephine. "Where did you get that ring from?"

"Which ring?" she said, stretching out on the desk like a cat.

"Makeda's ring."

She swallowed, the loopy, dreamy look dropping from her face as one of fear replaced it. "How you know about that?" The silky tone of her voice roughened as some pretense was dropped.

"How'd you get it?" His voice was amiable and calm.

She shook her head. "Can't talk about that. Can't take it off either.

I've tried everything. Even tried cutting my finger off, but it won't go. Only *she* can take it off."

Israel shot a look at Jesse Lee. "*She?*"

Josephine rolled to her side and propped her head on her hand. "Lilia."

Both Clara and Uncle Nazareth hissed. The old man must have dealt with that Enigma as well, or at least heard of her.

"Lilia? Who is that?" Israel asked.

"I been knowing Lilia for years." Josephine waved a hand in the air.

"Is she…is she an Enigma?" The woman nodded. "She gave you your talent? Singing opera?"

Josephine grew agitated. "No. I worked hard. Studied. Trained. Toured all over the world. *Madame Josephine.*" She lifted her arm, tracing her name on an imaginary marquee. Then her expression sobered. "But I got older. My voice started to get weak. Too much liquor, maybe." She laughed without humor.

"Lilia promised me a wealthy man who would love me and take care of me. 'Course she didn't say he'd be a gangster. But Mo loves me true." Her voice got dreamy. "Yet and still, she taught me how to manage things if he ever left. I am a rich woman now."

"And the Trick?" Israel's tone was cautious.

Josephine groaned dramatically. "Got to let her in. Let her Embrace me every few days. She takes over and does whatever she wants and I got to deal with the consequences." Her gaze grew sad and she struggled to right herself into a seated position.

Dread filled Clara. That was the worst Trick she'd ever heard.

Israel stood and helped Josephine, then handed her the scotch again. She downed it all in one gulp and smacked her lips. Then blinked, seeming like she was coming out of it.

Jesse Lee took a step forward and the woman's expression grew vacant again.

"Israel?" She grinned up at him. "You come here to take what I been offering you?" She looked over at Jesse Lee. "He can watch."

Israel's gaze shot down to his feet for a few moments. Clara imagined the embarrassed look on his face.

"You know what she does when she Embraces you?" Jesse Lee asked, voice low.

Josephine stood, wobbling, and headed over to refill her drink. "Makes me rich. Makes herself rich. She's still teaching me, so she says. A bigger operation, more workers, less cost. She just goes on and on and on about it."

"Wait, how can an Enigma be rich?" Jesse Lee asked.

"They deal in debts, Tricks. Tricking humans is a pastime, but tricking their own, that's real wealth. She steals our footsteps and promises them to the spirits."

"Our footsteps?" Both men looked at each other with confusion.

"The path we walk. Our destinies. Lilia says destinies are wasted on the no-count niggas who ain't got nothing going on in their lives. Says we don't deserve them." Josephine shrugged elaborately.

"She's giving human destinies to Enigmas?" Israel enunciated each word as if struggling to believe it.

"*Selling*, not giving. All them spirits owe her now. And she ain't done. Got a big sale coming up." She downed another glass of scotch and swayed where she stood. Israel leaped up and helped her back into her chair before she fell.

"You say you can't get the ring off?"

"Only *she* can take it off when she's wearing my skin." Josephine's eyes were closed now and it seemed as if she was slipping into sleep.

"And you can't undo what Lilia's done? Return the destinies? Restore the people?"

"Hmm? She bound me from using the ring at all. Only she can, when she's me." Her voice was slurred from both drunkenness and the effects of Israel's Charm. He must have turned it on high.

Israel shook her gently. "When is the big sale?"

"What's that?" She sniffed, opening a single eye to gaze up at him blearily.

"The big sale you said she's planning. When and where?"

"Oh, she's aiming higher now. Low-class Negroes got low-class destinies, she say. She wants more. Wants those uppity niggas who go to the galas at the Whitelaw. Those the destinies that will sell real big. She wants every single last one of them. Gonna auction them off."

Jesse Lee stared at his cousin in horror.

"She gon' kill me she finds out I told you." Her head fell back to the chair. "But maybe it's better that way. Can't live like this much longer." Tears slipped down her cheeks.

"How does she target the people she Afflicts?" Israel asked. "If you can't stop it, maybe there's another way."

Josephine opened her mouth to answer when gunshots rang out from downstairs. Clara jerked, startled. But Josephine just slid her eyes toward the door, an annoyed expression on her face.

Jesse Lee pulled the pistol from his holster.

"Take her memories," Israel hissed. "We can't let Lilia know she talked to us."

Jesse Lee nodded, gun in hand as he stared back at Josephine in concentration.

Another loud *pop, pop, pop* sounded downstairs and the door burst open. Thaniel Dawson had a battered Springfield 1903 rifle in his hands.

"It's Crooked Knee Willy's folks," he said, voice calm, though Clara noticed a splatter of blood on his shirt. Perhaps it wasn't his own. "Out the back way." He motioned with his head toward a curtain in the corner.

Jesse Lee raced over to slide open the curtain, revealing a scarred door with a number of dead bolts. Unlocking them all took precious moments that had Clara's stomach in knots. Finally, he wrenched open the door, which led onto a covered back porch.

Josephine, however, didn't look like she was ready to go. "That rat bastard Willy don't take no for an answer. He think he gon' come and shoot up *my* place?" She put her hands on her hips and looked like she was ready to meet bullets with a tongue-lashing. Clara felt a kinship with the woman.

Israel looped an arm around Josephine and began towing her toward the open door. She didn't resist, because of the Charm or her own good sense kicking in, Clara wasn't sure.

Jesse Lee led the way with Thaniel bringing up the rear as they hustled Josephine onto the porch and down the narrow metal stairs attached to it. The gunfire continued, growing louder as they hit the ground and raced down the alley.

"Into the Hudson," Thaniel shouted. Parked at the mouth of the alley was the gleaming red automobile. The bodyguards bundled Josephine into the car, with Israel watching the back of the building they'd emerged from.

Two figures dashed onto the porch, guns in hand. Clara recognized young Wallace Thurman and the other thug she'd seen at the Fairy Ball. Two more gangsters she didn't know followed behind them, but Josephine's Hudson was already peeling off down the street.

Israel melted into the foot traffic on V Street. Clara couldn't tell what he was feeling or see the expression on his face, but her own heart was racing. It probably wouldn't settle down for some time.

She straightened from her position, back stiff after leaning over the table to stare into the mason jar for so long. She took a ragged breath as the image in the water disappeared.

Uncle Nazareth's aged eyes held hers for a long moment. "Well, damn," he said, a haunted expression on his face.

"Damn is right."

26

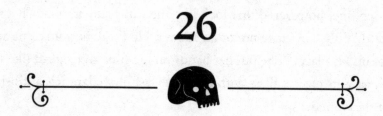

A RECKONING

Are you willing to pay?

The Empress's words echoed in Clara's mind once the spirit disappeared. Clara had raced home from Uncle Nazareth's and immediately called to the Enigma once again to try to get answers about Madame Josephine and Lilia. And once again, the spirit had left Clara more frustrated than ever—and worse than that, afraid.

"I told you that this was war," The Empress had hissed, the smoke growing denser and her form becoming more defined. "Lilia is my enemy."

"You could have told me that an Enigma was controlling the ring. That it can't be removed except when Lilia is Embracing Josephine." She recalled The Man in Black's warning that while Enigmas couldn't lie, the truth was a malleable thing.

But the Empress froze. That information appeared to come as a surprise to her. Then she chuckled. "Quite clever. Well, you'll have to take it from Lilia, then." She made it sound all so simple. "It should not be that difficult. The Charm I gave you is very powerful."

Clara wasn't touching that topic again. "And what will you do once I take the ring? How do you plan on using it given you don't have a corporeal form?" Her voice rose as The Empress's eyes narrowed.

"Focus on what you can control. Your task is to liberate the ring from that loathsome harpy Lilia. Place it in the box as I instructed. Gain your freedom."

"Will I?" Clara asked. "Gain my freedom?"

The Empress leveled her with a glare. "My word is my bond. I will remove your Charm *and* your Trick once this is done." Though the words should have been reassuring, they were anything but. Clara wanted to scream.

"And what about the destinies that Lilia is stealing? The people whose lives she's destroying? Are you going to restore them?"

"The only chance to save those people is to liberate the ring. Deliver it to me. I will end this war as well as their suffering." The Empress's voice softened to a purring coo. "Freedom has a cost, Clara. The cost of yours is this ring. The question now is, are you willing to pay?"

"I'm not sure anymore."

All pretense of softness crumbled and the Enigma's expression transformed into rage, showing her mercurial nature. "Well, maybe you need more incentive," she snapped. "If you go back on our deal and do not get me this ring, then I will take something from you as well."

Clara's breath caught. "What could you possibly take from me? You already have my debt."

"You humans only think of our power in your world, to help you get the things you want. But you have a spirit guardian, do you not? The essence of your grandmother exists in *my* world." Her voice grew cold and hard. "She has not chosen to move on to the Next Place. Her existence thus far has been calm and peaceful. Do you not wish for it to remain so?"

The smoky face smiled a terrifying grin that sent waves of alarm through Clara's body.

"You'd hurt Mama Octavia?" Her grandmother was already dead, but Clara wasn't so naïve as to assume that a ghost couldn't be harmed. That her spirit and soul weren't vulnerable to the whims of a powerful, angry Enigma. Thoughts of her grandmother's soul being tortured or going mad or even devolving to a Gray made Clara wince and clutch her stomach.

"Get me that ring!" The Empress faded away, snuffing out the candle on her exit.

Are you willing to pay?

The cost, as usual, was going to be great.

"Walters was a dead end," Aristotle announced as he entered the butcher shop's storage room and settled heavily onto the one wooden chair, blowing out a breath. Clara had been alone until his arrival, pacing the length of the small space. When she turned to him, she was surprised and gratified to find he wasn't glamoured. He wiped a hand across his weary face.

"The distillery manager? What happened?"

"Jesse Lee phoned me this afternoon saying that Walters was leaving Madame Josephine's office with one of the guards, heading to the new distillery. Thought if I followed, I could find out where the new setup is. Maybe even talk to Walters."

He crossed his legs, brushing imaginary lint off his trousers. "I took a chance when Walters stopped in at a drugstore. I approached the car where the guard was waiting and disguised myself as Walters. Tried to get him to spill the location of the new place, but the real man came back quicker than I'd thought." Aristotle chuckled. "Never seen somebody so confused. One minute, the poor guard was talking to who he thinks is Walters, then I drop to the ground and the real man comes out the store."

Clara smiled. "He must have thought he'd lost his mind."

"I know I would have." He started laughing again and pulled out a handkerchief to wipe his eyes. "But I didn't get the location. And it looks like Walters will be holed up there for the foreseeable future. I heard them saying he wasn't leaving for at least a couple weeks since they lost money after the raid and need to run the stills around the clock to make it up."

Disappointment settled over her. A dead end indeed.

"Did manage to find out that all the workers caught up in the police raid have been let go, odds are they're out at the new place now."

Just then Israel and Jesse Lee walked in, nonchalant as you please for having been in a gunfight earlier. Or at least in the vicinity of a gunfight.

Israel did a double take at the glare Clara directed his way and paused midstep. Zelda appeared right behind him, tugging off her blood-spattered apron. She scooted around him to sit on the crate next to Clara. At some point, Aristotle had donned his Clarence character and lounged in his seat in a sharp gray suit.

Looking only at Zelda, Clara relayed Aristotle's news about Walters and the Afflicted who'd been arrested.

Jesse Lee, oblivious to the tension crackling from Clara's direction, added, "Yeah, Madame Josephine is keeping all news of the new location locked up tight. She thinks one of her people tipped off the cops about the last place, so she's only using folks that have been with her a long time."

Clara crossed her arms. "Anything you boys want to share about where you been this afternoon?"

Israel removed his hat, then sat on a crate. "Seems you already know. I went to talk to Josephine." He related everything that had happened in Josephine's office. The only things he left out were the woman's more flirtatious comments and actions. Jesse Lee added some color to the story, making it sound like they had escaped under a hail of bullets from a squadron of trained militiamen. Clara rolled her eyes, but didn't begrudge him the enhancements.

"What did Crooked Knee Willy hope to gain by sending his thugs in like that?" Aristotle wondered.

Zelda had produced an apple and was busy chomping on it. "Intimidation. If he shoots up the place, maybe she'll get scared and leave. Though it don't sound like that's in danger of happening."

"She's a much tougher lady than I assumed," Clara said, still not looking at Israel.

He leaned over to her, trying to catch her eye. "I know you don't like it, but it needed doing. We never would have known about Lilia or the destinies or the gala otherwise."

She conceded his point, but wouldn't admit it. "You're lucky that you were talking to Josephine and not Lilia, weren't you?"

He took a deep breath. "Very lucky."

"Otherwise you'd be Lord knows where, bottling hooch and staring off into nothing all day. Not to mention all the holes you could be shot full of right now." She tapped her foot, continuing to look anywhere but at him.

Israel cleared his throat. "I didn't get a chance to ask her where the other Afflicted are being held or how she's targeting them in the first place."

"She said something about footsteps," Clara said. "Just like The Man in Black."

"The Man in Black?" Israel sat back, bewildered.

Clara realized she hadn't told any of them about how the Enigma had appeared to her and quickly ran it down. Israel's expression morphed from confused to horrified.

"*You're* lucky he was feeling helpful," he said. "Still don't see why he came to you with that."

"Me neither, but what he said matches up with what Josephine told you about Lilia. And it stands to reason that if *we* don't want to be indebted, then neither would the spirits. I suspect whatever she's charging them for a destiny is high."

"So it's not about the workers at all," Zelda said, still crunching her apple. "They're just the by-product of the destiny theft."

"Some extra bodies that Madame Josephine is taking advantage of," Aristotle added.

"She got more than she needs, that's for sure," Jesse Lee said.

The thought of an auction for destinies brought to mind the slave block. Their people in chains, sold like animals. Mama Octavia had been sold more than once, but didn't speak much of slavery days. Clara couldn't blame her.

"Well, she's about to get even more bodies if Lilia has her way. And there'll be no keeping Washington's elite in a bootlegging distillery." Clara's jaw tightened. "It would help if we knew how she was actually taking the destinies."

Aristotle tapped his foot on the ground in a rapid beat. "Footsteps? Didn't you say something about the shoes of the Afflicted in the warehouse?"

Clara turned to face him. "They had this grit they were all tracking around the place. We crawled through it."

Jesse Lee slapped his leg. "Foot track magic."

Clara swore. "Can't believe I didn't think of that."

"What's foot track magic?" Zelda asked, tossing her apple core into the bin in the corner.

Jesse Lee grew animated. "Old conjure man I met down in Louisiana talked about stealing the dirt from footprints, using it for hexes. Some folk deep in the country walk around with brooms to wipe away their prints so no one can steal them and get up to mischief."

"It's possible," Clara began, "that the Afflicted folks walked through some foot track powder somewhere and that's how the ring targeted them. A spell using footprints that targets their path of destiny."

Zelda frowned. "Since all the Afflicted folks we know or seen so far have been young and poor, could be somewhere they all go."

"Or a few somewheres," Clara said. "Maybe in the alleys or parks. If we go looking, we'll probably find the powder spread around places just waiting for folks to walk through it."

Israel's expression darkened. "Well, that would be almost impossible to stop. And can't be all that convenient... Explains why Lilia is planning to trap folks all in one place for her next big destiny haul. The Whitelaw Hotel is having one of their galas on Saturday, that's where Madame Josephine says Lilia's going to steal the destinies of the 'Luminous Four Hundred.'" He glanced at Clara as he used her terminology. "If she succeeds, she'll have full control over the Colored folks in this city."

Clara was feeling even more surly than usual. "Half of me wants to let them suffer. They don't care when people on 7th Street or the alley folk are in trouble, anyone they consider low-class, but we supposed to run to the rescue as soon as they're in harm's way?"

"How they act ain't always right," Israel said evenly, "but at the end of a white man's noose we're all the same."

Clara stiffened.

"The Klan don't care about a paper bag test," he continued. "They don't care what high school we went to, what our last name is, if our grandparents were free or slaves. Colored folks, no matter what class, need each other. Ain't nobody gonna stand up for us but us. In biology, it's called symbiosis. Two organisms living close together, working for the benefit of both. Professor Hansberry taught us about a concept they have in Africa—in Swahili it's called *utu*. In Zulu, the word is *ubuntu*. It translates to 'humanity,' but what it really means is 'community.' I am because we are. Our humanity is tied together."

"Our destinies are tied together too," Aristotle added. "That was in that research paper. The author mentioned another concept from the

Akan people in West Africa—the only way to discover your destiny is through your community." He looked around. "Our people were torn from their land, couldn't speak their language or pray to their gods anymore, got split into house Negroes and field Negroes, had their families torn apart and sold off, and then go on to perpetuate the same biases on each other. It's no wonder our destinies were ripe for the plucking. But we have to break the cycle."

They were all quiet as the weight of his words sank in. Some of Clara's vexation eased. Both men were right, of course.

"You think their destinies really are worth more?" Zelda asked softly. Eyes lowered, she played with the frayed edge of her apron. "I never thought too much about my own before, but I sure ain't saving the race or starting a bank or building grand buildings."

Her tone was more dejected than Clara had ever heard, and it abraded her skin. "Their destinies aren't worth more," she said quietly. "Being rich and educated and privileged don't make you a better person."

But she had been wondering more about her own purpose. Was she on the path she was supposed to be, and if not, how did she get back onto it? Dr. Woodson's words had never been far from her mind—*was* she pursuing happiness? What would that even look like? She'd never taken a moment to sit down and consider. But her freedom, just like that of her people, had come at a heavy price. Was she making the most of it?

"So what do we do?" Zelda asked, shoulders slumped.

Clara released the tight grip she'd had on her arms. "Lilia will be Embracing Madame Josephine at the gala for sure. She'll need to be if she's to steal the destinies there. We get ourselves into that party and stop her."

Everyone nodded in agreement, knowing that was far easier said than done.

Silence reigned again until Jesse Lee wiped a hand down his face and sagged back against the wall. "All this talk of destinies and souls and spirits got me feeling like I need to go to church more."

Israel snorted. "What do you think Pastor Montgomery back home would have to say about all this?"

Jesse Lee straightened, tucking his thumbs into the straps of his shoulder holster as if they were suspenders and affecting a marble-cheeked Southern drawl—an apparent impression of the pastor. "The Lord taketh and the Lord giveth away. Set your troubles on the hill and don't let them roll back down."

Zelda snickered. He was a good mimic and really got into the performance.

"If you pray twice on Sunday, pray three times on Monday, and don't let the devil catch you in your Friday drawers on Saturday."

Clara held back a laugh, turning it into a cough. Jesse Lee rocked back and forth on his heels and she got the impression that Pastor Montgomery was a rotund man, in danger of toppling over at any point while making the same movement.

"Even a Good Samaritan doesn't give away his last ear of corn, unless it's into the collection plate. But I don't want to see no corn in that plate, ya hear? Both Uncle Sam and the Lord on high require valid US tender."

Clara couldn't even hold back her laughter any longer.

"God made the world in seven days, but the church addition has been one step away from being built for seven years, and it don't take seven wise men to understand why. The good book says, 'Whoever sows sparingly will also reap sparingly,' and some of y'all are planting nothing but chaff in that collection plate. We need the wheat, my brothers and sisters, so that we may reap generously!"

Aristotle held up a hand to stop him, having nearly fallen out of his chair. Everyone else was holding their sides, gasping for breath.

"Now, I've gotten some complaints about the odor coming from some of our parishioners. Genesis tells us that the Lord God formed man out of the clay of the ground, and some of y'all think that means you need to be covered in dirt from sunup to sundown. Cast off the dust from your feet before you step into the Lord's house. And wash your behinds! Let us remember that cleanliness is next to godliness, and our good First Lady, Mrs. Montgomery, has no desire to smell the funk of all the Lord's children."

Clara looked around at the people gathered here and for the first time felt truly grateful to be a part of this team. Zelda caught her eye, as she wiped the tears from her own, and shook her head. Clara let the warmth fill her until it had nearly banished the fear.

At least for tonight.

27

A TRIP TO JAIL

"Associated Publishers, how can I help you?" After a brief pause, Mrs. Shuttlesworth held out the receiver. "Clara, it's for you."

Clara's head jerked back. She almost never got phone calls at the office. She crossed over to the office manager's desk and took the phone. "This is Clara Johnson."

"I've got us set up to visit Bowlegged Mo down at the jail. See if we can't find out where that new distillery is." Aristotle's voice resonated through the receiver with no preamble. "Israel wanted to make sure and let you know."

"What, was he too chicken to tell me himself?"

Mrs. Shuttlesworth's brows rose in chastisement of the obviously personal nature of the phone call. Clara offered an apologetic expression and ducked her head.

Aristotle chuckled. "Guess he didn't want his head taken off."

She sighed. It wasn't completely unreasonable.

Even though they couldn't free the Afflicted without the ring, finding all the missing people was still a priority. If they failed, at least they could let the families know what happened to their loved ones. And if they actually succeeded, they'd still need to locate the people to release them.

"You have a way in?" she asked.

"Officer Dudley is going to bring in two Colored lawyers to speak with Mo."

Mrs. Shuttlesworth took a stack of papers and left the room with a significant look at the clock on the wall, then back at Clara. The silent message: *Make this quick.*

Clara tapped her foot rapidly on the wood floor, then made a decision. "I'm going too."

Aristotle was quiet for a long moment. "Are you sure?"

The mere idea of going inside that building again made goose bumps rise all over, but she'd been having one of those feelings all morning. The ones she knew better than to ignore. At the mention of Israel's name it had flared brighter and hotter in her mind and she couldn't let it go.

"I need to be there," she told Aristotle. "Even if I don't want to ever go there again."

"You can get off work in about an hour?"

"I'll find a way."

They made plans to have Israel pick her up, and Clara hung up the phone. When Mrs. Shuttlesworth returned, Clara announced that she had to retrieve some documents from the print shop downtown that afternoon. With Samuel gone, she'd been taking on more and more errands for the office. Mrs. Shuttlesworth gave her a suspicious glare but didn't object, and before the hour was out, Clara gathered her things to go.

Israel's Ford pulled up in front of the office with Jesse Lee in the passenger seat. She squeezed between the two men again, both polite but subdued. She sensed it had more to do with where they were headed than anything directed at her.

They drove through the city, past the Capitol building to an area in Southeast overlooking the Anacostia River. The stone structure of the city's jail was fortresslike, not particularly tall, but cold, imposing, and harsh. Flashbacks of the night she'd been brought here in shackles replayed, unwanted.

Dragged from their house, bleeding and terrified, she and her father had been taken to the Emergency Hospital, where they patched her up quickly and deemed her well enough to be transported to jail. She had lived in this drafty building for almost two years.

The parking lot, located across from the building's wide front lawn, was half-full. The male prisoners were responsible for cutting the grass and pruning the large trees that shaded the narrow driveway to the main doors. A police wagon was parked in the small roundabout in front of the building, probably having dropped off a new prisoner.

Her breathing grew shallower as they sat in the car; Israel's gaze brushed against her. Fearing what he'd see if she met his eyes, she steadied her breath. "I'm ready. Let's go." He cut the ignition and they exited the vehicle.

Each step toward the imposing double doors was filled with dread. The lawn was parched in late summer and the strong smell from the river made her wrinkle her nose. But finally they were inside the lobby and "Officer Dudley" was there to greet them. His large belly strained against the buttons of his police uniform, and his craggy, sunburned face made him look the part, but the finger he swiped against his nose identified him as Aristotle.

"This way," he said brusquely, likely for the benefit of the front desk attendant who'd signed them in. He led them to the visiting room, a place Clara knew well. The chipped walls and flooring hadn't changed in three years and the peculiar smell—some mix of cleaning solution, body odor, and misery—clung in her nasal passages. Inhaling it again made her stumble. Israel, walking behind her, lent a steadying hand. She nodded in acknowledgment and worked to pull herself together.

"Only two are allowed to visit at a time," Dudley said. "You'll have to wait here." He motioned Clara to a seating area at the far wall of the visiting room. Small tables with three chairs each were clustered across the wide space. About half of them contained people, solemn prisoners with weeping or equally solemn family members, or harried-looking attorneys.

Clara sat as Dudley led the men to a table. A few minutes later, Bowlegged Mo was brought out by a guard. He was a large man with a medium-brown complexion. His hair was overly long and lye-straightened, but neatly combed. A well-connected gangster would enjoy certain privileges and deference in prison, and his clean, pressed shirt and dungarees were evidence of that. From her position, she couldn't tell if his legs really were all that bowed or if the nickname was an ironic joke like so many others.

She also couldn't hear their conversation, and since Israel's back was to her, didn't know how he was spinning his Charm—probably whistling again—but Mo sat and soon began to speak.

She kept her eyes on Israel's broad back, afraid to look away as fear and anxiety speared her. Maybe it had been a mistake to come, but she felt much better having her eyes on him as the feeling she'd woken up with intensified.

Something moved in her periphery and she reluctantly turned her head to find herself staring into the clear blue gaze of the dead policeman. He stood over her, somewhat menacingly, but she didn't look away, holding her ground until he blinked first. The fact that ghosts blinked almost made a chuckle rise from her chest, but she was in no mood to laugh.

Why was he here? What did he want? There was no point in asking, he'd never answered before. But today it seemed like he wanted something from her. He faded almost to nothing and then back into view once, then twice, tilting his head as if entreating her to follow. She wondered if he *couldn't* speak any longer, not just that he chose not to. Many ghosts who lingered lost the ability to communicate. Where was Mama Octavia when she needed her?

Clara shook her head, spreading her arms, communicating the fact that she didn't understand what he wanted. Then he faded in and out again, beckoning her forward.

He wants me to look Over There.

In this place? Full of misery and death? Though it wasn't as bad as the building it replaced a few decades earlier—one that had also held slave pens and was so poorly made that prisoners had regularly frozen to death inside during the winter months—the spirits that occupied this land could not be friendly.

She shook her head more firmly. "Absolutely not," she hissed. She didn't want anything to do with the spirits hovering about here and couldn't imagine what he was trying to get her look there for.

The policeman disappeared, she hoped for good. Only he immediately popped up across the room, right behind Israel. Clara straightened, dropping her arms. The ghost hovered near Israel, then swooped toward him and disappeared.

What just happened?

Gritting her teeth, Clara opened her second sight, removing the protective barriers and looking Over There. The spirit world lay over our own and, as she had expected, the jail was full of spirits. Ghosts of all kinds surrounded her, both human-looking and those so old they'd lost their forms and begun to decay, leached of all color. Using skills honed over a lifetime, she tuned them out, muting their spectral voices in her mind until she could focus on only one.

The policeman was clearly visible swirling around Israel, whose orange aura was bright and strong where it wasn't clouded by his

Enigma debt. Mo's shone with a calming yellow-green all the way through, while Jesse Lee's was a surprising gold.

Her sight gave her access to abilities long unused, and she managed to push out a repelling force to get the policeman away from Israel. The energy generated was stronger than she'd anticipated and the ghost blew away like tissue paper on the wind, disappearing from view. She shuttered her sight, closing a curtain on the auras and spirits and sinking safely back into the human world.

Except that her skin began to chill. She rubbed her arms for warmth, as a blast of cold air assaulted her. *Oh, no.* She stood suddenly, taking a final glance at Israel and Jesse Lee in deep conversation with Mo, and fled the building.

The searing heat hit her, but didn't penetrate. Today was the first day of September and it must be ninety degrees outside, but her teeth were chattering. Bright afternoon sunlight dimmed as the Grays surrounded her, blocking out the light. At least they'd followed her and not targeted the poor souls in the prison. She walked briskly underneath the trees until she was halfway down the main driveway before turning to face her pursuers. "What do you want? Why can't you leave me alone?"

No one was around to witness her talking to thin air, fortunately. She had no matches on her, nothing to create a ward with, and was sure that opening her sight again would only make things worse. She crumpled against the base of a leafy black oak, curling into a ball and resting her forehead on her knees.

"Go away! Please, just go away."

The icy chill that had overtaken her retreated a fraction. She shivered, but a hint of humidity managed to break through the cold. Clara lifted her head, surprised to see that even the darkness had abated a bit.

Dark gray cloudy energy still surrounded her like dense fog, but it wasn't on top of her, suffocating her, trying to strangle the life from her. She blinked, looking around.

"Farther away," she said uncertainly. The heavy mist retreated even more, leaving a perimeter of light and heat around her for several feet. Confusion and hope bubbled inside her, but before she could consider what this meant, the policeman was back, scowling at her from just inside the Grays-free area.

"You did this on purpose," she hissed. His eyes narrowed, but his expression was smug.

Anger drove out what was left of her fear. She wanted to scream, wished he was substantial so she could punch him. Wished she could shoot him again.

"I was in my home! In my bedroom!" she screamed, not caring if anyone could hear her. "You came to kill me!" Rage and pain and grief overflowed and her emotions seemed to agitate the Grays, whose swirling mass started to churn and heave.

They were the eye of a terrible storm. Crackles of power like flashes of lightning illuminated the thick fog.

"Leave. Me. Alone." Clara's voice boomed and the swelling mass of gray energy, the jumble of spirits which had invaded this world rippled, then shot out to the policeman, covering him completely. Tendril-like arms wrapped around him and sucked him back into their midst.

He disappeared from view. Clara's breathing came hard and fast. She was having trouble gulping down enough air. What was that? She'd never seen Grays act like that before... Were they *helping* her? Shaking, she leaned back against the tree and closed her eyes.

She didn't know how much time passed before the approaching footsteps crunching on the gravel drew her attention. Had she fallen asleep? When she looked up, the Grays were gone and Israel stood a few feet away. He was alone. He took one look at her and whatever he saw had him crossing the distance, crouching down, and drawing her into his arms. Part of her wanted to protest, but the larger part enjoyed melting into him as he tightened strong bands of protection around her.

Thankfully, no tears fell, but she was still shaken to her core. She buried her face in Israel's chest and breathed him in. Once she'd gotten herself together, she pulled away.

Unable to speak and put into words what she was feeling, she nodded at him in gratitude. He stared at her with soft eyes, but didn't speak. He merely helped her up and led her to the car.

"Jesse Lee?" she asked as she slid into the sun-heated seat.

"He's taking the streetcar back to Madame Josephine's. Didn't want to be seen with me right now. There could be questions."

"So what did Mo say?"

"He doesn't know anything about the Afflicted, or where they might be—it must have started after he was arrested. In fact, I'm starting to wonder if Lilia wasn't responsible for having Crooked Knee Willy *get* Mo arrested so that she could have control over his business."

"Wow, that would be smart."

"Yeah. He told us where the new distillery was, though. He'd been setting it up before he went down. Wasn't sure he'd have the workers to staff it and was scheming to bring up folks from down South—planning to keep them quiet by keeping them in debt to him like sharecroppers."

"Can't say I feel sorry for the man, then. But Lilia did him one better, she doesn't have to pay her workers."

Israel grunted. "Want to swing by the new place and take a look?"

She agreed and twenty minutes later they were idling at an intersection in Southwest, catty-corner to a large brick building. It was much bigger than the distillery on V Street and much more remote. The structure took up an entire block and stood between an empty lot and a grassy field. No signs of life dotted the neighborhood—this wasn't a residential area and the nearest buildings were boarded up.

Israel's grip tightened on the steering wheel. "There's no way to approach without them seeing you. No alleys to hide in. Nothing."

"Yeah, and no point in getting inside anyway until we have that ring. We should get going. Someone is sure to notice."

Israel gave the building a final appraisal before driving away. It was obvious they wouldn't be able to pull another stunt like the one they had the last time. Their only chance to free those people was to retrieve the ring at the Whitelaw gala.

The drive home was quiet, Israel leaving her to her own thoughts. When she realized they'd stopped moving for a long time, she looked up to find he'd parked in front of her building.

"Thank you for the ride," she said.

"We should talk, lioness."

Given his tone, whatever he wanted to talk about had nothing to do with the gala and their mission.

"I'm tired, so talk fast."

In her periphery, he shook his head slowly, but smiled. "You still mad at me?"

She snorted and rolled her eyes.

"I understand that you were worried about me talking to Josephine yesterday, but that's not everything, is it?"

She sat as far away as she could from him on the bench seat, pressed up against the window, but it was still close enough to feel the heat emanating from his body. Finally she turned to face him. "You did it and you walked away. If you hadn't, we'd be in dire straits right now. What else do you think it is?"

"I don't know."

Why'd he have to be so even-tempered all the time? The least he could do was get upset. But no, Israel Lee was almost always an unruffled sea. At least compared to her.

"What are you really upset about, Clara?"

Her nostrils flared as his dark brown eyes pinned her in place. "I. Told. You."

"And it has nothing to do with that kiss the other day?"

She blew out a breath and moved to open the door, but Israel stilled her with a hand on her arm. She froze at the touch and the reaction she had to it. "You're awfully full of yourself. I know women fall down at your feet on a daily basis, but that kiss wasn't nothing to write home about." Her voice didn't even quaver on the lie, for which she was proud.

Israel searched her eyes, his mouth offering just the hint of a curve. She pulled out of his grasp and scrambled out of the car before she did something she'd regret again. However, he got out as well, walking her to her door.

"I don't need your help walking twenty steps," she grumbled.

"I'm doing it anyway."

Arrowing her gaze into a fine point, she shot out, "I was worried about you. I didn't like that heifer draping herself across you and I was afraid. There, are you happy?"

Her anger dissolved under the force of her admission, leaving her bared. Exposing her soft underbelly felt wrong on many levels. She took a step away from his heart-melting expression, shaking her head.

"Don't come any closer, Israel Lee. You stay just where you are. We finish this thing on Saturday one way or another. Then I don't expect to see you darkening my doorstep again." Her back was pressed against her door and he stood in place, not moving a muscle, but gazing at her with that small smile that seemed to be growing.

"And don't think you can take liberties just because I kissed you. That doesn't mean anything and it's not going to happen again."

His smile only widened.

She spun around and fumbled to get her key in the lock. Finally, she wrenched the door open and stepped inside.

222222222222

Leslye Penelope

"Good evening," she said firmly and slammed the door.

She peeked through the window to find him standing there, brows raised, amusement coloring his features.

Again, she raced up the steps like she was on fire to get away from him.

272

28

CINDERELLA

W e need to talk fast, the fellas will be here in about fifteen minutes and doors open at nine," Israel said, checking his watch. The team was gathered in Room 5 of the True Reformer Hall, one of the smaller ballrooms available for rent. The District Rumblers were booked solid with back-to-back gigs the next three days, so their time for planning was tight.

Israel was dapper as always in a sharp gray suit. His tie was loosened and the top buttons of the creamy-white shirt undone. Clara did her best to focus her attention anywhere but on that bare triangle of skin.

"Where's Aristotle?" Zelda asked, looking around.

"Washing goofer dust off his hands," Clara said, wrangling her focus. Her own palms still stung from the stuff, though she'd washed her hands twice.

"Do I want to know why he was covered in graveyard dirt?" Jesse Lee asked, raising his brows.

The ballroom doors swung open to reveal a lithe, gray-haired white man in a crumpled tan suit. He had an aristocratic sort of face with cold blue eyes that swept over them all as he entered then shut the door behind him. Everyone froze, staring at the newcomer with a mix of confusion and shock. Everyone except for Clara.

"Still stuck?" she asked.

The man rolled his eyes. "Damned hoodoo hex dirt," he grumbled.

"Aristotle?" Zelda blurted, looking him up and down.

Clara twisted her hands together. "He came with me to get what we need for the glove and box to store the ring in. But we, ah, had a little accident with some of the conjuration materials. Turns out rootwork and Charms don't mix well. He can't change his glamour."

"It's happened before," Aristotle said, stuffing his hands in his pockets. "Should wear off in a few hours. Until then..." He shrugged. Israel shot him an apologetic look.

"But why were you a white man in the first place?" Jesse Lee asked, perplexed.

"Had to go over to Brookland to get what Clara needed for the work. Thought it would be easier if we went as a white man and his maid. Two unknown Negroes alone in that neighborhood...Didn't want to take the chance."

"Uncle Nazareth didn't have the particular elements that The Empress asked for," Clara continued. "Pointed me in the direction of a lady who would. An old-style conjure woman who works as a cook over there in Northeast, one of them big houses."

"Apparently she works with more dangerous tools than he does," Aristotle said. "Should have been our first clue."

"Can't tell you how sorry I am." Guilt made her ears burn, but he waved her off. To the others she explained, "In the taxi back over here, we hit a bump. The jar with the dust wasn't shut tight—my fault—and it got all over him."

Mama Octavia flickered into view. "Might could use some sulfur soap and rosemary water," she said, stroking her chin.

"After we get done here we can try that," Clara said. By this time, no one even fluttered an eyelid at her responding to thin air. "So how does everyone stand with our plan?"

Israel had moved to a chair in front of the low stage, tuning his guitar. "Wasn't no trouble to get the Rumblers swapped in to play at Saturday's gala. The real problem will be getting the band that had been booked there another gig. Don't like taking work away from anyone. Times out here are too tight."

"They should be glad they won't be there to get their destiny taken," Clara murmured.

"Might be, if they know," he responded amiably.

"Let me shake some trees," Aristotle said. "I know plenty of folks needing professional music, if the players aren't too high-minded about their clientele."

"I know these fellas, they're, ah, used to a variety of audiences," Israel said diplomatically. "Long as it's paying."

"Another Fairy Ball?" Zelda asked, perking up.

Aristotle chuckled. "Not quite so grand as all that. But they'd appreciate an upgrade from the old Victrola."

"Well, *I* got a problem," Jesse Lee announced. Everyone swiveled toward him. "Josephine's brought in some outside security for this weekend. A trio of heavy hitters down from Chicago."

"You think she suspects anything? Could she remember something about you from the other day?" Clara asked.

"Not possible. The memories of me and Israel are gone. I think this has more to do with Crooked Knee Willy. Thaniel says these Chicago niggas are some real roughnecks. *He* doesn't even want to be working with them."

Clara swore under her breath. Jesse Lee needed to be in place at the gala. As close to Josephine as possible.

"You any good at waiting tables?" Zelda asked. "That seems to be

Clara's go-to for these types of things." She smirked at Clara's unamused expression.

"You think a Pullman porter is just there to carry luggage?" Jesse Lee teased before sobering. "But I would hate to step on Miss Clara's toes." The words were said amiably, but there was a challenge in his eyes.

"An event this big, they'll need to hire on a lot of staff," she said. "No reason we can't both do it."

"Have you figured out how to get hired on yet?" Aristotle asked. "Old Louis Gaines runs things at the Whitelaw. It's a pretty tight ship down there. You need at least three references and an in-person interview just to sweep the floors."

Clara's mouth worked. She'd been unceremoniously shown the door that afternoon when she'd stopped by the hotel to inquire about employment for the gala. Unlike most places, which used an agency to staff big events, Louis Gaines acted like he was interviewing potential disciples for Christ.

Aristotle continued, a gleam in his eye. "Now, maybe if someone were to mess with the man's memories a little bit, make him forget a few things, he wouldn't notice one of his new employees was a mite unfamiliar."

Clara ground her teeth as smiles popped up all around her. She narrowed her eyes at everyone until their faces were wiped clean of all mirth.

"Such a thing might could work for one, but not two," Jesse Lee said, stroking his chin. Clara could swear the hint of a smile was trying to break through.

Zelda leaned forward, obviously enjoying this. "Sounds like everything is falling into place. The District Rumblers will be playing, Aristotle will do what he does best—provided no one's working any hoodoo—and Jesse Lee will get hired on as staff. That leaves you,

Clara." Her eyes blinked innocently, but the devil hid in her smile. "You gonna test old Mr. Gaines's memory or you gonna take a chance?"

Those were fighting words if Clara ever heard them.

When she returned to Henry's tailor and dress shop, the owner was at the cash register checking out a dapper gentleman who couldn't keep his eyes off the man's gorgeous face. For his part, Henry was very businesslike and professional, giving the customer a warm—but not too warm—smile as he left, garment bag in hand.

"Well, if it isn't Cinderella," Henry exclaimed, expression much brighter as he came around the counter, pulling a wrapped piece of candy out of his pocket. She smiled sheepishly. "Are you finally ready to take your place at the ball?"

Throat nearly closed because of nerves, she merely nodded. Her so-called team had neatly boxed her in and the only way to fight them was, in essence, to fight herself.

"Bit-O-Honey?" Henry asked, offering her a sweet.

"No thank you," she replied as he popped one into his mouth.

"I still have those gowns I picked for you." He paused, eyeing the tension in her limbs. "Or would you prefer something a little more... benign?"

Clara took a deep breath and shook off the fear. "I trust you, Henry. Whatever you think would look best."

The smile that overtook his face made her think of angels singing. It was no wonder Aristotle was smitten, it was hard not to be. He disappeared into the back and emerged with the same brightly colored gowns that looked more like sweet confections than clothing.

You can do this, she told herself and kept chanting the mantra when she stepped into the dressing room and tried on the first dress.

In front of the three-way mirror, Clara gazed at her reflection. Henry had pinned up her hair to get it off her neck and given her a gorgeous sparkly necklace to try out with the dress, which was in a shade he called periwinkle. The soft blue-violet fabric floated around her legs like spun sugar. She felt like a stranger was looking back at her.

"This dress looks like it was made for you. You're quite lovely, Miss Clara Johnson." She felt the sincerity in his voice. His words echoed Israel's from days ago; she still wasn't sure she believed them, but she was trying.

Mama Octavia rippled into view next to Henry. Clara met her grandmother's gaze in the mirror and was shocked to see tears in the woman's eyes. She was the most stoic person Clara had ever met, but now she was blinking and shaking her head as if surprised at herself. She faded away a moment later, but Clara wasn't upset. Dealing with rogue emotions was difficult, especially when you'd spent your life protecting yourself from them.

"You sure it's all right to borrow this? It's so fine."

Henry's eyes glittered. "Sweetie, I might just let you have that one. I can't imagine anyone else being able to do it justice."

"Don't be daft. I wouldn't have anywhere else to wear it."

"One thing tends to lead to another. First a gala, then a cotillion, then a banquet." He ticked them off on his fingers. "Before you know it, you're dining with the king of England himself. I have a feeling you're destined for great things, Miss Johnson." His radiant smile cut through the caustic response she might have given.

Even with all that jive he was spewing, she was already thinking about ways to pinch her already thin pennies even further to be able to pay him back for the dress. It only needed minor alterations and Henry promised her it would be ready by Friday. After changing back into her own clothes and bidding him goodbye, she stood outside on the sidewalk feeling a bit lost. Like the clock had already struck twelve.

Mama Octavia returned, back to her formidable self. Her eyes were dry and their dark brown depths were fathomless. "I'm proud of you, child," she said, voice gravelly as always.

"Proud? What for?" Clara tilted her head.

"You're slaying dragons in there." She nodded to the dress shop. "I know that going to the gala as a guest isn't something that makes you comfortable. But you're rising to the challenge. You wasn't meant to hide yourself away like you do, missing out on all the world has to offer. You're a young woman, and you should live. Why else did you buy your life back?"

Clara wrung her hands, shaking her head slightly. "Sometimes it just feels wrong, rubbing noses with the talented tenth. Isn't that all Mama wanted to do? Isn't that why she left? Feels like I'm betraying Daddy—and maybe myself—by being around them, pretending I'm one of them." Her voice rasped with the admission.

Mama Octavia glided as close as she could. The faint wisp of a ghostly touch stroked Clara's face. "You don't have to hold yourself back because of what your mama done, gal. She wanted the high life to plug a hole in her soul, what you're doing is for other people, to help them. Even your Trick, much as you hate it, tries to help folks. It's all you ever done. Don't let what she did hold you back your whole life."

A tightness overwhelmed her throat and rose to tug at her eyes. Clara nodded, unable to speak.

Mama Octavia cleared her throat, retreating and straightening, done with the rare display of emotion. "But what I came to tell you was that Uncle Nazareth is looking for you. He asked me to come find you."

Clara frowned. "How?"

"Did a weak-ass summons, but I been keeping an eye on him, so I allowed him to call me. Says he's got something for you."

His shop wasn't far from Henry's place and she walked over with curiosity overflowing. When she opened the door, the bell danced and chimed; Uncle Nazareth was standing behind the counter looking like he expected her.

"Clara." It was the first time he'd ever greeted her civilly, and shock stole her voice. He looked to the space where Mama Octavia hovered and nodded. "Thank you, Miss Octavia."

Her grandmother snorted, and Clara approached. "Do you see spirits, Uncle Nazareth?"

"Not like you do. Wasn't born with the sight or nothing like that, but my granddaddy raised me. He was old when I was born and his father came over from Africa. Learned a lot at his knee, and I keep myself attuned to the spirit world in various ways."

As she drew near, she took in the solemn lines on his weathered face. A few wisps of gray hair poked out beneath his white turban. "I had a dream about you, Clara Johnson. Woke up this morning and made this." He held out a small pouch made of black flannel and tied with a red string. Even amid the scents of incense and candle wax permeating the shop, the pouch's odor was clear and sharp. Not precisely unpleasant, just strong and pungent.

He offered it to her and she scanned his face before accepting. "It's a protection mojo bag. The strongest I can make."

She was touched by the gesture, especially given their differences. Whatever was inside the bag had some weight to it, though it wasn't exactly heavy. The soft fabric of the flannel was old, the edges stitched up carefully. "What was your dream?"

Standing in front of his many product displays, including his personal dream book meant to translate images from folks' dreams into winning numbers in the local gambling racket, she held her breath awaiting his answer. Many so-called spiritualists had their own dream books and they were all filled with rubbish, but somehow she knew that right now Uncle Nazareth wasn't trying to sell her any chicanery.

He settled his old eyes on her, the whites yellowed with age, and squinted. Now he was seeing through her, back to the dream. "You were surrounded by storms. Twisters like I grew up with back in Kansas. Turning and churning and sweeping you up until you *were* the storm." He blinked, focusing back on her. "You were the storm, Clara, and it was tearing you apart."

She swallowed to clear the lump in her throat and stepped away.

"Wear that on you somewhere," he said. "For protection until this is all over. You got to fix it each time you expect to walk into danger. Repeat the ninety-first psalm at least three times to fix the conjure. And wear it as close to your heart as you can."

There was an artlessness to him that she'd never seen before. And while she didn't put stock into hoodoo and conjure and didn't think she needed his kind of protection, she nodded gratefully and grasped the pouch in her hand. Would it really do any harm? "Thank you. Do I owe you anything for this?"

He waved her off. "No. 'Course not." She turned to leave the shop. "Besides, the price you're about to pay is already plenty."

She spun around and stared, but his lips were now pressed together. A chill descended over her. Had she really heard that or were her ears playing tricks on her?

A little clay figurine on the shelf next to the door caught her attention. She paused, examining it. The doll was in the crude shape of a man lying down flat, arms at its sides. She'd seen something like that before, only a larger version.

"Uncle Nazareth, in the Bible, God made man out of the clay of the earth. You ever heard about spirits making their own bodies that way, so they could leave Over There and come live here?"

He tilted his head, thinking. "I reckon that might be possible, at least for a short time. Though to really live, a spirit would need more than just a body to house their soul."

Clara nodded. "They'd need a destiny."

Mama Octavia's gaze shot to her, and Clara flattened her lips.

"One more question. Do you know how to force an Enigma out of an Embraced person?"

As Uncle Nazareth spoke, Clara listened carefully, a plan coming together in her mind.

29

SHAVE AND A HAIRCUT

Israel Lee lived on the first floor of a row house on W Street. It was a quiet block with old, leafy trees shading the sidewalk from the setting sun's light. Clara climbed the steps and entered the building, pausing for a few moments before rapping her knuckles in a simple rhythm on his door.

After leaving Uncle Nazareth's she'd walked for a long time, thinking back on the last few weeks, the things she'd done, the things she'd seen. Then she'd turned her feet in this direction, reluctant at first, but with each step, her purpose shined brighter.

Israel answered the door wearing only his undershirt and trousers and a face full of shaving cream. His eyes widened to the size of saucers at the sight of Clara on his doorstep. Before he could utter a word, she held up a hand.

"I'm here to see Jesse Lee."

He blinked, then stepped aside, ushering her in. "He stepped out for groceries but should be back directly. That boy is trying to eat me out of house and home, so I made him go himself. I have a show in an hour, but you can wait... if you'd like." He sounded uncertain, and she paused just inside the doorway, inhaling his clean, spicy scent before stepping past him.

His apartment was neat but sparse. In many ways it mirrored her own with the couch, coffee table, armchair, and folded cot in the corner. Jesse Lee's open suitcase was on the floor beside it.

Israel only had a kitchenette with a two-burner hot plate, not a full kitchen, and along the wall where the table should be leaned a line of guitar cases. An upright piano blocked some of the light from the side window.

He stayed quiet as she looked around, taking in how he lived and what was important to him—all the little things you learn about a person from seeing their home. Her cheeks heated under his reciprocal perusal of her.

"It meet your approval?" he asked, a smile in his voice.

She shrugged, jutting her chin up. "It'll do."

He chuckled and shook his head, then went off down the hall to the bathroom. Clara followed. He left the door open as he finished shaving, all but inviting her to watch. She recalled crouching in the corner of the tiny bathroom at that G Street house, Mama sitting on the sink, eyes squinted in concentration as she ran the straight blade over her daddy's cheeks. Clara had loved the scraping sound it made. She'd been warned the razor was sharp and she should never touch it, so she would content herself with fading into the background while her parents shared a quiet moment with no arguing and fussing, no accusations or denials.

Clara watched Israel from the doorway, silent as a mouse, not wanting to interrupt or make any kind of noise that would leave her accidentally responsible for a slipup that might mar his perfect face. He leaned forward toward the mirror, eyes on his reflection, the scrape of the blade the only sound.

Entranced, she couldn't tear her eyes away. Now, as an adult, she recognized what an intimate activity shaving was, and why her parents had never fought while they did it. Israel's movements were controlled, precise, and for some reason had her blood heating to an uncomfortable temperature.

When he paused, she realized she had made a sound—something embarrassing—and rushed from the room, regretting coming here. She sank into the leather armchair, both dismayed and delighted to find it smelled of him.

In the bathroom, the water ran. Israel appeared a few minutes later, patting his newly shorn face with a towel.

"So what you need Jesse Lee for?" He perched on the coffee table just in front of her.

She swallowed. "Just wanted to go over something about the mission. An idea I had. But . . ."

He was sitting awfully close to her, staring at her with those liquid-chocolate eyes, warm and sweet. She lost her train of thought looking at him and tried to reel it back in.

She sat back in the chair as far as she could. He leaned forward, not letting her retreat. His scent was practically wrapped around her, loosening her tongue. "What do you want from me, Israel Lee?"

He tilted his head and grabbed both her hands, uncurling them so they fit in his own. "Anything you're willing to give. Your time . . . A smile . . . A scowl . . . I wouldn't be opposed to a kiss."

She obliged him with the scowl and he chuckled. "You think you can put up with me?" she asked.

A slow grin dawned on his face. "I think putting up with you would test any man's patience from now until kingdom come." He squeezed her hands. "But I was always good at tests."

That pulled a surprised laugh from her. And another unexpected emotion. She wasn't used to feeling wanted—or wanting in return. She'd turned that part of herself off to deal with a string of disappointments. Allowing it to flourish now, to admit that she wanted this man, was frightening and invigorating.

But if this was to go any further, then she had to come clean.

"If we get the ring, then one of us gets free and the other doesn't." She squeezed his hand to stop him when he went to speak. "We can flip a coin for it at the end, but if I don't lose my Charm, I need you to know what it is."

She took a deep, steadying breath. "I don't talk about it, and I don't use it, which makes The Empress angry. She says it's the greatest Charm she's ever given, though I suspect my natural-born gift had something to do with it, changed what she'd intended to give me and made it more powerful, but either way, it's something that nobody should ever have, so I'm glad she's not handing it out willy-nilly."

Israel listened, his attention focused and supportive, giving her the strength to continue. "With your Charm, you say you can't make folks do something they wouldn't have done anyway, right? You're just lowering their inhibitions?"

He nodded.

"Mine is different. With mine, I can get you to do whatever I want. Force you. Take over your free will and get you to do any one thing I tell you."

His face grew ashen, but he didn't let go.

"Judge Gould really did have a change of heart. He asked the courts to give me a new trial, I didn't have anything to do with that. But the new judge wasn't going to honor that request. Came all the way down to the jail, sat in that visitor room, and told me to my face, gloating. Didn't think I deserved one." She worked her jaw back and forth, hating the taste of the words she was about to say. "So I made him. Forced him to agree to the trial and allow me to plead self-defense. When he woke up from what I done, he tried to take it back, but it was too late. The district attorney knew he couldn't get a conviction again and let me go. Controlling the judge got me my freedom, but it stole a part of my soul. What *couldn't* I do? Who *couldn't* I control? I could get anyone to do anything once." She shook her head.

"No one was meant to be able to do what I did. Freedom or not. Even if it means we lose on Saturday and don't get the ring and everyone's destinies get stolen, I can't use it again. You understand? I can't." Her breathing had sped up and her voice started to shake.

Israel finally did what she'd been expecting him to—he released her hands and stood. But instead of walking away, he bent to scoop her into his arms, lifting her up and taking her spot in the chair, with her draped over him.

She wasn't crying, Clara Johnson didn't cry, but her emotions were running high. Now it wasn't just Israel's scent surrounding her, the man himself was everywhere, in contact with every part of her body. His strength and his soothing touch softened the rigidity in her muscles, causing her to sink into him like quicksand.

This time she didn't remember who kissed who. Their lips met and all thoughts blanked. If she didn't know better, she would have thought his cousin was here wiping away her memories.

Israel's hand cupped her jaw, then threaded through her hair to press her closer to him. She tightened her arms around his neck and let go of everything that had been holding her back.

Every sensation was magnified—his bare arms against hers, the smoothness of his cheeks gliding against her own, the slide of their tongues tangling together. Warmth in her center heated to boiling and she was completely lost.

When Israel pulled back, she went to chase him, not ready for it to be over yet, but the key turning in the lock shook her free of her stupor. They broke apart as if scalded and rushed to their feet.

When Jesse Lee walked in the door, Clara and Israel were standing awkwardly in the center of the living room, breathing hard. Jesse Lee took one look at her mussed hair and his cousin's twisted undershirt and turned right around again, ready to walk out.

Israel laughed. "Hold on, I'm late to my show, so you might as well stay. Besides, she came to see you." He turned to Clara. "You gonna come out tonight to hear me play?"

Her face was hot, her lips were swollen, and she'd forgotten why she'd come here in the first place. But reality made an appearance in her brain once more. "I won't be good to anybody tomorrow if I start keeping musician's hours."

Israel smiled, unoffended, and ran a hand through his hair, then appeared to realize he wasn't fully dressed and disappeared into the bedroom.

Jesse Lee moved to the kitchenette with his grocery bag and set it on the counter. "Glad to see y'all finally working it out," he said wryly, unpacking.

Shaking the dust from her mind, she was still catching her breath when Israel rushed out, nattily attired in a brown summer suit, and grabbed one of the guitar cases from its place against the wall. Jesse Lee's back was turned and so Israel stole a quick kiss from Clara before winking and heading out the door.

She leaned against the wall, fanning herself with her hand. "Y'all could stand to open a window in here."

Jesse Lee chuckled. "You want something to eat? I'm frying up some ham."

She *was* hungry and any meal she didn't have to make herself was welcome. "Thank you."

"So you came to see me?" he asked, still bustling around the tiny kitchenette.

Clara snorted. "I know we didn't quite get off on the right foot, and haven't always seen eye to eye..."

He grinned over his shoulder. "Don't reckon you see eye to eye with many. But that ain't necessarily a bad thing."

She shrugged. "I've been thinking some more about what we have planned for Saturday, and I need to ask you for a favor."

He raised his brows but listened without interrupting to what she had to say.

30

THE WHITELAW HOTEL

Didn't nobody quite believe that boy when he said he was going to start a bank. What kind of Negro *starts* a whole bank? Not the son of a railroad man who didn't have more than three months of schooling in his whole life. We shook our heads and scoffed and laughed behind, and in front of, his back. He'd been a farmer and worked in a sawmill. Carried hod for the bricklayers and ended up gathering those boys into a union. Managed to get their wages raised a dollar a day. Then convinced the workers to let him invest their money. Took thirteen dollars and fifty cents and turned it into thousands.

And sure enough, John Whitelaw Lewis started Industrial Savings Bank in 1913—the only Colored bank in Washington—just like he said he would. And he wasn't done.

When he came round selling twelve-dollar shares in the new hotel he meant to build, we already knew not to question it. Like with the bank, the hotel he named after his mama was designed by a Colored architect and built by Colored builders. It was the only first-class, luxury hotel for Negroes in Washington, and the largest in the entire country. And he built it entirely with Negro money.

And wasn't it grand? When it opened, there was a five-day celebration. Twenty thousand people came through that week, eyes sparkling with pride and jaws dropping at the splendor. *Look at what we built!* There were murals on the walls and ceilings, elaborate woodwork, stained art glass, and more. Guest rooms and apartments ready to house the folks turned away everywhere else in the city. Finery to rival any white hotel. Proof of what we could do for ourselves.

The Whitelaw Hotel had hosted many a gala, and didn't nobody expect for that evening in early September to be any different. Cars and limousines pulled up to the front door, depositing their elegant passengers. The event was being sponsored by one of those snooty social clubs to honor some-damn-body or another and all of Negro high society was on the guest list. Regular folks gathered across the street to get a glimpse of the big to-do.

By some miracle, the hottest band in town, Israel Lee and the District Rumblers, had been booked at the last minute. The volunteer in charge of entertainment still wasn't certain how it had happened, but she refused to look a gift horse in the mouth and basked in the praise of the entertainment committee and the other organizers. *What a coup!*

Inside, the places were set, the silver polished, and the staff suited up and ready to go. The dining room manager, a tight-jawed man named Mr. Gaines, walked the line of servers standing stick straight for inspection with their backs to the wall. Though he was getting on in years, his mind was still sharp as a tack. Or it least it had been until this week. He'd forgotten where he put his keys twice, and had arrived at his house with two full loaves of bread in his grocery bag. He also had no recollection of hiring the broad-shouldered, dark-skinned server on the end, but the young man's uniform was crisp, his shoes were shined with military precision, and his chin was high.

Gaines ran through his standard speech, the same one he'd often been given as a young man working downtown at the Willard Hotel where he'd served presidents and princes. Then he sent his staff on their way. Just another party at the Whitelaw. No reason to believe this night would be different than any other.

No reason at all.

Clara ran her hands up and down the soft material of her gown's skirt. Her head felt light and her palms had begun to sweat; she didn't want that distracting her from her mission. The mojo bag was tied to her brassiere, resting in the valley between her breasts, as close to her heart as she could get it in this outfit. She'd worried that the smell would be overpowering, but once she'd put it into place and repeated the ninety-first psalm like Uncle Nazareth had instructed, the odor dissipated, leaving a light, pleasant scent that she actually preferred to the cheap perfume she almost never wore.

Aristotle walked beside her along the sidewalk in front of the hotel. He was in character as the same famous vaudevillian performer he'd used at the Lincoln Theatre. She'd wondered about mimicking anything from that ill-fated evening, but he'd reasoned that the smart set knew and loved the character, and it would be easier for a minor celebrity to gain entrance without an invitation.

They swept through the double doors, held open by uniformed doormen, and entered a magnificent lobby. Overhead, the colorful art glass ceiling panels glowed. Her feet sank into thick carpeting and she wobbled on her brand-new strapped heels as they walked past columns sporting detailed plasterwork designs. As they neared the ballroom, lively music filled the air. Israel's band wasn't playing yet, or if they were, he wasn't using his Charm since her head wasn't aching.

She kept an eye out for Zelda and Jesse Lee. The last time she'd seen her roommate had been as they approached the building together.

Instead of joining her as a guest in another of Henry's fabulous dresses, Zelda had dressed in her black pajamas outfit.

"I'll be better use to you all if no one sees me," she'd reasoned at their planning session. Clara wasn't sure about that, but there'd been no dissuading the stubborn heifer. Zelda had disappeared around the side of the hotel, looking for another way in where she could stay hidden until she was needed. Clara just hoped she stayed out of trouble.

"You have the box, right?" she asked Aristotle for the third time.

He replied with the patience of a saint, "Still have it." He tapped the breast pocket of his jacket. "And you have the glove."

If it hadn't been literally sewn with the thread of a dead woman's burial clothes, she would have put it on then—her palms were slick enough to slide off any surface. With her nerves on fire, a wave of dizziness overtook her and she stopped for a moment to settle herself.

The ballroom was at the center of the building, down a short flight of steps. However, the entry was clogged with something of a logjam. Tall, tuxedoed figures stood before her, blocking her view, but when voices began to rise up ahead, the crowd quieted to listen in.

"Who is in charge here?" an imperious woman asked. "I demand to speak to the person responsible."

A tightly controlled male voice replied, "You aren't on the invitee list, Mrs. Redmon. I'm very sorry, there's nothing I can do."

Clara looked over at Aristotle nervously. These sorts of events were always technically invite-only, however, it was very rare for anyone important to be turned away.

"There are simply too many people expected tonight. The fire marshal has been giving us trouble, so we need to be certain not to overwhelm the space."

The irate woman was having none of it, obviously not caring about fire safety. More arguing ensued and others came in to calm the rejected guest.

Aristotle's eyes narrowed, taking in the scene. Apparently the woman being turned away was a prominent lawyer's wife. She'd been traveling overseas and not included on the list because the organizers hadn't thought she'd be back in the country. As profuse apologies were given, the event people stayed firm. No one not on the list was going to be able to enter.

Clara was ready to throw her hands up and turn around to leave, but Aristotle grabbed her arm. "I have an idea. Stay here." Then he disappeared around a hallway.

Clara stayed in line, sweat dampening her back. Was it her imagination or were people staring at her? Could they tell that despite the dress and the pretty clips in her hair and shiny necklace she didn't belong there?

Just as her anxiety was rising, a murmuring began behind her and people turned to see what the new ruckus was about. Glad to feel that the focus had turned from her, if it had ever even been on her, she finally turned around.

And tried to pick her jaw up from the ground.

W. E. B. Du Bois stood proudly, not fifteen feet away. He wore an impeccable tuxedo and greeted his fans and admirers graciously. The author, activist, and editor was like Negro royalty, and in a room of people consumed with their own self-importance, he loomed larger than all.

His presence was a shock to Clara's system. Her copy of his book *The Souls of Black Folk* was creased and worn from repeated readings. She blinked repeatedly, unable to control her shock as the thin, balding man accepted handshakes and claps on the back good-naturedly.

The crowd parted before him like the Red Sea, and Clara doused the urge to slink off and hide. She simply stared and was left nearly frozen in shock when he caught her eye. Before she could regain her breathing, he was standing before her.

"Miss Johnson. It's so lovely to see you again. I look forward to speaking with you about your work on Dr. Woodson's journal."

Shock mixed with confusion as Clara's tongue went dry. Just when she thought she was going to suffer an apoplexy, Dr. Du Bois scratched his ear then tapped his nose with his index finger.

Her eyes widened to the point where they nearly hurt, and she had the strongest urge to laugh. She squelched it, swallowing and looking around at the audience they'd gathered. A smug satisfaction came over her when she saw Addie Savoy and Dr. Alphonzo Harley toward the back of the crowd.

"Thank you, Dr. Du Bois," she said, pitching her voice loud enough for everyone to hear. "It would be my honor."

"Du Bois" offered her his arm and she accepted, allowing the riotous laughter to take over on the inside. Part of her was upset with Aristotle for not warning her, or more precisely with her own self for falling for the ruse, but the other part of her was enjoying this very much.

They approached the young man with the clipboard, who was just as awestruck as everyone else. Certainly Dr. Du Bois had been to Washington enough times and mingled with the Luminous Four Hundred, but he was still obviously the top rooster in this henhouse and everyone wanted to curry his favor.

"I don't believe I'm on the guest list," Aristotle said to the gaping man. "I apologize for the inconvenience and I completely understand if there isn't room for me here tonight."

The young man's face reddened and he began stammering. "Oh, oh, n-no. Of course there's room for you, sir. Please, we'll have you and your guest seated at the main table."

His head bobbed in a nod like it wasn't attached to his body properly and he waved a waiter over and whispered furiously at the man— probably with instructions to rearrange the seating.

Clara almost felt bad, but a glance back at Addie's and Harley's faces, both mottled with shock and jealousy, made it all better. Plus, they were ultimately doing this to save these people's lives. She didn't remember ever feeling so light and airy before.

Hope filled her, dissolving her nerves. They had managed to get into the gala, now they just had to get the rest of the plan in gear.

31

THE BALL

Entering the exquisitely decorated ballroom, Clara could see why the fire marshals would be concerned. Every inch of the space was filled with tables and chairs. She wasn't even certain how people could walk through the room to get to their seat, it was so crowded with furniture. Hundreds of people would be here tonight—so many destinies at risk all at once.

"Who are we honoring again?" Clara asked Aristotle as she clung to his arm, wending their way around the obstacles.

"No idea," he said through his smile as he acknowledged several more folks who'd greeted him.

Sure enough, the two of them were seated at the head table, positioned directly in front of the stage. It was actually the perfect placement and Clara was glad the change in plans had worked to their favor. Israel's band was on the stage playing the background music. She caught his eye as he sat strumming his guitar and he winked at her. Her cheeks heated before she turned away. The room itself was quite warm, the heat of the evening barely dissipated by the electric fans blowing from their perches near the ceiling.

Columns adorned with decorative gold filigree and elaborate cornices broke up the large ballroom. On the ceiling, a larger version of the intricately colored art glass from the lobby shone down upon the guests like a heavenly light.

Servers diligently marched to and fro, carrying hors d'oeuvres, pouring water into the glasses on the table, and adjusting place settings. Aristotle pulled out a chair for her and she settled into her seat, visually scanning the room and taking in all the various personalities present: a who's who of Colored Washington. There were teachers, preachers, principals, lawyers, professors, and prominent businesspeople. Researchers and historians, scholars and politicians—those who had held office under friendlier regimes. There were writers and artists and singers and so many others. People who kept the community going, like Israel had said, all working in their own way to improve the condition of the race, like cogs in a great machine.

Clara had always wanted to lump these folks in together, imagining they were all like Addie Savoy and Dr. Harley, snobbish social climbers. And while she still felt more of a kinship with the waiters and waitresses than those being served, everyone here was a link in the same chain. Many bridged the gap between the classes, having come up from poverty themselves and done work to lift others. Mr. Whitelaw himself was among that number. Certainly some were greedy and looked down upon those less fortunate, but to an angry mob of white folks they were all the same. And without a destiny they would all face the same terrible fate.

Clara settled, bringing her focus back to the task at hand. She had not yet spotted Madame Josephine. Could the woman have changed her plans?

The table filled with people who greeted Dr. Du Bois heartily and her warmly as well since she was his guest. Being in his orbit certainly changed how folks treated her. For his part, Aristotle played his role masterfully. He knew a great deal about the famous scholar he impersonated and was able to interact with others seamlessly, or at least it appeared that way. No one seemed suspicious at all and she was grateful for his Charm.

The soft dinner music continued and a woman in an impressive white gown full of crystal beading climbed the stage and stood before the podium.

"Welcome all. On behalf of the Oldest Inhabitants, the premier club of Colored Washington, we thank you so much for coming tonight. We have gathered to honor a great man, however, I would be remiss if we didn't acknowledge another very special guest. It has come to my attention that today is the birthday for Madame Josephine Lawrence, exemplar of the race and world-renowned operatic performer. Madame Josephine, please come join me."

Enthusiastic applause sounded and the woman in question emerged from a set of double doors behind the stage, making a grand entrance. She was surrounded by four guards all the size of Thaniel Dawson, who led them. This must be why Jesse Lee hadn't been asked to work this evening, for while he was tall and strong, these men looked like they ate whole cows for breakfast.

Josephine was a small figure in their midst, but they parted to let her through, one assisting her up the short staircase to the stage. She approached the podium and waved at the crowd, whose applause took a long time to die. She wore a formfitting red gown which glittered with sequins and crystals. A tiara graced her head and diamonds dripped from her ears and neck.

Clara immediately recognized what she hadn't before. This was obviously a different woman than the one Israel had spoken to in her office. Everything about her was changed, from the way she walked to the haughty way she turned her head. She was acting the role of the blushing coquette, but confidence and power oozed from her pores.

The real Madame Josephine covered her insecurity with vamping and flirtation. This creature barely managed to disguise her domineering nature behind a thin veneer of feminine wiles.

Jesse Lee appeared at the foot of the stage with an empty tray in his hand. He'd previously informed his fellow bodyguards that he was picking up other work to supplement his income, so there was no reason for him to hide from them. Israel, seated several feet behind Josephine on the stage, watched her warily.

"Thank you all for indulging me," Madame Josephine cooed. "I don't want to take any of the spotlight away from our honoree tonight, but I would love it if you all would help me celebrate my birthday. Each time I turn thirty is better than the last." She laughed prettily and the crowd joined her.

"And how wonderful is it that my favorite musician, Israel Lee, is here with the District Rumblers?" She turned, motioning to the band. Israel stood and executed a quick bow as the audience cheered. Then he signaled to his bandmates, who instantly took up a quick-tempo version of the "Happy Birthday" song.

Clara's head began to pound. She stood and excused herself from the table. Walking away, she met Aristotle's eye. He nodded at her and she took a deep breath, gathering her courage.

With slow, careful steps she approached the side of the stage where Jesse Lee stood near Thaniel Dawson and another guard. Josephine's other two guards were positioned on the other side of the small stage. The two men near Jesse Lee were ribbing him good-naturedly about his second job. Jesse Lee chuckled and shook his head, studiously ignoring Clara's approach.

Guests were still pouring into the ballroom and finding their seats. It wasn't odd at all for Clara to be standing here, as several others were gathered nearby as well, gaping at the celebrities onstage. After the band finished the song, and cheers of "happy birthday!" rose,

Madame Josephine broke into an impromptu operatic solo that held
the audience enraptured. Her voice was dulcet and rich. She sang in
Italian, and while Clara couldn't understand the words, the emotions
were clear. Aside from the ache in her head, she felt like her heart was
being ripped from her chest by the sorrow evident in the music.

The fact that Lilia could also make use of Josephine's talent while
Embracing her was doubly concerning. Again, dizziness spun Clara's
head. She planted her feet, breathing deeply until the spell faded.

When Josephine sang the last note, the audience exploded in thun-
derous applause. The standing ovation was unanimous and the singer
bowed, appearing truly touched by the praise.

As the crowd quieted, Josephine relinquished the podium back
to the emcee. The District Rumblers began playing their quiet dinner music. Israel's Charm filtered through every note. Jesse Lee surreptitiously slipped in his earplugs, and Clara sucked in deep breaths
through her mouth to withstand the pain.

The singer crossed the stage, nearing where Clara stood, as the music
wafted over the audience, calming them. Pushing them to relax and
not be alarmed, no matter what they saw. They would pay little attention to the events on and near the stage, lulled into complacency by the
gentle melodies on a night where they intended to relax anyway.

When Josephine had nearly reached the steps, Clara stepped forward and tapped Jesse Lee on his right arm three times. She thought he
was trying to catch her eye, but she kept her gaze locked on their target.

"Clara," he breathed, but she was already moving forward. If she
stopped now, she'd lose her nerve.

Thaniel and the other guard swayed on their feet, their shoulders
slackening as their memories blanked. Josephine stumbled, her eyes
going vacant. Clara raced up the steps onto the stage, steadying the
woman.

"Madame Josephine," she said, not wanting to reveal that she knew it was Lilia with whom she spoke. "Let me help you." She gently grasped the wrist of the hand bearing the ring of Makeda. This was the closest Clara had been to the ring. It looked so old and out of place there on her finger. Tarnished and dull amid the other glimmering precious gems. Displaying no hint of the power it contained. The mojo bag at Clara's breast warmed in the presence of danger.

Josephine came along compliantly, but Clara stopped just before descending the steps. "Will you take the ring off for me? Please?" The music swelled, Israel putting more power into it. It sizzled through Clara's skull like lightning and she sucked in a breath.

"Clara, I can't—" Jesse Lee's voice cut off, strangled. His forehead had broken out into a sweat from controlling the memories of the four guards, plus Josephine. He shook his head tightly, eyes wide and panicked. He couldn't hold them for long. They had to hurry.

She pulled on the delicate white glove she'd stuffed into her bosom. Her covered hand hovered over Josephine's ring finger. She brushed against the metal cautiously, then expelled a deep breath when she didn't fall down dead. The Empress was right about the glove's protection, and the ring was actually loose on the woman's finger. It should slide right off. Though she didn't have the specially prepared box still in Aristotle's pocket, she could at least hold the ring until she got back to him. She glanced up at Josephine's face to make sure she was still enthralled and met her empty gaze.

Suddenly, the emptiness filled and the woman's hollow expression became a sinister gleam.

Clara gasped and tried to pull her arm away from Josephine's grip, but the woman tightened her hold.

"Clara Johnson." The voice was hard and cold. Lilia was no longer playing a role. "Did you really think these meager Charms would work on an Enigma?"

Fear took over Clara's bones as Lilia began to laugh.

32

A DESTINY OF OUR OWN

Lilia shoved Clara away, forcing her to the floor. Then the Enigma shot Jesse Lee a quelling glare. "An impressive effort, Jesse Lee, but ultimately futile." With a flick of her bejeweled fingers, the guards on either side of him blinked, rapidly regaining their faculties. They looked around, confused.

Jesse Lee clutched at his throat as if unable to speak. Had she done something to him?

Clara struggled to get to her feet, but it was like she was moving through molasses. Behind her, Israel's guitar had stopped playing—the whole band was quiet—though she couldn't even turn her head to get a glimpse of him.

"Restrain him," Lilia said calmly, motioning to Jesse Lee. Thaniel frowned, but grabbed hold of the man.

"And her and him and him." Lilia pointed to Clara, "Dr. Du Bois," and Israel as Clara's hopes sank to the depths of hell. The guards fanned out to do her bidding, but from the corner of her eye she saw Aristotle drop his character completely and lower from his chair to the ground, crawling under the table.

"I should really be thanking you, all of you, but Israel especially," Lilia said, turning to face him. "For calming these people so well for me. Look at them all, meek as lambs." A disturbing grin split Josephine's face, twisting the woman's beauty with Lilia's warped intentions. "It is so much easier to take their destinies when they're not making a big to-do." She waggled her fingers.

Clara's guard had reached her and locked her in a tight embrace. As soon as he touched her, whatever spell Lilia had used to keep her from moving evidently expired. She struggled, kicking and writhing in his powerful hold, but given that his arms were the size of her thighs, her efforts didn't accomplish much.

The guard swung her around, and now she could see that Israel was restrained as well. The fourth guard was stalking through the narrow aisles between the tables, searching for Aristotle, who would be able to stay hidden from human eyes, though Lilia could no doubt still recognize him. The audience remained in Israel's thrall, sitting or standing calmly, many with little smiles on their faces as if they were enjoying their evening. How long would the hypnotism last now that he wasn't playing? He'd laid it on pretty thick, but eventually it would fade and hundreds of people would begin to panic.

Clara swallowed, her tongue thick and throat tight; she hated having the strange man's arms banding her. Fury mottled both Israel's and Jesse Lee's faces. Clara tried to contain the rage exploding from her and keep her mind working. Keep Lilia talking. At least then she couldn't start what she'd come to do, and maybe they could come up with a way out of this.

"You knew what we were planning?" she asked between gasped breaths.

Lilia snorted. "Josephine had a hole in her memory I didn't like the feel of. It didn't take much digging to figure out who could have put it there." She glanced at Jesse Lee and shook a manicured finger at him as if chastising a child. "And after that stunt at the distillery, I wasn't taking any chances."

She extended her hand to admire the ring and began removing all the other jewels from her fingers, tossing the expensive baubles away as if they were trash. "You could never have removed this ring from my finger, Clara Johnson. With the wards I placed on it, only another Enigma would have the strength to do so, and none would dare challenge me when I hold the only possibility any of them have for a destiny." She turned her hand, flashing the ring and grinning triumphantly.

"You have power already, far more than any of us," Clara said through gritted teeth as the arms around her tightened. "Why do you need our destinies?"

"Humans have squandered them since the beginning of time. All that purpose and possibility wasted." Her voice was velvet and silk with the hint of something otherworldly in its depths. It slithered across Clara's skin like a snake and caused goose bumps to rise. "We are powerful, so much more than you, and yet we were denied the one thing that makes life really *mean* something." Her lips curled in disgust and she motioned to the body she wore.

"Embracing a human lets us live as you do for a time, but it ends all too soon when we exit your bodies. What we really crave are destinies of our own. Every spirit ever denied one has longed for it, and I now have the power to give it to them."

"For a price," Clara said wryly.

Lilia laughed. "Nothing in this world or the next is free, little girl."

"And if you kill the humans in the process?"

The Enigma shrugged. "You all are born dying. Speeding it up makes no difference in the long run. And now these destinies will go to those who can appreciate them. Those who understand their value. They're actually priceless." She admired the ring on her hand again, smiling fondly.

Clara couldn't move her head much with the immense barrier of the guard behind her. There were no weapons she could reach. Each table was decorated with several candles—she could use their smoke and fire to call to the spirit world, or she could use her own innate ability, but for what? Lilia's words resonated inside her mind—only an Enigma can remove the ring. Despair washed over Clara. Along with a realization. *Are you willing to pay?*

The destinies *were* priceless, but so were the lives of the people who would be sacrificed tonight and those all over the world who would doubtless suffer in the days to come. Why stop with the destinies of the Colored folks of Washington? Who would be next? Was Clara willing to pay the price for their freedom?

"Gathering everyone together here is such an expedient way of collecting destinies," Lilia said, sounding pleased. "I don't know why I didn't think of it before. It's been so tedious, sprinkling foot track powder here and there, waiting for people to walk through it." She scoffed.

"Of course, it was prudent to do a few test runs while perfecting the process. But now, I think I will take what I came here for." Lilia straightened and cleared her throat as if getting ready for another performance. She closed her eyes and began chanting, low and slow, in a language Clara had never heard before.

The lighting in the ballroom dimmed as the ring of Makeda started to glow. It gave off that same multicolored light she'd glimpsed when she'd looked Over There, only now it was visible. In addition to the tendrils reaching out to all the people whose destinies the ring had stolen, a single ball of intense, fractured light grew around the ring.

Trembling with fury and desperation, her heart raging inside her chest, Clara used her second sight to tear down the veil between here and Over There. She was compelled to at least monitor the ring's power, perhaps even find some last-ditch way to turn the tide, but what she found arrested her thoughts. Alongside the many people who filled this ballroom were just as many Enigmas. They hung in the air, or sat on top of the people, or clung to the ceiling. Spirits in many different forms, some humanlike, some animallike, more than she'd ever seen gathered anywhere before.

But ghosts had no need of a destiny, so they were not gathered here—except for the one that appeared suddenly beside her. Mama Octavia hovered at her side with fear in her eyes. Clara had so rarely seen her unflappable grandmother truly afraid.

"We failed, Grandma," she whispered, throat clogging. "We couldn't stop it."

Lilia continued to chant and the rainbow light grew and swirled around her, hiding her in its depths. The light was almost beautiful, a whirling, mobile thing that seemed to have a life all its own. Tendrils stretched out from it, hundreds of them, preparing to latch on to every person here and bind their destinies to the power of the ring.

Glowing, twisting threads snaked toward Jesse Lee and Israel. One was coming for her too. It hovered just in front of her chest and she braced herself for its impact.

"Clara, look at me, chile." Mama Octavia's words penetrated the fear. "You know what you need to do."

Clara blinked, watching the thin strand of light try again and again to enter her, but for some reason it couldn't. She shifted, trying to find some relief from the pressure of the man's arms, and felt the mojo bag move against her skin. Was Uncle Nazareth's gift really protecting her from the ring's magic?

She looked up at her grandmother again. "What do I need to do?"

Mama Octavia slid to the side to reveal a familiar form wreathed in white smoke. The Empress. She hovered there just at the edge of Clara's awareness.

The Enigma's voice was quiet, but cut through the air like a blade. "If you want to defeat Lilia, you must let me Embrace you."

33

A FLARE OF TEMPERS

Lilia's chanting grew louder as the tendrils of her spell flew out all around Clara. Fear and despair and anger warred within her.

"Is this really the only way?" Clara whispered. Mama Octavia nodded sadly. Both knew better than to trust the Enigma, but if Clara could use her to stop this, she needed to.

Feeling battered and bruised, she gazed at the spirit who had brought her so much pain. This, no doubt, would bring more. "All right, then."

An Embrace required affirmative consent. It had to be entered into of the Embraced one's own volition, with no coercion. Though The Empress was still just a smoky formation in the shape of a woman, her eyes seemed to gleam with promise as Clara spoke the words. "I give you permission to Embrace me one time only for the purpose of getting the ring of Makeda away from Lilia."

The Empress's hazy form shimmered with an inner light and then disappeared. A moment later, the massive arms of the man still restraining her were the least of her discomforts. It was like she'd been caught in an enormous vise and squeezed. Her consciousness was pushed and pressed inside herself as the Enigma took hold of her body.

Clara could see and hear and feel—all her physical senses were still sending her information—but she was merely a passenger. The Empress had control of her physical self, including her mouth and the words which came from them. Terror couldn't begin to describe the feeling.

In a swift move and with incredible strength, The Empress shook off the guard holding Clara's body and leapt to Lilia's side with a feat of athleticism Clara couldn't have performed. She wrapped a hand around Lilia's neck and the woman's chanting ceased abruptly.

"You!" Lilia spat like a curse, recognition lighting her eyes.

The Empress dragged the woman closer until they were nose to nose. "I told you this wasn't over."

Clara couldn't sense the Enigma's emotions, but she felt the smirk on her own face—an indescribably odd sensation. Lilia's fists beat at Clara's body as The Empress squeezed the woman's throat. Then Lilia changed tacks and brought her arms down hard on Clara's, causing Clara to howl in pain—something only she could hear. But Mama Octavia winced. Her grandmother could still hear her. The Empress remained silent, but her grip was broken and she pulled back. Lilia attacked.

Being a woman with a naturally choleric disposition, Clara had been in her share of fights. This one was about the nastiest she'd experienced, and not being in control was the single most agonizing thing she'd ever been through. Worse than the terror she'd felt the night of the riots when she thought she would die, or the days and months spent languishing in jail. She'd gotten into several fights there as well, with hard women torn down by life. Other murderers: a woman who'd killed her abusive husband and one who'd stabbed her own father in the back. That opponent had been damn near six feet tall and strong as an ox and Clara had quickly regretted losing her temper with her.

This fight was different.

The opponents didn't care about the bodies they used—maybe they intended to heal themselves with their Enigma magic, or maybe, being incorporeal, they paid no heed to the physical damage they took— they fought in a way Clara had only witnessed before in the unhinged and mentally unstable. Whenever she used her own fists, she knew that even coming out on top, she'd be in pain. These spirits evidenced no such knowledge.

Clara howled into a void as the blows landed one after another, The Empress doing little to protect herself while seeking to rain pain down on Lilia. To distract herself from the frustration of not even being able to turn her own head to look around, Clara focused on Over There. Since the two Enigmas had Embraced humans, their spirits were locked in the human world, visible mainly as churning, darkened auras. The other gathered Enigmas watched the fight with excitement. However, dread thickened into a solid mass inside her when she found Grays swirling around, their presence growing.

The undulating mass of dark energy filled the ballroom like fog. The other spirits ignored it and none of the humans could even sense it, but Clara felt the cold on her skin, even through the pain of another blow to her face from Lilia. As the fighting Enigmas rounded each other, Clara caught glimpses of Israel and Jesse Lee struggling against their captors. With the destiny spell on hold while Lilia faced off against The Empress, the multicolored threads were still visible, but the ring hadn't yet completed its work.

Lilia kicked The Empress backward, laying Clara flat on her ass, so she got a good glimpse of the ceiling and the large grate above the door just behind the stage. She thought it was her imagination when the grate was shoved aside and a black-clad figure crouched there, inside some sort of hidden ventilation chamber, before leaping down.

Zelda landed on Thaniel Dawson's back, wrenching the man backward and forcing him to release his hold on Jesse Lee. The Empress rose again and the two Enigmas circled each other, so Clara only got glimpses of Jesse Lee and Zelda both fighting the guard. Zelda was doing her flowing martial arts moves and Jesse Lee looked like a bare-knuckle boxer, punching and ducking; they came at the man from both sides and appeared to be holding their own.

When she spotted Israel, he had finally managed to get free of his own guard—maybe Zelda's arrival was the distraction he'd needed—and the two of them were trading blows. Meanwhile, the Grays had completely filled the ballroom, though they stayed away from the stage. Were they avoiding the dueling Enigmas?

Instead of attacking Clara, which would have been bad enough—her worst fears were being realized—they were overtaking the crowd of humans, who had finally begun shaking off the effects of Israel's Charm. All too quickly the room devolved into chaos as the Grays did what they did best. The glittering, rich, and well-mannered "Luminous Four Hundred" of Washington began to pick fights with one another. The influence of the Grays was maddening them, making them lose their faculties and their inhibitions and inciting them to violence. Fists flew. Tuxedoed men and women in expensive gowns began wrestling, grappling, punching, exchanging slaps and scratches.

Meanwhile, Clara's body was reeling from the damage of the Enigma fight. All around was violence and she could do nothing about it.

The Empress danced away from Lilia's kick, but Madame Josephine's face still looked triumphant. "You will never get this ring. What would you even do with it? You don't have the same arrangement I have with my darling Josephine. Once you leave that body, do you really think that child will let you wear her again? Or will you content yourself with a body made of clay like the others?"

The Empress shook Clara's head and curled her split lips. "Do you really think I will *leave* this body? Once I get that ring, I will take this body's destiny as my own—use it properly—and all those who owe you for the destinies you've promised will then owe me. I will not make the same mistake as you, valuing wealth above all. You should have stolen your host's destiny first instead of waiting."

Lilia's smile dropped, and if Clara had control of her own heart, it would have stopped beating. She knew she couldn't trust The Empress, but she had stupidly not expected *this* betrayal. She had entered into the Embrace willingly, but had not given it a time limit. She'd thought her parameters were enough to ensure that she would get herself back, but apparently not. In the heat of the moment, she'd made a grave error.

Lilia began chanting again, backing away quickly, no doubt trying to fix her mistake and steal Josephine's destiny for good. But The Empress rushed her, tackling her to the ground and gripping Lilia's hand with Clara's ungloved one. Where her skin met the metal surface of the ring, it burned, but apparently whatever protections the ring bore truly didn't affect Enigmas the same way, for it didn't kill her. The Empress gripped Lilia's hand, twisting and trying to break her fingers.

"I will have this ring," The Empress seethed.

Clara's consciousness pushed outward, desperate to regain command of her body. But try as she might, she had no control. She had willingly given it to her enemy. Her mind spun.

The sounds of fighting surrounded her and Clara quieted her mind, looking out Over There once more, searching for anything that could help.

She spotted The Man in Black not far away, a dark, shadowy form in the shape of a large man, the outline of a top hat visible on his head. He was little more than black smoke, but she could feel his gaze on her. He was deeply invested in the outcome of this fight, yet hadn't intervened. Maybe he couldn't since the battle was in the physical world.

Inspiration struck. She couldn't control her body but she still had her mind and her power. She could still communicate with the spirits. Using all her strength, she summoned The Man in Black.

The Empress stumbled. "What are you doing?"

Lilia grinned. "Defeating you!"

"Not you, idiot. Clara. What are you doing?"

Clara didn't answer, watching as The Man in Black's form slid closer. He was a silent force next to her. Though he didn't speak, she could sense him waiting to know what she sought.

"I know you don't want either of them to have this ring," she said.

Lilia kicked out and Clara's leg crumpled beneath her. The Empress must have figured out this body wouldn't last much longer, and healing energy went through her limbs, restoring some of her strength and dampening the pain.

The Man in Black tilted his head. His glittering eyes studied her from beneath the brim of his shadow hat. Clara raised her voice, audible only in the spirit world.

"You want to prevent the war, right? The other Enigmas won't be content to be in debt to *either* Lilia *or* The Empress. To be their masters now like Solomon was so long ago. They will fight back."

She had the uncomfortable sensation of hundreds of Enigmas focused on her for the first time. Something she'd striven her whole life to avoid. But it was necessary. Even the Grays seemed to take note; their writhing forms paused and all the violence occurring amid the gala attendees halted.

Nerves wracked Clara. She focused again on The Man in Black. "I can't do this alone. I need help."

"You traitorous, foolish child," The Empress hissed as she battled Lilia.

He was even closer now, his presence intense, bearing down on her like a physical weight. The shadows lightened so that she could just make out the outline of his face. The shape of his sharp and sparkling onyx eyes. She willed him to understand and to help, if not for her good or the good of humanity, then at least for his own. Her only chance was in creating as much chaos Over There as was currently happening in the human world.

A pair of dark lips curved upward, and The Man in Black tipped his hat toward her. Then he disappeared.

She wasn't sure what happened, whether he was going to assist or had just washed his hands of the whole thing. The gamble had not paid off.

Pain overwhelmed her, tearing her attention from Over There back to the human world, where she reeled from a punch that tore the breath from her lungs. The Empress quickly straightened and with a shriek launched herself once again at Lilia, catching hold of her hand and twisting it with a sickening crack. Then The Empress wrenched the ring from Josephine's finger, pulling off a significant amount of skin along with it. She held it up, a bloody smile spreading across Clara's lips.

Clara's spirit shuddered.

They had lost.

As her own ungloved fist closed around the coveted ring, despair overwhelmed her. Mama Octavia's voice whispered in her ear. "Don't give up yet, chile."

But it was already too late.

34

OUR PRECIOUS BLOOD

A wave of dizziness swamped her. Clara was losing consciousness. Perhaps, even now, The Empress was stealing her destiny, starting the process to detach it from her soul and eventually take it for her own.

Darkness overtook her, interrupted by a flashing, multicolored light bobbing in and out of view. Her head swam and dipped; she was light-headed, and her body felt weightless as well.

Slowly, images and sounds returned. But she was no longer in the ballroom in the Whitelaw Hotel. She sat in Israel's apartment, in the armchair that bore his scent, with Jesse Lee across from her on the couch, plates of fried ham and eggs on the coffee table in front of them.

"You want me to do what?" Jesse Lee asked, incredulous.

"Take my memories," Clara replied, "of this conversation and a few other things. Can you pinpoint exactly what you take? Make it so I don't notice they're missing?"

He scratched his chin. "I've never done it to someone voluntarily before—other than myself—but I think so. Why, though?"

"I think I've figured out The Empress's plan, and I don't want her to know I know."

His eyes rounded and his body stilled. "Wait, The Empress can read your mind?"

She shook her head. "But when she Embraces me, she'll know all my thoughts and memories."

His fork clattered to the ground. "Embraces you?"

Clara gripped her hands together to stop their shaking. Just thinking about it made her anxious. "It's the only way to get the ring. Listen, Josephine said that only Lilia could take the ring off when she was wearing her skin. Anyone else who touches it will die, aside from the one wearing it. The Empress gave me a list of instructions of how to get around that, but here's the thing, I think her plan has always been to get me close to the ring and in a situation where I can't possibly get it, then bargain with me to let her Embrace me and take it herself. If only Lilia can remove the ring, I think it means an Enigma has to do it."

Jesse Lee sat back, shaking his head. "But The Empress had to know you'd never let her Embrace you."

"You know how there are times when you can't reach Josephine's memories, they're hidden from you?"

He nodded.

"Do those times coincide with the times she's a raging witch and not the fake princess version of herself?"

He snapped his fingers. "When Lilia Embraces her, I can't take her memories."

Clara smiled humorlessly. "Charms don't work on an Enigma. But The Empress has been leading me to believe they would. She's been wanting me to use my Charm on Josephine since the beginning. She can't lie, but like The Man in Black said, there are different kinds of truths. I think she believed if I found out none of our Charms work, I'd have no choice but to accept her Embrace."

"An offer you can't refuse." They shared a long look, Jesse Lee's expression tinged with horror. "All right. So I take your memories and she can't see what you've got planned, then what?"

"Then when The Empress gets the ring, you give them back to me."

He wiped a hand down his face, still a bit flummoxed. "And how will that help?"

"Because now I know how to get rid of her."

"How?"

She hedged. "I probably shouldn't tell you, just in case. If any of them find out..."

He held up his hands. "I get it. But what about the rest of our plan?"

"Goes on just the same. We just don't tell the others it won't work." She held his eye. "Not even Israel. If any of them know..."

"They could give it away."

"Or be compromised somehow."

"But, Clara, this might not work either."

She took in a slow breath. "I know. If it don't, then I'm gone, you're gone, and so is everyone else, so there won't be nobody left to be mad at us."

Silence descended as Jesse Lee stared sightlessly in front of him, fingers tapping a rhythm on his thigh. "You sure you can force The Empress out once you let her in?"

Clara's voice was low when she responded. "I think I can, if I slay one more dragon."

The dizziness that affected those targeted by Jesse Lee's power hit her again, bringing back other memories. Recollections of putting the pieces together, ideas colliding in her mind, her chat with Uncle Nazareth, who knew a surprising amount about the spirit world. Even Mama Octavia had been impressed at the old man.

And then with a snap, she was back in the present, the holes in her mind filled once again. A feeling of gratitude for Jesse Lee came over her as the pain in her body made itself known once more.

The Empress held Clara's hand above her, triumphant, the ring still clutched in her grasp. It didn't burn or hurt at all, it vibrated, making a soft humming sound barely audible above the noise in the ballroom.

The Empress rewrote the wards surrounding the ring, tuning them from Lilia and Josephine to herself and Clara. The energy of the spell wafted out, visible to Clara's second sight. Touching the ring was still deadly to all others, and now no other Enigma would be able to wield it without overcoming the powerful magic.

Knowing what she had to do, Clara gathered her inner strength and settled into her focus. The other Enigmas present watched silently, motionless as The Empress spun her web. The Grays clogged the ballroom and restarted their mischief with the partygoers. The hubbub all around rose to a dull roar.

When Clara was little and the Grays had swarmed over her, cutting off her air, she'd been afraid, convinced they were trying to kill her. That fear had permeated her life from that day to this. But what if it was based on a misunderstanding? What if they weren't trying to kill her at all?

"One with the sight, such as yourself," Uncle Nazareth had said, "gets spirits seeking you out, 'cause you can hear them. It's a great comfort to them to be seen and understood."

Mama Octavia had listened on quietly, nodding her head in agreement.

"When a baby with the sight is born, it sends out signals, they ripple out Over There, and keep rippling for your whole life. You see the ones who need help, the angry ones, the dangerous ones, sure. But you also got a layer of protection around you, Clara Johnson."

His rheumy eyes had gone soft, wistful. "I sense a powerful energy looking after you. They're old, lost their consciousness, maybe lost their souls, but that don't mean they evil. They can't talk to you like your granny do, but they can listen. They been feeding off your energy—your anger and fear. You feed them something else, you give them a purpose, and they can be a powerful army. They can help you—if you let them."

The memory echoed softly in Clara's mind as she drew deeply on her power, the gift she'd been born with that she'd spurned, not understanding. Shouting out Over There, she focused her will on the Grays.

"I need your help."

The thronging mass of chaotic fog paused, tuned in to her, the way they had outside the prison. The way they always had if she looked back at all her encounters with them without the haze of terror.

"I need you to free me."

The response was immediate. The mist of spirits coalesced, then pressed against her like a vise.

After a lifetime of avoiding the attention of the spirits, today she welcomed them.

A spirit attack was an entirely different animal to a physical attack. A storm battered Clara as the Grays surrounded her. They pressed in on her body from all sides, squeezing her lungs and forcing the breath out. Instead of reacting with fear, she relaxed into it, knowing they meant her no harm.

The Empress, however, shrieked, and so did Lilia, who was caught up in the swarm as well. The Grays pummeled and battered the Enigmas, focusing their attention on them, tearing at them, thrashing and ripping in an uncontrolled frenzy like a pack of rabid dogs.

But they left Clara untouched. The Empress flapped her arms about her as if she could shoo the spirits away, but it was no use. The attack was happening Over There, and by the time the Enigma had the presence of mind to ready some kind of spiritual weapon, it was already over.

The Grays quickly overwhelmed The Empress and dragged her

spirit out of Clara's body. They took Lilia as well, leaving Josephine lying in a heap on the ground.

Over There, the familiar smoky form of The Empress and the sinuous, snakelike embodiment of Lilia were wrapped in dark tendrils of energy, binding them. The Man in Black flowed into existence nearby, his glittering eyes focused on Clara. The other Enigmas who filled the ballroom closed in as well, a dangerous energy rippling out from them.

The Empress and Lilia struggled against their bonds but soon were blocked from view by the hordes of encroaching Enigmas. The same Enigmas that both spirits had tried to manipulate, forcing them into debt with the promise of a stolen destiny hanging before them.

Clara, once again in control of her body, quickly catalogued its various aches and pains. Nothing was broken, but many, many things hurt. She stood up groggily, head still swimming.

Her grandmother's shout was her only warning. The only indication that she had looked away too quickly. Over There, The Empress had grown in size, battling her attackers. She had one smoky arm free of the bindings and threw a wave of dark energy in Clara's direction.

The blast hit her, knocking her back onto the ground violently. Her head banged against the wood; her arms and legs splayed out in all directions. Zelda was at her side in an instant, kneeling over her.

Clara blinked, the ache in her skull pounding like a drum. She didn't make the same mistake twice and looked Over There, but all she saw was the angry crowd of Enigmas, their rage still palpable, surrounding the two unseen targets. The Empress must have used the last of her strength for that attack and then been subdued. The Grays had retreated completely, leaving The Empress and Lilia to the wrath of the others.

Clara sat up, rubbing her chest. That's when she discovered the ring was no longer clutched in her palm.

She scrambled to her knees, scanning the floorboards of the stage.

Zelda helped her to her feet and Clara turned in a circle, then stopped, horrified, jaw hanging open.

Several feet away, Israel stood, his hair mussed and face ashen, hand in the air clamped into a fist. The bodyguard he'd been fighting lay on the ground, unconscious. Israel locked eyes with Clara and slowly uncurled his fingers. Sitting in the center of his palm was the ring.

35

THE RING OF MAKEDA

Israel's bare skin touched the ring, but he was alive. However, his movements were stilted and choppy, like a marionette. His head tilted down, like it was being pushed, and Clara's worry grew. She realized she'd closed her second sight out of habit. Now she looked through the veil again only to stumble backward.

Israel was possessed by the Grays.

Unlike Enigmas, or any spirit with a soul, the Grays didn't need permission to Embrace a person. They were, after all, pure chaos. They took what they wanted, generally wreaking havoc wherever they went. Clara stared at Israel, her heart breaking into tiny pieces. His gaze met hers again, holding anguish and intelligence. And fear.

"Israel?" she called out.

"I caught it," he whispered, and her heartbeat picked up. He was still him. The Grays hadn't stolen his mind or his consciousness, just his body. She wasn't sure what was happening, had no idea of the rules anymore.

"When you fell, you flung it away, but I caught it," he continued. "I can't move. What's happening to me?"

She took a step forward, hands out. "You've been possessed. By a kind of spirit—not an Enigma. Something different." Israel nodded in a way that indicated he didn't understand.

Why had they taken him over? They must be what was keeping him alive, since the ring should have killed him—the dark cloud of its wards still pulsed in her second sight.

"I need you to give it to me," Clara said slowly.

His brow descended. "Is it safe for you to have it?"

She'd been fine in the moments after The Empress had been forced from her body. The wards had been tuned to her, after all. But before she could respond, the overhead lighting flickered and faded. Shadows overtook the ballroom. Israel stiffened even more, if that were possible.

The shadows on the stage grew darker and larger and shifted until The Man in Black emerged from their depths. Israel's gaze shot to him as the Enigma approached.

"If you allow me to Embrace you," the Enigma said, "I will protect the ring. Keep it out of the hands of the others who will come for it." The rumble of his voice vibrated the soles of her feet.

Israel's brow furrowed. "I'm not sure that's an option right now."

The Man in Black was still an opaque mass, his features indistinct, though his eyes glittered like diamond chips. "The things that hold you have no consciousness of their own. They will not resist me if I Embrace you. Say yes. It is the only way to end this."

Israel's gaze returned to Clara. If he agreed to The Man in Black's request, would the Enigma double-cross him like The Empress had planned with her? Or would agreeing ensure his freedom, removing his Trick and allowing him to live a normal life? One where he could actually be happy?

"Word your agreement to ensure I cannot take your destiny, son. With that ring, your bargain is at an end." The Man in Black's words cracked open a hole inside Clara. She closed her eyes for a long moment, then opened them and nodded at Israel. She understood. If he chose freedom, she would not blame him.

Still unable to move, Israel looked at her, a tear slipping down his cheek. An unusual wetness rimmed her eyes as well. It was always only going to be one of them able to live free and happy. *Are you pursuing happiness?* The place in her heart that he occupied wanted him to pursue it and find it too. Maybe The Man in Black would want to auction the destinies like the others, and maybe this was leaving the frying pan for the fire, but she could not fault Israel for wanting his life back—one that he deserved.

She nodded at him again, but Israel's focus had strayed. He looked to the side, squinting as if listening to something. Then his expression cleared before turning steely. Resolve coated him. Clara took a deep breath and braced herself for his decision.

"Clara," he said, dark eyes boring holes in her. "Catch." He threw the ring to her.

She reached up and plucked the ring out of the air with her gloved hand. She stood there, her injuries still screaming at her, and opened her palm to stare incredulously at it. The ballroom remained dark and quiet around her—the madness the Grays had incited seemed to have subsided once again and turned into a stupor which overtook the gala guests.

Over There, the other Enigmas were still clustered in masses around Lilia and The Empress. Clara could see nothing of the imprisoned spirits.

The low hum she'd heard and felt before when The Empress had first grabbed the ring started up again. It grew louder, rising to a purring drone and then a whisper.

"Put it on."

Clara startled at the unseen voice, slowly realizing it was coming from the ring itself. "Put the ring on and keep it out of their hands."

The rainbow-colored threads of light still connected the ring to every destiny it had taken and was taking, the ones it was slowly severing until the recipients would be left with a hole in their souls that they'd never recover from.

But just as when Lilia began the spell to steal the destinies of the gala attendees, a brighter light surrounded the ring, a glow that pulsed, engulfing Clara's hand.

Over There, the Enigmas seemed to have gotten wind of what was happening. It was eerie how she could feel their attention swinging to her—homing in on the power of the ring. Clara could even sense the Grays that had Embraced Israel leaving him, fading back into the mass that still filled the ballroom. They had protected him—was it because they knew he was important to her?

"Keep the ring safe for us, Clara," the ring murmured.

"Who—who are you?" Her voice wobbled.

"We are the hope of Makeda." The fragile whisper buzzed through Clara's veins like a flutter in her eardrums. "Our Queen Mother poured much of herself into the crafting of this ring to protect her daughters. The ones who could never be ruled. Who could never be manipulated. Her sacrifice is embedded in its power." There was both a beauty and a sadness in the gentle rasp of the soft voice. Clara hung on the words.

"You are who we are meant for, Clara. The ring can only be borne by a woman such as you. It is now yours to bear and to protect."

"What do you mean, a woman such as me?" she said around the lump in her throat.

"Powerful. Fearless. Unable to be controlled."

"But—but I'm always afraid."

"It was meant for you to bear. Wear it always. Keep it safe. Protect it from harm."

Mama Octavia stepped into Clara's line of sight. Her frown was worried and her gaze heavy. Clara raised her brows in silent question, but her grandmother shook her head. She did not know what Clara should do.

Indecision battled within her. There were sure to be consequences if she wore the ring, but if she didn't, how could she end this? How could she protect the destinies of those gathered here and restore the Afflicted to their lives?

"The ring can never be destroyed; it will always be coveted by those without destinies," the voice announced. "Step into your purpose and wear it."

Clara took a steadying breath and met her grandmother's petrified gaze. She slid the ring onto the third finger of her ungloved right hand, then flexed her fingers. As heavy as it had felt sitting in her palm, it was surprisingly insubstantial once actually on her finger. The light surrounded her hand.

"Do not take it off," the voice warned, growing weaker. "Do not allow yourself to be Embraced. You are its steward now. Wear it well."

The ball of light faded, absorbed back into the dull metal of the ring. Clara turned on shaky legs back toward Israel. Now that he was free, his body under his control again, he rushed to her and pulled her roughly, almost desperately, into his arms. His scent washed over her and she took long moments to breathe him in. This embrace represented nothing but comfort with no hint of pain.

Finally she forced herself to pull away. This wasn't over yet.

36

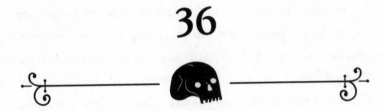

BARGAINS

Over There, the denizens of the spirit world were focused on her, but this time without a sense of malice. In their midst, The Empress's form was visible with some kind of magic binding keeping her captive. It looked like a band of darkness wrapped around her middle, with threads leading to a dozen spirits—those must be her guards.

Clara raised her right hand into the air, and while the ring was plain and didn't so much as glimmer in the low lighting, every spirit's focus turned to it.

"This ends today," she said. "I don't know why you were created without destinies, and I am sorry if it pains you, but if you are meant for them, there must be some other way to obtain them. You cannot steal ours."

Each barely visible strand of multicolored light that led to a missing and Afflicted person reminded her of the task ahead. As soon as she could figure out how to release the spell and restore everyone affected, she would.

She turned to the Enigma to whom she was indebted. "You made a vow, Empress," Clara called out. "You must abide by it. I have the ring. I completed our bargain."

The Enigma's face was indistinct at first, clouded over with rage at her current position. However, it soon solidified into the same regal visage Clara was used to. The one she'd made the deal with years ago. The Empress was bound by her vow, but that didn't mean she might not try to slip out of it. Clara held her breath, waiting for the spirit's response.

"Very well," she said, tilting her smoky head up. "You and your friends are released from your Tricks. The mighty gifts you have received from us are no more. My vow to you, and the ones their Enigmas made to me, is complete."

Clara turned to where Jesse Lee stood. Zelda had rejoined him and, at some point, Aristotle had arrived too. They all stood shoulder to shoulder, Jesse Lee and Zelda a bit battered after the fight with the human guards and the chaos from the Grays. Even Aristotle was disheveled and looked like he'd traded some blows with someone.

Slowly, the older man's aura cleared, leaving behind a gleaming dark pink. Jesse Lee's gold aura shone brilliantly beside him. Tears came to Clara's eyes as she felt her own burden lift. She would never have said her Charm and Trick *felt* like anything, but she certainly noticed the absence. The weight removed from her shoulders.

Jesse Lee and Aristotle grinned and clasped each other in an emotional hug. A smile on her face, Clara turned to Israel. He looked at his cousin with tears in his own eyes, but his orange aura still bore the same murky dimness of his debt. The smile dropped from Clara's face.

Israel put an arm around her, pulling her against him. She leaned on him, resting a hand on his chest, but he didn't look at her. In the shadows of the stage, The Man in Black still hovered.

Clara pinned him with her gaze. "Release him as well. You have what you wanted, The Empress and Lilia will face whatever justice your kind has. The war you feared has been avoided."

Israel finally met her eyes. The defeat and resignation within them drove sharp claws into her middle.

"He got the ring," Clara continued. "Did your deal specify that he had to keep it?"

Israel blinked, then his gaze shot to The Man in Black. The Enigma drew nearer until his features came into sharper focus. He was coated in midnight with stars for eyes. He even had a scent, which shouldn't be possible, but he smelled of cinnamon and cloves. Was that her imagination? Israel tried to push her behind him, standing between the two of them, but Clara refused. The Enigma drew so close that she had to lean back or else risk brushing her face against him. He peered at her like he was viewing her very soul. Maybe he was.

His voice reverberated, rattling around inside her rib cage. "I will release him as he met the letter of our deal, if not the spirit of it." The Man in Black smiled, revealing a glittering mouth of teeth even brighter than his eyes. The effect was alarming and she couldn't help cringing back into Israel's firm chest.

"You are free, Israel Lee," the spirit said. "But beware, the woman you have chosen has just accepted a dangerous mission. One that she does not truly understand. When you find out what that ring can actually do—" He shifted away, gliding across the stage. "Do not hesitate to call me. I would be happy to assist."

The Enigma left them with a sparkling and somewhat ominous grin, fading back into the shadows completely. In the ballroom, the artificial darkness lifted, leaving the electric lighting and the flickering of candlelight from the tables. The Empress was dragged off by the gang of spirits who'd bound her, and even farther away, Clara spotted Lilia, similarly bound, with an even larger group of spirits surrounding her, leading her away.

There was no sign of the Grays.

Israel's aura was a bright, clean orange and his smile was, for the first time, not tinged in sadness. His fingertips trailed down her arm until he grasped her gloved hand and squeezed gently. They crossed the stage, both moving gingerly because of their injuries, and went down the steps to where their friends waited.

Aristotle and Jesse Lee had an arm around each other and were laughing like madmen. Jesse Lee had an entire bottle of champagne in his other hand and took a generous swig before passing it to his new best friend.

Zelda had lost her black stocking cap in the melee, and her blonde hair was all over her head. She was having a silent conversation with Thaniel Dawson, who stared down at her with a bewildered expression. He wasn't restrained in any way, and the other guards were nowhere to be seen. Neither was their boss.

"Where did Madame Josephine go?" Clara had lost track of the woman at some point in the confusion. They all looked around, searching the stage and the area nearby for a glimpse of her.

It was Thaniel who finally answered, tearing his gaze from Zelda. "She slipped out the back with the other guards," he rumbled.

"Why are you still here?" Jesse Lee asked.

Murmurs rose across the rest of the ballroom as folks, now back in their right minds, picked themselves up and worked to understand what had happened. Their beautiful clothes and careful hairstyles were a total mess. Many sported bloody noses and swollen knuckles. Women cried softly and waiters were scurrying around, bringing out ice to help people tend to their various wounds.

Thaniel's gaze returned to Zelda. "I couldn't leave without knowing how this little thing was able to take me down." There was no animosity in his voice, merely curiosity. And maybe a little awe.

Zelda grinned broadly and looked Thaniel up and down appreciatively. "I can show you if you want. Back at your place?" She fluttered her eyelashes and tilted her head in a mockery of flirtation. Thaniel's brown skin warmed with a blush. His response was too low for Clara to hear, but Zelda's smile intensified. She linked her arm through the large man's and turned them toward the door.

"Don't wait up!" she called over her shoulder, then paused and looked back at Clara. "Unless you need me?"

Clara shook her head. "No, go have...fun." Zelda winked and managed to tug a man at least three times her size out the nearest door. The rest of them were speechless for a moment.

"I think we should make our exit as well," Aristotle said as the noise in the ballroom increased. Arguments were now breaking out. Folks had no idea what had just happened and would want answers. It was best to escape before any questions fell their way.

The four of them slipped out after Zelda.

37

NEGRO HISTORY WEEK

Clara's fingers flew over the typewriter, finishing the last page of her document. The thin black gloves she wore didn't impede her movement as much as she feared they would. Since an accidental touch of the ring by anyone she encountered would be deadly, her hands were always covered now, a small price to pay for her freedom. One day, she hoped to be able to change the potent wards still surrounding the ring, but they also served to protect it.

Monday morning had risen bright and sunny, as if even the weather knew there was no room for rain when Clara was feeling so good. She was determined to grab hold of her freedom with both hands, though she was still figuring out what that meant. The fan in the corner agitated the air, bringing a soft breeze, and as she pulled the page from her typewriter, she smiled.

The front door opened and Samuel Foster marched in, mail in hand.

"Good morning, Samuel," Mrs. Shuttlesworth called.

"Morning, Mrs. S. Clara." The grinning boy tossed mail on their desks. Another young man hovered in the entryway.

"Wallace Granger, is that you?" Clara called.

Wallace, who she'd previously seen waving a gun at Madame Josephine, now had his hands tucked into his pockets and his head lowered. Samuel stepped up beside him.

"Wally's looking for work and I thought I'd see if Dr. Woodson needed any more help."

Clara shot a glance at Mrs. Shuttlesworth, whose eyes were already large and warm, ready to help. Clara stood and crooked a finger at Wallace, who stared at her, expression dejected. He followed her to the window, where she spoke quietly.

"You done playing gangster or is this some type of scam?"

Wallace shook his head. "It's not a scam. I . . . I want to go straight."

"Why?" Clara crossed her arms.

"Bowlegged Mo got out of jail last week and Crooked Knee Willy done packed up and left town. I . . . want to do something else with myself."

"Lots of jobs you could have. Why here?"

Wallace shrugged. "Samuel's always going on and on about helping the race and how great Dr. Woodson is. Thought I could do something good for a change."

Clara didn't trust it, but Mrs. Shuttlesworth was already walking over with a big smile on her face. "Wallace, was it? I'm sure we can find something for you to do here."

She wrapped an arm around the teen and guided him deeper into the office. Wallace looked back over his shoulder and Clara narrowed her eyes. She'd be watching him carefully, making sure he didn't get out of line, but she figured everybody deserved a second chance.

Samuel bustled around picking up papers and straightening them out, and her heart filled to bursting. After they'd released the Afflicted from the new distillery and a few other of Josephine's businesses, figuring out how to restore the lost destinies had not been easy. And there were some people she hadn't been able to save. Those for whom the separation had lasted too long. A half dozen men and women had been admitted to Freedmen's Hospital in comas as their bodies shut down slowly. Their souls were too damaged and their destinies already gone. Both Clara and Uncle Nazareth had used every tool in their arsenal to try and bring them back, but nothing had worked. She suspected that, somewhere, six Enigmas in clay bodies with stolen destinies were walking around, pretending to be human. But that was a problem for another time.

Everyone else had gone back to their regular lives. They had no recollection of where they'd been or what they'd been doing for the past days or weeks, though many of their clothes stank of alcohol. But the sheer number of missing folks who had returned had given rise to all kinds of gossip. Theories ranged from some kind of medical experiment done by the government to a plot by the Klan to brainwash Negroes. Nobody knew where their loved ones had been, but they were all happy to get them back.

The front door opened again and Dr. Harley waltzed in with Addie Savoy at his side. When he caught sight of Clara, he froze, causing Addie to bump into him. The man had a fading shiner that still took up half his face, the bruising purple on his pale skin. Addie had a scratch on her cheek that she tried to mask with makeup, though she wore a veil attached her cloche hat to further hide it.

Clara viewed them both coolly, then turned her attention back to her work. As she stacked the typewritten pages, the two of them approached her desk.

"Miss Johnson," Harley said.

"Dr. Harley. Addie." She nodded at both politely.

"How are you this morning?"

She narrowed her eyes. "Fine, thank you. What can I do for you?"

"Oh, nothing, nothing." He paused, looking over at Addie, whose expression was pinched. "We were just wondering if you knew how Dr.

Du Bois was doing after the events a week ago. It was quite a ruckus and an unusual situation. It would be a shame if that taints his view of Washington."

Clara suppressed a grin, then thought better of it and let it out. These two were actually acting polite now because they thought she was a personal friend of Dr. Du Bois. Laughter bubbled up and she saw no need to hide it. But a glance from Mrs. Shuttlesworth as she walked back into the room had her suppressing her glee.

She cleared her throat. "Dr. Du Bois was certainly as shocked and confused as everyone else, but he was relatively unscathed. I see the same can't be said for you."

Dr. Harley touched his eye and winced. It was probably the first shiner he'd ever gotten. Clara could empathize; she'd had more black eyes than she could even count.

"I heard they're saying it was a gas leak," Addie piped in. "All those fumes just made people go a little mad." She tittered and then looked away.

"I heard that too," Clara said.

"Addie and I were wondering... That is, we're sending out our wedding invitations." Harley looked discomposed, not just because of his black eye, but his entire demeanor had lost that superior quality. Clara sat back, enjoying this.

He held up two cream-colored envelopes. "We were planning the nuptials for February, but then Dr. Woodson had the brilliant idea to create a Negro History Week which happened to coincide with our dates, and so we've pushed our ceremony to the beginning of March." He held out an envelope to her.

Clara blinked, staring at it.

"We have one for Dr. Du Bois as well. We were wondering if you could give it to him."

This time she did manage to restrain herself from guffawing

outright. She had no desire to attend the Jackass's wedding, but she made a mental note to do something extra nice for Aristotle.

"Well, Dr. Du Bois is a busy man. I'm sure you could send the invitations in the mail."

Addie's eyes grew wide. "Well, it's because he's so busy that we thought a more personal touch would be in order."

Enjoying herself more than she had in a while, Clara reached out and plucked the envelopes from Harley's hand. "I'll see what I can do."

Addie grinned and Dr. Harley nodded. "We'd be grateful."

At the next desk, Mrs. Shuttlesworth's jaw hung open. Clara shot her a glance and the woman worked to get herself together.

"Harley!" Dr. Woodson called from the other room. "I need to speak with you."

The man scurried off to see what Dr. Woodson wanted, and Addie looked around nervously, clutching her purse to her.

Clara was going to let her linger, but Mrs. Shuttlesworth took pity on the woman. "Why don't you wait in the kitchen, dear?" she said, rising to lead her there.

When the older woman returned, she was shaking her head. "Wonders never cease."

Clara chuckled. "Strange things are happening all across this city. Must be something in the air. Maybe swamp gas."

"Speaking of which, Langston quit this morning."

Clara's brows rose.

"Apparently he wanted to find an easier job, as a janitor or bussing tables or something. Said all the reading and editing was bad on his eyes. That boy is only twenty-three years old. But I told him they were hiring down at the Wardman Park Hotel. Maybe he can find something there."

"Hopefully he'll be happier than he was here," Clara mused.

"I sure hope that boy gets himself together. He has a lot of potential."

Clara shrugged. She couldn't say she'd miss Langston, but she wished him the best.

"Do you think you'd like his role?"

Clara jerked backward. "As Dr. Woodson's assistant?"

The woman nodded. Clara had been thinking a lot about destiny and purpose these days. The work at the journal was important, but she didn't want to be a typist forever. Was being the assistant of a great man where her future lay? She had no idea.

"Thank you, Mrs. Shuttlesworth. I'll think on it. You know, I've been considering taking night classes."

"Oh?"

"Mr. Hart, my lawyer, he teaches the law to folks. Opened up his own evening school. I think perhaps I could become a lawyer too. Help people in trouble. People with no hope."

Mrs. Shuttlesworth smiled her warm, open smile. "I think you'd be good at that, Clara. I think you'd make a real good lawyer."

Clara smiled in return, feeling a little hopeful herself.

At the end of the day, she said goodbye to her coworkers and stepped out into the heat. A shiny black Ford was waiting at the curb, partially hidden by the lounging form of a long-legged guitar player leaning against its door.

There was no crowd of admirers around him today. He certainly got a few looks from women passing, but that was always going to happen with such a handsome man. Fortunately for him and them, his eyes were only for Clara.

She walked into his waiting arms.

EPILOGUE

J esse Lee Stewart had walked this path many times before. For many
years with joy, and then for a time with dread. Now every step was a
mix of the two, each one warring for dominance. What would her face
be like when he saw her again? The years had made him quieter, softened the loud edges of him a bit. Would it be too much?

The little one-room house hadn't changed much since he'd last seen it.
There was a mason jar filled with yellow flowers on the windowsill, and
the porch had been swept scrupulously clean. He stood in front of the
door for ten minutes, afraid to knock, his bones locked up tight. Then he
finally brought his knuckles to the aged wood for three quick raps.

When she opened the door, he held his breath. And waited.

The woman in front of him had graced his dreams every night since
he'd last seen her. She hadn't changed a bit and he longed to pull her to
him. But not yet.

She blinked rapidly as her eyes filled with tears. "Jesse Lee?"

And he could finally breathe again.

He wrapped her in his arms and they cried together, right there on
the porch, for a long, long time.

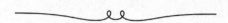

Aristotle walked into the dress shop on R Street more nervous than he'd been since he auditioned for his first show. He brushed imaginary lint off his trousers and inspected his suit in the mirror by the door. Today, he wasn't playing a character. Today, he was himself. And the chill that went through his bones reminded him that he was just beginning to figure out who that was.

Maybe he should have waited longer, but it had been weeks and he couldn't bear it anymore. He had to know one way or the other.

The curtain leading to the back shifted and Henry emerged with a mouth full of pins and a purple ribbon around his neck. His dress shirt was crisp and unbuttoned at the top, revealing the strong column of his neck. Aristotle nearly swallowed his tongue. He was an old fool to come here, but he could never tear himself away.

Henry removed each pin from between his lips and placed them in a pincushion attached to his wrist. Then he gave Aristotle a slow once-over. "You looking for a dress?"

"Um," Aristotle responded, suddenly nervous. He was sixty years old, for Chrissakes, where were these damned nerves coming from?

He cleared his throat. "My name is Aristotle." Then he paused, at a loss for how to continue.

"That's a whole lot of name," Henry said with a chuckle. He extended his hand. "Henry Jameson."

When they shook hands, Aristotle's vision whited out. He wasn't sure he would be able to remember his own name after today. Henry frowned down at his hand before meeting Aristotle's eyes. Confusion painted his expression.

"Have we met before?" Henry asked, searching Aristotle's face.

"I've...seen you around." He was feeling fidgety and stuck his hands in his pockets to quiet them. Then remembered that he'd brought something, a very small something, but hopefully it would break the ice.

"Would you like a Bit-O-Honey?" He held out the wrapped candy.

Henry's eyes lit up. "These are my favorites!" He grabbed the candy and had it unwrapped and in his mouth in seconds. "Keep bringing me these and we'll be best friends in no time."

Aristotle smiled.

Clara tapped her foot as Zelda took her sweet time perusing the display of apples, peaches, and plums at the grocery store. "You not painting a picture, just pick one," she finally erupted.

Zelda raised a single brow and continued her inspection. "I don't want no worms."

"When's the last time you had an apple with worms?"

Zelda narrowed her eyes and finally made her selection. A young mother with a toddler in tow rounded the corner and did a double take at Zelda's wardrobe. Instead of her black pajamas outfit, today she wore an almost identical version in white.

Clara glared at the woman, who turned tail and headed in the other direction, dragging her babbling baby.

"You finding everything okay, Miss Clara? Miss Zelda?"

The teenage boy who had ambled over was small and fine boned. Acne scars grazed his face and healing scars covered his knuckles, but his eyes were bright and lively—his destiny was his own again.

"Titus Monroe, can you tell this one that none of Miss Ruby's apples have worms?"

His eyes widened, and he held up his hands. "We got the finest produce in the entire District, Miss Zelda. Fresh off the truck this morning—I set them all out myself." His obvious pride in his work dampened Clara's annoyance.

"But Miss Ruby won't be pleased about folks shopping in their pajamas." The boy appeared sheepish.

"Don't worry, we're leaving," Clara said.

"And they're not pajamas!" Zelda added.

After she had paid for her fruit and they were back on the street, Clara regarded the woman's outfit again. "Is there a reason you couldn't change when you got there?"

"There really isn't anywhere for me to change clothes there," Zelda responded breezily.

"At the YWCA?" Clara's brows rose. "Why not?"

"No, not the YWCA, the YMCA. And they don't have women's changing rooms. I asked."

Clara stopped in the middle of the sidewalk. "Why on earth are you going to take a class at the YMCA?"

"They've started teaching jujitsu down there."

"Joo what?"

"It's a Japanese martial art. They brought in a master from San Francisco."

"And will they even teach women?"

"They'll teach me," Zelda said, grinning. "You doubt me?"

Clara eyed her dubiously.

"Well, do you doubt him?" She pointed to the corner where Thaniel Dawson stood, dressed in an identical outfit. His must have been made from bedsheets or something, he was so large, but he waited patiently for them to approach and then caught Zelda when she jumped into his arms.

Though his manner was gentle and his disposition at odds with his appearance, Clara suspected that if Thaniel put his mind to something, he could bend it to his will as strongly as Zelda did. Shaking her head, she bid them goodbye and good luck and continued on her way.

She would miss this block, although the new two-bedroom apartment she and Zelda were moving into was only a couple of blocks away on 13th Street. Still, the noise of the pool hall below and the chemical smell wafting up from Ruth Anne's beauty parlor wouldn't be there. Of course, there would be new smells and new neighbors. Hopefully they wouldn't annoy her too much.

A late-summer breeze rippled across her skin. People greeted her as she walked down U Street. Some of them knew her from her infamy from the riots—none knew of her more recent efforts, but it didn't matter. This was her city, and for now, it was peaceful again.

When she got to the Republic Gardens, the same bouncer who had kept her out a few weeks ago now smiled and opened the door for her. Though she was prone to holding grudges, the day was too nice for her to rib the man. She breezed through the interior, following the music to the back patio overlooking the garden, where the District Rumblers had just begun their set.

"Miss Johnson," a waitress said. "Your table is over here." She led her to a seat right in front of the band. The guitar player winked at her as he strummed. Clara enjoyed finally being able to listen to him perform. And Israel, she knew, enjoyed playing his beloved music and afterward being treated like a real person and not an object to be awed.

In the corner, the spectral figure of a pale policeman flickered into existence, staring at her with singular focus, but she ignored it, choosing instead to take her seat and let the music flow over her. She rubbed a gloved hand over the slight bump that the ring made. She was often drawn to it, stroking it or touching it, liking the feel of it against her fingertips when she was alone and removed her gloves. One day she would need to unlock its secrets. But this afternoon, she was happy just listening to the music. She closed her eyes and let it take her away.

Author's Note

I first learned about Clara "Carrie" Minor Johnson in an article in the *Washington Post Magazine*, "The DC Race War of 1919: And the forgotten story of one African American girl accused of murdering a police officer" by Jefferson Morley (wapo.st/1919). I'd set myself the task of writing a fantasy heist novel set during the Harlem Renaissance and was searching for the characters and story in the research. Originally the book was going to take place in New York City, but due to travel restrictions during the 2020 pandemic, I decided to set the tale a bit closer to home in Washington, DC, and I'm certain the novel is better for it. In Carrie, I discovered a fascinating young woman who inspired a character who has quickly become one of my favorites.

"Girl Kills Detective," "Sniping Negress Held for Slaying"—the headlines of the newspaper articles from that time tell their version of the story of seventeen-year-old Carrie, who was arrested during the Red Summer riots of 1919 for killing a policeman.

She would sit in jail for the next two years, becoming, as one writer put it, a "cause célèbre" in the Black community. She was a modern folk hero, and money was raised for her defense fund. A lady's charity group sponsored a fashion show in her honor (young Duke Ellington hand-painted placards and slides for the event). A Black newspaper printed a poem written by an eleven-year-old girl: *You have heard about the riot in Washington DC.... You read about Carrie Johnson who was only 17. She killed a detective, wasn't she brave and keen.*

That detective had been one of the two policemen who burst into

Carrie's bedroom during the middle of the riot. Police claimed there had been a sniper shooting from the roof—neighbors dispute this. Carrie and her father hid under the bed. They fired shots at the intruders, and the police fired back, injuring both father and daughter. They lived; Detective Harry Wilson died. Eighteen bullet holes were left in the door to Carrie's bedroom.

Carrie Johnson. Breonna Taylor. The comparisons jump to mind immediately. Cops in her bedroom. An exchange of gunfire. This incident took place over one hundred years ago, but it also happened yesterday. And there's little reason to believe it won't occur again tomorrow.

A jury convicted Carrie of manslaughter, but she was eventually given a new trial and finally allowed to plead self-defense. A new district attorney dropped the charges, tacitly admitting the young woman had been in fear for her life and he would not get another conviction.

At the age of nineteen, she was freed from jail and then disappeared from history. She may have become a janitor. She likely got married, had children, worked to put this incident behind her. But it certainly had a cost.

Six years after Red Summer, in August of 1925, the Ku Klux Klan marched down Pennsylvania Avenue. The climate of oppression and terror for Black Americans had changed little. How might Carrie at twenty-three have viewed her world? She was free but still locked in the chains of terror and Jim Crow. She lived in a city that had once been the center of Black society but also housed a sharply divided caste system within the race. She lived in a time of change, in a time of the "New Negro" and a cultural renaissance taking place not just in Harlem but on "Black Broadway," right there in the District of Columbia. What might she have done with her second chance?

My personal connection to this story exists on multiple levels. I went to Howard University and spent a fair amount of time on the U Street of the late 1990s, which, after the destruction of the riots in the

1960s, had emerged once again as a center for Black music and art. My mother's family hails from Washington, DC. One of the branches of the organization that Dr. Carter G. Woodson founded, now called the Association for the Study of African American Life and History (ASALH), is named after my grandfather: the Bethel Dukes Branch. While researching for this novel, I got the opportunity to dive deeper into my own family history as well as the city of my grandmother's youth, where my great-grandparents settled as part of the Great Migration.

For this fictionalized version of Carrie Johnson, I chose to use her given name, Clara, instead of the nickname she went by for most of her life. And while the vast majority of the named locations are real places, I took some creative license with certain dates.

For information on DC's Black Broadway, check out *Washington's U Street: A Biography* by Blair A. Ruble. And for a look at the city's alley communities, *Alley Life in Washington: Family, Community, Religion, and Folklife in the City, 1850–1970* by James Borchert.

While the era's drag balls in Harlem were well documented, I could find no existing record of any such events held in DC, though there were drag shows held at Republic Gardens. For more on Black gay and drag queen history in DC, there is *House of Swann: Where Slaves Became Queens* by Channing Gerard Joseph, forthcoming at the time I write this.

A great resource on the unique history of African Americans in the city and their social caste system is *The Original Black Elite: Daniel Murray and the Story of a Forgotten Era* by Elizabeth Dowling Taylor.

And for a harrowing tale of the lives of two Black brothers with albinism who were taken as children to be circus performers, please see *Truevine: Two Brothers, a Kidnapping, and a Mother's Quest: A True Story of the Jim Crow South* by Beth Macy.

Acknowledgments

Every book is a battlefield, but one written during a global pandemic has endured a special kind of struggle in order to exist. A historical novel written when all libraries are closed and travel is impossible deserves its own category of hardship. I need to thank my sister circle mastermind crew, Ines Johnson and Cerece Rennie Murphy, for keeping me sane and on track and for talking me off more ledges than I can count.

Arley Sorg and the Friday Afternooners deserve all my thanks. Accountability and community are vital for writers, even if they're just faces on Zoom staring at their own screens at the same time you are.

Special gratitude goes to Effie Sieberg for her resources, heist and caper tips, and amazing feedback.

To the Vermont Retreaters, Denny S. Bryce, Brenda Drake, and Deborah Ahern Evans: hope to see you in another hot tub soon!

My agent Sara Megibow's unfailing enthusiasm and support are so vital that I can never thank her enough. My editor, Nivia Evans, is an absolute joy to work with. I'm not sure how many times she has to tell an author to *add* twenty thousand words to a manuscript, but I deeply appreciate her guidance and efforts to improve each of those words. And to everyone at Orbit, thank you so much! I've really enjoyed becoming a part of this team.

My family's support keeps me reloading my pens each day to fight the good fight. Thank you to Paul, my brother, first reader, and brainstorm partner, for giving me additional perspective. And to my husband, Jared, who uncomplainingly grants me the resource of time and is always up for helping me research, especially when that research includes watching a dozen heist films.

And to my mother, Josephine, who allowed me to use her name for my antagonist when I couldn't find another one that had the right energy. I told her, "She's a villain, but she's a great character," and my mother gamely agreed to have her name immortalized on the page. A lifetime of love and support from my parents has helped me to live my dreams.

To the readers, endless thanks for your time. As they say in the friendly skies, I know you have many choices in your reading material, so thank you for choosing to spend some of your precious hours on this planet with my words.

Meet the Author

LESLYE PENELOPE has been writing since she could hold a pen and loves getting lost in the worlds in her head. She is an award-winning author of fantasy and paranormal romance. Equally left- and right-brained, she studied filmmaking and computer science at Howard University and sometimes dreams in HTML. She hosts the *My Imaginary Friends* podcast and lives in Maryland with her husband and furry dependents.

Interview

Your debut series, the Earthsinger Chronicles, is a traditional epic fantasy series set in a secondary world. What was it like transitioning to historical fantasy set in our world? How did the creative process differ?

The major difference in going from epic fantasy to historical fantasy was the research. I actually did a fair amount of research for the Earthsinger Chronicles, a series set in an alternate 1920s time period, to make sure my worldbuilding was robust and well reasoned. However, setting a story in the real world in 1925 required me to seriously level up my research abilities. Also, I discovered much of the story and characters from what I learned during my research. Truth is really stranger than fiction and it's amazing how fascinating history can be. I was surprised by how much inspiration I found in old newspapers and relatively obscure research papers.

When you build a world from scratch, there are so many decisions to make, and all of those have ripple effects for the story. However, it's not necessarily easier to set a novel in the real world, because now there are readers who are familiar with the settings that I mention or may be history aficionados who can pick apart the details and let me know when I've gotten something wrong. While dramatic license is definitely necessary sometimes, especially considering the magical aspects I've added, I still tried my best to make the world of the story grounded and real. And adhering to real-life events and incorporating real people into the story allowed me to stretch my creativity in very fun ways.

Where did the initial idea for The Monsters We Defy *come from,* *and how did the story begin to take shape?*

The initial idea was sparked by a social media post I saw, a reading wish list for a Harlem Renaissance fantasy heist. I'd never attempted a heist story before and didn't know if I could even pull something like that off—so I had to challenge myself. Also, the idea of setting a fantasy novel in the real world was very attractive after spending the better part of a decade meticulously crafting a secondary world.

I had done research on the Harlem Renaissance era for another project that didn't end up moving forward, so I had a few books on the subject and its major players. I fell deep into the research rabbit hole, firmly believing that I would discover who was doing the stealing and what were they after if I just knew more about the time period and historical events. And that turned out to be true.

Setting the story in Washington, DC, instead of Harlem helped as well. At the turn of the twentieth century, DC had the largest Black population of any American city—Black culture has so many roots here, as do many figures well known in the Harlem Renaissance and early Civil Rights movement, from Duke Ellington, to Langston Hughes, to Carter Woodson and many of the founders of the NAACP.

Before reading the newspaper article in which I found Clara Johnson's story, I didn't even know that DC had its own Red Summer riot in 1919. And of course, once I learned about Clara, the story took shape quickly.

What was the most challenging moment of writing The Monsters We Defy?

Since research was such an important part of the process, writing this book during the height of the pandemic lockdowns of 2020, when all libraries were closed and travel was, if not impossible, extremely inadvisable, was the most difficult part. There were certain resources that I couldn't get access to and would have loved to use. Especially since I live outside of Washington, DC, and in normal times would be able to visit places like the Library of Congress and the Moorland-Spingarn Research Center at my alma mater, Howard University.

The characters in your novel are vibrant and compelling. If you had to pick, who would you say is your favorite? Who did you find the most difficult to write?

Picking a favorite is so difficult! Zelda was definitely the most fun to write. Initially, I wanted to include a character who was passing for white in the story. Then I came across a vintage photograph of a young Black girl with albinism who was being exhibited in a museum. I love exploring identity in my writing, specifically Black identity. With Zelda, I got the chance to investigate the resilience of someone who was exploited all her life and will always stand out for her differences but is unapologetic, insanely talented, and always unbothered.

Clara was probably the most difficult to write because we view the world quite differently. She's very in touch with her anger in a way that I admire. I was constantly having to ask myself if I was writing reactions that were true to her or seeking to avoid conflict in a very Leslye-like way. There were many rewrites as I continued to push myself out of my own comfort zone to bring her to life more authentically.

What do you hope people will walk away with after reading The Monsters We Defy?

I hope people will have a great time with the characters and walk away knowing a little more about Washington, DC, and its place in Black history. I also hope that readers might find some of the same inspiration that I did in imagining the lives of of those who came before us. Though there are unfortunate parallels between the injustices of one hundred years ago and those of today, we, like our parents and grandparents, still find joy in community, friendship, family—found and otherwise—and in overcoming the obstacles set before us. The defiance of the title, and of the inspiring poem in the epigraph, is for every kind of monster we encounter. If we don't stop fighting back, we will free ourselves. That's what I was hoping to say with Clara's story.

Without giving too much away, could you share what readers can expect in your next novel?

I'm working on another fantasy, this one blending historical and secondary-world elements, which explores the theme of Black self-sufficiency differently than *Monsters*. It's about a thriving Southern Black town being threatened with eradication the way so many were. A mysterious and magical stranger comes to town, upending the life of my heroine and jeopardizing her long-held, devastating secret.

And, finally, if you could have a Charm and a Trick, what would they be?

As someone who knows better, I hope I would never accept an Enigma debt. But if I were saddled with one, I think it would be helpful to always know when someone was lying. As for the Trick, maybe what would balance that power would be never being able to lie myself. Or never being able to tell the truth. That would definitely be more painful, and I think an Enigma would get a kick out of it.

if you enjoyed
THE MONSTERS WE DEFY

look out for

THE BALLAD OF
PERILOUS GRAVES

by

Alex Jennings

Nola is a city full of wonders. A place of sky trolleys and dead cabs, where haints dance the night away, Wise Women keep the order, and songs walk, talk, and keep the spirit of the city alive. To those from Away, Nola might seem strange. To failed magician Perilous Graves, it's simply home. Then the rhythm stutters.

Nine songs of power have escaped from the magical piano that maintains the city's beat, and without them, Nola will fail. Unexpectedly, Perry and his sister, Brendy, are tasked with saving the city. But a storm is brewing, and the Haint of All Haints is awake. Even if they capture the songs, Nola's time might be coming to an end.

1

Here I'm Is!

Perry Graves tried not to think about summer's arrival—the heat devils hovering, breathless, over the blacktop as if waiting for something to happen—or even about the city streets. Tomorrow was the last day of school, and he'd be free to roam the neighborhood soon enough... But it *wouldn't* be soon enough. Perry and his little sister, Brendy, sat cross-legged on the living room floor watching Morgus the Magnificent on the TV. The unkempt, hollow-eyed scientist was trying to convince a gray-haired opera singer to stick his head into a machine that would allow Morgus to amputate the singer's voice with a flip of the switch. From here, Perry could hear his parents and their friends gabbing on the front porch as they sipped sweet tea and played dominoes.

"Why you ain't laughing?" Brendy said.

"Don't talk like that," Perry said. "Daddy hears you, he'll get you good." Then, "I don't always have to laugh just because something's funny."

"Oh, I know, Perry-berry-derry-larry." Brendy stuck her tongue out at him. "You in a *mood* 'cause you ain't seen Peaches in a week. You don't want me talkin' like her because it remind you of the paaaaaain in yo heaaaaaaaaart!"

Perry scowled. "Shut up."

"I'm sorry," Brendy said. "I'm sorry you luuuuuuuvs Peaches like she yo wiiiiiiiiife!"

"Little bit, you be sorry you don't shut your mouth," Perry threatened. He had no idea what he could do to silence her without getting into trouble.

"*Nyeeeeowm! Zzzzzrack!*" For a moment, Brendy absently imitated the sound effects from Morgus. "You just want her to say 'Oh! Perilous! I luuuuuvs yew tew! Keeeeeeess me, Perry! Like zey do een—'" Perry was ready to grab his baby sister, clap his hand over her mouth at least, but before he could, a clamor rose up outside. "Looka there!" some grown-up shouted from the porch, his voice marbling through a hubbub of startled adult exclamations.

Whatever was going on out there had nothing to do with Perry, so he ignored it. He was sure that someone had just walked through some graffiti, or that a parade of paintbodies was making its way down Jackson Avenue. He grabbed Brendy's wrist, all set to give her a good tickle, but when the first piano chord sounded on the night air, Perry's body took notice.

Perry let go of his sister, and his legs unfolded him to standing. By the time the second bar began, his knees had begun to flex. He danced in place for a moment before he realized what was happening, then turned and made for the front door. Brendy bounced along right beside him, her single Afro pouf bobbing atop her little round head.

Ooooooh—ooh-wee!
Ooooooh—ooh-wee!
Ooo-ooh baby, oooooh—ooh-wee!

Outside, Perry's parents and their friends had already descended to the street. Perry's grandfather, Daddy Deke, stood at the base of the porch steps, pumping his knees and elbows in time with the music.

"Something ain't right!" he shouted. "He don't never show up this far uptown—not even at Mardi Gras!"

Perry bounced on his toes in the blast of the electric fan sitting at the far end of the porch. The night beyond the stream of air was hot and close—like dog breath, but without the smell. As soon as Perry left the breeze, dancing to the edge of the porch steps, little beads of sweat sprang out on his forehead and started running down.

From here, as he wobbled his legs and rolled his shoulders, Perry saw a shadow forming under the streetlight. It was the silhouette of a man sitting at a piano, and the music came from him. The spirit's piano resolved into view. It was a glittery-gold baby grand festooned with stickers and beads, its keys moving on their own. Shortly thereafter, Doctor Professor himself appeared, hunched over, playing hard as he threw his head back in song. He wore a fuzzy purple fur hat, great big sunglasses with star-shaped lenses, and a purple-sequined tuxedo jacket and bow tie. Big clunky rings stood out on his knuckles as his hands blurred across the keyboard, striking notes and chords. Perry smelled licorice, but couldn't tell whether the smell came from Doctor Professor or from somewhere else. The scent was so powerful, it was almost unpleasant.

All Perry's senses seemed sharper now, and he tried to drink in every impression. He danced in place to the piano and the bass, but as he did, guitars and horns played right along, their sound pouring right out of Fess's mouth.

Ooh-wee, baby, ooooooh—wee
What did you done to meeeee…!

By now, everyone for blocks around had come out of their houses and onto the blacktop. A line of cars waited patiently at Carondelet Street, their doors open, their drivers dancing on the hoods and on the roofs. It was just what you did when Doctor Professor appeared, whatever time of day or night. They danced along to the music, and those who knew the lyrics even sang along.

You told me I'm yo man
You won't have nobody else
Now I'm sittin' home at night
With nobody but myself—!

Perry gave himself up to the sound and the rhythm of the music. The saxophone solo had begun, and it spun Perry around, carried him down the steps and across the yard. His feet swiveled on the sidewalk, turning in and out as he threw his arms up above his head.

Just as quickly as he'd come, Doctor Professor began to fade from sight. First, the man disappeared except for his hands, then his stool disappeared, and then the piano itself. He had become another disturbance in the air—a weird blot of not-really-anything smudged inside the cone cast by the streetlight, and just before he had gone entirely away, Perry heard another song starting up. The music released him, and the crowd stopped moving.

"Oh, have mercy!" Perry's mother crowed. "That's what I needed, baby!"

"That Doctor Professor sure can play."

"Baby, you know it. Take your bounce, take your zydeco—this a jazz city through and through!"

Wilting in the heat, Perry turned to head back inside and saw Daddy Deke still standing by the porch. The old man wore a black-and-crimson zoot suit, and now that he'd finished his dance, he took off his broad-brimmed hat and held it in his left hand. He looked down his beaky nose at Perry, staring like a bird. "Things like that don't happen for no reason," he said. "Something up."

"Something bad?" Perry asked.

"Couldn't tell ya, baby," he said. "Daddy Deke don't know much about magic or spirits. But I gotta wonder...why *that* streetlight in particular? That one right there in front of Peaches's house?"

Now Perry turned to look back at the space where Doctor Professor had appeared. Daddy Deke was right. It stood exactly in front of Peaches's big white birthday cake of a house.

"I didn't see her dancing," Perry said. "Did you?"

"If she'da been there, we'da known it," Daddy Deke said. "Can't miss that Peaches, now, can you?"

Perry and Brendy's parents resumed their seats on the porch, but Daddy Deke headed past them into the house. Perry and his sister followed. In the foyer, Daddy Deke paused to breathe in the cool of the AC and mop his brow with a handkerchief. "Ain't danced like that in a minute," he said.

The living room TV was still gabbling away. Brendy twirled and glided over to shut it off—and Perry wasn't surprised. After seeing Doctor Professor, the idea of staring at the TV screen seemed terminally boring—but so did porch-sitting.

"What you doing tonight anyhows, Daddy Deke?" Brendy asked.

"Caught a couple bass in the park this morning," the old man said. "Might as well fry some up and eat it."

"You went fishing without us?"

"Y'all had school," Daddy Deke said. "If you comin', come on."

Daddy Deke's house sat around the corner on Brainard Street, a stubby little avenue that ran from St. Andrew to Philip, parallel with St. Charles. The low, ranch-style bungalow with the terra-cotta roof and stucco walls looked a little out-of-place for the Central City—it was the kind of place Perry would expect to see in Broadmoor, crouching back from the street like ThunderCats Lair.

As Perry and Brendy crossed the lawn, Daddy Deke broke away to head for his car, an old Ford Comet that seemed like a good match for the house in that it was also catlike. But instead of ThunderCats Lair, it reminded Perry of Panthor, Skeletor's evil-but-harmless familiar. Daddy Deke turned to look at his grandchildren over his narrow shoulder. "Gwan, y'all. I just gotta stash something real quick, me."

As always, the door to Daddy Deke's house was unlocked. Perry let himself and Brendy inside and took a deep breath. Daddy Deke's place had a smell he couldn't quite identify, but it was unmistakable. A mix of incense, frying oil, and Daddy Deke's own particular aroma—the one he wore beneath his cologne and his mouthwash, the scent that was only his.

At one time, the house had been a doubled shotgun. Daddy Deke had had the central dividing wall and a couple others knocked down, but the second front door remained. Perry and Brendy took off their shoes and stored them in the cubby underneath the coat rack. By then, Daddy Deke had followed them inside.

"Do the fish need scaling?" Perry asked. Daddy Deke had shown him how to descale, gut, and fillet a fish, but Perry was still refining his grasp on the process. There was something about it he enjoyed; figuring out how to get rid of all those fins, bones, and scales felt a little like alchemy—transmuting an animal into food. It made Perry think of the Bible story where Jesus fed thousands on a couple fish and two loaves.

"Naw," Daddy Deke said. "Did it my own self this time—wanted to get them heads in the freezer. Gonna make a stew later on."

Perry's mouth watered. Daddy Deke's fish-head stew was legendary—no matter what form it took. He could make it French-style, Cajun, or even Thai. On those nights when Daddy Deke made a pot for the family and carried it around the corner, the family would eat in near silence, punctuated with satisfied grunts and hums of approval.

"Why I can't never fix the fishes?" Brendy asked. "I wanna help make dinner!"

"You didn't want to learn," Perry said. "You said it was gross."

A flash of anger lit Brendy's face, but it blinked away as quickly as it had come.

"You promise to be careful with the knife," Daddy Deke said, "and we put you on salad duty, heard?"

"Yesss!" Brendy hissed. "Knife knife knife knife *knife*!"

"Lord," Perry said with a roll of his eyes.

In the kitchen, Daddy Deke turned on the countertop radio and stride piano poured forth to fill the room like water. "You know who that is?" Daddy Deke said.

Perry listened closely. He recognized the song—"Summertime"— but not the expert hands that played it. Hearing it made him feel a sharp pang of loss. He hadn't touched a keyboard in more than a year. He pushed that thought away—thinking about playing was a dark road that led nowhere good. "No," Perry said. "Who is it?"

"That's Willie 'The Lion' Smith," Daddy Deke said, "outta New Jersey. Used to work in a slaughterhouse with his daddy when he was a boy. He said it was horrible, hearing them animals done in, but there was something musical about it, too. That's the thing about music, about a symphony: destruction, war, peace, and beauty all mixed up, ya heard?"

Perry frowned and shut his eyes, listening more closely. He could hear it. At first the tone of the music reminded him of water, and it was still liquid, but now he imagined a bit of darkness and blood mixed in. He saw flowers unfurling to catch rain in a storm. Some of them were destroyed, pulverized by the water or swept away in the high wind.

"That's the thing about music," Daddy Deke said. "It can destroy as much as it creates. It's wild and powerful, dig?"

Perry opened his eyes. "Yes," he said, trying to keep the sadness from his voice. "I understand—a little bit, I think."

———— ❧ ————

"Hey, now," Daddy Deke said.

Perry shook his head. His attention had been off in the ozone some-where as he, Daddy Deke, and Brendy played rummy. Perry liked rummy okay—he liked the shape of the rules, the feel of the game itself—the cards against his palms, raising and lowering them to the table, keeping track of points—but tonight, he'd been going through the motions. "I'm sorry," he said. "What's going on?"

"What's going on is you won and you don't even care!" Brendy huffed.

"Y'all, I'm sorry," Perry said. "I just—I still feel the music on me. I'm thinking about what it means and what Doctor Professor wants with Peaches."

Brendy rolled her eyes. "'And where she at? What she doing? She thinking bout me?' Blah blah blippity."

Daddy Deke laid down his cards and shook his head. "Don't tease ya brother for caring—and besides, Perry ain't the only one miss Peaches when she gone. Is he?"

Brendy pulled a face where she flexed her neck muscles and drew her mouth into a flat, toadish line. Then she let the expression go and sucked in a huge mouthful of air to pooch out her checks. She let that go, too. "Okay, no he ain't," she said. "We all be missing Peaches. I get left alone, too, but I don't make a big deal. Just like when—"

Perry knew his expression must have darkened because Brendy cast aside whatever she'd meant to say next. "En EE ways, Peaches *always* go away for a lil bit after a fight."

This was true. Thirteen days ago, Peaches had fought Maddy Bombz on the roof of One Shell Square after Perry and Peaches figured out how to predict the location of her next display. Each of her fusillades was part of a grander display—similar to the ones above the Missus Hipp on Juneteenth or on New Year's—and since she didn't care about

365

the safety of her "audience," of course she intended to launch her grand finale atop the tallest building in Nola. Perry and Brendy watched from a Poydras Street sidewalk as one of the explosions tossed Peaches down to the street.

She hit hard and lay still for a moment, then sat up, shaking her head angrily. A glance into the parking lot to his right told Perry what she'd do next. Peaches pushed up imaginary sleeves and bounded over to a big green dumpster. She lifted the bulky metal thing over her head easy-as-you-please and jumped. *Hard.* Watching her reminded Perry of the moon landing videos. It was as if gravity simply worked differently for her when she wanted it to.

When she leaped back to the street, the dumpster she carried had been crimped closed like a pie crust. She set it down right there on the pavement.

"Five-oh on the way," she said. "I seen 'em from up above. Let's get to steppin'." And they had. Perry and Brendy had spent the night at Peaches's house, watching TV and eating huckabucks and Sixlets late into the night because there was no school the next day.

Perry and his sister awakened the next morning to find Peaches's pocket of pillows and blankets empty—and nobody had seen her since.

"I know she coming back," Perry said.

"I know you know," Daddy Deke said. "But I'll tell you sumn for free—there ain't nothing wrong with the feelings you having, but them feelings are yours. Ain't nobody else responsible for 'em, dig? You can't carry nothing for nobody else, and cain't nobody carry what's yours for you."

Perry frowned. In the past, Daddy Deke had never failed to offer him comfort when he was feeling low, but this advice seemed important. He turned Daddy Deke's words over in his mind for the rest of the night. *Cain't nobody carry what's yours for you.* What burdens did he carry, and why? Well, there was the dream he'd had... but some dark, quiet presence in the back of Perry's mind told him that it hadn't been a dream, it had been a warning, and he'd be a fool not to heed it.

Music might be the most powerful magic in Nola, but it couldn't help Perry—not really.

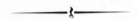

Dryades Academy was an old square-built art deco building that looked more like a courthouse than a place of learning. Its façade was a riot of ivy, full of ladybugs the size of baseballs, which marched up and down the outer walls, keeping them clean. Chickens roosted in the trees out front, and one of the substitute teachers, Mr. Ghiazi, had told Brendy that every evening, after hours, when the last students and teachers had gone home, the chickens would come inside and hold their own lessons, learning about corn and how to find the best worms and bugs. Something about the way he said it made Brendy think Mr. Ghiazi was probably joking—or at least that he thought he was.

Inside, the building boasted green marble floors, old-fashioned mosaics, and vintage furniture maintained by an invisible custodial staff. What Brendy loved most about the place, what she couldn't imagine ever parting with, was its smell. Crayons, glitter, oil soap, and cooking. It smelled best on cold winter days, but even on the last day of school, Dryades Academy smelled like home. How her brother could leave it made no sense to her.

This year, Perry and Brendy had attended separate schools. Last summer, Perry abruptly asked to transfer out of Dryades Academy and wound up at a new school over on Esplanade Avenue. Brendy didn't understand the choice, and she knew she should have asked Perry about it, but every time she tried to bring it up, Perry's face took on a lost, hunted look, and she backed down. Still, it made her sad and angry to be without him, and sometimes those feelings formed a little knot of tension in her throat—like she'd tried to swallow a pill and failed.

All year she had avoided thinking about it, but now, as she sat at her desk by the window in Mr. Evans's class, ignoring the movie playing on the classroom livescreen in favor of a Popeye the Sailor Man coloring book, she wondered whether Perry had decided to leave because he wasn't good at music.

Brendy bore down with her Fuzzy Wuzzy brown, filling in the outline of Popeye's left arm as he slung a string of chained-together oil barrels over his head. She'd taught herself a trick earlier this year: She liked to color in her figures hard, in layer after layer—careful, of course, to stay inside the lines—then go back with a plastic lunch knife and scrape away the wax. The process resulted in smoother, richer colors that had won her an award from the Chamber of Commerce in its Carnival Coloring Competition. The grand prize had been a beautiful purple-and-white bicycle that Daddy Deke taught her to ride without training wheels.

Brendy frowned, listening hard, as she finished coloring Popeye's exposed skin and tried to decide what color Olive Oyl should be this time. The chickens in the tree outside had gone quiet. Brendy had earned the right to sit by the broad classroom window because Mr. Evans thought she did such a good job fighting the temptation to stare outside at the trees and the play yard, and the neighborhood beyond. This was only partly true. Brendy found it easy to keep from staring out the window because she tended to listen out it instead. Most of the time she spent at her desk found her listening to the swish of cars on the street, the noise of other classes bouncing balls and running riot on the play yard blacktop, the squabbles of the chickens and the neighborhood cats—who seemed, lately, to have resolved their differences by banding together against the raccoons and possums.

Hey, girl!

Was that Peaches? Brendy raised an eyebrow.

Hey, girl. Hey!

Brendy frowned and selected another crayon. "Peaches?" she whispered.

Yeah, girl. Come on. We gots to go!

Brendy considered briefly, then raised her hand.

It took a while, but Mr. Evans noticed. "Brendy?"

"Can I go use it?"

Mr. Evans nodded curtly. "Two minutes." But he'd never remember.

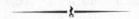

Jelly Roll Morton Memorial Academy was abuzz with the news that Doctor Professor had appeared at Jackson and Brainard last night, right in front of Perry's house, and that Perry himself had been there.

"What did you do?" kids asked.

"Oh, you know," Perry said, basking in his fame. "I do like you do. I danced."

"What song he played?"

" 'Missed Yo Chance,' " Perry answered. "It happens to be a favorite of mine."

"Who else was there? The backup singers? Any P-bodies?"

"At this time of year?" Perry asked. "It ain't Mardi Gras, you know."

"My daddy says it couldna been him," Mickey Ledoux said with a shake of his head. It was just after nine that morning, and the fifth grade was putting the finishing touches on that year's Learning System. The project was designed to represent everything the fifth-grade class had learned—about the Huey Long Bridge, about the Chinese Revolution, about fractions, adding and subtracting time, and about Albert Einstein.

The fifth-grade students had been divided into teams of five, and each student was responsible for designing and creating a representational planetoid to affix to the System—a giant mobile where every planet was an idea. Perry and Mickey were on the math team, and

Perry had made an abacus from Ping-Pong balls and PVC pipe, papered with cutouts from magazines and show flyers featuring musicians and clubs from around town. It had taken Perry weeks to come up with the design, and weeks more to execute it. Daddy Deke had brought him every magazine he could find that had even a mention of a Nola musician, but here it was, complete, staring him right in the face.

When Perry looked at Mickey's sculpture, he felt like he'd been duped. Mickey had made a sundial that looked like it had taken him maybe twenty minutes to put together—or no time at all if, as Perry suspected, Mickey's older brother had just done it for him.

Now, the entire fifth grade had taken over the cafeteria under the supervision of the art teacher, Miss Erica, and were completing the final assembly so that the project could be hoisted on wires and suspended from the cafeteria's high ceiling until next year's fifth-grade class completed its own. The usual lunch tables were absent—there'd be no lunch at school since today was a half day—and instead they stood at beige folding tables wearing their fathers' cast-off dress shirts backward to avoid messing up their uniforms.

Mickey himself had already started puberty, and his long legs combined with his light musculature made him the fastest runner at Morton Academy. When Mickey kept his mouth shut, running or playing ball, Perry envied the way he impressed everyone—especially the girls. When Mickey talked, though, it was usually to parrot something some dumb grown-up had said.

"You think anyone in Nola could mistake anybody else for Doctor Professor?" Perry asked.

Mickey considered. "Not really," he said slowly. "But what if it was a trick? What if it was somebody else impressonating him?"

"'Impersonating,'" Perry corrected without meaning to. "Why would anybody who could play like that pretend to be anybody else?"

"I don't know," Mickey said with an irritated shake of his

peanut-shaped head. "But it couldn't be him. It ain't Mardi Gras, and Jackson is too far uptown for Doctor Professor to just show up there."

Perry didn't answer right away. Biting his lip, he finished duct-taping a plastic coat hanger to the top of his abacus and picked it up by the hook, testing the hanger against the sculpture's weight. The hold seemed more than secure, and he sighed softly at the culmination of his efforts. Carefully, he laid the sculpture on the work table.

"Maybe he didn't just appear," he said, still staring at his work. "Maybe he wanted something. Or he was looking for somebody."

"Like who?"

Perry found it hard to keep the exasperation out of his voice. "Like Peaches, that's who! Important people come looking for her all the time."

"I heard Peaches don't live there no more anyhow," Mickey said. "I heard she left town."

Now Perry's face heated, and his fingers twitched. His hands wanted to curl into fists. "Oh yeah, Mickey?" he said, turning to face the other boy. "Who you heard that from? Cuz Peaches my best friend, and she wouldna left without telling me, ya heard?"

"Sure she is," Mickey said. "If she's such a good friend, when's the last time you seen her?"

Perry's heart sank. It had been a while. Two weeks, at least. What if Mickey was right? What if Peaches had run out on Perry? What if she'd run out on Nola?

"I see her every damn day, dummy," Perry said. "She lives two houses down from me. You don't never know what you're talking about. All you do is run fast and talk out your ass, and everybody knows it."

"Hey!" Mickey said, balling his own fists. "You take that back!"

"Sure I will," Perry said. "As soon as you admit you don't know nothing about nothing—and neither does your stupid daddy!"

Mickey actually drew back his fist to throw a punch, but Miss Erica had appeared behind him like magic. She caught Mickey's wrist and held it. "Boys!" she barked.

Miss Erica was a tallish white woman with dark hair and great big eyes. Today she wore a poet's blouse with frilly cuffs and a long crimson skirt that looked like a giant upside-down rose. "It's the last day of school. There will be no fussing and *no fighting*!"

"He called my daddy stupid!" Mickey said.

"Perry," Miss Erica said. "Is that true?"

"I didn't—I didn't start it," Perry said. "I called his daddy stupid, but it was because...I said it because..."

Perry couldn't find the words. He felt like the last boy on Earth.

"Apologize to Mickey."

Perry knew what Brendy or Peaches would say in his place: *Mickey Ledoux, I'm sorry you and yo daddy is so-o-o-o stoopid.* But he wasn't Brendy, and he certainly wasn't Peaches.

"I'm sorry," he said. "I'm just—I didn't mean it."

Deflated, Perry Graves went back to work.